OXFORD WORLD'S CLASSICS

THE PILGRIM'S PROGRESS

JOHN BUNYAN (1628–88) was born at Elstow, near Bedford, the eldest son of a brazier. He learned to read and write at the village school, and prepared to follow his father's trade. In 1644, however, he was swept up in the Civil War, and served as a soldier in the Parliamentary army. After leaving the army in 1647, he underwent a prolonged and agonizing spiritual crisis. Following his religious conversion he joined an Independent church in Bedford, and before long began to preach. This led, in 1656, to the beginning of a literary career in the course of which he would publish some sixty works of controversial, expository, and practical divinity, marked by an uncompromising zeal and trenchant directness of style. In 1660, following the Restoration of Charles II, he was imprisoned for twelve years in Bedford gaol because of his refusal to stop preaching. While in prison he published several books, among them *Grace Abounding to the Chief of Sinners* (1666), now recognized as one of the classics of Puritan spiritual autobiography. It was not, however, until the publication in 1678 of *The Pilgrim's Progress* that his genius fully declared itself. The imaginative intensity and authenticity of his allegory of the Christian life made the book an extraordinary best-seller, and has earned Bunyan a unique place in literary history. It was followed in 1680 by its sequel, *The Life and Death of Mr Badman*, by the elaborate multi-level allegory *The Holy War* in 1682, and by Part Two of *The Pilgrim's Progress* in 1684, works which substantiate Bunyan's claim to be among the founders of the English novel.

W. R. OWENS is Professor of English Literature at the University of Bedfordshire. His publications include two volumes in the Oxford edition of *The Miscellaneous Works of John Bunyan* (1994) and a co-edited collection of essays, *John Bunyan and his England, 1628–88* (1990). He is the editor of *The Gospels* in the Oxford World's Classics series (2011). He is co-author, with P. N. Furbank, of *The Canonisation of Daniel Defoe* (1988), *Defoe De-Attributions* (1994), *A Critical Bibliography of Daniel Defoe* (1998) and *A Political Biography of Daniel Defoe* (2006). They are joint General Editors of *The Works of Daniel Defoe* (44 vols., 2000–9).

OXFORD WORLD'S CLASSICS

For over 100 years Oxford World's Classics have brought readers closer to the world's great literature. Now with over 700 titles—from the 4,000-year-old myths of Mesopotamia to the twentieth century's greatest novels—the series makes available lesser-known as well as celebrated writing.

The pocket-sized hardbacks of the early years contained introductions by Virginia Woolf, T. S. Eliot, Graham Greene, and other literary figures which enriched the experience of reading. Today the series is recognized for its fine scholarship and reliability in texts that span world literature, drama and poetry, religion, philosophy and politics. Each edition includes perceptive commentary and essential background information to meet the changing needs of readers.

OXFORD WORLD'S CLASSICS

JOHN BUNYAN

The Pilgrim's Progress

Edited with an Introduction and Notes by

W. R. OWENS

UNIVERSITY PRESS

OXFORD
UNIVERSITY PRESS

Great Clarendon Street, Oxford OX2 6DP

Oxford University Press is a department of the University of Oxford.
It furthers the University's objective of excellence in research, scholarship,
and education by publishing worldwide in
Oxford New York

Auckland Bangkok Buenos Aires Cape Town Chennai
Dar es Salaam Delhi Hong Kong Istanbul Karachi Kolkata
Kuala Lumpur Madrid Melbourne Mexico City Mumbai Nairobi
São Paulo Shanghai Taipei Tokyo Toronto

Oxford is a registered trade mark of Oxford University Press
in the UK and in certain other countries

Published in the United States
by Oxford University Press Inc., New York

Text and index © Oxford University Press 1966
Editorial matter © W. R. Owens 2003

The moral rights of the author have been asserted

Database right Oxford University Press (maker)

First published as a World's Classics paperback 1984
Reissued as an Oxford World's Classics paperback 1998
New edition 2003
Reissued 2008

All rights reserved. No part of this publication may be reproduced,
stored in a retrieval system, or transmitted, in any form or by any means,
without the prior permission in writing of Oxford University Press,
or as expressly permitted by law, or under terms agreed with the appropriate
reprographics rights organizations. Enquiries concerning reproduction
outside the scope of the above should be sent to the Rights Department,
Oxford University Press, at the address above

You must not circulate this book in any other binding or cover
and you must impose this same condition on any acquirer

British Library Cataloguing in Publication Data
Data available

Library of Congress Cataloging in Publication Data
Data available

ISBN 978-0-19-953813-3

18

Printed and bound in Great Britain by Clays Ltd, Elcograf S.p.A.

To my parents
Thomas and Maria Owens
and
in memory of my grandparents
Robert and Rachel Owens

ACKNOWLEDGEMENTS

EVERY student of Bunyan owes an enormous debt to the late Roger Sharrock. In my own case the debt is a very personal one: he guided my early postgraduate studies with unfailing kindness and encouragement, and generously invited me to edit two volumes in his edition of Bunyan's *Miscellaneous Works* while I was still very much an apprentice scholar. I owe him a more particular debt in the preparation of the present edition. The text here is based upon his Oxford English Texts edition of *The Pilgrim's Progress*, and the index is the one he prepared for that edition. In preparing my own explanatory notes I have drawn with profit and gratitude upon his extensive scholarly commentary on the text, as well as upon his many other publications on Bunyan.

I am also greatly indebted to Professor N. H. Keeble, who edited the previous Oxford World's Classics edition of *The Pilgrim's Progress*, and from whose scholarship I have learned much. The glossary included here is a somewhat revised and enlarged version of one he prepared for his edition. I am grateful to him for allowing me to make use of it, and for many other kindnesses.

The chronology here is an adapted and revised version of one I prepared for a collection of essays, *John Bunyan and his England, 1628–88* (London, 1990), co-edited with Anne Laurence and Stuart Sim. It is a pleasure to acknowledge here my gratitude to them both for friendship and support over many years.

The Open University W. R. OWENS

CONTENTS

LIST OF ILLUSTRATIONS

INTRODUCTION

FROM the moment of its publication, *The Pilgrim's Progress* has appealed to an extraordinarily large and varied readership. No other work in English, except the Bible, has been so widely read over such a long period. First published in 1678, with a second part added in 1684, the book has never been out of print. It has been published in innumerable editions, and has been translated into over 200 languages. Such was its success that imitations, adaptations, abridgements, and translations began to appear almost immediately, a publishing phenomenon that has continued to this day. During the eighteenth and nineteenth centuries it became established as a classic book for children. So widespread was its influence in the nineteenth century that it has been described as one of the 'foundation texts of the English working-class movement'.[1] British soldiers in the First World War drew upon memories of reading *The Pilgrim's Progress* in trying to understand and express what was happening to them.[2] Images, names, and phrases from it are part of the common currency of the English language. Even those who have not read the book recognize 'the wilderness of this world', 'Vanity Fair', 'the Slough of Despond', 'Doubting Castle', 'the Delectable Mountains', 'Great-heart', 'Valiant-for-Truth', 'So he passed over, and the trumpets sounded for him on the other side'. A set of verses included in Part Two, 'Who would true valour see, | Let him come hither', is among the best-known hymns in English. If ever a book deserved to be described as one of the 'world's classics', it is *The Pilgrim's Progress*.

Bunyan's Life and Times

John Bunyan, the author of this famous book, lived from 1628 to 1688—a period witnessing some of the most turbulent and momentous events in English history. In 1642, while he was a boy of 14,

[1] E. P. Thompson, *The Making of the English Working Class* (1963; Harmondsworth, 1968), 34. See also Jonathan Rose, *The Intellectual Life of the British Working Classes* (New Haven, 2001), 93–6, 104–6.

[2] See Paul Fussell, *The Great War and Modern Memory* (Oxford, 1975; repr. 2000), 137–44.

tensions between King Charles I and Parliament erupted into a bloody civil war, which ended with the defeat and execution of the king. The institution of monarchy was abolished, together with the House of Lords, and England became a republic governed by Oliver Cromwell with the support of the army. The whole structure of the Church of England was dismantled: bishops, the Prayer Book, the Thirty-Nine Articles, and ecclesiastical courts were all swept away. The wearing of surplices, the playing of organs, and the use of baptismal fonts were prohibited, and the church festivals of Christmas, Easter, and Whitsuntide were abolished. These radical changes horrified many traditional Anglicans, but were supported by Puritan clergy and laity favouring a Presbyterian form of church government instead of episcopacy (rule by bishops). Most Puritans, however, believed in the concept of a state church, and were dismayed when the formal disestablishment of the Church of England allowed the emergence of independent congregations and new religious groups who declared themselves separate from any established church.

Bunyan had grown up in the village of Elstow, near Bedford, the son of a brazier, or tinker. Despite being relatively poor, his parents were able to send him to a local school, where he received a rudimentary education. In November 1644, shortly after his sixteenth birthday, he left home to become a foot soldier in the Parliamentary army, stationed at the nearby garrison town of Newport Pagnell in Buckinghamshire. Little is known about his military service, but though it seems unlikely that he was involved in much actual fighting, the experience of being a soldier must have made a considerable impression on him. In the army the young country boy was mixing with men who were vigorously propounding revolutionary new political and religious ideas. During these years, groups like the Levellers were putting forward detailed and far-reaching proposals for political and constitutional reform, and radical religious sects like Baptists and Quakers were demanding the right to worship freely.

On leaving the army in 1647, Bunyan returned to Elstow to take up his father's trade as a tinker. The next few years were ones of intense spiritual crisis for him, later described in harrowing detail in his spiritual autobiography, *Grace Abounding to the Chief of Sinners* (1666). Ever since childhood he had suffered from nightmares about devils trying to draw him down into Hell, and was terrified at the prospect that he might be marked out for damnation. As a youth he became, in his own estimation, a ringleader in wickedness, one who 'delighted in transgression against the Law of God'. Attempts to reform his life seemed hopeless, but a moment of revelation came when he heard 'three or four poor women' in Bedford talking about their experience of religion, and how 'God had visited their souls with his love in the Lord Jesus'. To Bunyan, 'they spake as if joy did make them speak . . . as if they had found a new world'. He was 'greatly affected with their words', and began to read the Bible in the hope of finding there 'the way to heaven and glory'.[3] In *Grace Abounding* he charts the slow and agonizing progress of his spiritual quest, his prolonged struggle with doubt and despair, and his eventual conviction of God's mercy towards him. An important stage in his conversion came when he made contact with the Independent (or congregational) church in Bedford that had been formed in 1650 under the leadership of an ex-Royalist convert, John Gifford. Bunyan joined this congregation in 1653, and within a few years began to preach in public. His sermons drew on his own spiritual experiences: 'I preached what I felt, what I smartingly did feel.'[4] The right of unlearned and unordained men to preach was a matter of fierce controversy in the seventeenth century. To many conservatives, Presbyterian as well as Anglican, the activities of 'mechanick preachers', as they were scornfully termed, posed a real threat to the whole social and ecclesiastical order. Cromwell, however, believed that 'liberty of conscience is a natural right',[5] and under his tolerant rule in the 1650s sects which were law-abiding were permitted to worship freely under the ministry of their own pastors.

Bunyan's most important intellectual development took place in the context of the radical preaching and pamphleteering, the dramatic political changes, and the extraordinary ideological struggles that characterized the English Revolution.[6] In the atmosphere of religious toleration during the 1650s, he began to write. His early

[3] John Bunyan, *Grace Abounding with Other Spiritual Autobiographies*, ed. John Stachniewski with Anita Pacheco (Oxford World's Classics, 1998), 7, 14, 17. Future references will be cited as *GA*.

[4] Ibid. 78.

[5] Cited in Roger Howell, Jr., 'Cromwell and English Liberty', in R. C. Richardson and G. M. Ridden (eds.), *Freedom and the English Revolution* (Manchester, 1986), 25–44 (31).

[6] The classic account of these years is Christopher Hill, *The World Turned Upside Down: Radical Ideas during the English Revolution* (1972; Harmondsworth, 1975).

publications—sermons, theological treatises, and controversial works—reveal that he shared many of the ideas and attitudes that had become widespread during the revolutionary decades. For example, he was a millenarian, who thought that the return of Christ to rule for a thousand years with his saints on earth was imminent.[7] He also shared some of the social attitudes of radical thinkers. In a work published in 1658, *A Few Sighs from Hell*, he vigorously castigated the rich for their pride and covetousness, and for their oppression of the poor.[8]

Oliver Cromwell died in 1658, and was succeeded as Lord Protector by his son Richard. However his Protectorate quickly collapsed, and in 1660 Charles II was restored to the throne. Bunyan was still a comparatively young man. His greatest works were yet to be written, and to a large extent these works, including *The Pilgrim's Progress*, can be seen as products of the aftermath of revolution, when gains in religious freedom enjoyed by people like Bunyan were abruptly reversed. The Restoration brought back not just the monarchy, but the whole traditional ruling establishment. The Church of England was re-established with the full apparatus of episcopacy, and the House of Lords restored, with seats for bishops. At first it seemed as if there might continue to be some limited form of religious toleration. Charles, in a Declaration issued from Breda in Holland in April 1660, promised 'a liberty to tender consciences . . . no man shall be disquieted or called in question, for differences of opinion in matters of religion which do not disturb the peace of the kingdom'.[9] But when a new House of Commons was elected early in 1661 its members proved to be stridently Anglican, and in no mood to bring in a bill for religious toleration as the king wished. Instead, one of their first actions was to pass an Act of Uniformity, enforcing the use of the Book of Common Prayer in all places of worship. As a result of their refusal to conform, over 1,000 Puritan clergymen were ejected from the Church of England and deprived of their livings.

[7] See W. R. Owens, 'John Bunyan and English Millenarianism', in David Gay, James G. Randall, and Arlette Zinck (eds.), *Awakening Words: John Bunyan and the Language of Community* (Newark, Del., 2000), 81–96.

[8] *A Few Sighs from Hell* (1658), in *The Miscellaneous Works of John Bunyan*, gen. ed. Roger Sharrock, 13 vols. (Oxford, 1976–94), i. 230–382. Future references to this edition will be cited as *Misc. Works*.

[9] Cited in Michael R. Watts, *The Dissenters: From the Reformation to the French Revolution* (Oxford, 1978), 221.

Having purged nonconformity from the Church of England, Parliament set about suppressing every trace of religious dissent in England. There was already a body of legislation under which nonconformists could be punished, notably the Elizabethan Act against Conventicles, whose penalties extended to banishment and death. To this was now added the savage series of statutes that came to be known collectively as the 'Clarendon Code', forbidding all religious meetings not conducted according to the liturgy of the Church of England, and punishing offenders with fines, imprisonment, and transportation. For the next thirty years Dissenters in England endured what came to be known as the 'Great Persecution'. The duration and severity of persecution fluctuated: it was fierce, though patchy, in the 1660s; restrained for most of the 1670s, following a royal Declaration of Indulgence in 1672 which allowed for nonconformist worship in licensed meeting-houses; ferocious again during the first half of the 1680s. In general Dissenters had more freedom in towns, where the corporation often turned a blind eye, than in country areas, where the magistrates were local gentry appointed by the crown. Many Dissenters adopted ingenious stratagems to avoid arrest, and often received help from sympathetic neighbours. When all this is said, however, the fact remains that the human cost of the state repression of Dissent that followed the collapse of the revolution was enormous. Hundreds died, and many more had their health broken in the foul, overcrowded conditions of Restoration prisons.[10]

Bunyan's fate was particularly hard, and indeed in some ways his punishment was an exemplary one. He was to spend over twelve years in prison, one of the longest sentences served by any Dissenter. In November 1660 he had gone to preach at a meeting in Lower Samsell in Bedfordshire. He had been warned that a warrant was out for him, and could have evaded arrest if he had wished. Instead, he chose to offer himself as an example, believing that he had been singled out by God to suffer persecution for the faith. He was duly arrested and brought before the local magistrate.

By good fortune, Bunyan's own account of his arrest and subsequent trial has survived in a series of letters written to his friends in the Bedford congregation. These were not published until long

[10] See Gerald R. Cragg, *Puritanism in the Period of the Great Persecution, 1660–1688* (Cambridge, 1957), 1–127.

after his death, no doubt because they are full of reported speech and vivid detail about the personalities involved. He was charged under the old Elizabethan Conventicle Act with non-attendance at the established church, and with preaching to unlawful assemblies, or 'conventicles'. The five judges before whom he appeared had themselves suffered fines, sequestration of property, and even imprisonment under Cromwell. As became clear in the course of the trial, their object was not so much to 'try' Bunyan in a legal sense, as to beat down his religious arguments and force him to return to his lawful calling as a tinker. The trial developed into a heated debate over the scriptural authority for the use of the Book of Common Prayer, with Bunyan repeatedly getting the better of the argument. When one of the judges thought to clinch the case, declaring that 'we know the Common Prayer-Book hath been ever since the Apostles time', Bunyan swiftly invited him to point out where in the New Testament the Prayer Book is mentioned.[11] In the end they lost patience, and sentenced Bunyan to remain in prison for three months. After that time, if he had not agreed to attend the established church and cease preaching, he would be banished from the realm. If he dared to return thereafter, he would, in the words of the judge, 'stretch by the neck for it'.[12]

In the event Bunyan was not banished, but remained in Bedford gaol. He was no blind fanatic, careless of his own safety, and he writes most movingly in *Grace Abounding* of the distress his imprisonment would bring to his family. 'The parting with my Wife and poor Children hath oft been to me in this place, as the pulling the flesh from my bones . . . O I saw in this condition I was as a man who was pulling down his house upon the head of his Wife and Children; yet thought I, I must do it, I must do it.'[13] He spent his time in prison making shoelaces and writing books, among them *The Pilgrim's Progress*. His release came as a result of a royal pardon granted in May 1672, following a second royal Declaration of Indulgence. Shortly before this he had been appointed pastor of the Bedford congregation. He obtained a licence to preach under the terms of the Indulgence, and became an active leader of the Dissenters, travelling throughout Cambridgeshire, Hertfordshire, and Bedfordshire, and earning for himself the nickname 'Bishop

[11] *GA*, 108–9. [12] Ibid. 110. [13] Ibid. 89–90.

Bunyan'. He was never free of the threat of further imprisonment. A warrant was issued for his arrest in 1675, but seemingly not put into effect. He was gaoled again for six months in 1677, and it was almost certainly during this second period of imprisonment that he put the finishing touches to *The Pilgrim's Progress*. He went on to publish a sequel to his allegory of the Christian life, under the title *The Life and Death of Mr Badman* (1680), an unsparing critique of what Bunyan regarded as the vices of Restoration society. Two years later he published *The Holy War*, a complex and ambitious allegory, weaving together the conversion of Mansoul, the history of the world, and the divine plan for humanity. In 1684, following the appearance of spurious 'continuations', he published his own 'Second Part' of *The Pilgrim's Progress*.

Bunyan's fame as the author of *The Pilgrim's Progress* brought him many invitations to preach at Dissenting meeting-houses in London and elsewhere. He also continued to write and publish. The list of his works runs to nearly sixty titles, of which fourteen were published posthumously. The latter years of Charles II's reign saw renewed persecution of Dissenters, and Bunyan's fears for his safety may be indicated by the deed of gift he had drawn up in 1685, making over all his possessions to his wife. In 1687 the political situation was abruptly reversed, when James II offered toleration to both Protestant and Roman Catholic Dissenters. Bunyan, however, did not live to see the 'Glorious Revolution', when James II was overthrown and replaced by William III, and religious toleration was at last granted to Protestant Dissenters. His death in August 1688 was brought about by a fever contracted while riding from Reading to London in heavy rain. He was buried in the famous Dissenting burial ground at Bunhill Fields, Finsbury.

Allegory

> There was some books too . . . One was 'Pilgrim's Progress', about a man that left his family it didn't say why. I read considerable in it now and then. The statements was interesting, but tough.[14]

Like Huck Finn, modern readers of *The Pilgrim's Progress* are liable

[14] Mark Twain, *Adventures of Huckleberry Finn*, ed. Emory Elliott (Oxford, 1999), 99.

to find it interesting, but also tough to come to terms with as a literary text. One reason for this may be that it is presented as an allegory, a literary form very popular in the Middle Ages and down to the end of the seventeenth century, but which is much less commonly used now. Characters and places are given names indicating that they are not actual individuals but personify or represent abstract qualities or ideas. *The Pilgrim's Progress* may seem to be about a journey from one city to another, but is 'really' about the Christian experience of conversion leading to salvation.

The story is presented as a dream in which the dreamer sees a man (later called Christian) with a book in his hand and a heavy burden on his back, in great distress because the book tells him he lives in the City of Destruction, and is condemned to death and judgment. Advised by Evangelist to flee towards a Wicket Gate, he sets out forthwith, leaving behind his wife and children who refuse to accompany him. The course of his subsequent pilgrimage is full of danger and adventure. It takes him through the Slough of Despond, past the Burning Mount, thence to the Wicket Gate, the Interpreter's House, the Cross (where his burden rolls away), the Hill Difficulty, the House Beautiful, the Valley of Humiliation, the Valley of the Shadow of Death, Vanity Fair, Lucre Hill, By-Path Meadow, Doubting Castle, the Delectable Mountains, the Enchanted Ground, and the country of Beulah. On the way he is helped by trusty companions, first Faithful, who is put to death at Vanity Fair, and then Hopeful, who accompanies him to the end. They have to face enemies, such as the foul fiend Apollyon who is slain by Christian, Lord Hategood who presides over the trial of Faithful in Vanity Fair, and Giant Despair, who imprisons Christian and Hopeful in Doubting Castle. They also encounter false friends like Mr Worldly-Wiseman, Talkative, By-ends, and Ignorance, who give them dangerous advice. At length their pilgrimage ends when they pass over the River and enter the Celestial City. In Part Two, Christian's wife Christiana sets out on pilgrimage, together with her children and their neighbour Mercy. Escorted by Great-heart, who slays various giants and monsters, they follow in Christian's footsteps, witnessing the scenes of his trials and victories. Their pilgrimage is a leisurely one, and on the way they are joined by a great number of fellow-pilgrims, such as Mr Feeble-mind, Mr Ready-to-halt, Mr Honest, Mr Valiant-for-Truth, Mr Stand-fast, Mr Despondency, and his daughter Much-afraid. At the end they too pass safely over the River one by one.

In the verse 'Apology' which prefaces the book, Bunyan explains and defends his use of allegory, noting that the Bible offers a precedent for the use of metaphor and parable for religious ends: 'I find that holy Writ in many places, | Hath semblance with this method, where the cases | Doth call for one thing to set forth another' (p. 7).[15] But Bunyan certainly does not think of the literary form of his work as a worthless husk, to be discarded for its kernel. On the contrary, he speaks of his own pleasure in writing the book:

> I only thought to make
> I knew not what: nor did I undertake
> Thereby to please my Neighbour; no not I,
> I did it mine own self to gratifie.
>
> . . . .
>
> Thus I set Pen to Paper with delight,
> And quickly had my thoughts in black and white.
> For having now my Method by the end,
> Still as I pull'd, it came . . . (p. 3)

In this description of the creative process, Bunyan expresses his sense of writing as a form of experiment or exploration in which, like many artists, he only discovers in the course of his practice what it is he is trying to say. Throughout these prefatory verses, he stresses that writing communicates through a shared enjoyment, and is of value for its own sake. Indeed he ends by highlighting the pleasure his readers can expect:

> Would'st thou divert thy self from Melancholly?
> Would'st thou be pleasant, yet be far from folly?
>
> . . . .
>
> Would'st thou be in a Dream, and yet not sleep?
> Or would'st thou in a moment Laugh and Weep?
> Wouldest thou loose thy self, and catch no harm?
> And find thy self again without a charm?
> Would'st read thy self, and read thou know'st not what
> And yet know whether thou are blest or not,
> By reading the same lines? O then come hither,
> And lay my Book, thy Head and Heart together. (pp. 8–9)

[15] Page references in parentheses are to the present edition of *The Pilgrim's Progress*.

These jauntily confident lines show that Bunyan is alive to the affective power of his language and imaginative creation, and recognizes that the literal 'surface' of the story he is telling is itself of value. C. S. Lewis has rightly emphasized that allegory should not be regarded as a cryptogram, existing only to be decoded and then cast aside. 'We ought not to be thinking "This green valley, where the shepherd boy is singing, represents humility"; we ought to be discovering, as we read, that humility is like that green valley. That way, moving always into the book, not out of it, from the concept to the image, enriches the concept.'[16]

The opening paragraph of *The Pilgrim's Progress*, one of the most famous in all literature, is a good example of Bunyan's narrative method.

As I walk'd through the wilderness of this world, I lighted on a certain place, where was a Denn; And I laid me down in that place to sleep: And as I slept I dreamed a Dream. I dreamed, and behold *I saw a Man cloathed with Raggs, standing in a certain place, with his face from his own House, a Book in his hand, and a great burden upon his back*. I looked, and saw him open the Book, and Read therein; and as he Read, he wept and trembled: and not being able longer to contain, he brake out with a lamentable cry; saying, *what shall I do?* (p. 10)

What most strikes us here is the simple but powerful portrayal of a man in great distress of mind, not knowing what to do or where to turn. The rhythms of the prose, its subtle use of alliteration and repetition of key words, strike an intensely urgent and personal note. It is no abstract theological dogma that lays hold of our attention and makes us want to read on: we are taken immediately into a very particular human situation.

At the same time, however, we know from the title of Bunyan's book that this man in distress is also 'representative' in some larger sense: the pilgrim's progress is 'from this world, to that which is to come'. And if we are alert to the language we begin to sense wider resonances. The phrase 'the wilderness of this world', for example, evokes the whole Christian concept of the fallen world inhabited by humankind after Adam and Eve are driven from Eden, and more specifically the biblical account of the 'great and terrible wilderness'

[16] C. S. Lewis, 'The Vision of John Bunyan', in Roger Sharrock (ed.), *The Pilgrim's Progress: A Casebook* (London, 1976), 198.

that the Children of Israel had to pass through before they could enter the Promised Land.[17]

There is, in fact, a tension—a creative tension—in *The Pilgrim's Progress* and in Bunyan's attitude to his book. On the one hand it is an allegory designed to assert the prime reality of a religious view based on a supreme confidence in a world that is to come. On the other hand (and at the same time) it is a very specific and concretely realized product of *this* world at a particular moment in its history. The episode where Christian passes through the Valley of the Shadow of Death provides an excellent example of this. It would be hard to think of a more completely allegorical and non-realist passage. Much of its power and effect depends on the sense it evokes of the danger and closeness of Hell. The two men Christian meets running away from it use traditional imagery to describe it for him. It is full of hobgoblins, satyrs, and dragons: 'we heard also . . . a continual howling and yelling, as of a People under unutterable misery' (p. 62). And yet the passage is also full of effects that can be called 'realist'. The dialogue between Christian and the two men comes across as actual, colloquial speech. 'But what have you seen?' said Christian. 'Seen! Why the Valley it self, which is as dark as pitch' (p. 62). We have a strong sense of the physical effort of Christian's walk along the pathway in the dark: 'oft times when he lift up his foot to set forward, he knew not where, or upon what he should set it next' (p. 63). But what most of all strikes us about the passage is its portrayal of a psychological experience of great force and realism. As he goes through the Valley, Christian is terrified by flames and smoke, and hears dreadful noises. What Bunyan conveys is the effort of mental will that enables him to continue:

> coming to a place, where he thought he heard a company of *Fiends* coming forward to meet him, he stopt; and began to muse what he had best to do. Sometimes he had half a thought to go back. Then again he thought he might be half way through the Valley; he remembred also how he had already vanquished many a danger: and that the danger of going back might be much more, then [than] for to go forward; so he resolved to go on. Yet the *Fiends* seemed to come nearer and nearer, but when they were come even almost at him, he cried out with a most vehement voice, *I will walk in the strength of the Lord God*; so they gave back, and came no further.
>
> (p. 63)

[17] See Deut. 1: 19.

Part of what Christian learns is how to conquer the deadly fears conjured up in his imagination. In the next paragraph, a marginal note tells us that Satan had all the time been trying to make Christian speak blasphemies. But when we read that poor Christian 'did not know his own voice', we recognize an experience we can all share: of hearing oneself say things that one does not fully understand or even want to say.

The Bible

One of the more unusual features of *The Pilgrim's Progress* for modern readers is that the margins of the text are filled with a series of notes, some of them commenting on what is happening, but often also referring to biblical texts. These notes have several functions, but one is to offer us interpretative keys to the deeper meaning of the narrative.[18] So, for example, if we look again at the opening paragraph, we see in the margin a whole series of references to the Bible. If we look up these texts in the Authorized Version, we discover the sources of the images of the rags and the great burden. In Isaiah 64: 6 we find that 'we are all as an unclean thing, and all our righteousnesses are as filthy rags'. Again, in Psalm 38: 4 we read, 'mine iniquities are gone over mine head: as an heavy burden they are too heavy for me.' Thus the rags represent worthless claims to righteousness, and the great burden represents the weight of human sinfulness.

The importance of the Bible in *The Pilgrim's Progress*, and in Bunyan's thought more generally, cannot be overemphasized. He frequently quotes from it explicitly, but often we find that he has absorbed biblical phrasing into his own prose.[19] The Bible was absolutely central to religious thought and practice in the seventeenth century, and to artistic, scientific, and political thought as well. For the learned John Milton as much as for the unlearned Bunyan, it was 'that book within whose sacred context all wisdom is enfolded'.[20] 'Thou must give more credit to one syllable of the written Word of the Gospel', Bunyan asserts, 'then [than] thou must give to all the

[18] See Maxine Hancock, *The Key in the Window: Marginal Notes in Bunyan's Narratives* (Vancouver, 2000).

[19] Many examples of this are given in the Explanatory Notes to the present edition.

[20] Cited in Christopher Hill, *The English Bible and the Seventeenth-Century Revolution* (1993; Harmondsworth, 1994), 21.

Saints and Angels in Heaven and Earth.'[21] In *Grace Abounding*, he gives a fascinating account of the development of his Bible reading, and of the effect this had on him during the period of his conversion. Sometimes he was terrified by texts that seemed to offer him no hope of salvation; at other times he would be comforted by texts such as 'that blessed sixth of *John, And him that comes to me, I will in no wise cast out!* [John 6: 37]'.[22]

One of the themes of *Grace Abounding* is how Bunyan learned to interpret the Bible, and this is a point of some significance in understanding *The Pilgrim's Progress*. In his 'Apology' he speaks of how, in the Old Testament, the gospel is 'held forth | By Types, Shadows and Metaphors' (p. 5). What he is referring to is a method of interpretation of the Bible by which persons, events, and things in the Old Testament are regarded as 'types' or 'shadows' of persons, events, and things in the Christian dispensation, the latter being referred to as 'antitypes' or 'fulfilments' of the types. The authority for this goes back to the New Testament. So, for example, we read in the Gospels and the Pauline epistles that Adam is a type of Christ; the crossing of the Red Sea by the Israelites is a type of Christian baptism; and the brazen serpent lifted up in the wilderness is a type of Christ's crucifixion.[23] In the seventeenth century typology was the standard method of interpreting Scripture, and of applying it to the lives and experiences of the church and individual believers. As the Puritan preacher Herbert Palmer put it, 'the Records of Holy Scripture . . . are not only Stories of things done in that Age, but Prophecies also of future events in succeeding Generations'.[24] For another Puritan, Thomas Taylor, the Bible was 'a notable guide through this pilgrimage of our life'. In reading it the Christian 'shall be able to parallel his Estate in some of the Saints, he shall see his own case in some of them, and so shall obtain instruction, direction, and consolation by them'.[25] George Herbert is saying the same in his typological poem 'The Bunch of Grapes':

[21] *The Doctrine of the Law and Grace Unfolded* (1659), in *Misc. Works*, ii. 191.
[22] *GA*, 70.
[23] See Rom. 5: 14; 1 Cor. 10: 1–4, 11; John 3: 14–15.
[24] Herbert Palmer, *The Glasse of Gods Providence Towards His Faithfull Ones* (1644), 'The Epistle Dedicatorie'.
[25] Thomas Taylor, *The Works* (1659), 89, 93.

For as the Jews of old by Gods command
Travell'd, and saw no town:
So now each Christian hath his journeys spann'd:
Their storie pennes and sets us down.[26]

For Bunyan, as for others in the seventeenth century, his own spiritual experiences could be intimately paralleled by and patterned on the experiences of the stories of the Jews in the Old Testament, and the prophetic books of the Old and New Testaments. We can see examples of this application of Bible stories in *The Pilgrim's Progress*. When Christian loses his Roll and has to go back for it, his experience is explicitly compared to the Exodus narrative: 'Thus it happened to *Israel* for their sin, they were sent back again by the way of the Red-Sea' (p. 44). In his journey through the Valley of the Shadow of Death, Christian passes 'that Quagg', into which '*King* David *once did fall*' (p. 63). Judge Hategood in Vanity Fair refers to acts passed by Pharaoh, Nebuchadnezzar, and Darius, thus linking himself to these persecutors and their eventual fates, and associating Christian and Faithful with Moses, who led his people out of Egypt; with the three young Hebrews who faced the fiery furnace and were delivered; and with Daniel who survived the lion's den (p. 94).

Even the basic metaphor of the Christian life as a pilgrimage, or journey, would have come to Bunyan from the Bible. In Hebrews 11: 13–16, for example, the Old Testament patriarchs are described as 'strangers and pilgrims on the earth' who desired 'a better country, that is, an heavenly'. He had often employed the metaphor in his earlier writings. The life of the church, he says, is a 'journying from *Egypt* to *Canaan*, from *Babylon* to this *Jerusalem-state*'.[27] The path trodden by believers is '*the way for the wayfaring men, even the way of holiness* . . . in which every one walks that entereth in by the Gates of New *Jerusalem*'.[28] Closest of all to *The Pilgrim's Progress* is a passage from a work which may indeed have given Bunyan the idea for his allegory, a sermon-treatise entitled *The Heavenly Footman*:

Because the *way is long* . . . and there is many a dirty step, many a high Hill, much Work to do, a wicked Heart, World and Devil to overcome . . . thou must Run a long and tedious Journey, thorow the wast howling

[26] *The English Poems of George Herbert*, ed. C. A. Patrides (London, 1974), 139.
[27] *The Holy City* (1665), in *Misc. Works*, iii. 97.
[28] Ibid. 150–1.

Wilderness, before thou come to the Land of Promise . . . Beware of by-paths . . . There are crooked Paths, Paths in which Men go astray, Paths that lead to Death and Damnation: But take heed of all those . . .[29]

As these examples suggest, Bunyan's purpose in writing *The Pilgrim's Progress* was no different from his purpose in more straightforwardly homiletic works. He was no art-for-art's-sake aesthete, but was writing with an urgent message: 'This Book will make a Travailer [traveller] of thee, | If by its Counsel thou wilt ruled be' (p. 8). In an important sense all of Bunyan's works are about the same single theme: the experience of religious conversion. The idea of conversion—a turning away from sin and towards God—is of course central to the message of the New Testament. Only by forgiveness of sin can eternal life be gained. In the sixteenth and seventeenth centuries Protestant theologians developed an elaborate account of the process by which conversion was supposed to take place. According to these theologians, humankind since the Fall of Adam and Eve is under bondage to sin, and unable to enter into a proper relationship with God. Salvation cannot be merited by any amount of 'good works' on the part of sinners, but is a free gift of God alone. This offer of salvation is not open to all, but operates within a framework of predestination whereby some are 'elected' by God to be saved and brought to Heaven, while others will be left in their sinful state and will end up in Hell for ever. Those elected to salvation would be enabled by God's grace to live holy lives on earth, doing God's will and bearing witness to the gospel. Conversion would proceed through a series of defined steps. The first of these would be 'effectual calling', by which the Holy Spirit would 'call' the sinner to repentance, and bring about conversion, or new birth. This would lead on to 'justification', by which the newly converted sinner would be made just before God, and forgiven and acquitted of the punishment due to sin, through the merits of Christ. Then would follow 'sanctification', the continuing supply of divine grace which would enable the convert to 'persevere' in faith, struggling against sin and endeavouring to lead a life of holiness acceptable to God. Finally would come 'glorification', the reward of eternal life in heaven.

This is the scheme of salvation that Christian's experiences exemplify in *The Pilgrim's Progress*. It is represented allegorically,

[29] *The Heavenly Footman* (1698), in *Misc. Works*, v. 150, 155.

but is also discussed openly at various points in the text. Hopeful, for example, gives a straightforward account of his conversion, one resembling closely the account of Bunyan's own conversion given in *Grace Abounding*. Like Bunyan, Hopeful describes how he had been awakened to a sense of his guilt as a sinner, and at first tried to reform his life, but soon realized that he could never by his own efforts become truly righteous in the sight of a wrathful God. After being told by Faithful about the work of Jesus on the cross, he came to see that only through believing in Christ would he be saved: 'I must look for righteousness in his person, and for satisfaction for my sins by his blood' (p. 136). Similarly, in Part Two, Great-heart offers a detailed exposition of the doctrine of justification, and how this is accomplished by the 'imputation' of Christ's righteousness to the sinner (pp. 197–9).[30]

Literature and Theology

The theology underlying *The Pilgrim's Progress* is perhaps the 'toughest' aspect of the work for some readers. Their problem is in accepting what was for Bunyan an absolutely crucial point about salvation: that attempts to earn it by 'good works', or living a morally upright life, are doomed. George Bernard Shaw indeed remarked admiringly that 'the whole allegory is a consistent attack on morality and respectability, without a word that one can remember against vice and crime'.[31] Many of the characters the pilgrims meet are not, on the face of it, wicked people deserving damnation: indeed most of them think they are on the path to Heaven. But what Bunyan insists upon, again and again, is that there is only *one* way to Heaven and only those justified by faith will get there. Those who trust in 'morality', like Mr Worldly-Wiseman, or who are downright hypocrites, like By-ends and his friends, or who only have a 'head' knowledge of religion, like Talkative, are not going to get to the Celestial City. Even ignorance of the truth will be no excuse. The character of that name, Ignorance, is quite convinced that he is not a bad man: 'I have

[30] For accounts of Bunyan's theological views, see Richard L. Greaves, *John Bunyan* (Abingdon, 1969), and Pieter de Vries, *John Bunyan on the Order of Salvation*, trans. C. van Haaften (New York, 1994).

[31] Shaw, 'Epistle Dedicatory' to *Man and Superman* (1907), in Sharrock (ed.), *The Pilgrim's Progress: A Casebook*, 118.

been a good Liver . . . I Pray, Fast, pay Tithes, and give Alms' (p. 120). But when he gets to the gates of the City, he is not admitted, but is bound and carried off to Hell.

Coleridge praised *The Pilgrim's Progress* as 'teaching and enforcing the whole saving truth according to the mind that was in Christ Jesus'. In his view it was 'incomparably the best *Summa Theologiae Evangelicae* ever produced by a writer not miraculously inspired'. However he also introduced what would become a vastly influential distinction between Bunyan the literary artist and Bunyan the theologian:

In that admirable Allegory, the first Part of the Pilgrim's Progress, which delights everyone, the interest is so great that in spite of all the writer's attempts to force the allegoric purpose on the Reader's mind by his strange names . . . his piety was baffled by his genius, and the Bunyan of Parnassus had the better of the Bunyan of the Conventicle—and with the same illusion as we read any tale known to be fictitious, as a novel,—we go on with the characters as real persons.[32]

Critics less sympathetic to Bunyan's theology than Coleridge have seized on the distinction between 'Parnassus' and 'Conventicle' to explain how a believer in what they regard as a narrow and abhorrent set of beliefs could nevertheless have produced such a masterpiece of literary art. F. R. Leavis, for example, found it hard to imagine how Bunyan's 'polemical and damnation-dispensing theology' could ever have been conducive to the 'generous creative power' which is 'beyond question there in *The Pilgrim's Progress*'. He admitted that he read the book 'without any thought of its theological intention'.[33] Others have taken the line that the 'redeeming literary quality of *The Pilgrim's Progress* resides in the fact that Bunyan's imagination transcends his theological convictions'.[34]

More recent critics have argued that what they see as Bunyan's harsh and inhumane theology cannot be set aside so easily, and have dwelt at some length on the tortuous paradoxes and 'persecutory fears' that they find dramatized in the allegory. Thomas Luxon, for

[32] Cited in Sharrock (ed.), *The Pilgrim's Progress: A Casebook*, 52–3.

[33] F. R. Leavis, 'Bunyan's Resoluteness', ibid., 204–20.

[34] Gordon Campbell, 'Fishing in Other Men's Waters: Bunyan and the Theologians', in N. H. Keeble (ed.), *John Bunyan: Conventicle and Parnassus* (Oxford, 1988), 137–51 (150). The same argument is put at greater length in an earlier essay by Campbell, 'The Theology of *The Pilgrim's Progress*', in Vincent Newey (ed.), *The Pilgrim's Progress: Critical and Historical Views* (Liverpool, 1980), 251–62.

example, speaks of Bunyan's Christianity as 'more a religion of brutality than of love, of metaphysics than of mercy'.[35] John Stachniewski, for his part, lays great emphasis on the doctrine of predestination, seeing this as central to *The Pilgrim's Progress*: 'Christian devotes most of his energy to sizing up the meaning, in the light of the decrees of election and reprobation, of each step in his journey.'[36] In the most extensive discussion of the whole issue to date, Michael Davies has argued that such critics are mistaken in seeing Bunyan as obsessed with predestination and morose introspection. 'Far from dismissing the sinner's role in his or her own salvation', Davies says, 'Bunyan's doctrine of salvation accords the human will a particularly positive role in its spiritual wayfaring.' He finds *The Pilgrim's Progress* to be 'more testing than terrifying, more accommodating than accusatory'.[37]

There is no doubt that Bunyan's theological system included the doctrine of predestination. He was very far from being alone in believing this: it was the agreed doctrine of the Church of England up to the middle of the seventeenth century (and even today remains in the Thirty-Nine Articles). But in *The Pilgrim's Progress*, as opposed to his non-fictional works, Bunyan is not so much concerned with theological doctrine itself (though there is plenty of discussion of that), as with the consequences of that doctrine for the ways in which his characters live their lives. Christian and his pilgrim companions may in theory have been predestined by God to be saved. In practice, they doubt their salvation all the way and never achieve certainty, and at every point they seem to be freely choosing how to act.

What *The Pilgrim's Progress* shows us, it may be argued, is how characters holding what may seem a remote and in some ways unappealing set of beliefs may nevertheless display a whole range of human virtues and frailties: courage, solidarity, friendship, presumption, fear, and so on. Bunyan's achievement, we might say, is to contrive to make his vision of the Christian life seem attractive, and his characters ones with whom we can sympathize. He shows us how

[35] Thomas H. Luxon, *Literal Figures: Puritan Allegory and the Reformation Crisis in Representation* (Chicago, 1995), 200.

[36] John Stachniewski, *The Persecutory Imagination: English Puritanism and the Literature of Religious Despair* (Oxford, 1991), 169.

[37] Michael Davies, *Graceful Reading: Theology and Narrative in the Works of John Bunyan* (Oxford, 2002), 5 and *passim*.

what seems, at first sight, to be a totally selfish and egocentric decision—ruthlessly to pursue one's *own* salvation at the expense of all one's human ties (to family, friends, and community)—bears fruit in a quite unexpected way. Christian discovers that pilgrims like himself are actually able to help one another; indeed (though never taking their eyes off their own personal salvation), they absolutely need one another.

This emphasis on human companionship and mutual support is the dominant theme of Part Two. The plot here, in which the itinerary of Christian's earlier progress is repeated in a calmer and much more protected atmosphere, has often been criticized as inferior to Part One.[38] In some ways, however, it can be regarded as a very fine invention on Bunyan's part. What he shows is how Christian's struggles and defeats and heroic persistence have blazed a trail and made the way altogether easier for Christiana and their children, and for all the weaker pilgrims who follow: Mr Fearing, Mr Feeble-mind, Mr Ready-to-halt, Mr Despondency and his daughter Much-afraid, and the rest. We might indeed think that this makes great psychological sense; at any rate it brings home to us the great gulf between *Grace Abounding* and *The Pilgrim's Progress*. Bunyan's own agonizing solitary battles with despair, as described in *Grace Abounding*, turn out, when recreated in allegorical romance, to bring benefit to weaker mortals. He makes things easier for all the many readers who have suffered from similar dark nights of the soul.

There may indeed be an element of self-portrait in Great-heart, as the pastor of the little flock of pilgrims in Part Two, who guides and protects them from harm. Not surprisingly, modern readers have reacted against what they see as the patriarchal aspects of Bunyan's presentation of his female pilgrims, as weak, timid, and in need of instruction suited to their lowly capacities. Margaret Olofson Thickstun has argued forcefully that 'Bunyan's belief in the spiritual inferiority of women makes it impossible for him to assign positive allegorical significance to a female character'.[39] N. H. Keeble has also stressed the extent to which Bunyan's discourse 'habitually construes and images the spiritual life in terms of masculine

[38] See N. H. Keeble, 'Christiana's Key: The Unity of *The Pilgrim's Progress*', in Newey (ed.), *The Pilgrim's Progress: Critical and Historical Views*, 1–20.

[39] Margaret Olofson Thickstun, *Fictions of the Feminine: Puritan Doctrine and the Representation of Women* (Ithaca, NY, 1988), 88.

achievement . . . and so fails to offer a positive view of femininity to set beside the dynamic image of masculinity. His imaginative sympathy for women is never so intense as to jeopardise patriarchy.'[40] Other critics have argued that the gender politics of *The Pilgrim's Progress* are more complicated than these readings suggest. Tamsin Spargo sees Bunyan's female characters as 'disrupting to varying degrees the discursive framework in which they are contained', and stresses the process of 'identification and self-recognition within the text' that occurs for female readers.[41] Similarly, Stuart Sim and David Walker have pointed to what they see as a contradiction between Bunyan's conventional patriarchal views of women, and his nonconformist stress on spiritual liberation. 'His beliefs are pulling him in different directions: trying to keep women subordinate, while also having to acknowledge that "God is no respecter of persons".'[42] Kathleen Swaim, in a notably sympathetic reading of Part Two, argues that Mercy, in particular, 'goes well beyond what is usually defined as the female role'. 'By the end she has translated the theoretical theology of part I into a full program of works and thereby subsumed the mode of masculine achievement within a fully realized, empowered, comprehensive, and multiplying feminine heroism.'[43]

Social Satire and Psychological Realism

The Pilgrim's Progress is a book strongly marked by the context within which it was produced, and by Bunyan's own experiences as a prisoner of conscience. In *Grace Abounding*, he described the crisis with which he was faced as he contemplated prolonged imprisonment, and even the gallows. Why was he doing it? What if, after all, his conversion was not secure? What if he should bring dishonour to the cause by displaying fear as he was about to be hanged?

[40] N. H. Keeble, '"Here is her Glory, even to be under Him": The Feminine in the Thought and Work of John Bunyan', in Anne Laurence, W. R. Owens, and Stuart Sim (eds.), *John Bunyan and his England, 1628–88* (London, 1990), 131–47 (147).

[41] Tamsin Spargo, *The Writing of John Bunyan* (Aldershot, 1997), 95, 125.

[42] Stuart Sim and David Walker, *Bunyan and Authority: The Rhetoric of Dissent and the Legitimation Crisis in Seventeenth-Century England* (Bern, 2000), 170.

[43] Kathleen Swaim, *Pilgrim's Progress, Puritan Progress: Discourses and Contexts* (Urbana, Ill., 1993), 191.

Wherefore I prayed to God that he would comfort me, and give me strength to do and suffer what he should call me to; yet no comfort appear'd . . . I was also at this time so possessed with the thought of death, that oft I was as if I was on the Ladder, with the Rope about my neck . . . I thought also, that God might chuse whether he would give me comfort now, or at the hour of death . . . 'twas my dutie to stand to his Word, whether he would ever look upon me or no, or save me at the last: Wherefore, thought I, the point being thus, I am for going on, and venturing my eternal state with Christ, whether I have comfort here or no; if God doth not come in, thought I, I will leap off the Ladder even blindfold into Eternitie, sink or swim, come heaven, come hell; Lord Jesus, if thou wilt catch me, do; if not, I will venture for thy Name.[44]

This passage brings home vividly—even a touch melodramatically—the seriousness of the decision that faced Dissenters: to conform, and lead a quiet life; or not to conform, and face constant persecution, with fines, imprisonment, and even death. The failure of the revolution brought not just political defeat, but a determined effort by the state to secure the total extermination of that feature of the revolutionary decades that had meant most to Bunyan and his kind, the freedom to worship as their conscience dictated.

The experience of state repression lies at the very heart of *The Pilgrim's Progress*. In the first sentence of the book, the world is described as a 'wilderness', and the narrator is in 'a Denn', or gaol as the margin glosses it. Christian, setting out on his pilgrimage, is warned by Mr Worldly-Wiseman of the dangers ahead: '*thou art like to meet with . . . Wearisomness, Painfulness, Hunger, Perils, Nakedness, Sword, Lions, Dragons, Darkness; and in a word, death*' (p. 19). Evangelist likewise warns of the 'many tribulations' Christian and Faithful will have to endure: 'you will be hardly beset with enemies, who will strain hard but they will kill you . . . one or both of you must seal the testimony which you hold, with blood' (p. 85). When they get to Vanity Fair, it happens as Evangelist has predicted. The pilgrims are set upon, beaten, thrown into a cage, and finally brought to trial before Lord Hategood. One of the witnesses, Envy, testifies that Faithful 'neither regardeth Prince nor People, Law nor Custom; but doth all that he can to possess all men with certain of his disloyal notions' (p. 91). Another witness, Pickthank, alleges that the pilgrims have 'railed on our noble Prince *Beelzebub*, and hath spoke

[44] *GA*, 91–2.

contemptibly of his honourable Friends, whose names are the Lord *Old man*, the Lord *Carnal delight*, the Lord *Luxurious*, the *Lord Desire of Vain-glory*, my old Lord *Lechery*, Sir *Having Greedy*, with all the rest of our Nobility' (p. 92).

The allegation that the pilgrims have 'bespattered most of the Gentry of our town' enrages Lord Hategood, and indeed it has often been noted that the ungodly in *The Pilgrim's Progress* are of the gentry or nobility, while pilgrims are among the poor and despised in society.[45] What is remarkable about the whole episode, indeed, is the toughness and defiance of Bunyan's social satire. He relates the deliberations of the jury with wonderful comic zest:

And first Mr. *Blind-man*, the foreman, said, *I see clearly that this man is an Heretick*. Then said Mr. *No-good, Away with such a fellow from the Earth. Ay*, said Mr. *Malice, for I hate the very looks of him.* Then said Mr. *Love-lust, I could never indure him. Nor I*, said Mr. *Live-loose, for he would alwayes be condemning my way. Hang him, hang him*, said Mr. *Heady. A sorry Scrub*, said Mr. *High-mind. My heart riseth against him*, said Mr. *Enmity. He is a Rogue*, said Mr. *Lyar. Hanging is too good for him*, said Mr. *Cruelty. Lets dispatch him out of the way*, said Mr. *Hate-light*. Then said Mr. *Implacable, Might I have all the World given me, I could not be reconciled to him, therefore let us forthwith bring him in guilty of death*. (p. 95)

The trial of Faithful at Vanity Fair dramatizes, in part, the experience of persecution in Restoration England. The concept of justice is simply not relevant here: indeed Faithful admits the truth of the charges brought against him and Christian. The pilgrims and the people of Vanity Fair speak a different language and have totally opposing values. What this brief passage also brings out is the brilliance of Bunyan's handling of names and speech. The characters in *The Pilgrim's Progress* are presented not so much as allegorical embodiments of a single abstract quality, but as types associated with particular characteristics and activities and who are brought to life in the way they speak.

How did the oppressed Dissenters survive the successive waves of persecution? Here again, *The Pilgrim's Progress* gives us some of the answers. One of the most important sources of strength was the

[45] See Christopher Hill, *A Turbulent, Seditious, and Factious People: John Bunyan and his Church* (Oxford, 1988), 214–15.

sense of fellowship, of belonging to a community of believers. In Bunyan's allegory, the 'gathered church' is represented as the Palace Beautiful, to which Christian is admitted after his burden has rolled off his back. It is not easy to enter this church—there are lions of persecution outside, which Mistrust and Timorous have been too afraid to pass—but it has been built by the Lord of the Hill 'for the relief and security of Pilgrims' (p. 47). Christian arrives 'weary, and benighted', having just ascended the Hill Difficulty and suffered the distress of losing his Roll, and is in need of rest and comfort. He is greeted by the 'Grave and Beautiful Damsel, named *Discretion*', who fetches others of 'the Family', Prudence, Piety, and Charity. They bring him in and converse graciously with him, before setting him down to supper at a table 'furnished with fat things, and with Wine that was well refined' (p. 52). Afterwards he is put to bed in 'a large upper Chamber, whose window opened towards the Sun rising; the name of the Chamber was *Peace*' (p. 53).

This picture of the church as a *family* was central to the way in which Dissenters of all denominations conceived of the bonds between members. It was, moreover, a family that had come together by free choice, not by custom or compulsion. They were a society of friends, as the Quakers later came to call themselves. Through the loving support of these 'good Companions' (p. 55) Christian is provided with the clothing and equipment to continue on his way to the Celestial City. Much of Bunyan's writing, including *Grace Abounding* and *The Pilgrim's Progress*, was designed, in part, to help bind Dissenters together in the face of efforts to fragment and annihilate them. Despite the imposition of censorship, writing was one of the most powerful weapons of resistance of Dissenters. The authorities tried to stamp out illegal printing—two of Bunyan's publishers were tried for seditious libel—but their efforts were never very effective. Dissenters were able to publish books and pamphlets defending themselves, challenging the government's representation of them as seditious rebels, and exhorting their supporters to remain steadfast.[46]

Much of *The Pilgrim's Progress* is given over to a portrayal and examination of the doubts, fears, temptations, and enemies—both external and internal—that Dissenters would have to face. The

[46] See N. H. Keeble, *The Literary Culture of Nonconformity in Later Seventeenth-Century England* (Leicester, 1987), ch. 3, 'Nonconformity and the Press'.

temptation to give way to doubt and despair is one Bunyan himself was especially prone to. *Grace Abounding* is unique among spiritual autobiographies in the seventeenth century in the amount of space it devotes to descriptions of repeated waves of despair. The problem is dramatized most memorably in *The Pilgrim's Progress* when Christian and Hopeful are imprisoned by Giant Despair in Doubting Castle. The pilgrims leave the narrow pathway they are travelling to take a short-cut through By-Path Meadow. Discovering their mistake, they try to find their way back, but night falls and they cannot retrace their steps, so they decide to wait for daybreak.

> Now there was not far from the place where they lay, a *Castle*, called *Doubting-Castle*, the owner whereof was *Giant Despair*, and it was in his grounds they now were sleeping; wherefore he getting up in the morning early, and walking up and down in his Fields, caught *Christian* and *Hopeful* asleep in his grounds. Then with a *grim* and *surly* voice he bid them awake, and asked them whence they were? and what they did in his grounds? They told him, they were Pilgrims, and that they had lost their way. Then said the *Giant*, You have this night trespassed on me, by trampling in, and lying on my grounds, and therefore you must go along with me. So they were forced to go, because he was stronger than they. They also had but little to say, for they knew themselves in a fault. The *Giant* therefore drove them before him, and put them into his Castle, into a very dark Dungeon, nasty and stinking to the spirit of these two men. (pp. 109–10)

The whole episode is a wonderful example of Bunyan's literary method, with its vividly naturalistic language, strong narrative drive, and easy incorporation of elements from folk-tale and popular romance. It is noteworthy, also, that Giant Despair 'walking up and down in his fields' suggests the power of the landowning gentry. His country estate is marked out by the stile and fence, and is defended by the laws of trespass. He is perfectly within his legal rights in arresting the pilgrims.[47]

We can also see in this episode some of the qualities of psychological realism that we noticed earlier in the Valley of the Shadow of Death episode. Although Giant Despair is an externalized figure he is also, in a sense, a manifestation of the pilgrims' own feelings of guilt and fear at having left the true pathway. Bunyan here

[47] On this see James Turner, 'Bunyan's Sense of Place', in Newey (ed.), *The Pilgrim's Progress: Critical and Historical Views*, 91–110.

dramatizes very powerfully and acutely the ways in which states of psychological torment are not so much fallen into as created in the mind.[48] What happens during their period of imprisonment and self-doubt is that the pilgrims manage to control their anxieties. Giant Despair, urged on by his wife, tells them that they may as well kill themselves, and Christian is at first ready to take this advice. Hopeful, however, in keeping with his name, counsels patience and courage:

> *My Brother . . . remembrest thou not how valiant thou has been heretofore;* Apollyon *could not crush thee, nor could all that thou didst hear, or see, or feel in the Valley of the shadow of Death; what hardship, terror, and amazement hast thou already gone through, and art thou now nothing but fear? . . . let's exercise a little more patience. Remember how thou playedst the man at* Vanity-Fair, *and wast neither afraid of the Chain nor Cage; nor yet of bloody Death: wherefore let us . . . bear up with patience as well as we can.* (p. 113)

Through a process of rational deliberation and a consideration of the lessons learned from experiences in the past, the pilgrims manage to control their fears and prevent themselves giving way to abject terror. It is worth noting, too, that their eventual release from captivity comes not by the intervention of any supernatural agency, but from resources found within Christian's own breast: '*What a fool, quoth he, am I, thus to lie in a stinking Dungeon, when I may as well walk at liberty?* I have a *Key* in my bosom, called *Promise*, that will, (I am perswaded) open any Lock in *Doubting-Castle*' (p. 114).

In the end, what kept Dissenters like Bunyan battling on during the long years of persecution was the conviction that their suffering and constancy would be rewarded in the next world, if not in this, and that ultimately good would win out over evil. Both parts of *The Pilgrim's Progress* end with descriptions of the entry of the pilgrims into the Celestial City. What is most impressive about Bunyan's handling of this is the way he manages to render the City and its inhabitants conceivable in human terms. When Christian and Hopeful have crossed the River, he arranges for the 'shining ones' to come and escort them up to the city, answering their questions about what they can expect. It is impossible not to feel the joy, the mounting

[48] This point is explored in Vincent Newey, 'Bunyan and the Confines of the Mind', ibid. 21–48.

excitement, the triumph of this consummation of the pilgrims' struggle, and the equivalent passage in Part Two is one of the great set pieces of the book. Bunyan's poetic vision of eternal felicity is not a morbid rejection of life here and now. His characters are certainly travelling through this earthly life towards an eternal life in Heaven, and in Bunyan's view there was no doubt that then the wicked would be punished and the righteous exalted. But the central, enduring quality of his book lies in its portrayal of the pilgrims' lives in this world.

As we know, *The Pilgrim's Progress* has had a most amazing world-wide impact. The reasons for its extraordinary success are many and complex. Much of its attraction lies in the beauty and simplicity of Bunyan's prose, and in the vividness with which he brings his allegorical characters to life, acutely catching the rhythms of colloquial speech. Its wide readership in languages other than English may be explained by the folk-tale elements in its structure—the story of a man in search for the truth is one that crosses cultural boundaries. It may also, no doubt, be attributed to the activities of Christian missionaries and imperialists. As Christopher Hill has put it, 'translations of *The Pilgrim's Progress* followed trade, the flag, and missionaries'. But as he has also noted, 'books create their own audiences, and readers transform what they read'.[49] The heroes of *The Pilgrim's Progress* are ordinary people striving to hold on to their beliefs in a hostile and uncomprehending world. Their story might offer consolation and inspiration to oppressed people in any society.

[49] Hill, *A Turbulent, Seditious, and Factious People: John Bunyan and his Church*, 376.

NOTE ON THE TEXT

THE text of *The Pilgrim's Progress* in this new Oxford World's Classics edition is based upon that established by the late Roger Sharrock, in his revision of the Oxford English Texts (OET) edition edited by James Blanton Wharey in 1928. Sharrock's edition was published in 1960, and reprinted with corrections in 1967 and 1975. His introduction provides a full discussion of the circumstances and date of composition of *The Pilgrim's Progress*, and a detailed analysis of all the editions published in Bunyan's lifetime. The text here has been set from the 1975 corrected reprint, omitting the textual apparatus, and altering the marginal page references to Part One in Part Two to correspond with the new pagination. In a few cases, noted below, I have ventured to restore first edition readings that had been emended by Sharrock. The only other departure from his text is the insertion here of illustrations, with accompanying verses, that were included in early editions. There seems little doubt that Bunyan himself was the author of the verses, and the illustrations they were written to accompany were an important part of the experience of the book for contemporary readers. Further details are given below.

Asterisks in the text are those used in the first edition to refer the reader to some of the scriptural references in the margins. Daggers (†) are used to indicate the presence of Explanatory Notes provided at the end of the text.

The Pilgrim's Progress was first published in 1678. The publisher, Nathaniel Ponder, was frequently in trouble with the authorities for publishing nonconformist writings. Among his authors were the celebrated nonconformist theologian John Owen, and the poet Andrew Marvell. *The Pilgrim's Progress* was the first work of Bunyan's that he published, and he evidently sensed that it was likely to be a popular book, for he went to the trouble of having it licensed, thus establishing his copyright in it. Eleven further editions had appeared before Bunyan's death in August 1688.

For the second edition, which appeared before the end of 1678, Bunyan added many new passages. The most important of these are:

1. Christian's attempt to explain his situation to his wife and children (from p. 10, l. 14, 'In this plight', to p. 11, l. 13, '*do to be saved?*').
2. His meeting with Mr Worldly-Wiseman and second meeting with Evangelist (from p. 18, l. 3, 'Now as Christian', to p. 25, l. 25, 'Mr. *Worldly-Wiseman's* counsel').
3. His discussion with Good-will (from p. 28, l. 5, '*Chr.* Truly, said *Christian*', to p. 28, l. 31, '*in no wise are cast out*').
4. His answers to Charity's question about his wife and children (from p. 51, l. 6, 'Then said *Charity*', to p. 52, l. 15, '*delivered thy soul from their blood*').
5. A sentence introducing verses about Faithful's encounter with Shame, 'And when I had shaken him off, then I began to sing' (p. 73, l. 26).
6. Evangelist's meeting with Christian and Faithful (from p. 83, l. 27, 'Now when they', to p. 85, l. 24, 'unto a faithful Creator').
7. Their memory of this while in the cage at Vanity Fair (from p. 90, l. 13, 'Here also they called', to p. 90, l. 22, 'should be otherwise disposed of').
8. By-ends' account of his kindred (from p. 97, l. 27, 'Almost the whole Town', to p. 97, l. 32, 'by Father's side: And').
9. The monument to Lot's wife and Christian and Hopeful's discussion about this (from p. 105, l. 22, 'Now I saw', to p. 107, l. 8, 'remember *Lot's* Wife').
10. Giant Despair's wife (from p. 110, l. 13, 'Now *Giant Despair* had a Wife', to p. 114, l. 17, 'search them in the morning').
11. The appearance of trumpeters to welcome Christian and Hopeful to the Celestial City (from p. 152, l. 3, 'There came out also at this time', to p. 152, l. 28, 'can their glorious joy be expressed').

The only further addition of any substance made by Bunyan appeared in the third edition (1679). He inserted here the long conversation between By-ends and his three companions, Mr Hold-the-World, Mr Money-love, and Mr Save-all (from p. 99, l. 10, 'Now I saw in my dream', to p. 103, l. 31, 'rebuked by the flames of a devouring fire').

The Second Part of *The Pilgrim's Progress* was published in 1684, and there was a second edition in 1686. These were the only two editions to be published in Bunyan's lifetime. The only substantive alteration in the second edition is the addition of a great many marginal notes.

A detailed analysis of the twelve editions of Part One, and the two editions of Part Two, issued before Bunyan's death was undertaken by Roger Sharrock. Unlike Wharey, who had based his text of Part One on the third edition, Sharrock returned to the first edition, incorporating into this the new material added by Bunyan in the second and third editions. For Part Two he based his text on the first edition, but incorporating the additional marginalia of the second. His reasons for going back to the earliest editions are given at length in his introduction. As he says, it has been a general principle in modern scholarly editing that a first edition is likely to represent most closely the intentions of the author, and in the case of *The Pilgrim's Progress* there are particularly strong reasons for regarding the first editions as superior. It is abundantly clear that the earliest editions are the most faithful to Bunyan's own style, which was characterized by the use of unconventional spellings, 'loose' grammar, and colloquial or dialect forms of speech. Examples include his fondness for the colloquial 'a' for the verb 'have' and the pronoun 'he' ('would a done', 'a came', etc.), and his use of archaic or provincial forms of words such as 'drownded' for drowned, 'strodled' for straddled, 'strook' for struck. As Sharrock demonstrates, in editions after the first these characteristic Bunyan idioms were normalized to more modern or correct forms, losing in the process some of the freshness and originality of his style. Although he added new material in the second and third editions of Part One, Bunyan did not supervise closely these or later reprints, and the changes were almost certainly introduced by the printers.

In most cases the old spelling and typographical conventions—use of capitalization and italicization—cause little problem for readers. (The Glossary at the back of the present edition includes obsolete, archaic, and dialect words, together with words spelled in unfamiliar ways.) The original punctuation may perhaps strike a modern reader as unusually heavy, but the reason is that Bunyan is almost certainly writing his text to be heard, not just read silently with the eye. He is using punctuation in a *rhythmically* correct way, rather than a strictly syntactically correct way.

The present text differs from OET in two respects. In his edition, Roger Sharrock corrected what were evident inaccuracies in the original texts, providing details in his textual apparatus at the foot of the page. In most cases the inaccuracy is plain to be seen, and the emendation is evidently justified. In a very few cases, however, emendations were introduced where the first edition reading seems perfectly acceptable. In the present text, first edition readings have been restored in the following instances:

1. On p. 8, l. 17: *Travailer*] *Traveller* (OET, p. 6, l. 33).
2. On p. 10, l. 14: restrained] refrained (OET, p. 8, l. 12).
3. On p. 29, l. 20: Travailer] Traveller (OET, p. 28, l. 21).
4. On p. 61, l. 3: *Christian* for a season saw] *Christian* saw (OET, p. 60, l. 8).
5. On p. 71, l. 3: made a hand of] made an end of (OET, p. 70, l. 36).
6. On p. 74, l. 7: *valiant for the Truth*] *valiant for Truth* (OET, p. 74, l. 25).
7. On p. 83, l. 8: to stink] so stink (OET, p. 85, l. 14).

The other way in which the present text differs from OET is by including all the illustrations appearing in texts published in Bunyan's lifetime. The first illustration was the famous 'sleeping portrait' of Bunyan engraved by Robert White. This appeared as the frontispiece to the third edition of Part One, published in 1679. In later editions Ponder inserted further illustrations, accompanied by four-line verses at the bottom, in the body of the text. These first began to appear in the fifth edition of 1680, which includes a woodcut of the martyrdom of Faithful, together with a number of other copper plate illustrations. These copper engravings were themselves subsequently reproduced as woodcuts in later editions. There were fifteen illustrations in all:

1. Christian meeting Evangelist.
2. Christian meeting Mr Worldly-Wiseman.
3. Christian at the Wicket Gate.
4. Christian losing his burden.
5. Christian in the arbour.
6. Christian passing the lions.
7. Christian in his armour.

8. Christian's fight with Apollyon.
9. Christian in the Valley of the Shadow of Death.
10. Christian and Faithful chained in Vanity Fair.
11. Faithful appearing before Lord Hategood.
12. The martyrdom of Faithful.
13. Giant Despair before his castle.
14. The pilgrims with the shepherds at the Delectable Mountains.
15. The pilgrims riding the clouds.

In the first edition of Part Two, two illustrations were included:

1. Great-heart leading the pilgrims.
2. The pilgrims dancing round the head of Giant Despair.

There was also a new version of the frontispiece sleeping portrait, showing Christiana, Mercy, and the four boys above the dreamer. All these illustrations, together with copies of the title pages of the first edition, have been included in the present edition, at the appropriate points in the text. Because the state of many of the originals is poor, it has been decided to reproduce instead highly accurate nineteenth-century facsimiles. These were made for George Offor's edition of *The Works of John Bunyan*, 3 vols. (Glasgow, Edinburgh, and London, 1860–2), and placed by him as a complete set at the start of the text of *The Pilgrim's Progress* in volume iii, pp. 79–84.

SELECT BIBLIOGRAPHY

A CHRONOLOGICAL list of responses to Bunyan from 1656 up to 1980 is presented in James F. Forrest and Richard L. Greaves, *John Bunyan: A Reference Guide* (Boston, 1982). This may be supplemented by Beatrice Batson, *John Bunyan's 'Grace Abounding' and 'The Pilgrim's Progress': An Overview of Literary Studies 1960–1987* (New York, 1988). In the sections that follow I refer for the most part to works published after 1980.

Texts of Bunyan's Works

Grace Abounding to the Chief of Sinners, ed. Roger Sharrock (Oxford, 1962).

Grace Abounding to the Chief of Sinners, ed. W. R. Owens (Harmondsworth, 1987).

Grace Abounding with Other Spiritual Autobiographies, ed. John Stachniewski with Anita Pacheco (Oxford, 1998).

The Holy War, ed. Roger Sharrock and James F. Forrest (Oxford, 1980).

The Life and Death of Mr. Badman, ed. James F. Forrest and Roger Sharrock (Oxford, 1988).

The Miscellaneous Works of John Bunyan, gen. ed. Roger Sharrock, 13 vols. (Oxford, 1976–94): vol. i, ed. T. L. Underwood and Roger Sharrock (1980); vol. ii, ed. Richard L. Greaves (1976); vol. iii, ed. J. Sears McGee (1987); vol. iv, ed. T. L. Underwood (1989); vol. v, ed. Graham Midgley (1986); vol. vi, ed. Graham Midgley (1980); vol. vii, ed. Graham Midgley (1989); vol. viii, ed. Richard L. Greaves (1979); vol. ix, ed. Richard L. Greaves (1981); vol. x, ed. Owen Watkins (1988); vol. xi, ed. Richard L. Greaves (1985); vol. xii, ed. W. R. Owens (1994); vol. xiii, ed. W. R. Owens (1994).

The Pilgrim's Progress, ed. James Blanton Wharey, 2nd edn. rev. Roger Sharrock (Oxford, 1960).

The Pilgrim's Progress, ed. Roger Sharrock (Harmondsworth, 1965; rev. 1987).

The Pilgrim's Progress, ed. N. H. Keeble (Oxford, 1984).

Biographical Studies

Brown, John, *John Bunyan: His Life, Times and Work* (1885; rev. F. M. Harrison, London, 1928).

Hill, Christopher, *A Turbulent, Seditious, and Factious People: John Bunyan and his Church, 1628–1688* (Oxford, 1988).

Mullett, Michael A., *John Bunyan in Context* (Keele, 1996).

Critical Studies: Books and Collections of Essays

Batson, E. Beatrice, *John Bunyan: Allegory and Imagination* (London, 1984).

Collmer, Robert (ed.), *Bunyan in our Time* (London, 1989).

Davies, Michael, *Graceful Reading: Theology and Narrative in the Works of John Bunyan* (Oxford, 2002).

de Vries, Pieter, *John Bunyan on the Order of Salvation*, trans. C. van Haaften (New York, 1994).

Gay, David, Randall, James G., and Zinck, Arlette (eds.), *Awakening Words: John Bunyan and the Language of Community* (Newark, Del., 2000).

Greaves, Richard L., *John Bunyan* (Abingdon, 1969).

—— *John Bunyan and English Nonconformity* (London, 1992).

Hancock, Maxine, *The Key in the Window: Marginal Notes in Bunyan's Narratives* (Vancouver, 2000).

Johnson, Barbara A., *Reading Piers Plowman and The Pilgrim's Progress: Reception and the Protestant Reader* (Carbondale, Ill., 1992).

Kaufmann, U. Milo, *The Pilgrim's Progress and Traditions in Puritan Meditation* (New Haven and London, 1966).

Keeble, N. H. (ed.), *John Bunyan: Conventicle and Parnassus* (Oxford, 1988).

—— (ed.), *John Bunyan: Reading Dissenting Writing* (Bern, 2002).

Laurence, Anne, Owens, W. R., and Sim, Stuart (eds.), *John Bunyan and his England, 1628–1688* (London, 1990).

MacDonald, Ruth K., *Christian's Children: The Influence of John Bunyan's 'The Pilgrim's Progress' on American Children's Literature* (Bern, 1989).

Newey, Vincent (ed.), *The Pilgrim's Progress: Critical and Historical Views* (Liverpool, 1980).

Sharrock, Roger, *John Bunyan* (London, 1954; repr. 1968).

—— *John Bunyan: The Pilgrim's Progress* (London, 1966).

—— (ed.), *The Pilgrim's Progress: A Casebook* (London, 1976).

Sim, Stuart, *Negotiations with Paradox: Narrative Practice and Narrative Form in Bunyan and Defoe* (London, 1990).

—— and Walker, David, *Bunyan and Authority: The Rhetoric of Dissent and the Legitimation Crisis in Seventeenth-Century England* (Bern, 2000).

Spargo, Tamsin, *The Writing of John Bunyan* (Aldershot, 1997).

Swaim, Kathleen M., *Pilgrim's Progress, Puritan Progress: Discourses and Contexts* (Urbana, Ill., 1993).

Talon, Henri, *John Bunyan: The Man and his Works*, trans. Barbara Wall (London, 1951).

Tindall, William York, *John Bunyan, Mechanick Preacher* (New York, 1934; repr. 1964).

van Os, M., and Schutte, G. J. (eds.), *Bunyan in England and Abroad* (Amsterdam, 1990).

Wakefield, Gordon, *John Bunyan: The Christian* (London, 1992; repr. 1994).

Critical Studies: Articles and Chapters in Books

(articles in the volumes of essays noted above are not included here)

Alexander, J. H., 'Christ in *The Pilgrim's Progress*', *Bunyan Studies*, 2 (1989), 22–9.

Berger, Benjamin Lyle, 'Calvinism and the Problem of Suspense in *The Pilgrim's Progress*', *Bunyan Studies*, 8 (1998), 28–35.

Breen, Margaret Soenser, 'The Sexed Pilgrim's Progress', *Studies in English Literature*, 32 (1992), 443–60.

—— 'Christiana's Rudeness: Spiritual Authority in *The Pilgrim's Progress*', *Bunyan Studies*, 7 (1997), 96–111.

Damrosch, Leopold, Jr., 'Experience and Allegory in Bunyan', in *God's Plot and Man's Stories: Studies in the Fictional Imagination from Milton to Fielding* (Chicago, 1985).

Finley, C. Stephen, 'Bunyan among the Victorians: Macaulay, Froude, Ruskin', *Journal of Literature and Theology*, 3 (1989), 77–94.

Fish, Stanley E., 'Progress in *The Pilgrim's Progress*', in *Self-Consuming Artifacts: The Experience of Seventeenth-Century Literature* (Berkeley and Los Angeles, 1972), 224–64.

Forrest, James F., 'Conspectus: The Critical Reception of *The Pilgrim's Progress*, Second Part', *Bunyan Studies*, 1 (1988), 36–42.

Freeman, Thomas S., 'A Library in Three Volumes: Foxe's "Book of Martyrs" in the Writings of John Bunyan', *Bunyan Studies*, 5 (1994), 47–57.

Greaves, Richard L., 'Bunyan through the Centuries: Some Reflections', *English Studies*, 64 (1983), 113–21.

Hancock, Maxine, 'Folklore and Theology in the Structure and Narrative Strategies of *The Pilgrim's Progress*', *Bunyan Studies*, 9 (1999/2000), 7–24.

Hofmeyr, Isabel, 'Bunyan in Africa: Text, Translation, Transition', *African Studies Association of the UK: Biennial Conference*, 1 (1998), 1–14.

Iser, Wolfgang, 'Bunyan's *Pilgrim's Progress*: The Doctrine of Predestination and the Shaping of the Novel', in *The Implied Reader: Patterns of Communication in Prose Fiction from Bunyan to Beckett* (Baltimore, 1974), 1–28.

Johnson, Galen, ' "Be Not Extream": The Limits of Theory in Reading John Bunyan', *Christianity and Literature*, 49 (2000), 447–64.

Keeble, N. H., '*The Pilgrim's Progress*: A Puritan Fiction', *Baptist Quarterly*, 28 (1980), 321–36.

—— 'The Way and the Ways of Puritan Story: Biblical Patterns in Bunyan and his Contemporaries', *English*, 33 (1984), 209–32.

Knott, John R., 'Bunyan and the Holy Community', *Studies in Philology*, 80 (1983), 200–25.

Luxon, Thomas H., 'The Pilgrim's Passive Progress: Luther and Bunyan on Talking and Doing, Word and Way', *English Literary History*, 53 (1986), 73–98.

—— 'Calvin and Bunyan on Word and Image: Is there a Text in Interpreter's House?', *English Literary Renaissance*, 18 (1988), 438–59.

Manlove, C. N., 'The Image of the Journey in *Pilgrim's Progress*: Narrative versus Allegory', *Journal of Narrative Technique*, 10 (1988), 16–38.

Michie, Allen, 'Between Calvin and Calvino: Postmodernism and Bunyan's *The Pilgrim's Progress*', *Bucknell Review*, 41 (1998), 37–56.

Pooley, Roger, 'The Wilderness of This World', *Baptist Quarterly*, 27 (1978), 290–9.

—— 'The Structure of *The Pilgrim's Progress*', *Essays in Poetics*, 4 (1979), 59–70.

Sim, Stuart, ' "Vertuous Mediocrity" and "Fanatic Conventicle": Pilgrimage Styles in John Bunyan and Bishop Simon Patrick', *English Studies*, 68 (1987), 316–24.

—— 'Bunyan, Lyotard, and the Conflict of Narratives (or, Postmodernising Bunyan)', *Bunyan Studies*, 8 (1998), 67–81.

Slights, William W. E., 'Bunyan on the Edge', *Bunyan Studies*, 10 (2001/2), 29–45.

Spargo, Tamsin, 'The Purloined Postcard: Waiting for Bunyan', *Textual Practice*, 8 (1994), 79–96.

Stachniewski, John, '*The Pilgrim's Progress*: Allegory and the Persecutory Imagination', in *The Persecutory Imagination: English Puritanism and the Literature of Religious Despair* (Oxford, 1991), 169–216.

Stranahan, Brainerd P., 'Bunyan's Special Talent: Biblical Texts as Events in *Grace Abounding* and *The Pilgrim's Progress*', *English Literary Renaissance*, 11 (1981), 329–43.

—— 'Bunyan and the Epistle to the Hebrews: His Source for the Idea of Pilgrimage in *The Pilgrim's Progress*', *Studies in Philology*, 79 (1982), 279–96.

—— ' "With Great Delight": The Song of Solomon in *The Pilgrim's Progress*', *English Studies*, 68 (1987), 220–7.

Thickstun, Margaret Olofson, 'From Christiana to Stand-fast: Subsuming the Feminine in *The Pilgrim's Progress*', in *Fictions of the Feminine:*

Puritan Doctrine and the Representation of Women (Ithaca, NY, 1988), 87–104.

Titlestad, P. J. H., 'The "pretty young man Civility": Bunyan, Milton and Blake and Patterns of Puritan Thought', *Bunyan Studies*, 6 (1995/6), 34–43.

Van Dyke, Carolynn, 'Allegory and Experience: *The Pilgrim's Progress*', in *The Fiction of Truth: Structures of Meaning in Narrative and Dramatic Allegory* (Ithaca, NY, 1985).

General Historical, Literary, and Theological Studies

Coolidge, John S., *The Pauline Renaissance in England: Puritanism and the Bible* (Oxford, 1970).

Cragg, G. R., *Puritanism in the Period of the Great Persecution, 1660–1688* (Cambridge, 1957).

Greaves, Richard L., *Deliver Us from Evil: The Radical Underground in Britain, 1660–1663* (New York, 1986).

—— *Enemies under his Feet: Radicals and Nonconformists in Britain, 1664–1667* (Stanford, Calif., 1990).

—— *Secrets of the Kingdom: British Radicals from the Popish Plot to the Revolution of 1688–1689* (Stanford, Calif., 1992).

Haller, William, *The Rise of Puritanism* (1938; repr. New York, 1957).

—— *Liberty and Reformation in the Puritan Revolution* (New York, 1955).

Harris, Tim, Seaward, Paul, and Goldie, Mark (eds.), *The Politics of Religion in Restoration England* (Oxford, 1990).

Hill, Christopher, *The World Turned Upside Down: Radical Ideas during the English Revolution* (1972; repr. Harmondsworth, 1975).

Keeble, N. H., *The Literary Culture of Nonconformity in Later Seventeenth-Century England* (Leicester, 1987).

—— (ed.), *Writing of the English Revolution* (Cambridge, 2001).

Knott, John R., *The Sword of the Spirit: Puritan Responses to the Bible* (Chicago, 1980).

—— *Discourses of Martyrdom in English Literature, 1563–1694* (Cambridge, 1993).

McGregor, J. F., and Reay, Barry (eds.), *Radical Religion in the English Revolution* (Oxford, 1984).

Nuttall, Geoffrey F., *The Holy Spirit in Puritan Faith and Practice*, 2nd edn. (1947; repr. Chicago, 1992).

Smith, Nigel, *Perfection Proclaimed: Language and Literature in English Radical Religion 1640–1660* (Oxford, 1989).

—— *Literature and Revolution in England, 1640–1660* (New Haven, 1994).

Spufford, Margaret, *Small Books and Pleasant Histories: Popular Fiction and its Readership in Seventeenth-Century England* (London, 1981).

Wallace, Dewey D., *Puritans and Predestination: Grace in English Protestant Theology, 1525–1695* (Chapel Hill, NC, 1982).

Watkins, Owen C., *The Puritan Experience* (London, 1972).

Watts, Michael R., *The Dissenters: From the Reformation to the French Revolution* (Oxford, 1978).

Further Reading in Oxford World's Classics

The Bible: Authorized King James Version, ed. Robert Carroll and Stephen Prickett.

Bunyan, John, *Grace Abounding with other Spiritual Autobiographies*, ed. John Stachniewski with Anita Pacheco.

The Gospels, ed. W. R. Owens.

CHRONOLOGY OF BUNYAN'S LIFE AND TIMES

	Life	*Times*
1628	Born at Elstow in Bedfordshire (baptized 30 November), first of three children of Thomas Bunyan (1603–76), a brazier, and his second wife Margaret Bentley (1603–44).	Petition of Right, an early attempt by Parliament to limit the royal prerogative. Assassination of the Duke of Buckingham.
1629–40		Personal rule of Charles I.
1630s	Attends local school for a short period. Upon leaving, follows father's trade and becomes a brazier (or 'tinker')	
1633		William Laud appointed Archbishop of Canterbury. Posthumous publication of *Poems* by John Donne, and *The Temple* by George Herbert.
1637		Trial of Prynne, Burton, and Bastwick, Puritan pamphleteers.
1637–8		Trial of John Hampden over Ship Money. John Milton publishes *Lycidas*.
1639		First Bishops' War with Scotland.
1640		Second Bishops' War. The Long Parliament meets. Impeachment of Laud. Press censorship breaks down.
1640		'Root and Branch' petition discussed in the Commons. Grand Remonstrance passed. Rebellion in Ireland.
1642		Attempt by king to arrest the 'five members'. Bishops' Exclusion Bill passed, suspending their authority. First Civil War begins. Battle of Edgehill. Parliament closes theatres.
1643		Westminster Assembly opens to discuss religious settlement. Parliament concludes Solemn League and Covenant with Scots. Censorship revived.

	Life	*Times*
1644	Mother and sister Margaret die (in June and July); father remarries within two months. (November) mustered in the parliamentary forces stationed in the garrison town of Newport Pagnell, Buckinghamshire.	Parliamentary victory at Marston Moor. Milton publishes *Areopagitica*, in protest against censorship.
1645		Archbishop Laud executed. Formation of New Model Army. Parliamentary victory at Battle of Naseby. Use of Prayer Book prohibited by Parliament.
1646		Charles I surrenders to Scots. Oxford surrenders to Parliament. End of First Civil War. Abolition of feudal tenures and the Court of Wards. Parliament orders setting up of a Presbyterian church system in England. Offices of bishop and archbishop abolished.
1647	Demobilized and returns to Elstow.	Election of 'Agitators' in New Model Army. At the 'Putney Debates', Army Council and Leveller leaders discuss extension to the franchise. King escapes from custody.
1648	Marries first wife and sets up house in Elstow. Her name is unknown, but, according to Bunyan in *Grace Abounding*, her father 'was counted godly', and she brought as her dowry two religious books: Arthur Dent's *The Plaine Mans Path-way to Heaven* (1601) and Lewis Bayly's *The Practice of Piety* (1612).	Second Civil War (April to August). Pride's Purge of Parliament.
1649		'Rump' of the House of Commons assumes supreme power. Trial and execution of Charles I. Abolition of monarchy and House of Lords. England proclaimed a free commonwealth. Levellers suppressed at Burford. Cromwell in Ireland, takes Drogheda and Wexford. Milton publishes *The Tenure of Kings and Magistrates*, defending the regicide.

	Life	*Times*
1650	Undergoes spiritual crisis lasting for nearly three years. Receives counsel from John Gifford, pastor of the Independent congregation in Bedford. First child, Mary, born blind (baptized 20 July); three other children follow.	Cromwell defeats the Scots. Diggers suppressed. Abolition of compulsory attendance at parish church. Blasphemy Act directed against Ranters. Andrew Marvell writes *Horatian Ode*.
1651		Attempted invasion by Charles II defeated at Battle of Worcester. Fifth Monarchist movement active. Navigation Act passed. Thomas Hobbes publishes *Leviathan*.
1652		War with the Dutch. Gerrard Winstanley publishes *The Law of Freedom in a Platform*.
1653	Becomes member of John Gifford's congregation in Bedford (is baptized and becomes full member in 1655).	Cromwell expels the Rump. Barebone's Parliament (July–December). Instrument of Government, a written constitution for Britain. Cromwell becomes Lord Protector.
1654		First Protectorate Parliament. Cromwellian state church created on loosely Presbyterian lines.
1655	Moves to live in Bedford, and begins to preach, first to the Bedford church and then more widely in the locality.	Cromwell dismisses First Protectorate Parliament. Rule of the major-generals. Readmission of Jews to England.
1656	Involved in controversy with Quakers, and as a result publishes first work, *Some Gospel-Truths Opened*.	Second Protectorate Parliament. Parliament tries the Quaker James Nayler for blasphemy. James Harrington publishes *Oceana*.
1657	Publishes *A Vindication of Some Gospel-Truths Opened*.	Major-generals abolished. Cromwell refuses the crown.
1658	First wife dies. Publishes first of his sermon-treatises, *A Few Sighs from Hell*.	Death of Oliver Cromwell, succeeded as Protector by son Richard.
1659	Marries second wife, Elizabeth; three children are born of this marriage. Publishes *The Doctrine of the Law and Grace Unfolded*, the most important of his theological treatises.	Abdication of Richard Cromwell. Royalist rebellion by Sir George Booth defeated. Renewed threat of civil war.

	Life	*Times*
1660	Arrested (November) for preaching illegally and held in custody. Wife gives birth prematurely to first baby, which dies.	General Monck leads the army south to London. The Long Parliament is dissolved. Charles II returns to England and is proclaimed king (May). House of Lords and episcopacy restored. Regicides executed.
1661	Tried in Bedford and sentenced, initially to three months' imprisonment. Continued refusal to give undertaking to stop preaching leads to his remaining in gaol for twelve years. Wife appeals for his release at the assizes in August, to no avail. Supports family by making shoelaces, and continues to write. Publishes first prison book, a poem entitled *Profitable Meditations*.	Fifth Monarchist uprising in London. Election of 'Cavalier' Parliament. Widespread persecution of Dissenters begins.
1662	Publishes *I Will Pray with the Spirit*, an attack on the use of the Book of Common Prayer.	Act of Uniformity, requiring conformity to a newly published Book of Common Prayer, leads to the ejection of over 1,000 clergy from Church of England. Charles II's first Declaration of Indulgence overruled by Parliament.
1663	Publishes *Christian Behaviour*, a conduct manual, and another poem, *Prison Meditations*.	
1664		Triennial Act. First Conventicle Act.
1665	Publishes two poems, *One Thing is Needful* and *Ebal and Gerizzin*; a millenarian treatise, *The Holy City*; and a sermon-treatise, *The Resurrection of the Dead*.	Five Mile Act. Anglo-Dutch war begins. The Great Plague.
1666	Publishes spiritual autobiography, *Grace Abounding to the Chief of Sinners*.	Great Fire of London.
1667		Milton publishes *Paradise Lost*.
1670		Second Conventicle Act. Persecution of Dissenters worsens.

	Life	*Times*
1671	Probably writes *The Heavenly Footman* (published posthumously in 1698).	Milton publishes *Paradise Regained* and *Samson Agonistes*.
1672	Elected pastor of the Bedford congregation (January). Released from prison (March), and licensed (May) to preach. Congregation purchase barn in Bedford as a meeting place. Publishes *A Defence of the Doctrine of Justification by Faith*, an attack on the Anglican Edward Fowler's *Design of Christianity* (1671), and *A Confession of my Faith and A Reason of my Practice in Worship*.	Charles II issues Second Declaration of Indulgence. Marvell publishes (anonymously) *The Rehearsal Transpros'd*.
1673	Publishes *Differences in Judgment about Water-Baptism no Bar to Communion*, arising from dispute with some London Baptists, and a sermon, *The Barren Fig-Tree*.	Declaration of Indulgence is withdrawn. Renewed persecution of nonconformists. Test Act compels all civil and military office-holders to take communion according to rites of the Book of Common Prayer. James, Duke of York, declares himself a Roman Catholic. Wren begins rebuilding St Paul's.
1674	Publishes *Peaceable Principles and True*, answering attacks by Baptist leaders Thomas Paul and Henry Danvers.	
1675	Publishes doctrinal catechism, *Instruction for the Ignorant*, and a sermon, *Light for Them that Sit in Darkness*.	
1676	Publishes two sermon-treatises, *Saved by Grace* and *The Strait Gate*. Father dies.	
1677	Imprisoned again during the first six months of the year.	
1678	Publishes *Come, and Welcome, to Jesus Christ*, and *The Pilgrim's Progress*.	The Popish Plot. Second Test Act excludes Roman Catholics from Parliament.
1679	Publishes *A Treatise of the Fear of God*.	'Cavalier' Parliament is dissolved. Censorship lapses with expiry of the Licensing Act.

	Life	*Times*
1679–81		Three 'Exclusion' Parliaments pass bills to exclude James, Duke of York, from the succession, because he is a Roman Catholic.
1680	Publishes *The Life and Death of Mr Badman*.	
1681–5		Charles II rules without Parliament. Persecution of Dissenters is intensified. John Dryden publishes *Absalom and Achitophel* (1681).
1682	Publishes *The Holy War* and *The Greatness of the Soul.*	Thomas Sherman publishes his *The Second Part of the Pilgrim's Progress*, a spurious continuation of Bunyan's work.
1683	Publishes *A Case of Conscience*, an attack on separate meetings by women, and *A Holy Life*.	Rye House Plot. Execution of leading Whigs. Purges of corporations.
1684	Publishes *Seasonable Counsel, or Advice to Sufferers; A Caution to Stir up to Watch against Sin;* and *The Pilgrim's Progress, Second Part*	
1685	Makes a deed of gift of all his property to his wife, in fear of further persecution. Publishes *A Discourse upon the Pharisee and the Publicane* and *Questions about the Nature and Perpetuity of the Seventh-Day Sabbath*.	Death of Charles II and accession of James II. Monmouth's rising is defeated at Sedgemoor. Revocation of Edict of Nantes and arrival of Huguenot refugees in England.
1686	Publishes *A Book for Boys and Girls*.	
1687		James II issues Declaration of Indulgence granting freedom of worship to Dissenters. Purge of corporations. Sir Isaac Newton publishes his *Principia Mathematica*.
1688	Publishes five works: *The Advocateship of Jesus Christ*; *The Jerusalem Sinner Saved*; *A Discourse of the Building . . . of the House of God*; *The Water of Life*; and *Solomon's Temple Spiritualized*. Dies (31	James II reissues Declaration of Indulgence. Trial and acquittal of seven bishops for their opposition to the Declaration. William of Orange lands at Torbay; James flees to France.

	Life	*Times*
	August) from a fever contracted while riding from Reading to London in heavy rain. Buried (3 September) in Bunhill Fields, Finsbury.	
1689	Two works published posthumously: *The Acceptable Sacrifice* and *Last Sermon*.	William and Mary are proclaimed king and queen. Toleration Act grants freedom of worship to Protestant Dissenters, but not civil rights. John Locke publishes *Letter on Toleration*.
1692	Publication of first volume of projected folio edition of Bunyan's works, including twelve unpublished pieces: *An Exposition on the Ten First Chapters of Genesis*; *Of Justification by an Imputed Righteousness*; *Paul's Departure and Crown; Of the Trinity and a Christian*; *Of the Law and a Christian*; *Israel's Hope Encouraged*; *The Desire of the Righteous Granted*; *The Saints Privilege and Profit*; *Christ a Complete Saviour*; *The Saints Knowledge of Christ's Love*; *Of the House of the Forest of Lebanon*; *Of Antichrist, and his Ruine*.	

Printed for Nat: Ponder in the Poultry:

THE

Pilgrim's Progress

FROM

THIS WORLD,

TO

That which is to come:

Delivered under the Similitude of a

DREAM

Wherein is Discovered,

The manner of his setting out,

His Dangerous Journey; And safe

Arrival at the Desired Countrey.

I have used Similitudes, Hos. 12. 10.

By *John Bunyan.*

Licensed and Entred according to Order.

LONDON,

Printed for *Nath. Ponder* at the *Peacock* in the *Poultrey* near *Cornhil*, 1678.

THE AUTHOR'S *APOLOGY* FOR HIS BOOK

WHEN at the first I took my Pen in hand,
Thus for to write; I did not understand
That I at all should make a little Book
In such a mode; Nay, I had undertook
To make another, which when almost done,
Before I was aware, I this begun.
And thus it was: I writing of the Way
And Race of Saints† *in this our Gospel-Day,*
Fell suddenly into an Allegory
About their Journey, and the way to Glory,
In more than twenty things, which I set down;
This done, I twenty more had in my Crown,
And they again began to multiply,
Like sparks that from the coals of Fire do flie.
Nay then, thought I, if that you breed so fast,
I'll put you by your selves, lest you at last
Should prove ad infinitum, *and eat out*
The Book that I already am about.
Well, so I did; but yet I did not think
To shew to all the World my Pen and Ink
In such a mode; I only thought to make
I knew not what: nor did I undertake
Thereby to please my Neighbour; no not I,
I did it mine own self to gratifie.
Neither did I but vacant seasons spend
In this my Scribble; Nor did I intend
But to divert my self in doing this,
From worser thoughts, which make me do amiss.
Thus I set Pen to Paper with delight,
And quickly had my thoughts in black and white.
For having now my Method by the end,
Still as I pull'd, it came;† *and so I penn'd*
It down, until it came at last to be
For length and breadth the bigness which you see.

Well, when I had thus put mine ends together,
I shew'd them others, that I might see whether
They would condemn them, or them justifie:
And some said, let them live; some, let them die:
Some said, John, *print it; others said, Not so:*
Some said, It might do good; others said, No.
Now was I in a straight, and did not see
Which was the best thing to be done by me:
At last I thought, Since you are thus divided,
I print it will, and so the case decided.
For, thought I; Some I see would have it done,
Though others in that Channel do not run;
To prove then who advised for the best,
Thus I thought fit to put it to the test.
I further thought, if now I did deny
Those that would have it thus, to gratifie,
I did not know, but hinder them I might,
Of that which would to them be great delight.
For those that were not for its coming forth;
I said to them, Offend you I am loth;
Yet since your Brethren pleased with it be,
Forbear to judge, till you do further see.
If that thou wilt not read, let it alone;
Some love the meat, some love to pick the bone:
Yea, that I might them better palliate,
I did too with them thus Expostulate.
May I not write in such a stile as this?
In such a method too, and yet not miss
Mine end, thy good? why may it not be done?
Dark Clouds bring Waters, when the bright bring none;
Yea, dark, or bright, if they their silver drops
Cause to descend, the Earth, by yielding Crops,
Gives praise to both, and carpeth not at either,
But treasures up the Fruit they yield together:
Yea, so commixes both, that in her Fruit
None can distinguish this from that, they suit
Her well, when hungry: but if she be full,
She spues out both, and makes their blessings null.
You see the ways the Fisher-man doth take

To catch the Fish; what Engins doth he make?
Behold! how he ingageth all his Wits;
Also his Snares, Lines, Angles, Hooks and Nets:
Yet Fish there be, that neither Hook, nor Line,
Nor Snare, nor Net, nor Engin can make thine;
They must be grop't for, and be tickled too,
Or they will not be catcht, what e're you do.
  How doth the Fowler seek to catch his Game,
By divers means, all which one cannot name?
His Gun, his Nets, his Lime-twigs, light and bell:†
He creeps, he goes, he stands; yea, who can tell
Of all his postures? Yet there's none of these
Will make him master of what Fowls he please.
Yea, he must Pipe, and Whistle to catch this;
Yet if he does so, that *Bird he will miss.*
  If that a Pearl may in a Toads-head dwell,†
And may be found too in an Oister-shell;
If things that promise nothing, do contain
What better is then Gold; who will disdain,
(That have an inkling of it,) there to look,
That they may find it? Now my little Book,
(Tho void of all those paintings that may make
It with this or the other man to take,)
Is not without those things that do excel,
What do in brave, but empty notions dwell.
  Well, yet I am not fully *satisfied,*
That this your Book will stand, when soundly try'd.
  Why, what's the matter? It is dark, *what tho?*
But it is feigned, *what of that I tro?*
Some men by feigning words as dark as mine,
Make truth to spangle, and its rayes to shine.
  But they want solidness: *Speak man thy mind:*
They drown'd the weak; Metaphors make us blind.
  Solidity, indeed becomes the Pen
Of him that writeth things Divine to men:
But must I needs want solidness, because
By Metaphors I speak; was not Gods Laws,
His Gospel-laws in older time held forth
By Types, Shadows† *and Metaphors? Yet loth*

Will any sober man be to find fault
With them, lest he be found for to assault
The highest Wisdom. No, he rather stoops,
And seeks to find out what by pins and loops
By Calves, and Sheep; by Heifers, and by Rams;
By Birds and Herbs, and by the blood of Lambs;†
God speaketh to him: And happy is he
That finds the light, and grace that in them be.
Be not too forward therefore to conclude,
That I want solidness, that I am rude:
All things solid in shew, not solid be;
All things in parables despise not we,
Lest things most hurtful lightly we receive;
And things that good are, of our souls bereave.†
My dark and cloudy words they do but hold
The Truth, as Cabinets inclose the Gold.
The Prophets used much by Metaphors
To set forth Truth; Yea, who so considers
Christ, his Apostles too, shall plainly see,
That Truths to this day in such Mantles be.
Am I afraid to say that holy Writ,
Which for its Stile, and Phrase, puts down all Wit,
Is every where so full of all these things,
(Dark Figures, Allegories,)† *yet there springs*
From that same Book that lustre, and those rayes
Of light, that turns our darkest nights to days.
Come, let my Carper, to his Life now look,
And find There darker Lines, then in my Book
He findeth any. Yea, and let him know,
That in his best things there are worse lines too.
May we but stand before impartial men,
To his poor One, I durst adventure Ten,
That they will take my meaning in these lines
Far better then his lies in Silver Shrines.†
Come, Truth, although in Swadling-clouts, I find
Informs the Judgement, rectifies the Mind,
Pleases the Understanding, makes the Will
Submit; the Memory too it doth fill
With what doth our Imagination please;

Likewise, it tends our troubles to appease.
Sound words I know Timothy *is to use;*
And old Wives Fables he is to refuse,†
But yet grave Paul *him no where doth forbid*
The use of Parables; in which lay hid
That Gold, those Pearls, and precious stones that were
Worth digging for; and that with greatest care.
Let me add one word more, O Man of God!
Art thou offended? dost thou wish I had
Put forth my matter in another dress,
Or that I had in things been more express?
Three things let me propound, then I submit
To those that are my betters, (as is fit.)
1. *I find not that I am denied the use*
Of this my method, so I no abuse
Put on the Words, Things, Readers, or be rude
In handling Figure, or Similitude,
In application; but, all that I may,
Seek the advance of Truth, this or that way:
Denyed did I say? Nay, I have leave,
(Example too, and that from them that have
God better pleased by their words or ways,
Then any Man that breatheth now adays,)
Thus to express my mind, thus to declare
Things unto thee that excellentest are.
2. *I find that men (as high as Trees) will write*
Dialogue-wise;† *yet no Man doth them slight*
For writing so: Indeed if they abuse
Truth, cursed be they, and the craft they use
To that intent; but yet let Truth be free
To make her Salleys upon Thee, and Me,
Which way it pleases God. For who knows how,
Better then he that taught us first to Plow,†
To guide our Mind and Pens for his Design?
And he makes base things usher in Divine.
3. *I find that holy Writ in many places*
Hath semblance with this method, where the cases
Doth call for one thing to set forth another:
Use it I may then, and yet nothing smother

Truths golden Beams; Nay, by this method may
Make it cast forth its rayes as light as day.
And now, before I do put up my Pen,
I'le shew the profit of my Book, and then
Commit both thee, and it unto that hand
That pulls the strong down, and makes weak ones stand.
This Book it chaulketh out before thine eyes
The man that seeks the everlasting Prize:†
It shews you whence he comes, whither he goes,
What he leaves undone; also what he does:
It also shews you how he runs, and runs
Till he unto the Gate of Glory comes.
It shews too, who sets out for life amain,
As if the lasting Crown they would attain:
Here also you may see the reason why
They loose their labour, and like fools do die.
This Book will make a Travailer of thee,
If by its Counsel thou wilt ruled be;
It will direct thee to the Holy Land,
If thou wilt its Directions understand:
Yea, it will make the sloathful, active be;
The Blind also, delightful things to see.
Art thou for something rare, and profitable?
Wouldest thou see a Truth within a Fable?
Art thou forgetful? wouldest thou remember
From New-years-day *to the last of* December?
Then read my fancies, they will stick like Burs,†
And may be to the Helpless, Comforters.
This Book is writ in such a Dialect,
As may the minds of listless men affect:
It seems a Novelty, and yet contains
Nothing but sound and honest Gospel-strains.
Would'st thou divert thy self from Melancholly?
Would'st thou be pleasant, yet be far from folly?
Would'st thou read Riddles, and their Explanation,
Or else be drownded in thy Contemplation?
Dost thou love picking meat?† *or would'st thou see*
A man i' th Clouds, and hear him speak to thee?
Would'st thou be in a Dream, and yet not sleep?

Or would'st thou in a moment Laugh and Weep?
Wouldest thou loose thy self, and catch no harm?
And find thy self again without a charm?
Would'st read thy self, and read thou know'st not what
And yet know whether thou art blest or not,
By reading the same lines? O then come hither,
And lay my Book, thy Head and Heart together.

JOHN BUNYAN

THE PILGRIM'S PROGRESS: IN THE SIMILITUDE OF A DREAM

The *Gaol.† As I walk'd through the wilderness of this world, I lighted on a certain place, where was a *Denn; And I laid me down in that place to sleep: And as I slept I dreamed a Dream. I dreamed, and behold *I saw a Man *cloathed with Raggs, standing in a certain place, with his face from his own House, a Book in his hand, and a great burden*† *upon his back*. I looked, and saw him open the Book, and Read therein; and as he Read, he wept and trembled: and not being able longer to contain, he brake out with a lamentable cry; saying, **what shall I do?*†

* Isa. 64. 6. Luke 14. 33. Psal. 38. 4. Hab. 2. 2. Act. 16. 31.

* His Out-cry.

In this plight therefore he went home, and restrained himself as long as he could, that his Wife and Children should not perceive his distress; but he could not be silent long, because that his trouble increased: wherefore at length he brake his mind to his Wife and Children; and thus he began to talk to them, *O my dear Wife*, said he, *and you the Children of my bowels, I your dear friend am in my self undone, by reason of a burden that lieth hard upon me: moreover, I am for certain informed, that this our City will be burned with fire from Heaven, in which fearful overthrow, both my self, with thee, my Wife, and you my sweet babes, shall miserably come to ruine; except (the which, yet I see not) some way of escape can be found, whereby we may be delivered*. At this his Relations were sore amazed; not for that they believed, that what he said to them was true, but because they thought, that some frenzy distemper had got into his head: therefore, it drawing towards night, and they hoping that sleep might settle his brains, with all hast they got him to bed; but the night was as troublesome to him as the day: wherefore instead of sleeping, he spent it in sighs and tears. So when the morning was come, they would know how he did; and he told them worse and worse. He also set to talking to them again, but they began to be hardened; *they also thought to drive away his distemper by harsh and surly carriages to him: sometimes they would deride, sometimes they would chide, and sometimes they would quite neglect him: wherefore he began to retire himself to his Chamber to pray for, and pity them; and also to condole his own misery: he would also walk solitarily in the Fields, sometimes reading, and sometimes praying: and thus for some days he spent his time.

* Carnal Physick for a Sick Soul.

Now, I saw upon a time, when he was walking in the Fields, that he was (as he was wont) reading in his Book, and greatly distressed in his mind; and as he read, he burst out, as he had done before, crying, *What shall I do to be saved?*

I saw also that he looked this way, and that way, as if he would run; yet he stood still, because, as I perceived, he could not tell which way to go. I looked then, and saw a man named *Evangelist*† coming to him, and asked, *Wherefore dost thou cry?* He answered, Sir, I perceive, by the Book in my hand, that I am Condemned to die, and *after that to come to Judgment; and I find that I am not *willing to do the first, nor * able to do the second.

* Heb. 9. 27.
* Job 16. 21, 22.
* Ezek. 22. 14.

Then said *Evangelist*, Why not willing to die? since this life is attended with so many evils? The Man answered, Because I fear that this burden that is upon my back, will sink me lower then the Grave; and I shall fall into **Tophet*.† And Sir, if I be not fit to go to Prison, I am not fit (I am sure) to go to Judgement, and from thence to Execution; and the thoughts of these things make me cry.

* Isa. 30. 33.

Then said *Evangelist*, If this be thy condition, why standest thou still? He answered, Because I know not whither to go; Then he gave him a **Parchment-Roll*, and there was written within, **Fly from the wrath to come*.

* *Conviction of the necessity of flying.*
* Mat. 3. 7.

The Man therefore Read it, and looking upon *Evangelist* very carefully; said, Whither must I fly? Then said *Evangelist*, pointing with his finger over a very wide Field, Do you see yonder **Wicket-gate*?† The Man said, No. Then said the other, Do you see yonder *shining light? He said, I think I do. Then said *Evangelist*, Keep that light in your eye, and go up

* Mat. 7.
Psal. 119. 105.
2 Pet. 1. 19.

Christian, no sooner leaves the world, but meets
Evangelist, who lovingly him greets,
With Tydings of another; And doth show
Him how to mount to that from this below.

directly thereto, *so shalt thou see the Gate; at which when thou knockest, it shall be told thee what thou shalt do. ** Christ and the way to him cannot be found without the Word.*

So I saw in my Dream, that the Man began to run; Now he had not run far from his own door, but his Wife and Children perceiving it, began to cry after him to return: *but the Man put his fingers in his Ears, and ran on crying, Life, Life, Eternal Life: so he looked not behind him, *but fled towards the middle of the Plain. * Luke 14. 26. * Gen. 19. 17.

The Neighbors also came out to *see him run, and as he ran, some mocked, others threatned; and some cried after him to return: Now among those that did so, there were two that were resolved to fetch him back by force. *The name of the one was *Obstinate*, and the name of the other *Pliable*. Now by this time the Man was got a good distance from them; But however they were resolved to pursue him; which they did and in little time they over-took him. Then said the Man, Neighbours, *Wherefore are you come?* They said, To perswade you to go back with us; but he said, That can by no means be: You dwell, said he, in the City of *Destruction*,† (the place also where I was born) I see it to be so; and dying there, sooner or later, you will sink lower then the Grave, into a place that burns with Fire and Brimstone: Be content good Neighbours, and go along with me. ** They that fly from the wrath to come, are a Gazing-Stock to the world.* Jer. 20. 10. * Obstinate *and* Pliable *follow him.*

**What!* said *Obstinate, and leave our Friends, and our Comforts behind us!* ** Obstinate.*

*Yes, said *Christian*,† (for that was his name) because, that all, which you shall forsake, is not *worthy to be compared with a little of that that I am seeking to enjoy, and if you will go along with me, and hold it, you shall fare as I my self; for there where I go, is *enough, and to spare; Come away, and prove my words. ** Christian.* * 2 Cor. 4. 18. * Luke 15.

Obst. *What are the things you seek, since you leave all the world to find them?*

Chr. I seek an **Inheritance, incorruptible, undefiled, and that fadeth not away*; and it is laid up in Heaven, *and fast there, to be bestowed at the time appointed, on them that diligently seek it. Read it so, if you will, in my Book. * 1 Pet. 1. 4. * Heb. 11. 16.

Obst. *Tush*, said *Obstinate, away with your Book; will you go back with us, or no?*

Chr. No, not I, said the other; because I have laid my hand to the *Plow.

* Luke 9. 62.

Obst. *Come then, Neighbour* Pliable, *let us turn again, and go home without him; there is a company of these Craz'd-headed Coxcombs, that when they take a fancy by the end, are wiser in their own eyes then seven men that can render a reason.*†

Pli. Then said *Pliable*, Don't revile; if what the good *Christian* says is true, the things he looks after are better then ours; my heart inclines to go with my Neighbour.

Obst. *What! more Fools still? be ruled by me and go back; who knows whither such a brain-sick fellow will lead you? Go back, go back, and be wise.*

* Christian *and* Obstinate *pull for* Pliable's *Soul.*

Chr. *Come with me Neighbour *Pliable*, there are such things to be had which I spoke of, and many more Glories besides; If you believe not me, read here in this Book; and for the truth of what is exprest therein, behold, all is confirmed by the *blood of him that made it.

* Heb. 13. 20, 21.

* Pliable *concented to go with* Christian.

Pli. **Well Neighbour* Obstinate (*said* Pliable) *I begin to come to a point; I intend to go along with this good man, and to cast in my lot with him: But my good Companion, do you know the way to this desired place?*

Chr. I am directed by a man whose name is *Evangelist*, to speed me to a little Gate that is before us, where we shall receive instruction about the way.

Pli. *Come then, good Neighbour, let us be going:* Then they went both together.

Obst. And I will go back to my place, said *Obstinate*: I will be no Companion of such mis-led fantastical Fellows.

* *Talk between Christian, and* Pliable.

Now I saw in my Dream, that when *Obstinate* was gon back, *Christian* and *Pliable* went *talking over the Plain; and thus they began their discourse,

Chr. Come Neighbour *Pliable*, how do you do? I am glad you are perswaded to go along with me; and had even *Obstinate* himself, but felt what I have felt of the Powers, and Terrours of what is yet unseen, he would not thus lightly have given us the back.

Pliable. *Come Neighbour* Christian, *since there is none but us two here, tell me now further, what the things are, and how to be enjoyed, whither we are going.*

Chr. I can better conceive of them with my Mind, then speak of them with my Tongue: But yet since you are desirous to know, I will read of them in my Book.

Pli. *And do you think that the words of your Book are certainly true?*

Chr. Yes verily, for it was made by him that *cannot lye. * Tit. 1. 2.

Pli. *Well said; what things are they?*

Chr. There is an *endless Kingdom to be Inhabited, and everlasting life to be given us; that we may Inhabit that Kingdom for ever. * Isa. 45. 17. John 10. 27, 28, 29.

Pli. *Well said, and what else?*

Chr. There are Crowns of Glory to be given us; *and Garments that will make us shine like the Sun in the Firmament of Heaven. * 2 Tim. 4. 8. Rev. 3. 4. Matth. 13.

Pli. *This is excellent; And what else?*

Chr. There shall be no more crying, *nor sorrow; For he that is owner of the place, will wipe all tears from our eyes. * Isa. 25. 8. Rev. 7. 16, 17. Chap. 21. 4.

Pli. *And what company shall we have there?*

Chr. There we shall be with *Seraphims*, *and *Cherubins*, Creatures that will dazle your eyes to look on them: There also you shall meet with thousands, and ten thousands that have gone before us to that place; none of them are hurtful, but loving, and holy; every one walking in the sight of God; and standing in his presence with acceptance for ever: In a word, there we shall see the *Elders with their Golden Crowns: There we shall see the Holy *Virgins with their Golden Harps. There we shall see *Men that by the World were cut in pieces, burnt in flames, eaten of Beasts, drowned in the Seas, for the love that they bare to the Lord of the place; all well, and cloathed with *Immortality, as with a Garment. * Isa. 6. 2. 1 Thess. 4. 16, 17. Rev. 5. 11. * Rev. 4. 4. * Chap. 14. 1, 2, 3, 4, 5. * John 12. 25. * 2 Cor. 5. 2, 3, 5.

Pli. *The hearing of this is enough to ravish ones heart; but are these things to be enjoyed? how shall we get to be Sharers hereof?*

Chr. The Lord, the Governour of that Countrey, hath Recorded *that* *in this Book: The substance of which is, If we be truly willing to have it, he will bestow it upon us freely. * Isa. 55. 12. John 7. 37. Chap. 6. 37. Rev. 21. 6. Chap. 22. 17.

Pli. *Well, my good Companion, glad am I to hear of these things: Come on, let us mend our pace.*

Chr. I cannot go so fast as I would, by reason of this burden that is upon my back.

Now I saw in my Dream, that just as they had ended this talk, they drew near to a very *Miry Slow* that was in the midst of the Plain, and they being heedless, did both fall suddenly into the bogg. The name of the Slow was *Dispond.*† Here therefore they wallowed for a time, being grievously bedaubed with the dirt; And *Christian*, because of the burden that was on his back, began to sink in the Mire.

Pli. *Then said* Pliable, *Ah, Neighbour* Christian, *where are you now?*

Chr. Truly, said *Christian*, I do not know.

Pli. At that *Pliable* began to be offended; and angerly, said to his Fellow, *Is this the happiness you have told me all this while of? if we have such ill speed at our first setting out, What may we expect, 'twixt this and our Journeys end? *May I get out again with my life, you shall possess the brave Country alone for me.* And with that he gave a desperate struggle or two, and got out of the Mire, on that side of the Slow which was next to his own House: So away he went, and *Christian* saw him no more.

* *It is not enough to be Pliable.*

Wherefore *Christian* was left to tumble in the Slow of *Dispond* alone; but still he endeavoured to struggle to that side of the Slow, that was still further *from his own House, and next to the Wicket-gate; the which he did, but could not get out, because of the burden that was upon his back: But I beheld in my Dream, that a Man came to him, whose name was *Help*, and asked him, *What he did there?*

* Christian *in trouble, seeks still to get further from his own House.*

Chr. Sir, said *Christian*, I was bid go this way, by a Man called *Evangelist*, who directed me also to yonder Gate, that I might escape the wrath to come: And as I was going thither, I fell in here.

Help. *But why did you not look for * the steps?*

* *The Promises.*†

Chr. Fear followed me so hard, that I fled the next way, and fell in.

Help. *Then*, said he, **Give me thy hand*; so he gave him his hand, and *he drew him out, and set him upon sound ground, and bid him go on his way.

* Help *lifts him out.*
* Psal. 40. 2.

Then I stepped to him that pluckt him out, and said; Sir,

Wherefore, (since over this place is the way from the City of *Destruction*, to yonder *Gate*,) is it, that *this* Plat is not mended, that poor Travellers might go thither with more security? And he said unto me, this *Miry slow*, is such a place as cannot be mended: It is the descent whither the *scum and filth that attends conviction for sin doth continually run, and therefore is it called the *Slow of Dispond*: for still as the sinner is awakened about his lost condition, there ariseth in his soul many fears, and doubts, and discouraging apprehensions, which all of them get together, and settle in this place: And this is the reason of the badness of this ground.

** What makes the Slow of Dispond.*

It is not the *pleasure of the King that this place should remain so bad; his Labourers also, have by the direction of His Majesties Surveyors, been for above this sixteen hundred years,† imploy'd about this patch of ground, if perhaps it might have been mended: yea, and to my knowledge, saith he, *Here* hath been swallowed up, at least, Twenty thousand Cart Loads; yea Millions of wholesom Instructions, that have at all seasons been brought from all places of the Kings Dominions; (and they that can tell, say, they are the best Materials to make good ground of the place,) If so be it might have been mended, but it is the *Slow of Dispond* still; and so will be, when they have done what they can.

* Isa. 35. 3, 4.

True, there are by the direction of the Law-giver, certain good and substantiall *steps, placed even through the very midst of this *Slow*; but at such time as this place doth much spue out its filth, as it doth against change of weather, these steps are hardly seen; or if they be, Men through the diziness of their Heads, step besides; and then they are bemired to purpose, notwithstanding the steps be there; but the ground is *good when they are once got in at the Gate.

** The Promises of forgiveness and acceptance to life by Faith in Christ.*

* 1 Sam. 12. 23.

Now I saw in my Dream, that by this time **Pliable* was got home to his House again. *So his Neighbours came to visit him; and some of them called him wise Man for coming back; and some called him Fool for hazarding himself with *Christian*; others again did mock at his Cowardliness; saying, Surely since you began to venture, I would not have been so base to have given out for a few difficulties. So *Pliable* sat sneaking among them. But at last he got more confidence, and

* Plyable *got home, and is visited of his Neighbors.*

**His entertainment by them at his return.*

then they all turned their tales, and began to deride poor *Christian* behind his back. And thus much concerning *Pliable*.

** Mr.* Worldly-Wiseman *meets with* Christian.

Now as Christian was walking solitary by himself, he espied one afar off, come crossing over the field *to meet him; and their hap was to meet just as they were crossing the way of each other. The Gentleman's name was, Mr. *Worldly-Wiseman*,† he dwelt in the Town of *Carnal-Policy*, a very great Town, and also hard by, from whence Christian came. This man then meeting with Christian, and having some inckling of him, for Christians setting forth from the City of *Destruction*, was much noised abroad, not only in the Town, where he dwelt, but also it began to be the *Town*-talk in some other places, Master *Worldly-Wiseman* therefore, having some guess of him, by beholding his laborious going, by observing his sighs and groans, and the like; began thus to enter into some talk with *Christian*.

Talk betwixt Mr. Worldly-Wiseman, *and* Christian.

World. *How now, good fellow, whither away after this burdened manner?*

Chr. A burdened manner indeed, as ever I think poor creature had. And whereas you ask me, *Whither away*, I tell you, Sir, I am going to yonder Wicket-gate before me; for there, as I am informed, I shall be put into a way to be rid of my heavy burden.

Worl. *Hast thou a Wife and Children?*

** 1 Cor. 7. 29.*

Chr. Yes, but I am so laden with this burden, that I cannot take that pleasure in them as formerly: methinks, I am as *if I had none.

Worl. *Wilt thou hearken to me, if I give thee counsel?*

Chr. If it be good, I will; for I stand in need of good counsel.

** Mr.* Worldly-Wiseman's *Counsel to* Christian.

Worl. **I would advise thee then, that thou with all speed get thy self rid of thy burden; for thou wilt never be settled in thy mind till then: nor canst thou enjoy the benefits of the blessing which God hath bestowed upon thee till then.*

Chr. That is that which I seek for, even to be rid of this heavy burden; but get it off my self I cannot: nor is there a man in our Country that can take it off my shoulders; therefore am I going this way, as I told you, that I may be rid of my burden.

Worl. *Who bid thee go this way to be rid of thy burden?*

Chr. A man that appeared to me to be a very great and honorable person; his name, as I remember is *Evangelist*.

Worl. **I beshrow him for his counsel; there is not a more dangerous and troublesome way in the world, than is that unto which he hath directed thee; and that thou shalt find, if thou wilt be ruled by his counsel: Thou hast met with something (as I perceive) already; for I see the dirt of the* Slow of Dispond *is upon thee; but that Slow is the beginning of the sorrows that do attend those that go on in that way: hear me, I am older than thou! thou art like to meet with in the way which thou goest, Wearisomness, Painfulness, Hunger, Perils, Nakedness, Sword, Lions, Dragons, Darkness; and in a word, death,*† *and what not? These things are certainly true, having been confirmed by many testimonies. And why should a man so carelessly cast away himself, by giving heed to a stranger?*

* *Mr.* Worldly-Wiseman *Condemned* Evangelists *Counsel.*

Chr. Why, Sir, this burden upon my back is more terrible to me than are all these things which you have mentioned: *nay, methinks I care not what I meet with in the way, so be I can also meet with deliverance from my burden.

* *The frame of the heart of young Christians.*

Worl. *How camest thou by thy burden at first?*

Chr. By reading this Book in my hand.

Worl. **I thought so; and it is happened unto thee as to other weak men, who meddling with things too high for them, do suddenly fall into thy distractions; which distractions do not only unman men, (as thine I perceive has done thee) but they run them upon desperate ventures, to obtain they know not what.*

* Worldly-Wiseman *does not like that Men should be Serious in reading the Bible.*

Chr. I know what I would obtain; it is ease for my heavy burden.

Worl. *But why wilt thou seek for ease this way, seeing so many dangers attend it, especially, since (hadst thou but patience to hear me) I could direct thee to the obtaining of what thou desirest, without the dangers that thou in this way wilt run thy self into: yea, and the remedy is at hand. Besides, I will add, that instead of those dangers, thou shalt meet with much safety, friendship, and content.*

Chr. Pray Sir open this secret to me.

Worl. **Why in yonder Village, (the Village is named* Morality*) there dwells a Gentleman, whose name is* Legality, *a very judicious man (and a man of a very good name) that has skill to help men off with such burdens as thine are, from their shoulders: yea, to my knowledge he hath done a great deal of good this way:*

* *Whether Mr.* Worldly *prefers Morality before the Straight Gate.*

Ai, and besides, he hath skill to cure those that are somewhat crazed in their wits with their burdens. To him, as I said, thou mayest go, and be helped presently. His house is not quite a mile from this place; and if he should not be at home himself, he hath a pretty young man to his Son, whose name is Civility, *that can do it (to speak on) as well as the old Gentleman himself: There, I say, thou mayest be eased of thy burden, and if thou art not minded to go back to thy former habitation, as indeed I would not wish thee, thou mayest send for thy wife and Children to thee to this Village, where there are houses now stand empty, one of which thou mayest have at reasonable rates: Provision is there also cheap and good, and that which will make thy life the more happy, is, to be sure there thou shalt live by honest neighbors, in credit and good fashion.*

* Christian *Snared by Mr.* Worldly Wisemans *Word.*

*Now was *Christian* somewhat at a stand, but presently he concluded; if this be true which this Gentleman hath said, my wisest course is to take his advice, and with that he thus farther spoke.

Chr. Sir, which is my way to this honest man's house?

* *Mount Sinai.*

Worl. *Do you see yonder *high hill?*†

Chr. Yes, very well.

Worl. By that *Hill* you must go, and the first house you come at is his.

* *Christian afraid that Mount* Sinai *would fall on his head.*

* Exod. 19. 18.

* Ver. 16.

* Heb. 12. 21.

So *Christian* turned out of his way to go to Mr. *Legality's* house for help: but behold, when he was got now hard by the *Hill*, it seemed so high, and also that side of it that was next the way side, did hang so much over, that Christian was *afraid to venture further, lest the *Hill* should fall on his head:† wherefore there he stood still, and wotted not what to do. Also his burden, *now*, seemed heavier to him, than while he was in his way. There came also *flashes of fire out of the Hill, that made **Christian* afraid that he should be burned: here therefore he swet, and did quake for *fear. And now he began to be sorry that he had taken Mr. *Worldly-Wisemans* counsel; and with that he saw **Evangelist* coming to meet him; at the sight also of whom he began to blush for shame. So *Evangelist* drew nearer, and nearer, and coming up to him, he looked upon him with a severe and dreadful countenance: and thus began to reason with *Christian*.

* Evangelist *findeth* Christian *under Mount* Sinai *and looketh severely upon him.*

When Christians unto carnal Men give ear,
Out of their way they go, and pay for't dear,
For Master *Worldly-Wiseman* can but shew
A Saint the way to Bondage and to Woe.

* Evangelist *reasons afresh with* Christian.

Evan. *What doest thou here? said he: at which word *Christian* knew not what to answer: wherefore, at present he stood speechless before him. Then said *Evangelist* farther, *Art not thou the man that I found crying, without the walls of the City of* Destruction?

Chr. Yes, dear Sir, I am the man.

Evan. *Did not I direct thee the way to the little Wicket-gate?*

Chr. Yes, dear Sir said *Christian.*

Evan. *How is it then that thou art so quickly turned aside, for thou art now out of the way?*

Chr. I met with a Gentleman, so soon as I had got over the *Slow of Dispond*, who perswaded me, that I might in the *Village* before me, find a man that could take off my burden.

Evan. *What was he?*

Chr. He looked like a Gentleman, and talked much to me, and got me at last to yield; so I came hither: but when I beheld this Hill, and how it hangs over the way, I suddenly made a stand, lest it should fall on my head.

Evan. *What said that Gentleman to you?*

Chr. Why, he asked me whither I was going, and I told him.

Evan. *And what said he then?*

Chr. He asked me if I had a Family, and I told him: but, said I, I am so loaden with the burden that is on my back, that I cannot take pleasure in them as formerly.

Evan. *And what said he then?*

Chr. He bid me with speed get rid of my burden, and I told him 'twas ease that I sought: And said I, I am therefore going to yonder *Gate* to receive further direction how I may get to the place of deliverance. So he said that he would shew me a better way, and short, not so attended with difficulties, as the way, Sir, that you set me: which way, said he, will direct you to a Gentleman's house that hath skill to take off these burdens: So I believed him, and turned out of that way into this, if haply I might be soon eased of my burden: but when I came to this place, and beheld things as they are, I stopped for fear, (as I said) of danger: but I now know not what to do.

Evan. *Then* (said Evangelist) *stand still a little, that I may shew thee the words of God.* So he stood trembling. *Then* (said

* Heb. 12. 25.

Evangelist) **See that ye refuse not him that speaketh; for if they* *escaped not who refused him that spake on Earth,* **much more shall not we escape, if we turn away from him that speaketh from Heaven. He said moreover,* **Now the just shall live by faith; but if any man draws back, my soul shall have no pleasure in him. He also did thus apply them, Thou art the man that art running into this misery, thou hast began to reject the counsel of the most high, and to draw back thy foot from the way of peace,*† *even almost to the hazarding of thy perdition.*

*Evangelist *Convinces* Christian *of his Error.*
* Chap. 10. 38.

Then *Christian* fell down at his foot as dead, crying, Woe is me, for I am undone: at the sight of which *Evangelist* caught him by the right hand, saying, All manner of sin and blasphemies shall be forgiven unto men; be not faithless, but believing; then did *Christian* again a little revive, and stood up trembling, as at first, before *Evangelist.*

Matth. 12. Mark 3.

Then *Evangelist* proceeded, saying, *Give more earnest heed to the things that I shall tell thee of.* I will now shew thee who it was that deluded thee, and who 'twas also to whom he sent thee. *The man that met thee, is one *Worldly-Wiseman*, and rightly is he so called; partly, *because he favoureth only the Doctrine of this World (therefore he always goes to the Town of *Morality* to Church) and partly *because he loveth that Doctrine best, for it saveth him from the Cross; and because he is of this carnal temper, therefore he seeketh to prevent my ways, though right. *Now there are three things in this mans counsel that thou must utterly abhor.

* *Mr.* Worldly-Wiseman *discribed by* Evangelist.
* 1 John 4. 5.
* Gal. 6. 12.
* Evangelist *discovers the deceit of* Mr. Worldly Wiseman.

1. His turning thee out of the way.
2. His labouring to render the Cross odious to thee.
3. And his setting thy feet in that way that leadeth unto the administration of Death.†

First, Thou must abhor his turning thee out of the way; yea, and thine own consenting thereto: because this is to reject the counsel of God, for the sake of the counsel of a *Worldly-Wiseman.* The Lord says, **Strive to enter in at the strait gate,* the gate to which I sent thee; **for strait is the gate that leadeth unto life, and few there be that find it.* From this little wicket-gate, and from the way thereto hath this wicked man turned thee, to the bringing of thee almost to destruction; hate therefore his turning thee out of the way, and abhor thy self for harkening to him.

* Luke 13. 24.
* Mat. 7. 13, 14.

Secondly, Thou must abhor his labouring to render the Cross odious unto thee; for thou art to *prefer it before the treasures in Egypt: besides the King of glory hath told thee, *that he that will save his life shall lose it: and *he that comes after him, and hates not his father and mother, and wife, and children, and brethren, and sisters; yea, and his own life also, he cannot be my Disciple. I say therefore, for a man to labour to perswade thee, that that shall be thy death, without which the truth hath said, thou canst not have eternal life, this Doctrine thou must abhor.

* Heb. 11. 25, 26.

* Mark 8. 34. John 13. 25. Mat. 10. 39.

* Luke 14. 26.

Thirdly, thou must hate his setting of thy feet in the way that leadeth to the ministration of death. And for this thou must consider to whom he sent thee, and also how unable that person was to deliver thee from thy burden.

He to whom thou wast sent for ease, being by name *Legality*, is the Son of the *Bond woman which now is, and is in bondage with her children, and is in a mystery this *Mount *Sinai*, which thou hast feared will fall on thy head. Now if she with her children are in bondage, how canst thou expect by them to be made free? This *Legality* therefore is not able to set thee free from thy burden. No man was as yet ever rid of his burden by him, no, nor ever is like to be: ye cannot be justified by the Works of the Law; for by the deeds of the Law no man living can be rid of his burden: therefore Mr. *Worldly-Wiseman* is an alien, and Mr. *Legality* a cheat: and for his Son *Civility*, notwithstanding his simpering looks, he is but an hypocrite, and cannot help thee. Believe me, there is nothing in all this noise, that thou hast heard of this sottish man, but a design to beguile thee of thy Salvation, by turning thee from the way in which I had set thee. After this *Evangelist* called aloud to the Heavens for confirmation of what he had said; and with that there came words and fire out of the Mountain under which poor Christian stood, that made the hair of his flesh stand. The words were thus pronounced, *As many as are of the works of the Law, are under the curse; for it is written, Cursed is every one that continueth not in all things which are written in the Book of the Law to do them.*

* Gal. 4. 21, 22, 23, 24, 25, 26, 27.

* *The Bond-Woman.*

Gal. 3. 10.

Now *Christian* looked for nothing but death, and began to cry out lamentably, even cursing the time in which he met with

Mr. *Worldly-Wiseman*, still calling himself a thousand fools for hearkening to his counsel: he also was greatly ashamed to think that this Gentlemans arguments, flowing only from the flesh, should have that prevalency with him as to cause him to forsake the right way. This done, he applied himself again to *Evangelist* in words and sense as follows.

Chr. *Sir, what think you? is there hopes? may I now go back and go up to the *Wicket-gate*? shall I not be abandoned for this, and sent back from thence ashamed? I am sorry I have hearkened to this man's counsel, but may my sin be forgiven.

* Christian *Enquired if he may yet be Happy.*

Evang. Then said *Evangelist* to him, Thy sin is very great, for by it thou hast committed two evils; thou hast forsaken the way that is good, to tread in forbidden paths: *yet will the man at the Gate receive thee, for he has *good will* for men; only, said he, take heed that thou turn not aside again, lest thou perish from the way when his wrath is *kindled but a little. Then did *Christian* address himself to go back, and *Evangelist*, after he had kist him, gave him one smile, and bid him God speed; so he went on with haste, neither spake he to any man by the way; nor if any man asked him, would he vouchsafe them an answer. He went like one that was all the while treading on forbidden ground, and could by no means think himself safe, till again he was got into the way which he left to follow Mr. *Worldly-Wiseman's* counsel: so in process of time *Christian* got up to the Gate. Now over the Gate there was Written, *Knock and it shall be opened unto you.* *He knocked therefore, more then once or twice, *saying*,

* Evangelist *comforts him.*

* Psal. 2 *last.*

* Mat. 7. 8.

May I now enter here? will he within
Open to sorry me, though I have bin
An undeserving Rebel? then shall I,
Not fail to Sing his lasting praise on high.

At last there came a grave Person to the Gate: named *Good-will*,† who asked, *Who was there? and whence he came? and what he would have?*

Chr. Here is a poor burdened sinner, I come from the City of *Destruction*, but am going to Mount *Zion*,† that I may be delivered from the wrath to come; I would therefore, Sir, since

He that will enter in must first without
Stand knocking at the Gate, nor need he doubt
That is a knocker but to enter in;
For God can love him and forgive his sin.

I am informed that by this Gate is the way thither, know if you are *willing* to let me in.

Good-Will. *I am *willing* with all my heart, said he; and with that he opened the Gate.

** The Gate will be opened to broken-hearted sinners.*

So when *Christian* was stepping in, the other gave him a pull: Then said *Christian*, what means that? The other told him, A little distance from this Gate, there is erected a strong Castle, of which **Belzebub*† is the Captain: from thence both he, and them that are with him, Shoot Arrows at those that come up to this Gate; if happily they may die before they can enter in. Then, said *Christian*, *I rejoyce and tremble. So when he was got in, the man of the Gate asked him, Who directed him thither?

** Satan envies those that enter the straight Gate.*

* Christian *Entred the Gate with Joy and trembling.*

Chr. **Evangelist* bid me come hither and knock, (as I did;) And he said, that you, Sir, would tell me what I must do.

* *Talke between* Good Will *and* Christian.

Good Will. *An open Door is set before thee, and no man can shut it.*†

Chr. Now I begin to reap the benefits of my hazzards.

Good Will. *But how is it that you came alone?*

Chr. Because none of my Neighbours saw their danger as I saw mine.

Good Will. *Did any of them know of your coming?*

Chr. Yes, my Wife and Children saw me at the first, and called after me to turn again: Also some of my Neighbours stood crying, and calling after me to return; but I put my Fingers in mine Ears, and so came on my way.

Good Will. *But did none of them follow you to perswade you to go back?*

Chr. Yes, both *Obstinate*, and *Pliable*: But when they saw that they could not prevail, *Obstinate* went railing back; but *Pliable* came with me a little way.

Good Will. *But why did he not come through?*

Chr. We indeed came both together, until we came at the Slow of *Dispond*, into the which, we also suddenly fell. And then was my Neighbour *Pliable* discouraged, and would not adventure further. *Wherefore getting out again, on that side next to his own House; he told me, I should possess the brave Countrey alone for him: So he went his way, and I came mine. He after *Obstinate*, and I to this Gate.

** A Man may have Company when he sets out for Heaven, & yet go thither alone.*

Good Will. Then said *Good Will*, Alas poor man, is the Cœlestial Glory of so small esteem with him, that he counteth it not worth running the hazards of a few difficulties to obtain it?

Chr. Truly, said *Christian*, I have said the truth of *Pliable*, and if I should also say all the truth of my self, it will appear there is *no betterment 'twixt him and my self. 'Tis true, he went back to his own house, but I also turned aside to go in the way of death, being perswaded thereto by the carnal arguments of one Mr. *Worldly Wiseman*.

* Christian *accuseth himself before the man at the Gate.*

Good Will. Oh, did he light upon you! what, he would have had you a sought for ease at the hands of Mr. *Legality*; they are both of them a very cheat: but did you take his counsel?

Chr. Yes, as far as I durst, I went to find out Mr. *Legality*, until I thought that the Mountain that stands by his house, would have fallen upon my head: wherefore there I was forced to stop.

Good Will. That Mountain has been the death of many, and will be the death of many more: 'tis well you escaped being by it dasht in pieces.

Chr. Why, truly I do not know what had become of me there, had not *Evangelist* happily met me again as I was musing in the midst of my *dumps*: but 'twas Gods mercy that he came to me again, for else I had never come hither. But now I am come, such a one as I am, more fit indeed for death by that Mountain, than thus to stand talking with my Lord: But Oh, what a favour is this to me, that yet I am admitted entrance here.

* Christian is *comforted again.*

* John 6. 37.

Good Will. *We make no objections against any, notwithstanding all that they have done before they come hither, **they in no wise are cast out*; and therefore, good *Christian*, come a little way with me, and I will teach thee about the way thou must go. *Look before thee; dost thou see this narrow way? That is the way thou must go. It was cast up by the Patriarchs,† Prophets, Christ, and his Apostles, and it is as straight as a Rule can make it: This is the way thou must go.

* Christian *directed yet on his way.*

Chr. But said *Christian, Is there no turnings nor windings, by which a Stranger *may loose the way?*

* Christian *afraid of losing his way.*

Good Will. Yes, there are many ways *Butt* down upon this;

and they are Crooked, and Wide: But *thus* thou may'st distinguish the right from the wrong, *That* only being *straight and narrow.

* Mat. 7. 14.

Then I saw in my Dream, *That *Christian* asked him further, If he could not help him off with his burden that was upon his back; For as yet he had not got rid thereof, nor could he by any means get it off without help.

* Christian *weary of his Burden.*

He told him, As to the burden, be content to bear it, until thou comest to the place of *Deliverance; for there it will fall from thy back it self.

* *There is no deliverance from the guilt, and burden of sin, but by the death and blood of Christ.*

Then *Christian* began to gird up his loins, and to address himself to his Journey. So the other told him, that by that he was gone some distance from the Gate, he would come at the house of the *Interpreter*;† at whose Door he should knock; and he would shew him excellent things. Then *Christian* took his leave of his Friend, and he again bid him God speed.

Then he went on, till he came at the house of the **Interpreter*, where he knocked over, and over: at last one came to the Door, and asked *Who was there?*

* Christian *comes to the House of the Interpreter.*

Chr. Sir, here is a Travailer, who was bid by an acquaintance of the Good-man of this House, to call here for my profit: I would therefore speak with the Master of the House: so he called for the Master of the House; who after a little time came to *Christian*, and asked him what he would have?

Chr. Sir, said *Christian*, I am a Man that am come from the City of *Destruction*, and am going to the Mount *Zion*, and I was told by the Man that stands at the Gate, at the head of this way, that if I called here, you would shew me excellent things, such as would be an help to me in my Journey.

Inter. Then said the *Interpreter*, *come in, I will shew thee that which will be profitable to thee.† So he commanded his man to *light the Candle, and bid *Christian* follow him; so he had him into a private Room, and bid his Man open a Door; the which when he had done, **Christian* saw a Picture of a very grave Person hang up against the wall, and this was the fashion of it, **It had eyes lift up to Heaven, the best of Books in its hand, the Law of Truth was written upon its lips,† the World was behind its back; it stood as if it pleaded with Men, and a Crown of Gold did hang over its head.*

* *He is entertained.*

* *Illumination.*

* Christian *sees a brave Picture.*

* *The fashion of the Picture.*

Chr. *Then said* Christian, *What means this?*

Inter. The Man whose Picture this is, is one of a thousand, he can *beget Children, Travel in birth with Children, and *Nurse them himself when they are born. And whereas thou seest *him with his eyes lift up to Heaven, the best of Books in his hand, and the Law of Truth writ on his Lips: it is to shew thee, that his work is to know, and unfold dark things to sinners; even as also thou seest *him stand as if he Pleaded with Men: And whereas thou seest the World as cast behind him, and that a Crown hangs over his head; that is, to shew thee, that slighting and despising the things that are present, for the love that he hath to his Masters service, he is sure in the world that comes next to have Glory for his Reward: Now, said the *Interpreter*, I have shewed thee this Picture first, *because the Man whose Picture this is, is the only Man, whom the Lord of the Place whither thou art going, hath Authorized, to be thy Guide in all difficult places thou mayest meet with in the way: wherefore take good heed to what I have shewed thee, and bear well in thy mind what thou hast seen; lest in thy Journey, thou meet with some that pretend to lead thee right, but their way goes down to death.

* 1 Cor. 4. 15.
* Gal. 4. 19.
* 1 Thes. 2. 7.
* *The meaning of the Picture.*
* *Why he shewed him the Picture first.*

Then he took him by the hand, and led him into a very large *Parlour* that was full of dust, because never swept; the which, after he had reviewed a little while, the *Interpreter* called for a man to *sweep*: Now when he began to sweep, the dust began so abundantly to fly about, that *Christian* had almost therewith been choaked: Then said the *Interpreter* to a *Damsel* that stood by, Bring hither Water, and sprinkle the Room; which when she had done, was swept and cleansed with pleasure.

Chr. Then said Christian, *What means this?*

In. The *Interpreter* answered; This Parlor, is the heart of a Man that was never sanctified by the sweet Grace of the Gospel: The *dust*, is his Original Sin, and inward Corruptions that have defiled the whole Man. He that began to sweep at first, is the Law; but She that brought water, and did sprinkle it, is the Gospel: Now, whereas thou sawest that so soon as the first began to sweep, the dust did so fly about, that the Room by him could not be cleansed, but that thou wast almost choaked therewith, this is to shew thee, that the Law, instead of cleansing the heart (by its working) from sin, *doth revive, put *strength into, and *increase it in the soul, even as it doth discover and forbid it, for it doth not give power to subdue.

* Rom. 7. 6.
* 1 Cor. 15. 56.
* Rom. 5. 20.

Again, as thou sawest the *Damsel* sprinkle the Room with Water, upon which it was cleansed with pleasure: This is to shew thee, that when the Gospel comes in the sweet and precious influences thereof to the heart, then I say, even as thou sawest the Damsel lay the dust by sprinkling the Floor with Water, so is sin vanquished and subdued, and the soul made clean, through the Faith of it; and consequently *fit for the King of Glory to inhabit.

* John 15. 3. Ephes. 5. 26. Acts 15. 9. Rom. 16. 25, 26. John 15. 13.

I saw moreover in my Dream, *that the *Interpreter* took him by the hand, and had him into a little Room, where sat two little Children, each one in his Chair: The name of the eldest was *Passion*, and of the other, *Patience; Passion* seemed to be much discontent, but *Patience* was very quiet. Then *Christian* asked, What is the reason of the discontent of *Passion*? The *Interpreter* answered, The Governour of them would have him stay for his best things till the beginning of the next year; but he will have all now: *But *Patience* is willing to wait.

* *He shewed him* Passion & Patience.

Passion *will have all now.*

* Patience *is for waiting.*

Then I saw that one came to **Passion*, and brought him a Bag of Treasure, and poured it down at his feet; the which he took up, and rejoyced therein, and withall, laughed *Patience* to scorn: But I beheld but a while, and he had *lavished all away, and had nothing left him but Rags.

* Passion *has his desire,*

* *And quickly lavishes all away.*

Chr. *Then said* Christian *to the* Interpreter, **Expound this matter more fully to me.*

* *The matter expounded.*

Int. So he said, These two Lads are Figures; *Passion*, of the Men of *this* World; and *Patience*, of the Men of *that* which is to come: For as here thou seest, *Passion will have all now*, this year; that is to say, in *this* World; *So* are the Men of this World: they must have all their good things now, they cannot stay till next *Year*; that is, untill the *next* World, for their Portion of good. That Proverb, **A Bird in the hand is worth two in the Bush*, is of more Authority with them, then are all the Divine Testimonies of the good of the world to come. But as thou sawest, that he had quickly lavished all away, and had presently left him, nothing but Raggs; So will it be with all such Men at the end of this world.

* *The Worldly Man for a Bird in the hand.*

Chr. *Then said* Christian; *Now I see that* Patience *has the best* *Wisdom, and that upon many accounts.* 1. *Because he stays for the best things.* 2. *And also because he will have the glory of* His, *when the other hath nothing but Raggs.*

* Patience *had the best Wisdom.*

In. Nay, you may add another; to wit, The glory of the *next* world will never wear out; but *these* are suddenly gone. Therefore *Passion* had not so much reason to laugh at *Patience*, because he had his good things first, as *Patience* will have to laugh at *Passion*, *because he had his best things *last*; for *first* must give place to *last*, because *last* must have his time to come, but *last* gives place to *nothing*; for there is not another to succeed: he therefore that hath his Portion *first*, must needs have a time to spend it; but he that has his Portion *last*, must have it lastingly. Therefore it is said of **Dives, In thy life thou receivedst thy good things, and likewise* Lazarus *evil things; but now he is comforted, and thou art tormented.*

* *Things that are first must give place, but things that are last are lasting.*

* Luke 16. Dives *had his good things first.*

Chr. *Then I perceive, 'tis not best to covet things that are* now, *but to wait for things to* come.

Int. You say the Truth, **For the things that are seen, are* Temporal; *but the things that are not seen, are* Eternal: But though this be so, yet since things present, and our fleshly appetite, *are such near Neighbours one to another*; and again, because things to come, and carnal sense, are such strangers one to another: therefore it is, that the first of these so suddenly fall into *amity*, and that *distance* is so continued between the second.

* 2 Cor. 4. 18. *The first things are but Temporal.*

Then I saw in my Dream, that the *Interpreter* took *Christian* by the hand, and led him into a place, where was a Fire burning against a Wall, and one standing by it always, casting much Water upon it to quench it: Yet did the Fire burn higher and hotter.

Then said Christian, *What means this?*

The *Interpreter* answered, This fire is the work of Grace that is wrought in the heart; he that casts Water upon it, to extinguish and put it out, is the *Devil*: but in that thou seest the fire, notwithstanding, burn higher and hotter, thou shalt also see the reason of that: So he had him about to the back side of the Wall, where he saw a Man with a Vessel of Oyl in his hand, of the which he did also continually cast, but secretly, into the fire. Then said *Christian, What means this?* The *Interpreter* answered, This is *Christ*, who continually with the Oyl of his Grace, maintains the work already begun in the heart; by the means of which, notwithstanding what the Devil can do, the souls of his people prove gracious still. And in that thou sawest, that the Man stood behind the Wall to maintain the fire; this is to teach thee, that it is hard for the tempted to see how this work of Grace is maintained in the soul. 2 Cor. 12. 9.

I saw also that the *Interpreter* took him again by the hand, and led him into a pleasant place, where was builded a stately Palace, beautiful to behold; at the sight of which, *Christian* was greatly delighted; he saw also upon the top thereof, certain Persons walked, who were cloathed all in gold. Then said *Christian*, May we go in thither? Then the *Interpreter* took him, and led him up toward the door of the Palace; and behold, at the door, stood a great company of men, as desirous to go in, but durst not. There also sat a Man, at a little distance from the door, at a Table-side, with a Book, and his Inkhorn before him, to take the Name of him that should enter therein: He saw also that in the doorway, stood many Men in Armour to keep it, being resolved to do to the Man that would enter, what hurt and mischief they could. Now was *Christian* somwhat in a muse; at last, when every Man started back for fear of the Armed Men; *Christian* saw a man of a very stout countenance come up to the Man that sat there to write; saying, **Set down my Name Sir*; the which when he had done, he saw the Man draw his Sword, and put an Helmet upon his Head, and rush toward the door upon the Armed Men, who laid upon him with deadly force; but the Man, not at all discouraged, fell to cutting and hacking most fiercely; so after he had *received and given many wounds to those that attempted to keep him out, he cut his way through them all, and pressed forward into the Palace; at which there was a pleasant voice heard from those that were within, even of the Three† that walked upon the top of the Palace, saying,

* *The valiant man.*†

* Acts 14. 22.

Come in, Come in;
Eternal Glory thou shalt win.

So he went in, and was cloathed with such Garments as they.

Then *Christian* smiled, and said, I think verily I know the meaning of this.

Now, said *Christian*, let me go hence: Nay stay (said the *Interpreter,*) till I have shewed thee a little more, and after that, thou shalt go on thy way. So he took him by the hand again, and led him into a very dark Room, where there sat a Man in an Iron *Cage.

** Despair like an Iron Cage.*

Now the Man, to look on, seemed very sad: he sat with his eyes looking down to the ground, his hands folded together; and he sighed as if he would break his heart. Then said *Christian, What means this?* At which the *Interpreter* bid him talk with the Man.

Chr. Then said *Christian* to the Man, *What are thou?* The Man answered, *I am what I was not once.*

Chr. *What wast thou once?*

* Luke 8. 13.

Man. The *Man* said, I was once a fair *and flourishing Professor,† both in mine own eyes, and also in the eyes of others: I once was, as I thought, fair for the Cœlestial City, and had then even joy at the thoughts that I should get thither.

Chr. *Well, but what art thou now?*

Man. I am *now* a Man of Despair, and am shut up in it, as in this Iron Cage. I cannot get out; O *now* I cannot.†

Chr. *But how camest thou in this condition?*

Man. I left off to watch, and be sober;† I laid the reins upon the neck of my lusts; I sinned against the light of the Word, and the goodness of God: I have grieved the Spirit, and he is gone; I tempted the Devil, and he is come to me; I have provoked God to anger, and he has left me; I have so hardened my heart, that I *cannot* repent.

Then said *Christian* to the *Interpreter*, But is there no hopes for such a Man as this? Ask him, said the *Interpreter*.

Chr. Then said *Christian, Is there no hope but you must be kept in this Iron Cage of Despair?*

Man. No, none at all.

Chr. *Why? The Son of the Blessed is very pitiful.*

* Heb. 6. 6.
* Luke 19. 14.
* Heb. 10. 28, 29.

Man. I have *Crucified him to my self afresh, I have despised *his Person, I have despised his Righteousness, I have counted his Blood an unholy thing, I have done despite *to the Spirit of Grace: Therefore I have shut my self out of all the

Promises; and there now remains to me nothing but threatnings, dreadful threatnings, fearful threatnings of certain Judgement and firy Indignation, which shall devour me as an Adversary.

Chr. *For what did you bring your self into this condition?*

Man. For the Lusts, Pleasures, and Profits of this World; in the injoyment of which, I did then promise my self much delight: but now even every one of those things also bite me, and gnaw me like a burning worm.

Chr. *But canst thou not now repent and turn?*

Man. God hath denied me repentance; his Word gives me no encouragement to believe; yea, himself hath shut me up in this Iron Cage: nor can all the men in the World let me out. O Eternity! Eternity! how shall I grapple with the misery that I must meet with in Eternity?

Inter. Then said the *Interpreter* to *Christian*, Let this mans misery be remembred by thee, and be an everlasting caution to thee.

Chr. Well, said *Christian*, this is fearful; God help me to watch and be sober; and to pray, that I may shun the causes of this mans misery. Sir, is it not time for me to go on my way now?

Int. Tarry till I shall shew thee one thing more, and then thou shalt go on thy way.

So he took *Christian* by the hand again, and led him into a Chamber, where there was one a rising out of Bed; and as he put on his Rayment, he shook and trembled. Then said *Christian*, Why doth this man thus tremble? The *Interpreter* then bid him tell to *Christian* the reason of his so doing: So he began, and said, This night as I was in my sleep, I Dreamed, and behold the Heavens grew exceeding black; also it thundred and lightned in most fearful wise, that it put me into an Agony.† So I looked up in my Dream, and saw the Clouds rack at an unusual rate, upon which I heard a great sound of a Trumpet, and saw also a Man sit upon a Cloud, attended with the thousands of Heaven; they were all in flaming fire, also the Heavens was on a burning flame. I heard then a voice, saying, *Arise ye Dead, and come to Judgement*; and with that the Rocks rent, the Graves opened, & the Dead that were therein came

1 Cor. 15. 1 Thess. 4. Jude 15. 2 Thess. 1. 8. John 5. 28. Rev. 20. 11, 12, 13, 14. Isa. 26. 21. Mich. 7. 16, 17.

Psal. 5. 1, 2, 3. forth; some of them were exceeding glad, and looked upward;
Dan. 7. 10. and some sought to hide themselves under the Mountains:
Then I saw the Man that sat upon the Cloud, open the Book;
Mal. 3. 2, 3. and bid the World draw near. Yet there was by reason of a Fiery
Dan. 7. 9, 10. flame that issued out and came from before him, a convenient
distance betwixt him and them, as betwixt the Judge and the
Prisoners at the Bar. I heard it also proclaimed to them that
* Mat. 3. 2. attended on the Man that sat on the Cloud, **Gather together*
Ch. 13. 30. *the Tares, the Chaff, and Stubble, and cast them into the burning*
Mal. 4. 1. *Lake*; and with that the Bottomless pit opened, just whereabout I stood; out of the mouth of which there came in an
abundant manner Smoak, and Coals of fire, with hideous
* Luke 3. 17. noises. It was also said to the same persons **Gather my Wheat*
* 1 Thess. 4. *into my Garner*. And with that I saw many catch'd up *and
16, 17. carried away into the Clouds, but I was left behind. I also
sought to hide my self, but I could not; for the Man that sat
upon the Cloud, still kept his eye upon me: my sins also came
Rom. 2. 14, into mind, and my Conscience did accuse me on every side.
15. Upon this I awaked from my sleep.

Chr. *But what was it that made you so afraid of this sight?*

Man. Why, I thought that the day of Judgement was come, and that I was not ready for it: but this frighted me most, that the Angels gathered up several, and left me behind; also the pit of Hell opened her mouth just where I stood: my Conscience too within afflicted me; and as I thought, the Judge had always his eye upon me, shewing indignation in his countenance.

Then said the *Interpreter to Christian, Hast thou considered all these things?*

Chri. Yes, and they put me in *hope* and *fear*.

Inter. Well, keep all things so in thy mind, that they may be as a *Goad* in thy sides, to prick thee forward in the way thou must go. Then *Christian* began to gird up his loins, and to address himself to his Journey. Then said the *Interpreter*, The Comforter† be always with thee good *Christian*, to guide thee in the way that leads to the City.

So *Christian* went on his way, saying,

Here I have seen things rare, and profitable;
Things pleasant, dreadful, things to make me stable

In what I have began to take in hand:
Then let me think on them, and understand
Wherefore they shewed me was, and let me be
Thankful, O good Interpreter, to thee.

Now I saw in my Dream, that the high way up which *Christian* was to go, was fenced on either side with a Wall, and that Wall is called **Salvation*. Up this way therefore did burdened *Christian* run, but not without great difficulty, because of the load on his back.

* Isa. 26. 1.

He ran thus till he came at a place somewhat ascending; and upon that place stood a *Cross*, and a little below in the bottom, a Sepulcher. So I saw in my Dream, that just as *Christian* came up with the *Cross*, his burden loosed from off his Shoulders, and fell from off his back; and began to tumble; and so continued to do, till it came to the mouth of the Sepulcher, where it fell in, and I saw it no more.

Then was *Christian* glad *and lightsom, and said with a merry heart, *He hath given me rest, by his sorrow; and life, by his death*. Then he stood still a while, to look and wonder; for it was very surprizing to him, that the sight of the Cross should thus ease him of his burden. He looked therefore, and looked again, even till the springs that were in his head sent the *waters down his cheeks. Now as he stood looking and weeping, behold three shining ones† came to him, and saluted him, with *Peace be to thee*: so the first said to him, **Thy sins be forgiven*. The second stript him of his Rags, and *cloathed him with change of Raiment. The third also set *a mark in his forehead, and gave him a Roll with a Seal upon it,† which he bid him look on as he ran, and that he should give it in at the Cœlestial Gate: so they went their way. Then *Christian* gave three leaps for joy, and went on singing.

* *When God releases us of our guilt and burden, we are as those that leap for joy.*

* Zech. 12. 10.

* Mark 2. 5.

* Zech. 3. 4.

* Eph. 1. 13.

Thus far did I come loaden with my sin,
Nor could ought ease the grief that I was in,
Till I came hither: What a place is this!
Must here be the beginning of my bliss?
Must here the burden fall from off my back?
Must here the strings that bound it to me, crack?
Blest Cross! blest Sepulcher! blest rather be
The Man that there was put to shame for me.

A Christian can sing tho alone, when God doth give him the joy of his heart.

Who's this; the Pilgrim. How! 'tis very true,
Old things are past away, all's become new.
Strange! he's another Man upon my word,
They be fine Feathers that make a fine Bird.

I saw then in my Dream that he went on thus, even untill he came at a bottom, where he saw, a little out of the way, three Men fast asleep, with Fetters upon their heels. The name of the one was **Simple*, another *Sloth*, and the third *Presumption*.

* *Simple, Sloth, and Presumption.*

Christian then seeing them lye in this case, went to them, if peradventure he might awake them. And cried, You are like them that sleep on the top of *a Mast, for the dead Sea is under you, a Gulf that hath no bottom: Awake therefore, and come away; be willing also, and I will help you off with your Irons. He also told them, If he that goeth about like *a roaring Lion, comes by, you will certainly become a prey to his teeth. With that they lookt upon him, and began to reply in this sort: **Simple* said, *I see no danger; Sloth* said, *Yet a little more sleep:* and *Presumption* said, *Every Fatt must stand upon his own bottom,*† *what is the answer else that I should give thee?* And so *they* lay down to sleep again, and *Christian* went on his way.

* Prov. 23. 34.

* 1 Pet. 5. 8.

* *There is no perswasion will do, if God openeth not the eyes.*

Yet was he troubled to think, That men in that danger should so little esteem the kindness of him that so freely offered to help them; both by awakening of them, counselling of them, and proffering to help them off with their Irons. And as he was troubled thereabout, he espied two men come tumbling over the Wall, on the left hand of the narrow way; and they made up a pace to him. The name of the one was *Formalist*,† and the name of the other *Hypocrisie*. So, as I said, they drew up unto him, who thus entered with them into discourse.

Chr. **Gentlemen, Whence came you, and whither do you go?*

* Christian *talked with them.*

Form. and *Hyp.* We were born in the Land of Vainglory, and are going for praise to Mount *Sion*.

Chr. *Why came you not in at the Gate which standeth at the beginning of the way? Know you not that it is written,* **That he that cometh not in by the door, but climbeth up some other way, the same is a thief and a robber.*

* John 10. 1.

Form. and *Hyp.* They said, That to go to the Gate for entrance, was by all their Countrey-men counted too far about; and that therefore their usual way was to make a short cut of it, and to climb over the Wall as they had done.

Chr. *But will it not be counted a Trespass, against the Lord of the City whither we are bound, thus to violate his revealed will?*

* *They that come into the way, but not by the door, think that they can say something in vindication of their own Practice.*

Form. and *Hyp.* They told him, *That as for that, he needed not to trouble his head thereabout: for what they did they had custom for; and could produce, if need were, Testimony that would witness it, for more then a thousand years.

Chr. *But said* Christian, *Will your Practice stand a Trial at Law?*

Form. & Hyp. They told him, That Custom, it being of so long a standing, as above a thousand years, would doubtless now be admitted as a thing legal, by any Impartial Judge. And besides, said they, so be we get into the way, what's matter which way we get in? if we are in, we are in: thou art but in the way, who, as we perceive, came in at the Gate; and we are also in the way that came tumbling over the wall: Wherein now is thy condition better then ours?

Chr. I walk by the Rule of my Master, you walk by the rude working of your fancies. You are counted thieves already, by the Lord of the way; therefore I doubt you will not be found true men at the end of the way. You come in by your selves without his direction, and shall go out by your selves without his mercy.

To this they made him but little answer; only they bid him look to himself. Then I saw that they went on every man in his way, without much conference one with another; save that these two men told *Christian*, That, as to *Laws and Ordinances*, they doubted not, but they should as consciensiously do them as he. Therefore said they, We see not wherein thou differest from us, but by the Coat that is on thy back, which was, as we tro, given thee by some of thy Neighbours, to hide the shame of thy nakedness.

* Gal. 2. 16.

Chr. By *Laws and Ordinances, you will not be saved, since you came not in by the door. And as for this Coat that is on my back, it was given me by the Lord of the place whither I go; and that, as you say, to cover my nakedness with. And I take it as a token of his kindness to me, for I had nothing but rags before; and besides, *thus I comfort my self as I go: Surely, think I, when I come to the Gate of the City, the Lord thereof will know me for good, since I have his Coat on my back; a *Coat* that he gave me freely in the day that he stript me

* Christian *has got his Lords Coat on his back, and is comforted therewith, he is comforted also with his Mark, and his Roll.*

of my rags. I have moreover a mark in my forehead, of which perhaps you have taken no notice, which one of my Lords most intimate Associates fixed there in the day that my burden fell off my shoulders. I will tell you moreover, that I had then given me a Roll sealed to comfort me by reading, as I go in the way; I was also bid to give it in at the Cœlestial Gate, in token of my certain going in after it: all which things I doubt you want; and want them, because you came not in at the Gate.

To these things they gave him no answer, only they looked upon each other, and *laughed*. Then I saw that they went on all, save that *Christian* kept before, who had no more talk but with himself, and that sometimes sighingly, and sometimes comfortably: also he would be often reading in the Roll, that one of the shining ones gave him, by which he was refreshed.

I believe then, that they all went on till they came to the foot of an Hill, *at the bottom of which was a Spring. There was also in the same place two other ways besides that which came straight from the Gate; one turned to the left hand, and the other to the right, at the bottom of the Hill: but the narrow way lay right up the Hill, (and the name of the going up the side of the Hill, is called *Difficulty*.) *Christian* now went to the *Spring and drank thereof to refresh himself, and then began to go up the Hill; saying,

* *He comes to the hill Difficulty.*

* Isa. 49. 10.

This Hill, though high, I covet to ascend,
The difficulty will not me offend:
For I perceive the way to life lies here;
Come, pluck up, Heart; lets neither faint nor fear:
Better, tho difficult, th' right way to go,
Then wrong, though easie, where the end is wo.

The other two also came to the foot of the Hill. But when they saw that the Hill was steep and high, and that there was two other ways to go; and supposing also that these two ways might meet again, with that up which *Christian* went, on the other side of the Hill: Therefore they were resolved to go in those ways; (now the name of one of those ways was *Danger*, and the name of the other *Destruction*) So *the one took the way which is called *Danger*, which led him into a great Wood; and the other took directly up the way to *Destruction*, which led

* *The danger of turning out of the way.*

him into a wide field full of dark Mountains,† where he stumbled and fell, and rose no more.

I looked then after *Christian*, to see him go up the Hill, where I perceived he fell from running to going, and from going to clambering upon his hands and his knees, because of the steepness of the place. Now about the midway to the top of the Hill, was a pleasant **Arbour*, made by the Lord of the Hill, for the refreshing of weary Travailers. Thither therefore *Christian* got, where also he sat down to rest him. Then he pull'd his Roll out of his bosom, and read therein to his comfort; he also now began afresh to take a review of the Coat or Garment that was given him as he stood by the Cross. Thus pleasing himself a while, he at last fell into a slumber, and thence into a fast sleep, which detained him in that place until it was almost night, and in his sleep his *Roll fell out of his hand. Now as he was sleeping, there came one to him & awaked him, saying **Go to the Ant, thou sluggard, consider her ways, and be wise*: and with that *Christian* suddenly started up, and sped him on his way, and went a pace till he came to the top of the Hill.

* *Award of grace.*

* *He that sleeps is a loser.*

* Prov. 6. 6.

Now when he was got up to the top of the Hill, there came two men running against him amain; the name of the one was **Timorous*, and the name of the other *Mistrust*. To whom *Christian* said, Sirs, what's the matter you run the wrong way? *Timorous* answered, That they were going to the City of *Zion*, and had got up that *difficult* place; but, said he, the further we go, the more danger we meet with, wherefore we turned, and are going back again.

* Christian *meets with* Mistrust *and* Timorous.

Yes, said *Mistrust*, for just before us lye a couple of Lions† in the way, whether sleeping or wakeing we know not and we could not think, if we came within reach, but they would presently pull us in pieces.

Chr. Then said *Christian*, You make me afraid, but whither shall I fly to be safe? If I go back to mine own Countrey, *That* is prepared for Fire and Brimstone; and I shall certainly perish there. If I can get to the Cœlestial City, I am sure to be in safety there. *I must venture: To go back is nothing but death, to go forward is fear of death, and life everlasting beyond it. I will yet go forward. So *Mistrust* and *Timorous* ran down the Hill;

* Christian *shakes off fear.*

Shall they who wrong begin yet rightly end?
Shall they at all have safety for their friend?
No, no, in head-strong manner they set out,
And headlong they will fall at last no doubt.

and *Christian* went on his way. But thinking again of what he heard from the men, he felt in his bosom for his Roll: that he might read therein and be comforted; but he felt, and *found it not. Then was *Christian* in great distress, and knew not what to do, for he wanted that which used to relieve him, and that which should have been his Pass into the Cœlestial City. Here therefore he began to be much *perplexed, and knew not what to do; at last he bethought himself that he had slept in the *Arbour* that is on the side of the Hill: and falling down upon his knees, he asked God forgiveness for that his foolish Fact, and then went back to look for his Roll. But all the way he went back, who can sufficiently set forth the sorrow of *Christians* heart? sometimes he sighed, sometimes he wept, and often times he chid himself, for being so foolish to fall asleep in that place which was erected only for a little refreshment from his weariness. Thus therefore he went back, carefully looking on this side, and on that, all the way as he went, if happily he might find his Roll, that had been his comfort so many times in his Journey. He went thus till he came again within sight of the *Arbour*, where he sat and slept; but that sight renewed *his sorrow the more, by bringing again, even a fresh, his evil of sleeping into his mind. Thus therefore he now went on, bewailing his sinful sleep, saying, *O wretched Man that I am*, that I should sleep in the day time! that I should sleep in the midst of difficulty! that I should so indulge the flesh, as to use that rest for ease to my flesh, which the Lord of the Hill hath erected only for the relief of the spirits of Pilgrims! How many steps have I took in vain! (Thus it happened to *Israel* for their sin, they were sent back again by the way of the Red-Sea†) and I am made to tread those steps with sorrow, which I might have trod with delight, had it not been for this sinful sleep. How far might I have been on my way by this time! I am made to tread those steps thrice over, which I needed not to have trod but once: Yea now also I am like to be benighted, for the day is almost spent. O that I had not slept! Now by this time he was come to the *Arbour* again, where for a while he sat down and wept, but at last (as *Christian* would have it) looking sorrowfully down under the Settle, there he *espied his Roll; the which he with trembling and haste catch'd up, and put it into

* Christian *missed his Roll, wherein he used to take comfort.*

* *He is perplexed for his Roll.*

* Christian *bewails his foolish sleeping.* Rev. 2. 2.

1 Thess. 5. 7, 8.

* Christian *findeth his Roll where he lost it.*

his bosom; but who can tell how joyful this man was, when he had gotten his Roll again? For this Roll was the assurance of his life, and acceptance at the desired Haven. Therefore he laid it up in his bosom, gave thanks to God for directing his eye to the place where it lay, and with joy and tears betook him self again to his Journey. But Oh how nimbly now did he go up the rest of the Hill! Yet before he got up, the Sun went down upon *Christian*; and this made him again recall the vanity of his sleeping to his remembrance, and thus he again began to condole with himself: *Ah thou sinful sleep! how for thy sake am I like to be benighted in my Journey! I must walk without the Sun, darkness must cover the path of my feet, and I must hear the noise of doleful Creatures,*† *because of my sinful sleep!* Now also he remembered the story that *Mistrust* and *Timorous* told him of, how they were frighted with the sight of the Lions. Then said *Christian* to himself again, These Beasts range in the night for their prey, and if they should meet with me in the dark, how should I shift them? how should I escape being by them torn in pieces? Thus he went on his way, but while he was thus bewayling his unhappy miscarriage, he lift up his eyes, and behold there was a very stately Palace before him, the name whereof was *Beautiful*,† and it stood just by the High-way side.

So I saw in my Dream, that he made haste and went forward, that if possible he might get Lodging there; Now before he had gone far, he entered into a very narrow passage, which was about a furlong off of the Porters Lodge, and looking very narrowly before him as he went, he espied two Lions in the way. Now, thought he, I see the dangers that *Mistrust* and *Timorous* were driven back by, (The Lions were chained, but he saw not the Chains) Then he was afraid, and thought also himself to go back after them, for he thought nothing but death was before him: But the *Porter* at the Lodge, whose name is **Watchful*, perceiving that *Christian* made a halt, as if he would go back, cried unto him saying, Is thy strength so small? fear not the Lions, for they are Chained; and are placed there for trial of faith where it is; and for discovery of those that have none: keep in the midst of the Path, and no hurt shall come unto thee.

* Mark 13. 34.

Then I saw that he went on, trembling for fear of the Lions;

Difficult is behind, Fear is before,
Though he's got on the Hill, the Lions roar;
A Christian man is never long at ease,
When one fright's gone, another doth him seize.

but taking good heed to the directions of the *Porter*; he heard them roar, but they did him no harm. Then he clapt his hands, and went on till he came and stood before the Gate where the *Porter* was. Then said *Christian* to the *Porter*, Sir, What house is this? and may I lodge here to night? The *Porter* answered, This House was built by the Lord of the Hill: and he built it for the relief and security of Pilgrims. The *Porter* also asked whence he was, and whither he was going?

Chr. I am come from the City of *Destruction*, and am going to Mount *Zion*; but because the Sun is now set, I desire, if I may, to lodge here to night.

Por. *What is your name?*

Chr. My name is, now, *Christian*; but my name at the first was *Graceless*: I came of the Race of **Japhet*, whom God will perswade to dwell in the Tents of *Shem*.† * Gen. 9. 27.

Por. *But how doth it happen that you come so late, the Sun is set?*

Chr. I had been here sooner, but that, wretched man that I am! I slept in the *Arbour* that stands on the Hill side; nay, I had notwithstanding that, been here much sooner, but that in my sleep I lost my Evidence, and came without it to the brow of the Hill; and then feeling for it, and finding it not, I was forced with sorrow of heart, to go back to the place where I slept my sleep, where I found it, and now I am come.

Por. Well, I will call out one of the Virgins of this place, who will, if she likes your talk, bring you in to the rest of the Family, according to the Rules of the House. So *Watchful* the *Porter* rang a Bell; at the sound of which, came out at the door of the House, a Grave and Beautiful Damsel, named *Discretion*, and asked why she was called.

The *Porter* answered, This Man is in a Journey from the City of *Destruction* to Mount *Zion*, but being weary, and benighted, he asked me if he might lodge here to night; so I told him I would call for thee, who after discourse had with him, mayest do as seemeth thee good, even according to the Law of the House.

Then she asked him whence he was, and whither he was going, and he told her. She asked him also, how he got into the way and he told her; Then she asked him, What he had seen, and met with in the way, and he told her; and last, she asked his name, so he said, It is *Christian*; and I have so much the more a desire to lodge here to night, because, by what I perceive, this place was built by the Lord of the Hill, for the relief and security of Pilgrims. So she smiled, but the water stood in her eyes: And after a little pause, she said, I will call forth two or three more of the Family. So she ran to the door, and called out *Prudence*, *Piety* and *Charity*, who after a little more discourse with him, had him in to the Family; and many of them meeting him at the threshold of the house, said, Come in thou blessed of the Lord; this house was built by the Lord of the Hill, on purpose to entertain such Pilgrims in. Then he bowed his head, and followed them into the House. So when he was come in, and set down, they gave him somthing to drink; and consented together, that until supper was ready, some one or two of them should have some particular discourse with *Christian*, for the best improvement of time: and they appointed *Piety* and *Prudence* and *Charity* to discourse with him; and thus they began.

Piety *discourses him.*

Piety. *Come good* Christian, *since we have been so loving to you, to receive you in to our House this night; let us, if perhaps we may better our selves thereby, talk with you of all things that have happened to you in your Pilgrimage.*

Chr. With a very good will, and I am glad that you are so well disposed.

Piety. *What moved you at first to betake yourself to a Pilgrim's life?*

* *How* Christian *was driven out of his own* Countrey.

Chr. I was *driven out of my Native Countrey, by a dreadful sound that was in mine ears, to wit, That unavoidable destruction did attend me, if I abode in that place where I was.

Piety. *But how did it happen that you came out of your Countrey this way?*

* *How he got into the way to* Sion.

Chr. It was as God would have it; for when I was under the fears of destruction, I did not know whither to go; but by chance there came a man, even to me, (as I was trembling and weeping) whose name is **Evangelist*, and he directed me to the Wicket-gate, which else I should never have found; and so set me into the way that hath led me directly to this House.

Piety. *But did you not come by the House of the Interpreter?*

Chr. Yes, and did see such things there, the remembrance of which will stick by me as long as I live; specially three *things; *to wit*, How Christ, in despite of Satan, maintains his work of Grace in the heart; how the Man had sinned himself quite out of hopes of Gods mercy; and also the Dream of him that thought in his sleep the day of Judgement was come.

** A rehearsal of what he saw in the way.*

Piety. *Why? Did you hear him tell his Dream?*

Chr. Yes, and a dreadful one it was, I thought. It made my heart ake as he was telling of it, but yet I am glad I heard it.

Piety. *Was that all that you saw at the house of the Interpreter?*

Chr. No, he took me and had me where he shewed me a stately Palace, and how the People were clad in Gold that were in it; and how there came a venturous Man, and cut his way through the armed men that stood in the door to keep him out; and how he was bid to come in, and win eternal Glory. Methought those things did ravish my heart; I could have staid at that good Mans house a twelve-month, but that I knew I had further to go.

Piety. *And what saw you else in the way?*

Chr. Saw! Why, I went but a little further, and I saw one, as I thought in my mind, hang bleeding upon the Tree; and the very sight of him made my burden fall off my back (for I groaned under a weary burden) but then it fell down from off me. 'Twas a strange thing to me, for I never saw such a thing before: Yea, and while I stood looking up, (for then I could not forbear looking) three shining ones came to me: one of them testified that my sins were forgiven me: another stript me of my rags, and gave me this Broidred Coat which you see; and the third set the mark which you see in my forehead, and gave me this sealed Roll (and with that he plucked it out of his bosom.)

Piety. *But you saw more then this, did you not?*

Chr. The things that I have told you were the best: yet some other matters I saw, as namely I saw three Men, *Simple*, *Sloth*, and *Presumption*, lye a sleep a little out of the way as I came, with Irons upon their heels; but do you think I could awake them? I also saw *Formalist* and *Hypocrisie* come tumbling over the wall, to go, as they pretended, to *Sion*, but they were quickly lost; even as I my self did tell them, but they would not believe: but, above all, I found it *hard* work to get up this Hill, and as *hard* to come by the Lions mouths; and truly if it had not been for the good Man, the Porter that stands at the Gate, I do not know, but that after all, I might have gone back again: but now I thank God I am here, and I thank you for receiving of me.

Prudence *discourses him.*

Then *Prudence* thought good to ask him a few questions, and desired his answer to them.

Pru. *Do you not think somtimes of the Countrey from whence you came?*

* Christians *thoughts of his Native Countrey.*

Heb. 11. 15, 16.

Chr. Yes, *but with much shame and detestation; *Truly, if I had been mindful of that Countrey from whence I came out, I might have had opportunity to have returned; but now I desire a better Countrey; that is, an Heavenly.*

Pru. *Do you not yet bear away with you some of the things that then you were conversant withal?*

* Christian *distasted with carnal cogitations.*

* Christians *choice.*

Chr. Yes but greatly against my will; especially my inward and *carnal cogitations; with which all my Countrey-men, as well as my self, were delighted; but now all those things are my grief: and might I but chuse mine own things, I would *chuse never to think of those things more; but when I would be doing of that which is best, that which is worst is with me.

Pru. *Do you not find sometimes, as if those things were vanquished, which at other times are your perplexity?*

* Christians *golden hours.*

Chr. Yes, but that is but seldom; but they are to me *Golden hours, in which such things happen to me.

Pru. *Can you remember by what means you find your anoyances at times, as if they were vanquished?*

* *How* Christian *gets power against his corruptions.*

Chr. Yes, when *I think what I saw at the Cross, that will do it; and when I look upon my Broidered Coat, that will do it; also when I look into the Roll that I carry in my bosom, that will do it; and when my thoughts wax warm about whither I am going, that will do it.

Pru. *And what is it that makes you so desirous to go to Mount* Zion?

* *Why* Christian *would be at Mount* Zion.

Chr. Why, *there I hope to see him *alive*, that did hang *dead* on the Cross; and there I hope to be rid of all those things, that to this day are in me, an anoiance to me; there they say there is no *death, and there I shall dwell with such Company as I like best. For to tell you truth, I love him, because I was by him eased of my burden, and I am weary of my inward sickness; I would fain be where I shall die no more, and with the Company that shall continually cry, **Holy, Holy, Holy.*†

* Isa. 25. 8. Rev. 21. 4.

* Charity *discourses him.*

Then said *Charity* to *Christian, Have you a family? are you a married man?*

Chr. I have a Wife and four small Children.†

Cha. *And why did you not bring them along with you?*

Chr. Then *Christian* *wept, and said, Oh how willingly would I have done it, but they were all of them utterly averse to my going on Pilgrimage.

* Christian's *love to his Wife and Children.*

Cha. *But you should have talked to them, and have endeavoured to have shewen them the danger of being behind.*

Chr. So I did, and told them also what God had shewed to me of the destruction of our City; but I seemed to them as one that mocked, and they believed me not.

Gen. 19. 14.

Cha. *And did you pray to God that he would bless your counsel to them?*

Chr. Yes, and that with much affection; for you must think that my Wife and poor Children were very dear unto me.

Cha. *But did you tell them of your own sorrow, and fear of destruction? for I suppose that destruction was visible enough to you?*

Chr. Yes, over, and over, and over. They might also *see my fears in my countenance, in my tears, and also in my trembling under the apprehension of the Judgment that did hang over our heads; but all was not sufficient to prevail with them to come with me.

* Christian's *fears of perishing might be read in his very countenance.*

Cha. *But what could they say for themselves why they came not?*

Chr. Why, *my Wife was afraid of losing this World; and my Children were given to the foolish delights of youth: so what by one thing, and what by another, they left me to wander in this manner alone.

* *The cause why his Wife and Children did not go with him.*

Cha. *But did you not with your vain life, damp all that you by words used by way of perswasion to bring them away with you?*

Chr. Indeed I cannot commend my life; for I am conscious to my self of many failings therein: I know also that a man by his conversation, may soon overthrow what by argument or perswasion he doth labour to fasten upon others for their good: Yet, this I can say, I was very wary of giving them occasion, by any unseemly action, to make them averse to going on Pilgrimage. Yea, for this very thing, they would tell me I was too precise,† and that I denied my self of things (for their sakes) in which they saw no evil. Nay, I think I may say, that, if what they saw in me did hinder them, it was my great tenderness in sinning against God, or of doing any wrong to my Neighbor.

Christian's *good conversation before his Wife and Children.*

* 1 John 3. 12.
Christian *clear of their blood if they perish.*
* Ezek. 3. 19.

Cha. *Indeed* *Cain *hated his Brother, because his own works were evil, and his Brothers righteous; and if thy Wife and Children have been offended with thee for this, they thereby shew themselves to be implacable to *good; and thou hast delivered thy soul from their blood.*

* *What* Christian *had to his supper.*
* *Their talk at supper time.*
* Heb. 2. 14, 15.

Now I saw in my Dream, that thus they sat talking together until supper was ready. So when they had made ready, they sat down to meat; Now the Table was furnished *with fat things, and with Wine that was well refined;† and all their talk *at the Table was about the Lord of the Hill: As namely, about what he had done, and wherefore he did what he did, and why he had builded that House: and by what they said, I perceived that he had been a *great Warriour*, and had fought with and slain *him that had the power of Death, but not without great danger to himself, which made me love him the more.

For, as they said, and as I believe, (said *Christian*) he did it with the loss of much blood; but that which put Glory of Grace into all he did, was, that he did it of pure love to his Countrey. And besides, there were some of them of the Household that said, they had seen, and spoke with him since he did dye on the Cross; and they have attested, that they had it from his own lips, that he is such a lover of poor Pilgrims, that the like is not to be found from the East to the West.

They moreover gave an instance of what they affirmed, and that was, He had stript himself of his glory that he might do this for the Poor;† and that they heard him say and affirm, That he would not dwell in the Mountain of *Zion* alone. They said moreover, That he had made many Pilgrims *Princes, though by nature they were *Beggars born, and their original had been the Dunghil.

* *Christ makes Princes of Beggars.*
* 1 Sam. 2. 8. Psal. 113. 7.

Thus they discoursed together till late at night; and after they had committed themselves to their Lord for Protection, they betook themselves to rest. The Pilgrim they laid in a large upper *Chamber, whose window opened towards the Sun rising; the name of the Chamber was *Peace*, where he slept till break of day; and then he awoke and sang,

* Christians *Bed-Chamber.*

Where am I now? is this the love and care
Of Jesus, for the men that Pilgrims are?
Thus to provide! That I should be forgiven!
And dwell already the next door to Heaven.

So in the Morning they all got up, and after some more discourse, they told him that he should not depart, till they had shewed him the *Rarities* of that place. And first they had him into the Study, *where they shewed him Records of the greatest Antiquity; in which, as I remember my Dream, they shewed him first the Pedigree of the Lord of the Hill, that he was the Son of the Ancient of Days,† and came by an eternal Generation. Here also was more fully Recorded the Acts that he had done, and the names of many hundreds that he had taken into his service; and how he had placed them in such Habitations that could neither by length of Days, nor decaies of Nature, be dissolved.

* Christian *had into the Study, and what he saw there.*

Then they read to him some of the worthy Acts that some of his servants had done: As how they had subdued Kingdoms, wrought Righteousness, obtained Promises, stopped the mouths of Lions, quenched the *violence of Fire, escaped the edge of the Sword; out of weakness were made strong, waxed valiant in fight, and turned to flight the Armies of the *Aliens*.

* Heb. 11. 33, 34.

Then they read again in another part of the Records of the House, where it was shewed how willing their Lord was to receive into his favour, any, even any, though they in time past had offered great affronts to his Person and proceedings. Here also were several other Histories of many other famous things; of all which *Christian* had a view. As of things both Ancient and Modern; together with Prophecies and Predictions of things that have their certain accomplishment, both to the dread and amazement of enemies, and the comfort and solace of Pilgrims.

The next day they took him, and had him into the *Armory; where they shewed him all manner of Furniture, which their Lord had provided for Pilgrims, as Sword, Shield, Helmet, Brest plate, *All-Prayer*, and Shooes† that would not wear out. And there was here enough of this, to harness out as many men for the service of their Lord, as there be Stars in the Heaven for multitude.

* Christian *had into the Armory.*

They also shewed him some of the Engines with which some of his Servants had done wonderful things. *They shewed him *Moses* Rod, the Hammer and Nail with which *Jael* slew *Sisera*, the Pitchers, Trumpets, and Lamps too, with which *Gideon* put to flight the Armies of *Midian*. Then they shewed him the Oxes goad wherewith *Shamger* slew six hundred men. They shewed him also the Jaw bone with which *Sampson* did such mighty feats; they shewed him moreover the Sling and Stone with which *David* slew *Goliah* of *Gath*: and the Sword also with which their Lord will kill the Man of Sin,† in the day that he shall rise up to the prey. They shewed him besides many excellent things, with which *Christian* was much delighted. This done, they went to their rest again.

* Christian *is made to see Ancient things.*

Then I saw in my Dream, that on the morrow he got up to go forwards, but they desired him to stay till the next day also; and then said they, we will, (if the day be clear) shew you the *delectable Mountains; which they said, would yet further add to his comfort; because they were nearer the desired Haven, then the place where at present he was. So he consented and staid. When the Morning was up, they had him to the top of the House, *and bid him look South; so he did; and behold at a great distance he saw a most pleasant Mountainous Country, beautified with Woods, Vinyards, Fruits of all sorts; Flowers also, with Springs and Fountains, very delectable to behold. Then he asked the name of the Countrey, they said it was *Immanuels Land*:† and it is as common, said they, as this *Hill* is to, and for all the Pilgrims. And when thou comest there, from thence, thou maist see to the Gate of the Cœlestial City, as the Shepherds that live there will make appear.

* Christian *shewed the delectable Mountains.*

* Isa. 33. 16, 17.

Now he bethought himself of setting forward, *and they were willing he should: but first, said they, let us go again into the Armory, so they did; and when he came there, they *harnessed him from head to foot, with what was of proof, lest perhaps he should meet with assaults in the way. He being therefore thus accoutred, walketh out with his friends to the Gate, and there he asked the *Porter* if he saw any Pilgrims pass by; then the *Porter* answered, Yes.

* Christian *sets forward.*

* Christian *sent away Armed.*

Ch. Pray did you know him?

Por. I asked his name, and he told me it was *Faithful.*

Chr. O, said *Christian*, I know him, he is my Townsman, my near Neighbour, he comes from the place where I was born: how far do you think he may be before?

Por. He is got by this time below the Hill.

Chr. Well, *said *Christian*, good Porter the Lord be with thee, and add to all thy blessings much increase, for the kindness that thou hast shewed to me.

* *How* Christian *and the Porter greet at parting.*

Then he began to go forward, but *Discretion, Piety, Charity*, and *Prudence* would accompany him down to the foot of the Hill. So they went on together, reiterating their former discourses till they came to go down the Hill. Then said *Christian*, as it was *difficult* coming up, so (so far as I can see) it is *dangerous* going down. Yes, said *Prudence*, so it is; for it is an hard matter for a man to go down into the valley of *Humiliation*, as thou art now, and to catch no slip by the way; therefore, said they, are we come out to accompany thee down the Hill. So he began to go down, but very warily, yet he caught a slip or two.

Then I saw in my Dream, that these good Companions (when *Christian* was gone down to the bottom of the Hill) gave him a loaf of Bread, a bottle of Wine, and a cluster of Raisins;† and then he went on his way.

But now in this Valley of *Humiliation* poor *Christian* was hard put to it, for he had gone but a little way before he espied a foul *Fiend* coming over the field to meet him; his name is *Apollyon*.† Then did *Christian* begin to be afraid, and to cast in his mind whether to go back, or to stand his ground. But he considered again, that he had no Armour for his back, and therefore thought that to turn the back to him, might give him greater advantage with ease to pierce him with his Darts;

Whilst *Christian* is among his godly friends,
Their golden mouths make him sufficient 'mends
For all his griefs, and when they let him go,
He's clad with northern steel from top to toe.

therefore he resolved to venture, and *stand his ground. For thought he, had I no more in mine eye, then the saving of my life, 'twould be the best way to stand.

* Christians *resolution at the approach of* Apollyon.

So he went on, and *Apollyon* met him; now the Monster was hidious to behold, he was cloathed with scales like a Fish (and they are his pride) he had Wings like a Dragon, feet like a Bear, and out of his belly came Fire and Smoak, and his mouth was as the mouth of a Lion.† When he was come up to *Christian*, he beheld him with a disdainful countenance, and thus began to question with him.

Apol. *Whence come you, and whither are you bound?*

Chr. I come from the City of *Destruction*, *which is the place of all evil, and am going to the City of *Zion*.

* *Discourse betwixt* Christian *and* Apollyon.

Apol. *By this I perceive thou art one of my Subjects, for all that Countrey is mine; and I am the Prince and God of it. How is it then that thou hast ran away from thy King? Were it not that I hope thou maiest do me more service, I would strike thee now at one blow to the ground.*

Chr. I was born indeed in your Dominions, but your service was hard, and your wages such as a man could not live on, **for the wages of Sin is death*; therefore when I was come to years, I did as other considerate persons do, look out, if perhaps I might mend my self.

* Rom. 6. 23.

Apol. *There is no Prince that will thus lightly lose his Subjects; neither will I as yet lose thee. But since thou complainest of thy service and wages, *be content to go back; what our Countrey will afford, I do here promise to give thee.*

* Apollyons *flattery.*

Chr. But I have let my self to another, even to the King of Princes, and how can I with fairness go back with thee?

Apol. *Thou hast done in this, according to the Proverb, *changed a bad for a worse:*† *but it is ordinary for those that have professed themselves his Servants, after a while to give him the slip; and return again to me: do thou so too, and all shall be well.*

* Apollyon *undervalues Christs service.*

Chr. I have given him my faith, and sworn my Allegiance to him; how then can I go back from this, and not be hanged as a Traitor?

Apol. *Thou didest the same to me, *and yet I am willing to pass by all, if now thou wilt yet turn again, and go back.*

* Apollyon *pretends to be merciful.*

Chr. What I promised thee was in my none-age; and besides, I count that the Prince under whose Banner now I stand, is able to absolve me; yea, and to pardon also what I did as to my compliance with thee: and besides, (O thou destroying *Apollyon*) to speak truth, I like his Service, his Wages, his Servants, his Government, his Company, and Countrey better then thine: and therefore leave off to perswade me further, I am his Servant, and I will follow him.

Apollyon *pleads the grievous ends of Christians, to diswade* Christian *from persisting in his way.*

Apol. *Consider again when thou art in cool blood, what thou art like to meet with in the way that thou goest. Thou knowest that for the most part, his Servants come to an ill end, because they are transgressors against me, and my ways: How many of them have been put to shameful deaths! and besides, thou countest his service better then mine, whereas he never came yet from the place where he is, to deliver any that serv'ed him out of our hands: but as for me, how many times, as all the World very well knows, have I delivered, either by power or fraud, those that have faithfully served me, from him and his, though taken by them; and so I will deliver thee.*

Chr. His forbearing at present to deliver them, is on purpose to try their love, whether they will cleave to him to the end: and as for the ill end thou sayest they come to, that is most glorious in their account: For, for present deliverance, they do not much expect it; for they stay for their Glory, and then they shall have it, when their Prince comes in his, and the Glory of the Angels.

Apol. *Thou hast already been unfaithful in thy service to him, and how dost thou think to receive wages of him?*

Chr. Wherein, O *Apollyon*, have I been unfaithful to him?

Apollyon *pleads* Christian's *infirmities against him.*

Apol. *Thou didst faint at first setting out, when thou wast almost choked in the Gulf of Dispond. Thou didst attempt wrong ways to be rid of thy burden, whereas thou shouldest have stayed till thy Prince had taken it off. Thou didst sinfully sleep, and loose thy choice thing: thou wast also almost perswaded to go back, at the sight of the Lions; and when thou talkest of thy Journey, and of what thou hast heard, and seen, thou art inwardly desirous of vain-glory*† *in all that thou sayest or doest.*

Chr. All this is true, and much more, which thou hast left out; but the Prince whom I serve and honour, is merciful, and ready to forgive: but besides, these infirmities possessed me in thy Countrey, for there I suckt them in, and I have groaned under them, been sorry for them, and have obtained Pardon of my Prince.

Apol. Then *Apollyon* broke out into a grievous rage, saying, *I am an enemy to this Prince: I hate his Person, his Laws, and People: I am come out on purpose to withstand thee.*

Apollyon *in a rage falls upon* Christian.

Chr. Apollyon, beware what you do, for I am in the Kings High-way, the way of Holiness,† therefore take heed to your self.

Apol. Then *Apollyon* strodled quite over the whole breadth of the way, and said, I am void of fear in this matter, prepare thy self to dye, for I swear by my Infernal Den, that thou shalt go no further, here will I spill thy soul: and with that he threw a flaming Dart at his brest; but *Christian* had a Shield in his hand, with which he caught it, and so prevented the danger of that. Then did *Christian* draw, for he saw 'twas time to bestir him; and *Apollyon* as fast made at him, throwing Darts as thick as hail; by the which, notwithstanding all that *Christian* could do to avoid it, **Apollyon* wounded him in his *head*, his *hand* and *foot*; this made *Christian* give a little back: *Apollyon* therefore followed his work amain, and *Christian* again took courage, and resisted as manfully as he could. This sore Combat lasted for above half a day, even till *Christian* was almost quite spent. For you must know, that *Christian*, by reason of his wounds, must needs grow weaker and weaker.

* Christian *wounded in his understanding, faith and conversation.*

Then *Apollyon* espying his opportunity, began to gather up close to *Christian*, and wrestling with him, gave him a dreadful fall; and with that *Christian's* Sword flew out of his hand. Then said *Apollion, I am sure of thee now*; and with that, he had almost prest him to death; so that *Christian* began to despair of life. But as God would have it, while *Apollyon* was fetching of his last blow, thereby to make a full end of this good Man, *Christian* nimbly reached out his hand for his Sword, and caught it, saying, **Rejoyce not against me, O mine Enemy! when I fall, I shall arise*; and with that, gave him a deadly thrust, which made him give back, as one that had received his mortal wound: *Christian* perceiving that, made at him again, saying, **Nay, in all these things we are more then Conquerours,*

Apollyon *casteth down to the ground* Christian.

Christians *victory over* Apollyon.

* Mich. 7. 8.

* Rom. 8. 37.

A more unequal match can hardly be,
Christian must fight an Angel; but you see,
The valiant man by handling Sword and Shield,
Doth make him, tho' a Dragon, quit the field.

through him that loved us. And with that, *Apollyon* spread forth his Dragons wings, and sped him away, that *Christian* for a season saw him no more.

James 4. 7.

In this Combat no man can imagine, unless he had seen and heard as I did, what yelling, and hideous roaring *Apollyon* made all the time of the fight, he spake like a Dragon: and on the other side, what sighs and groans brast from *Christians* heart. I never saw him all the while give so much as one pleasant look, till he perceived he had wounded *Apollyon* with his two-edg'd Sword, then indeed he did smile, and look upward: but twas the dreadfullest sight that ever I saw.

A brief relation of the Combat by the spectator.

So when the Battel was over, *Christian* said, I will here give thanks to him that hath delivered me out of the mouth of the Lion; to him that did help me against *Apollyon*: and so he did, saying,

Christian *gives God thanks for deliverance.*

Great Beelzebub, *the Captain of this Fiend,*
Design'd my ruin; therefore to this end
He sent him harnest out, and he with rage
That hellish was, did fiercely me Ingage:
But blessed Michael† *helped me, and I*
By dint of Sword did quickly make him flye;
Therefore to him let me give lasting praise,
And thank and bless his holy name always.

Then there came to him an hand with some of the leaves of the Tree of Life,† the which *Christian* took, and applyed to the wounds that he had received in the Battel, and was healed immediately. He also sat down in that place to eat Bread, and to drink of the Bottle that was given him a little before; so being refreshed, he addressed himself to his Journey, with his *Sword drawn in his hand; for he said, I know not but some other enemy may be at hand. But he met with no other affront from *Apollyon*, quite through this Valley.

* Christian *goes on his Journey with his Sword drawn in his hand.*

Now at the end of this Valley, was another, called the Valley of the *Shadow of Death*, and *Christian* must needs go through it, because the way to the Cœlestial City lay through the midst of it: Now this Valley is a very solitary place. The Prophet **Jeremiah* thus describes it, *A Wilderness, a Land of desarts, and of Pits, a Land of drought, and of the shadow of death, a Land*

* Jer. 2. 6.

that no Man (but a Christian) *passeth through, and where no man dwelt.*

Now here *Christian* was worse put to it then in his fight with *Apollyon*, as by the sequel you shall see.

I saw then in my Dream, that when *Christian* was got to the Borders of the Shadow of Death, there met him two Men,
* *The children of the Spies go back.* *Children of them that brought up an *evil report of the good Land, making haste to go back: to whom *Christian* spake
* Numb. 13. as follows.

Chr. *Whither are you going?*

Men. They said, Back, back; and would have you to do so too, if either life or peace is prized by you.

Chr. *Why? what's the matter? said* Christian.

Men. Matter! said they; we were going that way as you are going, and went as far as we durst; and indeed we were almost past coming back, for had we gone a little further, we had not been here to bring the news to thee.

Chr. *But what have you met with? said* Christian.

Psal. 44. 19. *Men.* Why we were almost in the Valley of the shadow of
Psal. 107. 14. Death, but that by good hap we looked before us, and saw the danger before we came to it.

Chr. *But what have you seen? said* Christian.

Men. Seen! Why the Valley it self, which is as dark as pitch; we also saw there the Hobgoblins, Satyrs,† and Dragons of the Pit: we heard also in that Valley a continual howling and yelling, as of a People under unutterable misery; who there sat bound in affliction and Irons: and over that Valley hangs the
* Job 3. 5. ch. 10. 22. discouraging *Clouds of confusion, death also doth always spread his wings over it: in a word, it is every whit dreadful, being utterly without Order.

Ch. *Then said* Christian, *I perceive not yet, by what you have*
* Jer. 2. 6. *said, but that *this is my way to the desired Haven.*

Men. Be it thy way, we will not chuse it for ours; so they parted, and *Christian* went on his way, but still with his Sword drawn in his hand, for fear lest he should be assaulted.

Psal. 69. 14. I saw then in my Dream, so far as this Valley reached, there was on the right hand a very deep Ditch; that Ditch is it into which the blind have led the blind† in all Ages, and have both there miserably perished. Again, behold on the left hand, there was a very dangerous Quagg, into which, if even a good Man falls, he can find no bottom for his foot to stand on: Into that Quagg *King* David *once did fall*,† and had no doubt therein been smothered, had not He that is able, pluckt him out.

The path-way was here also exceeding narrow, and therefore good *Christian* was the more put to it; for when he sought in the dark to shun the ditch on the one hand, he was ready to tip over into the mire on the other; also when he sought to escape the mire, without great carefulness he would be ready to fall into the ditch. Thus he went on, and I heard him here sigh bitterly: for, besides the dangers mentioned above, the path way was here so dark, that oft times when he lift up his foot to set forward, he knew not where, or upon what he should set it next.

About the midst of this Valley, I perceived the mouth of Hell to be, and it stood also hard by the way side: Now thought *Christian*, what shall I do? And ever and anon the flame and smoke would come out in such abundance, with sparks and hideous noises, (things that cared not for *Christians* Sword, as did *Apollyon* before) that he was forced to put up his Sword, and betake himself to another weapon called **All-prayer*: so he cried in my hearing, **O Lord I beseech thee deliver my Soul.* Thus he went on a great while, yet still the flames would be reaching towards him: also he heard doleful voices, and rushings too and fro, so that sometimes he thought he should be torn in pieces, or trodden down like mire in the Streets. This frightful sight was seen, and these dreadful noises were heard by him for several miles together: and coming to a place, where he thought he heard a company of *Fiends* coming forward to meet him, he ſtopt; and began to muse what he had best to do. Sometimes he had half a thought to go back. Then again he thought he might be half way through the Valley; he remembred also how he had already vanquished many a danger: and that the danger of going back might be much more, then for to go forward; so he resolved to go on. Yet the *Fiends* seemed to come nearer and nearer, but when they were come even almost at him, he cried out with a most vehement voice, *I will walk in the strength of the Lord God*;† so they gave back, and came no further.

* Ephes. 6. 18.

* Psal. 116. 4.

Christian *put to a stand, but for a while.*

Poor man where art thou now, thy day is night,
Good man be not cast down, thou yet art right,
Thy way to heaven lies by the gates of hell;
Chear up, hold out, with thee it shall go well.

One thing I would not let slip, I took notice that now poor *Christian* was so confounded, that he did not know his own voice: and thus I perceived it: Just when he was come over against the mouth of the burning Pit, one of the wicked ones got behind him, and stept up softly to him, and whisperingly suggested many grievous blasphemies to him,† which he *verily thought had proceeded from his own mind. This put *Christian* more to it than any thing that he met with before, even to think that he should now blaspheme him that he loved so much before; yet, could he have helped it, he would not have done it: but he had not the discretion neither to stop his ears, nor to know from whence those blasphemies came.

* Christian *made believe that he spake blasphemies, when 'twas Satan that suggested them into his mind.*

When *Christian* had travelled in this disconsolate condition some considerable time, he thought he heard the voice of a man, as going before him, saying, *Though I walk through the valley of the shaddow of death, I will fear none ill,*† *for thou art with me*.

Psalm 23. 4.

Then was he glad, and that for these reasons:

First, because he gathered from thence, that some who feared God were in this Valley as well as himself.

Secondly, For that he perceived, God was with them, though in that dark and dismal state; and why not, thought he, with me, though by reason of the impediment that attends this place, I cannot perceive it.

Job 9. 11.

Thirdly, For that he hoped (could he over-take them) to have company by and by. So he went on, and called to him that was before, but he knew not what to answer; for that he also thought himself to be alone: And by and by, the day broke; then said *Christian*, **He hath turned the shadow of death into the morning.*

* Amos 5. 8.

Christian *glad at break of day.*

Now morning being come, he looked back, not of desire to return, but to see, by the light of the day, what hazards he had gone through in the dark. So he saw more perfectly the Ditch that was on the one hand, and the Quag that was on the other; also how narrow the way was which lay betwixt them both; also now he saw the Hobgoblins, and Satyrs, and Dragons of the Pit, but all afar off; for after break of day, they came not nigh; yet they were discovered to him, according to that which is written, **He discovereth deep things out of darkness, and bringeth out to light the shadow of death*.

* Job 12. 22.

Now was *Christian* much affected with his deliverance from all the dangers of his solitary way, which dangers, though he feared them more before, yet he saw them more clearly now, because the light of the day made them conspicuous to him; and about this time the Sun was rising, and this was another mercy to *Christian*: for you must note, that tho the first part of the Valley of the shadow of Death was dangerous, *yet this second part which he was yet to go, was, if possible, far more dangerous: for from the place where he now stood, even to the end of the Valley, the way was all along set so full of Snares, Traps, Gins, and Nets here, and so full of Pits, Pitfalls, deep holes, and shelvings down there, that had it now been dark, as it was when he came the first part of the way, had he had a thousand souls, they had in reason been cast away; but, as I said, just now the Sun was rising. Then said he **His candle shineth on my head, and by his light I go through darkness*.

* *The second part of this Valley very dangerous.*

* Job 29. 3.

In this light therefore he came to the end of the Valley. Now I saw in my Dream, that at the end of this Valley lay blood, bones, ashes, and mangled bodies of men, even of Pilgrims that had gone this way formerly: And while I was musing what should be the reason, I espied a little before me a Cave, where two Giants, *Pope* and *Pagan*, dwelt in old time, by whose Power and Tyranny the Men whose bones, blood, ashes, *&c.* lay there, were cruelly put to death. But by this place *Christian* went without much danger, whereat I somewhat wondered; but I have learnt since, that *Pagan* has been dead many a day; and as for the other, though he be yet alive, he is by reason of age, and also of the many shrewd brushes that he met with in his younger dayes, grown so crazy and stiff in his joynts, that he can now do little more then sit in his Caves mouth, grinning at Pilgrims as they go by, and biting his nails, because he cannot come at them.

So I saw that *Christian* went on his way, yet at the sight of the *old Man* that sat in the mouth of the *Cave*, he could not tell what to think, specially because he spake to him, though he could not go after him; saying, *You will never mend, till more of you be burned*:† but he held his peace, and set a good face on't, and so went by, and catcht no hurt. Then sang *Christian*,

O world of wonders! (I can say no less)
That I should be preserv'd in that distress
That I have met with here! O blessed bee
That hand that from it hath delivered me!
Dangers in darkness, Devils, Hell, and Sin,
Did compass me, while I this Vale was in:
Yea, Snares, and Pits, and Traps, and Nets did lie
My path about, that worthless silly I
Might have been catch't, intangled, and cast down:
But since I live, let JESUS wear the Crown.

Now as *Christian* went on his way, he came to a little ascent, which was cast up on purpose, that Pilgrims might see before them: up there therefore *Christian* went, and looking forward, he saw *Faithful* before him, upon his Journey. Then said *Christian* aloud, Ho, ho, So-ho; stay, and I will be your Companion. At that *Faithful* looked behind him, to whom *Christian* cried again, Stay, stay, till I come up to you: but *Faithful* answered, *No*, I am upon my life, and the Avenger of Blood† is behind me. At this *Christian* was somwhat moved, and putting to all his strength, he quickly got up with *Faithful*, and did also over-run him, so the *last was first*.† Then did *Christian* vain-gloriously smile, because he had gotten the start of his Brother: but not taking good heed to his feet, he suddenly stumbled and fell, and could not rise again, until *Faithful* came up to help him.

Christian *overtakes* Faithful.

Christians *fal[l]* *makes* Faithf[ul] *and he go lovingly together.*

Then I saw in my Dream, they went very lovingly on together; and had sweet discourse of all things that had happened to them in their Pilgrimage: and thus *Christian* began.

Chr. *My honoured and well beloved Brother* Faithful, *I am glad that I have overtaken you; and that God has so tempered our spirits, that we can walk as Companions in this so pleasant a path.*

Faith. I had thought dear friend, to have had your company quite from our Town, but you did get the start of me; wherefore I was forced to come thus much of the way alone.

Chr. *How long did you stay in the City of* Destruction, *before you set out after me on your Pilgrimage?*

Faith. Till I could stay no longer; for there was great talk presently after you was gone out, that our City would in short time with Fire from Heaven be burned down to the ground.

Their talk about the Countrey from whence they came.

Chr. *What? Did your Neighbours talk so?*

Faith. Yes, 'twas for a while in every bodies mouth.

Chr. *What, and did no more of them but you come out to escape the danger?*

Faith. Though there was, as I said, a great talk thereabout, yet I do not think they did firmly believe it. For in the heat of the discourse, I heard some of them deridingly speak of you, and of your desperate Journey, (for so they called this your Pilgrimage) but I did believe, and do still, that the end of our City will be with Fire and Brimstone from above: and therefore I have made mine escape.

Chr. *Did you hear no talk of Neighbour* Pliable?

Faith. Yes, *Christian*, I heard that he followed you till he came at the Slough of *Dispond*; where, as some said, he fell in; but he would not be known to have so done: but I am sure he was soundly bedabled with that kind of dirt.

Chr. *And what said the Neighbours to him?*

How Plyable *was accounted of when he got home.*

Faith. He hath since his going back been had greatly in derision, and that among all sorts of People: some do mock and despise him, and scarce will any set him on work. He is now seven times worse then if he had never gone out of the City.

Chr. *But why should they be so set against him, since they also despise the way that he forsook?*

Faith. Oh, they say, Hang him; he is a Turn-Coat, he was not true to his profession: I think God has stired up even his enemies to hiss at him, and make him a Proverb, because he hath forsaken the way.

Prov. 15. 10.

Chr. *Had you no talk with him before you came out?*

Faith. I met him once in the Streets, but he leered away on the other side, as one ashamed of what he had done; so I spake not to him.

* 2 Pet. 2. 22. *The Dog and Sow.*

Chr. *Well, at my first setting out, I had hopes of that Man; but now I fear he will perish in the overthrow of the City, *for it is happened to him according to the true Proverb, The Dog is turned to his Vomit again, and the Sow that was Washed to her wallowing in the mire.*

Faith. They are my fears of him too: But who can hinder that which will be?

Chr. Well Neighbour *Faithful* said *Christian*, let us leave him, and talk of things that more immediately concern our selves. *Tell me now, what you have met with in the way as you came? for I know you have met with some things, or else it may be writ for a wonder.*†

Faith. I escaped the Slough that I perceive you fell into, and got up to the Gate without that danger; only I met with one whose name was *Wanton*, that had like to have done me a mischief.

Faithfull *assaulted by* Wanton.

Chr. *'Twas well you escaped her Net;* *Joseph *was hard put to it by her, and he escaped her as you did, but it had like to have cost him his life. But what did she do to you?*

* Gen. 39. 11, 12, 13.

Faith. You cannot think (but that you know something) what a flattering tongue she had, she lay at me hard to turn aside with her, promising me all manner of content.

Chr. *Nay, she did not promise you the content of a good conscience.*

Faith. You know what I mean, all carnal and fleshly content.

Chr. *Thank God you have escaped her: The *abhorred of the Lord shall fall into her Ditch.*

* Prov. 22. 14.

Faith. Nay, I know not whether I did wholly escape her, or no.

Chr. *Why, I tro you did not consent to her desires?*

Faith. No, not to defile my self; for I remembred an old writing that I had seen, which saith, *Her steps take hold of Hell.* So I shut mine eyes, because I would not be bewitched with her looks: then she railed on me, and I went my way.

Prov. 5. 5. Job 31. 1.

Chr. *Did you meet with no other assault as you came?*

Faith. When I came to the foot of the Hill called *Difficulty*, I met with a very aged Man, who asked me, *What I was, and whither bound?* I told him that I was a Pilgrim, going to the Cœlestial City: Then said the old Man, *Thou lookest like an honest fellow; Wilt thou be content to dwell with me, for the wages that I shall give thee?* Then I asked him his name, and where he dwelt? He said his name was *Adam the first,*† *and I dwell in the Town of *Deceit*. I asked him then, What was his work? and what the wages that he would give? He told me, That his work was *many delights; and his wages, that I should be*

He is assaulted by Adam *the first.*

* Eph. 4. 22.

his Heir at last. I further asked him, What House he kept, and what other Servants he had? so he told me, *That his House was maintained with all the dainties in the world, and that his Servants were those of his own begetting.* Then I asked how many children he had, He said, that he had but three Daughters, *The *lust of the flesh, the lust of the eyes, and the pride of life*, and that I should marry them all, if I would. Then I asked, how long time he would have me live with him? And he told me, *As long as he lived himself.*

* 1 Joh. 2. 16.

Chr. *Well, and what conclusion came the* Old Man, *and you to, at last?*

Faith. Why, at first I found my self somewhat inclinable to go with the Man, for I thought he spake very fair; but looking in his forehead as I talked with him, I saw there written, *Put off the old Man with his deeds.*†

Chr. *And how then?*

Faith. Then it came burning hot into my mind, whatever he said, and however he flattered, when he got me home to his House, he would sell me for a Slave. So I bid him forbear to talk, for I would not come near the door of his House. Then he reviled me, and told me, that he would send such a one after me, that should make my way bitter to my soul: So I turned to go away from him: but just as I turned my self to go thence, I felt him take hold of my flesh, and give me such a deadly twitch back, that I thought he had pull'd part of me after himself: This made me cry, **O wretched Man!* So I went on my way up the Hill.

* Rom. 7. 24.

Now when I had got about half way up, I looked behind me, and saw one coming after me, swift as the wind; so he overtook me just about the place where the Settle stands.

Chr. *Just there, said* Christian, *did I sit down to rest me; but being overcome with sleep, I there lost this Roll out of my bosom.*

Faith. But good Brother hear me out: So soon as the Man† over-took me, he was but a word and a blow: for down he knockt me, and laid me for dead. But when I was a little come to my self again, I asked him wherefore he served me so? he said, Because of my secret inclining to *Adam the first*; and with that, he strook me another deadly blow on the brest, and beat me down backward; so I lay at his foot as dead as before. So when I came to my self again, I cried him mercy; but he said, I know not how to show mercy, and with that knockt me down again. He had doubtless made a hand of† me, but that one came by, and bid him forbear.

Chr. *Who was that, that bid him forbear?*

Faith. I did not know him at first, but as he went by, I perceived the holes in his hands, and his side; then I concluded that he was our Lord. So I went up the Hill.

Chr. *That Man that overtook you, was* Moses, **he spareth none, neither knoweth he how to shew mercy to those that transgress his Law.*

* *The temper of* Moses.

Faith. I know it very well, it was not the first time that he has met with me. 'Twas he that came to me when I dwelt securely at home, and that told me, He would burn my house over my head, if I staid there.

Chr. *But did not you see the house that stood there on the top of that Hill on the side of which* Moses *met you?*

Faith. Yes, and the Lions too, before I came at it, but for the Lions, I think they were a sleep, for it was about Noon; and because I had so much of the day before me, I passed by the Porter, and came down the Hill.

Chr. *He told me indeed that he saw you go by, but I wish you had called at the House; for they would have shewed you so many Rarities, that you would scarce have forgot them to the day of your death. But pray tell me, did you meet no body in the Valley of* Humility?

Faithful *assaulted by* Discontent.

Faith. Yes, I met with one *Discontent*, who would willingly have perswaded me to go back again with him: his reason was, for that the Valley was altogether without *Honour*; he told me moreover, That there to go, was the way to disobey all my Friends, as Pride, Arrogancy, Self-conceit, worldly Glory, with others, who he knew, as he said, would be very much offended, if I made such a Fool of my self, as to wade through this Valley.

Chr. *Well, and how did you answer him?*

Faithfuls *answer to* Discontent.

Faith. I told him, that although all these that he named might claim kindred of me, and that rightly, (for indeed they were my Relations, *according to the flesh*) yet since I became a Pilgrim, they have disowned me, as I also have rejected them; and therefore they were to me now no more then if they had never been of my Linage; I told him moreover, That as to this Valley, he had quite mis-represented the thing: *for before Honour is Humility, and a haughty spirit before a fall.*† Therefore said I, I had rather go through this Valley to the Honour that was so accounted by the wisest, then chuse that which he esteemed most worth our affections.

Chr. *Met you with nothing else in that Valley?*

He is assaulted with Shame.

Faith. Yes, I met with *Shame*, But of all the Men that I met with in my Pilgrimage, he, I think, bears the wrong name: the other would be said nay, after a little argumentation (and some what else) but this bold faced *Shame* would never have done.

Chr. *Why, what did he say to you?*

Faith. What! why he objected against Religion it self; he said it was a pitiful, low, sneaking business for a man to mind Religion; he said that a tender conscience was an unmanly thing, and that for Man to watch over his words and ways, so as to tye up himself from that hectoring liberty, that the brave spirits of the times accustom themselves unto, would make him the Ridicule of the times. He objected also, that but few of
1 Cor. 1. 26. the Mighty, Rich, or Wise, were ever of my opinion; nor any of
ch. 3. 18. Phil. 3. 7, 8. them neither, before they were perswaded to be Fools, and to
be of a voluntary fondness, to venture the loss of all, *for no body*
* John 7. 48. *else knows what*. He moreover objected *the base and low estate and condition of those that were chiefly the Pilgrims; also their ignorance of the times in which they lived, and want of understanding in all natural Science.† Yea, he did hold me to it at that rate also, about a great many more things then here I relate; as, that it was a *shame* to sit whining and mourning under a Sermon, and a *shame* to come sighing and groaning home. That it was a *shame* to ask my Neighbour forgiveness for petty faults, or to make restitution where I had taken from any: He said also that Religion made a man grow strange to the great, because of a few vices (which he called by finer names) and made him own and respect the base, because of the same Religious fraternity. And is not this, said he, a *shame?*

Chr. *And what did you say to him?*

Faith. Say! I could not tell what to say at the first. Yea, he put me so to it, that my blood came up in my face, even this

Shame fetch'd it up, and had almost beat me quite off. But at last I began to consider, **That that which is highly esteemed among Men, is had in abomination with God.* And I thought again, this *Shame* tells me what men are, but it tells me nothing what God, or the Word of God is. And I thought moreover, That at the day of doom, we shall not be doomed to death or life, according to the hectoring spirits of the world; but according to the Wisdom and Law of the Highest. Therefore thought I, what God says, is best, though all the men in the world are against it. Seeing then, that God prefers his Religion, seeing God prefers a tender Conscience, seeing they that make themselves Fools for the Kingdom of Heaven, are wisest;† and that the poor man that loveth Christ, is richer then the greatest man in the world that hates him; *Shame* depart, thou art an enemy to my Salvation: shall I entertain thee against my Soveraign Lord? How then shall I look him in the face at his coming? Should I now be *ashamed* of his ways and Servants, how can I expect the blessing? But indeed this *Shame* was a bold Villain; I could scarce shake him out of my company; yea, he would be haunting of me, and continually whispering me in the ear, with some one or other of the infirmities that attend Religion: but at last I told him, Twas but in vain to attempt further in this business; for those things that he disdained, in those did I see most glory: And so at last I got past this *importunate* one:

* Luke 16. 15.

Mar. 8. 38.

And when I had shaken him off, then I began to sing.

The tryals that those men do meet withal
That are obedient to the Heavenly call,
Are manifold and suited to the flesh,
And come, and come, and come again afresh;
That now, or somtime else, we by them may
Be taken, overcome, and cast away.
O let the Pilgrims, let the Pilgrims then,
Be vigilant, and quit themselves like Men.

Chr. *I am glad, my Brother, that thou didst withstand this Villain so bravely; for of all, as thou sayst, I think he has the wrong name: for he is so bold as to follow us in the Streets, and to attempt to put us to* shame *before all men; that is, to make us*

ashamed *of that which is good: but if he was not himself audacious, he would never attempt to do as he does, but let us still resist him: for notwithstanding all his Bravadoes, he promoteth the Fool,*
Prov. 3. 35. *and none else.* The Wise shall Inherit Glory, said *Solomon*, but shame shall be the promotion of Fools.

Faith. *I think we must cry to him for help against shame, that would have us be valiant for the Truth upon the Earth.*†

Chr. *You say true. But did you meet no body else in that Valley?*

Faith. No not I, for I had Sun-shine all the rest of the way, through that, and also through the Valley of the shadow of death.

Chr. *'Twas well for you, I am sure it fared far otherwise with me.* I had for a long season, as soon almost as I entred into that Valley, a dreadful Combat with that foul Fiend *Apollyon*: Yea, I thought verily he would have killed me; especially when he got me down, and crusht me under him, as if he would have crusht me to pieces. For as he threw me, my Sword flew out of my hand; nay he told me, *He was sure of me:* but *I cried to God, and he heard me, and delivered me out of all my troubles.*† Then I entred into the Valley of the shadow of death, and had no light for almost half the way through it. I thought I should a been killed there, over, and over: but at last, day brake, and the Sun rise, and I went through that which was behind with far more ease and quiet.

Moreover, I saw in my Dream, that as they went on, *Faithful*, as he chanced to look on one side, saw a Man whose name is *Talkative*, walking at a distance besides them, (for in this place there was room enough for them all to walk). *He was a tall Man, and something more comely at a distance then at hand*, To this Man, *Faithful* addressed himself in this manner.

Talkative *described.*

Faith. *Friend, Whither away? Are you going to the Heavenly Countrey?*

Talk. I am going to that same place.

Faith. *That is well: Then I hope we may have your good company.*

Talk. With a very good will, will I be your companion.

Faithful *and* Talkative *enter discourse.*

Faith. *Come on then, and let us go together, and let us spend our time in discoursing of things that are profitable.*

Talk. To talk of things that are good, to me is very acceptable, with you or with any other; and I am glad that I have met with those that incline to so good a work. For to speak the truth, there are but few that care thus to spend their time (as they are in their travels) but chuse much rather to be speaking of things to no profit, and this hath been a trouble to me.

Talkatives *dislike of bad discourse.*

Faith. *That is indeed a thing to be lamented; for what things so worthy of the use of the tongue and mouth of men on Earth, as are the things of the God of Heaven?*

Talk. I like you wonderful well, for your saying is full of conviction; and I will add, What thing so pleasant, and what so profitable, as to talk of the things of God?

What things so pleasant? (that is, if a man hath any delight in things that are wonderful) for instance: If a man doth delight to talk of the History or the Mystery of things; or if a man doth love to talk of Miracles, Wonders, or Signs, where shall he find things Recorded so delightful, and so sweetly penned, as in the holy Scripture?

Faith. *That's true: but to be profited by such things in our talk, should be that which we design.*

Talk. That is it that I said; for to talk of such things is most profitable, for by so doing, a Man may get knowledge of many things; as of the vanity of earthly things, and the benefit of things above: (thus in general) but more particularly, By this a man may learn the necessity of the New-birth, the insufficiency of our works, the need of Christs righteousness, *&c.* Besides, by this a man may learn by *talk*, what it is to repent, to believe, to pray, to suffer, or the like: by this also a Man may learn what are the great promises & consolations of the Gospel, to his own comfort. Further, by this a Man may learn to refute false opinions, to vindicate the truth, and also to instruct the ignorant.

Talkatives *fine discourse.*

Faith. *All this is true, and glad am I to hear these things from you.*

Talk. Alas! the want of this is the cause that so few understand the need of faith, and the necessity of a work of Grace in their Soul, in order to eternal life: but ignorantly live in the works of the Law, by which a man can by no means obtain the Kingdom of Heaven.

Faith. *But by your leave, Heavenly knowledge of these, is the gift of God; no man attaineth to them by humane industry, or only by the talk of them.*

Talk. All this I know very well. For a man can receive nothing except it be given him from Heaven; all is of Grace, not of works:† I could give you an hundred Scriptures for the confirmation of this.

O brave Talkative.

Faith. *Well then, said* Faithful; *what is that one thing, that we shall at this time found our discourse upon?*

O brave Talkative.

Talk. What you will: I will talk of things heavenly, or things earthly; things Moral, or things Evangelical; things Sacred, or things Prophane; things past, or things to come; things forraign, or things at home; things more Essential, or things Circumstantial: provided that all be done to our profit.

Faithful *beguiled by* Talkative.

Faith. Now did *Faithful* begin to wonder; *and stepping to* Christian, (*for he walked all this while by himself*) *he said to him,* (*but softly*) *What a brave Companion have we got! Surely this man will make a very excellent Pilgrim.*

Christian *makes a discovery of* Talkative, *telling* Faithful *who he was.*

Chr. At this *Christian* modestly smiled, and said, This man with whom you are so taken, will beguile with this tongue of his, twenty of them that know him not.

Faith. *Do you know him then?*

Chr. Know him! Yes, better then he knows himself.

Faith. *Pray what is he?*

Chr. His name is *Talkative*, he dwelleth in our Town; I wonder that you should be a stranger to him, only I consider that our Town is large.

Faith. *Whose Son is he? And whereabout doth he dwell?*

Chr. He is the Son of one *Saywell*, he dwelt in *Prating-row*; and he is known of all that are acquainted with him, by the name of *Talkative* in *Prating-row*, and notwithstanding his fine tongue, he is but a sorry fellow.

Faith. *Well, he seems to be a very pretty man.*

Chr. That is, to them that have not through acquaintance with him, for he is best abroad, near home he is ugly enough: your saying, That he is a *pretty man*, brings to my mind what I have observed in the work of the Painter, whose Pictures shews best at a distance; but very near, more unpleasing.

Faith. *But I am ready to think you do but* jest, *because you* smiled.

Chr. God-forbid that I should *jest*, (though I smiled) in this matter, or that I should accuse any falsely; I will give you a further discovery of him: This man is for any company, and for any *talk*; as he *talketh now* with you, so will he *talk* when he is on the *Ale-bench*: And the more drink he hath in his crown, the more of these things he hath in his mouth: Religion hath no place in his heart, or house, or conversation; all he hath lieth in his *tongue*, and his Religion is to make a noise *therewith*.

Faith. *Say you so! Then I am in this man greatly deceived.*

Chr. Deceived? you may be sure of it. Remember the Proverb, *They say and do not: but the Kingdom of God is not in word, but in power*. He *talketh* of Prayer, of Repentance, of Faith, and of the New-birth: but he knows but only to *talk* of them. I have been in his Family, and have observed him both at home and abroad; and I know what I say of him is the truth. His house is as empty of Religion, *as the white of an Egg is of savour*. There is there, neither Prayer, nor sign of Repentance for sin: Yea, the bruit in his kind serves God far better than he. He is the very stain, reproach, and shame of Religion to all that know him; it can hardly have a good word in all that end of the Town where he dwells, through him. Thus say the common People that know him, *A* Saint *abroad, and a* Devil *at home*:† His poor Family finds it so, he is such a *churl*, such a railer at, and so unreasonable with his Servants, that they neither know how to do for, or speak to him. Men that have any dealings with him, say, 'tis better to deal with a *Turk* then with him, for fairer dealing they shall have at their hands. This *Talkative*, if it be possible, will go beyond them, defraud, beguile, and over-reach them. Besides, he brings up his Sons to follow his steps; and if he findeth in any of them *a foolish timorousness*, (for so he calls the first appearance of a tender conscience) he calls them fools and block-heads; and by no means will imploy them in much, or speak to their commendations before others. For my part I am of opinion, that he has, by his wicked life, caused many to stumble and fall; and will be, if God prevent not, the ruine of many more.

Mat. 23.
1 Cor. 4. 20.
Talkative *talks, but does not.*

His house is empty of Religion.

He is a stain to Religion, Rom. 2. 24, 25.

The Proverb that goes of him.

Men shun to deal with him.

Faith. *Well, my Brother, I am bound to believe you; not only because you say you know him, but also because like a Christian, you make your reports of men. For I cannot think that you speak these things of ill will, but because it is even so as you say.*

Chr. Had I known him no more than you, I might perhaps have thought of him as at the first you did: Yea, had he received this report, at *their* hands only, that are enemies to Religion, I should have thought it had been a slander: (A Lot that often falls from bad mens mouths upon good mens names and professions:) But all these things, yea, and a great many more as bad, of my own knowledge I can prove him guilty of. Besides, good men are ashamed of him, they can neither call him *Brother* nor *Friend*: the very naming of him among them, makes them blush, if they know him.

Faith. *Well, I see that Saying, and Doing are two things, and hereafter I shall better observe this distinction.*

The Carkass of Religion.

Chr. They are two things indeed, and are as diverse as are the Soul and the Body: For as the Body without the Soul, is but a dead Carkass; so, *Saying*, if it be alone, is but a dead Carkass also. The Soul of Religion is the practick part: *Pure Religion and undefiled, before God and the Father, is this, To visit the Fatherless and Widows in their affliction, and to keep himself unspotted from the World.* This *Talkative* is not aware of, he thinks that *hearing* and *saying* will make a good Christian and thus he deceiveth his own Soul. Hearing is but as the sowing of the Seed; talking is not sufficient to prove that fruit is indeed in the heart and life; and let us assure our selves, that at the day of Doom, men shall be judged according to their fruits. It will not be said then, *Did you believe?* but, Were you *Doers*, or *Talkers* only? and accordingly shall they be judged. The end of the world is compared to our Harvest, and you know men at Harvest regard nothing but Fruit. Not that any thing can be accepted that is not of Faith: But I speak this to shew you how insignificant the profession of *Talkative* will be at that day.

James 1. 27. *see ver.* 22, 23, 24, 25, 26.

See Mat. 13. *and ch.* 25.

Lev. 11. Deut. 14.

Faith. *This brings to my mind that of* Moses, *by which he describeth the beast that is clean. He is such an one that parteth the Hoof, and cheweth the Cud: Not that parteth the Hoof only, or that cheweth the Cud only. The Hare cheweth the Cud, but yet is unclean, because he parteth not the Hoof. And this truly resembleth* Talkative; *he cheweth the Cud, he seeketh knowledge,*

Faithful *convinced of the badness of* Talkative.

he cheweth upon the Word, but he divideth not the Hoof, he parteth not with the way of sinners; but as the Hare he retaineth the foot of a Dog, or Bear, and therefore he is unclean.

Chr. You have spoken, for ought I know, the true Gospel sense of those Texts;† and I will add an other thing. *Paul* calleth some men, yea, and those great Talkers too, *sounding Brass, and Tinckling Cymbals*; that is, as he Expounds them in another place, *Things without life, giving sound*. Things without life, that is, without the true Faith and Grace of the Gospel; and consequently, things that shall never be placed in the Kingdom of Heaven among those that are the Children of life: Though their *sound* by their *talk*, be as if it were the *Tongue*, or voice of an Angel.

1 Cor. 13. 1, 2, 3 ch. 14. 7. Talkative, *like to things that sound without life.*

Faith. *Well, I was not so fond of his company at first, but I am as sick of it now. What shall we do to be rid of him?*

Chr. Take my advice, and do as I bid you, and you shall find that he will soon be sick of your Company too, except God shall touch his heart and turn it.

Faith. *What would you have me to do?*

Chr. Why, go to him, and enter into some serious discourse about *the power of Religion*: And ask him plainly (when he has approved of it, for that he will) whether this thing be set up in his Heart, House, or Conversation.

Faith. Then *Faithful* stept forward again, and said to *Talkative: Come, what chear? how is it now?*

Talk. Thank you, well. I thought we should have had a great deal of *Talk* by this time.

Faith. *Well, if you will, we will fall to it now; and since you left it with me to state the question, let it be this: How doth the saving Grace of God discover it self, when it is in the heart of man?*

Talk. I perceive then that our talk must be *about the power of things*; Well, 'tis a very good question, and I shall be willing to answer you. And take my answer in brief thus. First, *Where the Grace of God is in the heart, it causeth* there *a great out-cry against sin.* Secondly——

Talkatives *false discovery of a work of grace.*

Faith. *Nay hold, let us consider of one at once: I think you should rather say, It showes it self by inclining the Soul to abhor its sin.*

Talk. Why, what difference is there between crying out against, and abhoring of sin?

To cry out against sin, no sign of Grace. Faith. *Oh! a great deal; a man may cry out against sin, of policy; but he cannot abhor it, but by vertue of a godly antipathy against it: I have heard many cry out against sin in the Pulpit, who yet can abide it well enough in the heart, and house, and* Gen. 39. 15. *conversation.* Josephs *Mistris cried out with a loud voice, as if she had been very holy; but she would willingly, notwithstanding that, have committed uncleanness with him. Some cry out against sin, even as the Mother cries out against her Child in her lap, when she calleth it slut, and naughty Girl, and then falls to hugging and kissing it.*

Talk. You lie at the catch,† I perceive.

Faith. *No not I, I am only for seting things right. But what is the second thing whereby you would prove a discovery of a work of grace in the heart?*

Talk. Great knowledge of Gospel Mysteries.

Great knowledge no sign of grace. 1 Cor. 13. Faith. *This sign should have been first, but first or last, it is also false; Knowledge, great knowledge may be obtained in the mysteries of the Gospel, and yet no work of grace in the Soul. Yea, if a man have all knowledge, he may yet be nothing, and so consequently be no child of God. When Christ said,* Do you know all these things? *And the Disciples had answered, Yes: He addeth,* Blessed are ye if ye do them.† *He doth not lay the blessing in the knowing of them, but in the doing of them. For there is a knowledge that is not attended with doing:* He that knoweth his Masters will and doth it not. *A man may know like an Angel, and yet be no Christian: therefore your sign is not true. Indeed to know, is a thing that pleaseth Talkers and Boasters; but to do, is that which pleaseth God. Not that the heart can be good without knowledge; for without that the heart is naught: There is therefore knowledge,* *Knowledge and knowledge.* *and knowledge. Knowledge that resteth in the bare speculation of things, and knowledge that is accompanied with the grace of faith and love, which puts a man upon doing even the will of God from the heart: the first of these will serve the Talker, but without the* *True Knowledge attended with endeavours.* *other the true Christian is not content.* Give me understanding, and I shall keep thy Law, yea, I shall observe it with my whole heart, *Psal.* 119. 34.

Talk. You lie at the catch again, this is not for edification.

Faith. *Well, if you please propound another sign how this work of grace discovereth it self where it is.*

Talk. Not I, for I see we shall not agree.

Faith. *Well, if you will not, will you give me leave to do it?*

Talk. You may use your Liberty.

One good sign of grace.

Faith. *A work of grace in the soul discovereth it self, either to him that hath it, or to standers by.*

John 16. 8. Rom. 7. 24. John 16. 9. Mark 16. 16. Psal. 38. 18. Jer. 31. 19. Gal. 2. 16. Acts 4. 12. Matth. 5. 6. Rev. 21. 6.

To him that hath it, thus. *It gives him conviction of sin, especially of the defilement of his nature, and the sin of unbelief, (for the sake of which he is sure to be damned, if he findeth not mercy at Gods hand by faith in Jesus Christ.) This sight and sense*† *of things worketh in him sorrow and shame for sin; he findeth moreover revealed in him the Saviour of the World, and the absolute necessity of closing with him, for life, at the which he findeth hungrings and thirstings after him, to which hungrings,* &c. *the promise is made. Now according to the strength or weakness of his Faith in his Saviour, so is his joy and peace, so is his love to holiness, so are his desires to know him more, and also to serve him in this World. But though I say it discovereth it self thus unto him; yet it is but seldom that he is able to conclude that this is a work of Grace, because his corruptions now, and his abused reason, makes his mind to misjudge in this matter; therefore in him that hath this work, there is required a very sound Judgement, before he can with steddiness conclude that this is a work of Grace.*

To others it is thus discovered.

Rom. 10. 10. Phil. 1. 27. Matth. 5. 9. John 24. 15. Psal. 50. 20. Job 42. 5, 6. Ezek. 29. 43.

1. *By an experimental confession of his Faith in Christ.* 2. *By a life answerable to that confession*, to wit, *a life of holiness; heart-holiness, family-holiness (if he hath a Family) and by Conversation-holiness in the world: which in the general teacheth him, inwardly to abhor his sin, and himself for that in secret, to suppress it in his Family, and to promote holiness in the World; not by talk only, as an Hypocrite or* Talkative *person may do: but by a practical Subjection in Faith, and Love, to the power of the word: And now Sir, as to this brief description of the work of Grace, and also the discovery of it, if you have ought to object, object: if not, then give me leave to propound to you a second question.*

Another good sign of grace.

Talk. Nay, my part is not now to object, but to hear, let me therefore have your second question.

Faith. It is this, *Do you experience the first part of this description of it? and doth your life and conversation testifie the same? or standeth your Religion* in Word, or in Tongue, *and not in* Deed *and* Truth: *pray, if you incline to answer me in this, say no more then you know the God above will say* Amen *to; and also, nothing but what your Conscience can justifie you in*. For, not he that commendeth himself is approved, but whom the Lord commendeth.† *Besides, to say I am thus, and thus, when my Conversation, and all my Neighbours tell me, I lye, is great wickedness.*

Talkative *not pleased with* Faithfuls *questions.*

Talk. Then *Talkative* at first began to blush, but recovering himself, thus he replyed, You come now to Experience, to Conscience, and God: and to appeals to him for justification of what is spoken: This kind of discourse I did not expect, nor am I disposed to give an answer to such questions, because, I count not my self bound thereto, unless you take upon you to be a *Catechizer*; and, though you should so do, yet I may refuse to make you my Judge: But I pray will you tell me, why you ask me such questions?

The reasons why Faithful *put to him that question.* Faithfuls *plain dealing* to *Talkative.*

Faith. *Because I saw you forward to talk, and because I knew not that you had ought else but notion. Besides, to tell you all the truth, I have heard of you, that you are a Man whose Religion lies in talk, and that your conversation gives this your Mouth-profession the lye. They say You are a spot among Christians, and that Religion fareth the worse for your ungodly conversation, that some already have stumbled at your wicked ways, and that more are in danger of being destroyed thereby; your Religion, and an Ale-house, and Covetousness, and uncleanness, and swearing, and lying, and vain Company-keeping*, &c. *will stand together. The Proverb is true of you, which is said of a Whore*; to wit, *That she is a shame to all Women; so you are a shame to all Professors.*

Talkative *flings away from* Faithful.

Talk. Since you are ready to take up reports, and to judge so rashly as you do; I cannot but conclude you are some peevish, or melancholly man not fit to be discoursed with, and so adieu.

Chr. Then came up *Christian* and said to his Brother, I told you how it would happen, your words and his lusts could not agree; he had rather leave your company, then reform his life: but he is gone as I said, let him go; the loss is no mans but his own, he has saved us the trouble of going from him: for he continuing, as I suppose he will do, as he is, he would have

A good riddance.

been but a blot in our Company: besides, the Apostle says, *From such withdraw thy self.*†

Faith. *But I am glad we had this little discourse with him, it may happen that he will think of it again; however, I have dealt plainly with him; and so am clear of his blood, if he perisheth.*†

Chr. You did well to talk so plainly to him as you did; there is but little of this faithful dealing with men now a days, and that makes Religion to stink in the nostrills of many, as it doth: for they are these *Talkative* Fools, whose Religion is only in word, and are debauched and vain in their Conversation, that (being so much admitted into the Fellowship of the Godly) do stumble the World, blemish Christianity, and grieve the Sincere. I wish that all Men would deal with such, as you have done, then should they either be made more conformable to Religion, or the company of Saints would be too hot for them. Then did Faithful say,

> *How* Talkative *at first lifts up his Plumes!*
> *How bravely doth he speak! how he presumes*
> *To drive down all before him! but so soon*
> *As* Faithful *talks of* Heartwork, *like the Moon*
> *That's past the full, into the wain he goes;*
> *And so will all, but he that* Heartwork *knows.*

Thus they went on talking of what they had seen by the way; and so made that way easie, which would otherwise, no doubt, have been tedious to them: for now they went through a Wilderness.

Now when they were got almost quite out of this Wilderness, *Faithful* chanced to cast his eye back, and espied one coming after them, and he knew him. Oh! said *Faithful* to his Brother, who comes yonder? Then *Christian* looked, and said, It is my good friend *Evangelist*. Ai, and my good friend too, said *Faithful*; for 'twas he that set me the way to the Gate. Now was *Evangelist* come up unto them, and thus saluted them.

Evangelist *overtakes them again.*

Evan. Peace be with you, dearly beloved, and, peace be to your helpers.†

They are glad at the sight of him.

Chr. *Welcome, welcome, my good* Evangelist, *the sight of thy countenance brings to my remembrance, thy ancient kindness, and unwearied laboring for my eternal good.*

Faith. *And, a thousand times welcome, said good* Faithful; *Thy company, O sweet* Evangelist, *how desirable is it to us, poor Pilgrims!*

Evan. Then, said *Evangelist*, How hath it fared with you, my friends, since the time of our last parting? *what* have you met with, and *how* have you behaved your selves?

Chr. *Then* Christian, *and* Faithful *told him of all things that had happened to them in the way; and* how, *and with* what *difficulty they had arrived to that place.*

His exhortation to them.

Evang. Right glad am I, said *Evangelist*; not that you met with trials, but that you have been victors; and for that you have (notwithstanding many weaknesses,) continued in the way to this very day.

John 4. 36. Gal. 6. 9. 1 Cor. 9. 24, 25, 26, 27. Rev. 3. 11.

I say, right glad am I of this thing, and that for mine own sake and yours; I have sowed, and you have reaped, and the day is coming, when both he that sowed, and they that reaped shall rejoyce together; that is, if you hold out: for, in due time ye shall reap, if you faint not. The Crown is before you, and it is an incorruptible one; so run that you may obtain it. Some there be that set out for this Crown, and after they have gone far for it, another comes in, and takes it from them; hold fast therefore that you have, let no man take your Crown; you are not yet out of the gun-shot of the Devil: you have not resisted unto blood, striving against sin: let the Kingdom be always before you, and believe stedfastly concerning things that are invisible. Let nothing that is on this side the other world get within you; and above all, look well to your own hearts, and to the lusts thereof; for they are deceitful above all things, and desperately wicked: set your faces like a flint, you have all power in Heaven and Earth on your side.†

** They do thank him for his exhortation.*

Chr. *Then *Christian thanked him for his exhortation, but told him withal, that they would have him speak farther to them for their help, the rest of the way; and the rather, for that they well knew that he was a Prophet, and could tell them of things that might happen unto them; and also how they might resist and overcome them. To which request* Faithful *also consented. So* Evangelist *began as followeth.*

*Evan.** My Sons, you have heard in the words of the truth of the Gospel, that you must through many tribulations enter into the Kingdom of Heaven. And again, that in every City, bonds and afflictions abide in you;† and therefore you cannot expect that you should go long on your Pilgrimage without them, in some sort or other. You have found something of the truth of these testimonies upon you already, and more will immediately follow: for now, as you see, you are almost out of this Wilderness, and therefore you will soon come into a Town that you will by and by see before you: and in that Town you will be hardly beset with enemies, who will strain hard but they will kill you: and be you sure that one or both of you must seal the testimony which you hold, with blood: but be you faithful unto death, and the King will give you a Crown of life.† *He that shall die there, although his death will be unnatural, and his pain perhaps great, he will yet have the better of his fellow; not only because he will be arrived at the Cœlestial City soonest, but because he will escape many miseries that the other will meet with in the rest of his Journey. But when you are come to the Town, and shall find fulfilled what I have here related, then remember your friend and quit your selves like men; and commit the keeping of your souls to your God, as unto a faithful Creator.

* *He predicteth what troubles they shall meet with in* Vanity Fair, *and encourageth them to stedfastness.*

* *He whose lot it will be there to suffer, will have the better of his brother.*

Then I saw in my Dream, that when they were got out of the Wilderness, they presently saw a Town before them, and the name of that Town is *Vanity*; and at the Town there is a *Fair* kept called *Vanity-Fair*:† It is kept all the year long, it beareth the name of *Vanity-Fair*, because the Town where tis kept, *is lighter then* Vanity; and also, because all that is there sold, or that cometh thither, is *Vanity*. As is the saying of the wise, *All that cometh is vanity*.†

Isa. 40. 17. Eccles. 1. ch. 2. 11, 17.

This Fair is no new erected business, but a thing of Ancient standing; I will shew you the original of it.

Almost five thousand years agone, there were Pilgrims† walking to the Cœlestial City, as these two honest persons are; and *Beelzebub*, *Apollyon*, and *Legion*,† with their Companions, perceiving by the path that the Pilgrims made, that their way to the City lay through *this Town* of *Vanity*, they contrived

The Antiquity of this Fair.

here to set up a Fair; a Fair wherein should be sold of *all sorts of Vanity*, and that it should last all the year long. Therefore at *this Fair* are all such Merchandize sold, as Houses, Lands, Trades, Places, Honours, Preferments, Titles, Countreys, Kingdoms, Lusts, Pleasures, and Delights of all sorts, as Whores, Bauds, Wives, Husbands, Children, Masters, Servants, Lives, Blood, Bodies, Souls, Silver, Gold, Pearls, Precious Stones, and what not.

The Merchandise of this Fair.

And moreover, at this Fair there is at all times to be seen Juglings, Cheats, Games, Plays, Fools, Apes, Knaves, and Rogues, and that of all sorts.

Here are to be seen too, and that for nothing, Thefts, Murders, Adultries, False-swearers, and that of a blood-red colour.

And as in other Fairs of less moment, there are the several Rows and Streets under their proper names, where such and such Wares are vended: So here likewise, you have the proper Places, Rows, Streets, (*viz.* Countreys, and Kingdoms) where the Wares of this Fair are soonest to be found: Here is the *Britain* Row, the *French* Row, the *Italian* Row, the *Spanish* Row, the *German* Row, where several sorts of Vanities are to be sold. But as in other *fairs*, some one Commodity is as the chief of all the *fair*, so the Ware of *Rome*† and her Merchandize is greatly promoted in *this fair*: Only our *English* Nation, with some others, have taken a dislike thereat.

The Streets of this fair.

Now, as I said, the way to the Cœlestial City lyes just thorow *this Town*, where this lusty Fair is kept; and he that will go to the City, and yet not go thorow this Town, must needs *go out of the World*. The Prince of Princes himself, when here, went through *this Town* to his own Countrey, and that upon a *Fair-day* too: Yea, and as I think it was *Beelzebub*, the chief Lord of this *Fair*, that invited him to buy of his *Vanities*; yea, would have made him Lord of the *Fair*, would he but have done him Reverence as he went thorow the *Town*. Yea, because he was such a person of Honour, *Beelzebub* had him from *Street* to *Street*, and shewed him all the Kingdoms of the World in a little time, that he might, if possible alure that Blessed One, to *cheapen* and *buy* some of his *Vanities*. But he had no mind to the Merchandize, and therefore left the *Town*; without

1 Cor. 5. 10. *Christ went through this Fair.*

Matth. 4. 8. Luk. 4. 5, 6, 7.

Christ bought nothing in this Fair.

laying out so much as one Farthing upon these *Vanities*. This *Fair* therefore is an Ancient thing, of long standing, and a very great *Fair*.

Now these Pilgrims, as I said, must needs go thorow this *Fair*: Well, so they did; but behold, even as they entered into the *Fair*, all the people in the *Fair* were moved, and the Town it self as it were in a Hubbub about them; and that for several reasons: For,

The Pilgrims enter the Fair.

The Fair in a hubbub about them.

First, The Pilgrims were cloathed with such kind of Raiment, as was diverse from the Raiment of any that traded in that *fair*. The people therefore of the *fair* made a great gazing upon them: Some said they were Fools, some they were Bedlams, and some they are Outlandish-men.

The first cause of the hubbub.

Secondly, And as they wondred at their Apparel, so they did likewise at their Speech; for few could understand what they said; they naturally spoke the Language of *Canaan*; But they that kept the *fair*, were the men of this World: So that from one end of the *fair* to the other, they seemed *Barbarians*† each to the other.

1 Cor. 2. 7, 8. *The second cause of the hubbub.*

Thirdly, But that which did not a little amuse the Merchandizers, was, that these Pilgrims set very light by all their Wares, they cared not so much as to look upon them: and if they called upon them to buy, they would put their fingers in their ears, and cry, *Turn away mine eyes from beholding vanity*; and look upwards, signifying that their Trade and Traffick was in Heaven.

Third cause of the hubbub.

Psal. 119. 37. Phil. 3. 19, 20.

One chanced mockingly, beholding the carriages of the men, to say unto them, What will ye buy? but they, looking gravely upon him, said, *We buy the Truth*. At that, there was an occasion taken to despise the men the more; some mocking, some taunting, some speaking reproachfully, and some calling upon others to smite them. At last things came to an hubbub, and great stir in the *fair*; insomuch that all order was confounded. Now was word presently brought to the *great one* of the *fair*, who quickly came down, and deputed some of his most trusty friends to take these men into examination, about whom the *fair* was almost overturned. So the men were brought to examination; and they that sat upon them, asked them whence they came, whither they went, and what they did

Fourth cause of the hubbub.

Prov. 23. 23.

They are mocked.

The fair in a hubbub.

They are examined.

** They tell who they are and whence they came.* Heb. 11. 13, 14, 15, 16.

there in such an unusual Garb? *The men told them, that they were Pilgrims and Strangers in the world, and that they were going to their own Countrey, which was the Heavenly *Jerusalem*; and that they had given none occasion to the men of the Town, nor yet to the Merchandizers, thus to abuse them, and to let them in their Journey. Except it was, for that, when one asked them what they would buy, they said, they would *buy the Truth*.

They are not believed.

But they that were appointed to examine them, did not believe them to be any other then Bedlams and Mad, or else such as came to put all things into a confusion in the *fair*. Therefore they took them, and beat them, and besmeared them with dirt, and then put them into the Cage, that they might be made a Spectacle to all the men of the *fair*.

They are put in the Cage.

There therefore they lay for some time, and were made the objects of any mans sport, or malice, or revenge, the great one of the *fair* laughing still at all that befel them.

Their behaviour in the Cage.

But the men being patient, and not rendering railing for railing, but contrarywise blessing,† and giving good words for bad, and kindness for injuries done: Some men in the *fair* that were more observing, and less prejudiced then the rest, began to check and blame the baser sort for their continual abuses done by them to the men:

The men of the Fair do fall out among themselves about these two men.

They therefore in angry manner let fly at them again, counting them as bad as the men in the Cage, and telling them that they seemed confederates, and should be made partakers of their misfortunes. The other replied, That for ought they could see, the men were quiet, and sober, and intended no body any harm; and that there were many that Traded in their *fair*, that were more worthy to be put into the Cage, yea, and Pillory too, then were the men that they had abused. Thus, after divers words had passed on both sides, (the men behaving themselves all the while very wisely, and soberly before them) they fell to some Blows, among themselves, and did harm one to another.

They are made the Authors of this disturbance.

Then were these two poor men brought before their Examiners again, and there charged as being guilty of the late Hubbub that had been in the *fair*.

They are led up and down the fair in Chaines, for a terror to others.

So they beat them pitifully, and hanged Irons upon them, and led them in Chaines up and down the *fair*, for an example and a terror to others, lest any should further speak in their behalf, or joyn themselves unto them. But *Christian and*

Behold *VANITY-FAIR*; the Pilgrims there
Are Chain'd and Ston'd beside;
Even so it was, our Lord past here,
And on Mount *Calvary* dy'd.

Faithful behaved themselves yet more wisely, and received the ignominy and shame that was cast upon them, with so much meekness and patience, that it won to their side (though but few in comparison of the rest) several of the men in the *fair*. This put the other party yet into a greater rage, insomuch that they concluded the death of these two men. Wherefore they threatned that the Cage, nor Irons, should serve their turn, but that they should die, for the abuse they had done, and for deluding the men of the *fair*.

Some of the men of the fair won to them.

Their adversaries resolve to kill them.

Then were they remanded to the Cage again, until further order should be taken with them. So they put them in, and made their feet fast in the Stocks.

They are again put into the Cage and after brought to Tryal.

Here also they called again to mind what they had heard from their faithful friend *Evangelist*, and was the more confirmed in their way and sufferings, by what he told them would happen to them. They also now comforted each other, that whose lot it was to suffer, even he should have the best on't; therefore each man secretly wished that he might have that preferment: but committing themselves to the All-wise dispose of him that ruleth all things, with much content they abode in the condition in which they were, until they should be otherwise disposed of.

Then a convenient time being appointed, they brought them forth to their Tryal in order to their Condemnation. When the time was come, they were brought before their Enemies and arraigned; the Judges name was Lord *Hate-good*. Their Indictment† was one and the same in substance, though somewhat varying in form; the Contents whereof was this.

That they were enemies to, and disturbers of their Trade; that they had made Commotions and Divisions in the Town, and had won a party to their own most dangerous Opinions, in contempt of the Law of their Prince.†

Their Indictment.

Then *Faithful* began to answer, That he had only set himself against that which had set it self against him that is higher then the highest.† And, said he, As for disturbance, I make none, being my self a man of Peace; the Party that were won to us, were won, by beholding our Truth and Innocence, and they are only turned from the worse to the better. And as

Faithfuls *answer for himself.*

to the King you talk of; since he is *Beelzebub*, the Enemy of our Lord, I defie him and all his Angels.

Then Proclamation was made, that they that had ought to say for their Lord the King against the Prisoner at the Bar, should forthwith appear, and give in their evidence. So there came in three Witnesses, to wit, *Envy, Superstition, and Pickthank.*† They was then asked, If they knew the Prisoner at the Bar? and what they had to say for their Lord the King against him.

Then stood forth **Envy*, and said to this effect; My Lord, I have known this man a long time, and will attest upon my Oath before this honourable Bench, That he is—

* Envy *begins.*

Judge. Hold, give him his Oath: So they sware him. Then he said, My Lord, this man, notwithstanding his plausible name, is one of the vilest men in our Countrey; He neither regardeth Prince nor People, Law nor Custom; but doth all that he can to possess all men with certain of his disloyal notions, which he in the general calls Principles of Faith and Holiness. And in particular, I heard him once my self affirm, *That Christianity, and the Customs of our Town of* Vanity, *were Diametrically opposite, and could not be reconciled.* By which saying, my Lord, he doth at once, not only condemn all our laudable doings, but us in the doing of them.

Judg. Then did the Judge say to him, Hast thou any more to say?

Envy. My Lord, I could say much more, only I would not be tedious to the Court. Yet if need be, when the other Gentlemen have given in their Evidence, rather then any thing shall be wanting that will dispatch him, I will enlarge my Testimony against him. So he was bid stand by. Then they called *Superstition*, and bid him look upon the Prisoner; they also asked, What he could say for their Lord the King against him? Then they sware him, so he began.

*Super;** My Lord, I have no great acquaintance with this man, nor do I desire to have further knowledge of him; However this I know, that he is a very pestilent fellow,† from some discourse that the other day I had with him in this *Town*; for then talking with him, I heard him say, That our Religion was naught, and such by which a man could by no means please

* Superstition *follows.*

God: which sayings of his, my Lord, your Lordship very well knows, what necessarily thence will follow, *to wit*, That we still do worship in vain, are yet in our Sins, and finally shall be damned; and this is that which I have to say.

Then was *Pickthank* sworn, and bid say what he knew, in behalf of their Lord the King against the Prisoner at the Bar.

Pickthanks *Testimony.*

Pick. My Lord, and you Gentlemen all, This fellow I have known of a long time, and have heard him speak things that ought not to be spoke. For he hath railed on our noble Prince *Beelzebub*, and hath spoke contemptibly of his honourable Friends, whose names are the Lord *Old man*, the Lord *Carnal delight*, the Lord *Luxurious*, the Lord *Desire of Vain-glory*, my old Lord *Lechery*, Sir *Having Greedy*, with all the rest of our Nobility; and he hath said moreover, that if all men were of his mind, if possible, there is not one of these Noblemen should have any longer a being in this Town. Besides, he hath not been afraid to rail on you, my Lord, who are now appointed to be his Judge, calling you an ungodly villain, with many other such like vilifying terms, with which he hath bespattered most of the Gentry of our Town. When this *Pickthank* had told his tale, the Judge directed his speech to the Prisoner at the Bar, saying, Thou Runagate, Heretick, and Traitor,† hast thou heard what these honest Gentlemen have witnessed against thee.

Sins are all Lords and Great ones.

Faith. *May I speak a few words in my own defence?*

Judg. Sirrah, Sirrah, thou deservest to live no longer, but to be slain immediately upon the place; yet that all men may see our gentleness towards thee, let us hear what thou hast to say.

Faithfuls *defence of himself.*

Faith. 1. I say then in answer to what Mr. *Envy* hath spoken, I never said ought but this, *That what Rule, or Laws, or Custom, or People, were flat against the Word of God, are diametrically opposite to Christianity.* If I have said a miss in this, convince me of my errour, and I am ready here before you to make my recantation.

2. As to the second, to wit, Mr. *Superstition*, and his charge against me, I said only this, *That in the worship of God there is required a divine Faith; but there can be no divine Faith, without a divine Revelation of the will of God: therefore whatever is thrust into the worship of God, that is not agreeable to divine Revelation,*

Now *Faithful* play the man, speak for thy God,
Fear not the wicked's malice, nor their rod;
Speak boldly man, the truth is on thy side,
Die for it, and to life in triumph ride.

cannot be done but by an humane Faith, which Faith will not profit to Eternal Life.

3. As to what Mr. *Pickthank* hath said, I say, (avoiding terms, as that I am said to rail, and the like) That the Prince of this Town, with all the Rablement his Attendants, by this Gentleman named, are more fit for a being in Hell, then in this Town and Countrey; *and so the Lord have mercy upon me.*

The Judge his speech to the Jury.

Then the Judge called to the Jury (who all this while stood by, to hear and observe;) Gentlemen of the Jury, you see this man about whom so great an uproar hath been made in this Town: you have also heard what these worthy Gentlemen have witnessed against him; also you have heard his reply and confession: It lieth now in your breasts to hang him, or save his life. But yet I think meet to instruct you into our Law.

Exod. 1. There was an Act made in the days of *Pharaoh* the Great, Servant to our Prince, That lest those of a contrary Religion should multiply and grow too strong for him, their Males
Dan. 3. should be thrown into the River. There was also an Act made in the days of *Nebuchadnezzar* the Great, another of his Servants, That whoever would not fall down and worship his golden Image, should be thrown into a fiery Furnace. There
Dan. 6. was also an Act made in the days of *Darius*, That who so, for some time, called upon any God but his, should be cast into the Lions Den. Now the substance of these Laws this Rebel has broken, not only in thought, (which is not to be born) but also in word and deed; which must therefore needs be intolerable.

For that of *Pharaoh*, his Law was made upon a supposition, to prevent mischief, no Crime being yet apparent; but here is a Crime apparent. For the second and third, you see he disputeth against our Religion; and for the Treason he hath confessed, he deserveth to die the death.

** The Jury and their names.*

Then went the Jury out, *whose names were Mr. *Blind-man*, Mr. *No-good*, Mr. *Malice*, Mr. *Love-lust*, Mr. *Live-loose*, Mr. *Heady*, Mr. *High-mind*, Mr. *Enmity*, Mr. *Lyar*, Mr. *Cruelty*, Mr. *Hate-light*, and Mr. *Implacable*, who every one gave in his private Verdict against him among themselves, and afterwards unanimously concluded to bring him in guilty

Every ones private verdict.

before the Judge. And first Mr. *Blind-man*, the foreman, said, *I see clearly that this man is an Heretick*. Then said Mr.

No-good, Away with such a fellow from the Earth. Ay, said Mr. *Malice, for I hate the very looks of him*. Then said Mr. *Love-lust, I could never indure him. Nor I*, said Mr. *Live-loose, for he would alwayes be condemning my way. Hang him, hang him*, said Mr. *Heady. A sorry Scrub*, said Mr. *High-mind. My heart riseth against him*, said Mr. *Enmity. He is a Rogue*, said Mr. *Lyar. Hanging is too good for him*, said Mr. *Cruelty. Lets dispatch him out of the way*, said Mr. *Hate-light*. Then said Mr. *Implacable, Might I have all the World given me, I could not be reconciled to him, therefore let us forthwith bring him in guilty of death*:* And so they did, therefore he was presently Condemned, To be had from the place where he was, to the place from whence he came, and there to be put to the most cruel death that could be invented.

* *They conclude to bring him in guilty of death.*

They therefore brought him out, to do with him according to their Law; and first they Scourged him, then they Buffetted him, then they Lanced his flesh with Knives; after that they Stoned him with Stones, then prickt him with their Swords, and last of all they burned him to Ashes at the Stake.† Thus came *Faithful* to his end. *Now, I saw that there stood behind the multitude, a Chariot and a couple of Horses,† waiting for *Faithful*, who (so soon as his adversaries had dispatched him) was taken up into it, and straightway was carried up through the Clouds, with sound of Trumpet, the nearest way to the Cœlestial Gate. But as for *Christian*, he had some respit, and was remanded back to prison; so he there remained for a space: But he that over-rules all things, having the power of their rage in his own hand, so wrought it about, that *Christian* for that time escaped them, and went his way.

The Cruel death of Faithful.

* *A Chariot and Horses wait to take away* Faithful.

Christian *is still alive.*

And as he went he Sang.

* *Well* Faithful, *thou hast faithfully profest*
Unto thy Lord: with him thou shalt be blest;
When Faithless *ones, with all their vain delights,*
Are crying out under their hellish plights.
Sing, Faithful, *sing; and let thy name survive;*
For though they kill'd thee, thou art yet alive.

* *The Song that* Christian *made of* Faithful *after his death.*

Now I saw in my Dream, that *Christian* went not forth alone, for there was one whose name was *Hopeful*, (being made so by the beholding of *Christian* and *Faithful* in their

Christian *has another Companion.*

Brave *Faithful*, Bravely done in Word and Deed!
Judge, Witnesses, and Jury, have instead
Of overcoming thee, but shewn their Rage,
When thou art dead, thoul't live from Age to Age.

words and behaviour, in their sufferings at the *fair*) who joyned himself unto him, and entring into a brotherly covenant, told him that he would be his Companion. Thus one died to make Testimony to the Truth, and another rises out of his Ashes to be a Companion with *Christian*. This *Hopeful* also told *Christian*, that there were many more of the men in the *fair* that would take their time and follow after.

There is more of the men of the fair *will follow.*

So I saw that quickly after they were got out of the *fair*, they overtook one that was going before them, whose name was *By-ends*;† so they said to him, What Countrey-man, Sir? and how far go you this way? He told them, That he came from the Town of *Fair-speech*, and he was going to the Cœlestial City, (but told them not his name.)

They overtake By-ends.

From *Fair-speech, *said* Christian; *is there any that be good live there?*

* Prov. 26. 25.

By-ends. Yes, said *By-ends*, I hope.

Chr. *Pray Sir, what may I call you?* said *Christian*.

By-ends. I am a Stranger to you, and you to me; if you be going this way, I shall be glad of your Company; if not, I must be content.

By-ends *loth to tell his name.*

Chr. *This Town of* Fair-speech *said* Christian, *I have heard of it, and, as I remember, they say its a Wealthy place.*

By-ends. Yes, I will assure you that it is, and I have very many Rich Kindred there.

Chr. *Pray who are your Kindred there, if a man may be so bold?*

By-ends. Almost the whole Town; and in particular, my Lord *Turn-about*, my Lord *Time-server*, my Lord *Fair-speech*, (from whose Ancestors that Town first took its name:) Also Mr. *Smooth-man*, Mr. *Facing-bothways*, Mr. *Any-thing*, and the Parson of our Parish, Mr. *Two-tongues*, was my Mothers own Brother by Father's side: And to tell you the Truth, I am become a Gentleman of good Quality; yet my Great Grand-father was but a Water-man, looking one way, and Rowing another:† and I got most of my estate by the same occupation.

Chr. *Are you a Married man?*

By-ends. Yes, and my Wife is a very Virtuous woman, the Daughter of a Virtuous woman: She was my Lady *Fainings* Daughter, therefore she came of a very Honourable Family,

The wife and Kindred of By-ends.

and is arrived to such a pitch of Breeding, that she knows how to carry it to all, even to Prince and Peasant. 'Tis true, we somewhat differ in Religion from those of the stricter sort, yet but in two small points: First, we never strive against Wind and Tide. Secondly, we are alwayes most zealous when Religion goes in his Silver Slippers; we love much to walk with him in the Street, if the Sun shines,† and the people applaud it.

Where By-ends *differs from others in Religion.*

Then *Christian* stept a little a toside to his fellow *Hopeful*, saying, It runs in my mind that this is one *By-ends*, of *Fair-speech*, and if it be he, we have as very a Knave in our company, as dwelleth in all these parts. Then said *Hopeful, Ask him; methinks he should not be ashamed of his name*. So *Christian* came up with him again; and said, Sir, you talk as if you knew something more then all the world doth, and if I take not my mark amiss, I deem I have half a guess of you: Is not your name Mr. *By-ends* of *Fair-speech?*

By-ends. That is not my name, but indeed it is a Nick-name that is given me by some that cannot abide me, and I must be content to bear it as a reproach, as other good men have born theirs before me.

How By-ends *got his name.*

Chr. *But did you never give an occasion to men to call you by this name?*

By-ends. Never, never! The worst that ever I did to give them an occasion to give me this name, was, that I had always the luck to jump in my Judgement with the present way of the times, whatever it was, and my chance was to get thereby; but if things are thus cast upon me, let me count them a blessing, but let not the malicious load me therefore with reproach.

Chr. *I thought indeed that you was the man that I had heard of, and to tell you what I think, I fear this name belongs to you more properly then you are willing we should think it doth.*

He desires to keep Company with Christian.

By-ends. Well, if you will thus imagine, I cannot help it. You shall find me a fair Company-keeper, if you will still admit me your associate.

Chr. *If you will go with us, you must go against Wind and Tide, the which, I perceive, is against your opinion: You must also own Religion in his Rags, as well as when in his Silver Slippers, and stand by him too, when bound in Irons, as well as when he walketh the Streets with applause.*

By-ends. You must not impose, nor Lord it over my Faith; leave me to my liberty, and let me go with you.

Chr. *Not a step further, unless you will do in what I propound, as we.*

Then said *By-ends*, I shall never desert my old Principles, since they are harmless and profitable. If I may not go with you, I must do as I did before you overtook me, even go by my self, until some overtake me that will be glad of my company.

Now I saw in my dream, that *Christian* and *Hopeful*, forsook him, and kept their distance before him, but one of them looking back, saw three men following Mr. *By-ends*, and behold, as they came up with him, he made them a very low *Conje*, and they also gave him a *Complement*. The mens names were Mr. *Hold-the-World*, Mr. *Mony-love*, and Mr. *Save-all*;† men that Mr. *By-ends*, had formerly bin acquainted with; for in their minority they were Schoolfellows, and were taught by one Mr. *Gripe-man*,† a Schoolmaster in *Love-gain*, which is a market town in the County of *Coveting* in the North. This Schoolmaster taught them the art of getting, either by violence, cousenage, flattery, lying or by putting on a guise of Religion, and these four Gentlemen had attained much of the art of their Master, so that they could each of them have kept such a School themselves.

Well when they had, as I said, thus saluted each other, Mr. *Mony-love* said to Mr. *By-ends*, Who are they upon the Road before us? for *Christian* and *Hopeful* were yet within view.

By-ends. They are a couple of far countrey-men, that after *their mode*, are going on Pilgrimage.

Mony-love. Alas, why did they not stay that we might have had their good company, for *they*, and *we*, and *you* Sir, I hope, are all going on Pilgrimage.

By-ends. We are so indeed, but the men before us, are so ridged, and love so much their own notions, and do also so lightly esteem the opinions of others; that let a man be never so godly, yet if he jumps not with them in all things, they thrust him quite out of their company.

Mr. *Save-all.* That's bad; But we read of some, *that are righteous over-much*,† and such mens ridgedness prevails with them to judge and condemn all but themselves. But I pray what and how many, were the things wherein you differed?

By-ends. Why they after their head-strong manner, conclude that it is duty to rush on their Journy *all* weathers, and I am for waiting for *Wind* and *Tide.* They are for hazzarding all for God,† at a clap, and I am for taking *all* advantages to secure my life and estate. They are for holding *their notions*, though all other men are against them, but I am for Religion in what, and so far as the times, and my safety will bear it. They are for Religion, when in rags, and contempt, but I am for him when he walks in his golden slipers in the Sunshine, and with applause.

Mr. *Hold-the-world.* Ai, and hold you there still, good Mr. *By-ends*, for, for my part, I can count him but a fool, that having the liberty to keep what he has, shall be so unwise as to lose it. Let us be wise *as Serpents*,† 'tis best to make hay when the Sun shines;† you see how the Bee lieth still all winter and bestirs her then only when she can have profit with pleasure. God sends sometimes Rain, and sometimes Sunshine;† if they be such fools to go through the first, yet let us be content to take fair weather along with us. For my part I like that Religion best, that will stand with the security of Gods good blessings unto us; for who can imagin that is ruled by his reason, since God has bestowed upon us the good things of this life, but that he would have us keep them for his sake. *Abraham* and *Solomon* grew rich in Religion. And *Job* saies, that a good man *shall lay up gold as dust.*† He must not be such as the men before us, if they be as you have discribed them.

Mr. *Save-all.* I think that we are all agreed in this matter, and therefore there needs no more words about it.

Mr. *Mony-love.* No, there needs no more words about this matter indeed, for he that believes neither Scripture nor reason (and you see we have both on our side) neither knows his own liberty, nor seeks his own safety.

Mr. *By-ends.* My Brethren, we are, as you see, going all on Pilgrimage, and for our better diversion from things that are bad, give me leave to propound unto you this question.

Suppose a man; a Minister, or a Tradesman, &c. *should have an advantage lie before him to get the good blessings of this life. Yet so, as that he can by no means come by them, except, in appearance at least, he becomes extraordinary Zealous in some points of Religion, that he medled not with before, may he not use this means to attain his end, and yet be a right honest man?*

Mr. *Mony-love*, I see the bottom of your question, and with these Gentlemens good leave, I will endeavour to shape you an answer. And first to speak to your question, as it concerns a *Minister* himself. *Suppose a Minister, a worthy man, possessed but of a very small benefice, and has in his eye a greater, more fat, and plump by far; he has also now an opportunity of getting of it; yet so as by being more studious, by preaching more frequently, and zealously, and because the temper of the people requires it, by altering of some of his principles, for my part I see no reason but a man may do this (provided he has a call.) Ai, and more a great deal besides, and yet be an honest man.* For why,

1. His desire of a greater benefice is lawful (this cannot be contradicted) since 'tis set before him by providence; so then, he may get it if he can, *making no question for conscience sake.*†

2. Besides, his desire after that benefice, makes him more studious, a more zealous preacher, *&c.* and so makes him a better man. Yea, makes him better improve his parts, which is according to the mind of God.

3. Now as for his complying with the temper of his people, by disserting, to serve them, some of his principles, this argueth, 1. That he is of a self-denying temper. 2. Of a sweet and winning deportment. 3. And so more fit for the Ministerial function.

4. I conclude then, that a Minister that changes a *small* for a *great*, should not for so doing, be judged as covetous, but rather, since he is improved in his parts and industry thereby, be counted as one that pursues his call, and the opportunity put into his hand to do good.

And now to the second part of the question which concerns the *Tradesman* you mentioned: suppose such an one to have but a poor imploy in the world, but by becoming Religious, he may mend his market, perhaps get a rich wife, or more and far better customers to his shop. For my part I see no reason but that this may be lawfully done. For why,

1. To become religious is a vertue, by what means soever a man becomes so.

2. Nor is it unlawful to get a rich wife, or more custome to my shop.

3. Besides the man that gets these by becoming religious, gets that which is good, of them that are good, by becoming good himself; so then here is a good wife, and good customers, and good gaine, and all these by becoming religious, which is good. Therefore to become religious to get all these is a good and profitable design.

This answer, thus made by this Mr. *Mony-love*, to Mr. *By-ends'* question, was highly applauded by them all; wherefore they concluded upon the whole, that it was most wholsome and advantagious. And because, as they thought, no man was able to contradict it, and because *Christian* and *Hopeful* was yet within call; they joyfully agreed to assault them with the question as soon as they overtook them, and the rather because they had opposed Mr. *By-ends* before. So they called after them, and they stopt, and stood still till they came up to them, but they concluded as they went, that not *By-ends*, but old Mr. *Hold-the-world* should propound the question to them, because, as they supposed, their answer to him would be without the remainder of that heat that was kindled betwixt Mr. *By-ends* and them, at their parting a little before.

So they came up to each other and after a short salutation, Mr. *Hold-the-world* propounded the question to *Christian* and his fellow, and bid them to answer it if they could.

Chr. Then said *Christian*, Even a babe in Religion may answer ten thousand such questions. For if it be unlawful to follow Christ for loaves, as it is, *Joh.* 6.† How much more abominable is it to make of him and religion a stalking horse† to get and enjoy the world. Nor do we find any other than Heathens, Hypocrites, Devils and Witches that are of this opinion.

1. *Heathens*, for when *Hamor* and *Shechem* had a mind to the Daughter and Cattle of *Jacob*, and saw that there was no waies for them to come at them, but by becoming circumcised, they say to their companions; If every male of us be circumcised, as they are circumcised, shall not their Cattle, and their substance, and every beast of theirs be ours? Their Daughters and

their Cattle were that which they sought to obtain, and their Religion the stalking horse they made use of to come at them. Read the whole story, *Gen.* 34. 20, 21, 22, 23.

2. The Hypocritical Pharisees were also of this Religion, long prayers were their pretence, but to get widdows houses were their intent, and greater damnation was from God their Judgment, *Luke* 20. 46, 47.

3. *Judas* the Devil was also of this Religion, he was religious for the bag, that he might be possessed of what was therein, but he was lost, cast away, and the very Son of perdition.†

4. *Simon* the witch was of this Religion too, for he would have had the Holy Ghost, that he might have got money therewith, and his sentence from *Peters* mouth was according, *Act.* 8. 19, 20, 21, 22.

5. Neither will it out of my mind, but that that man that takes up Religion for the world, will throw away Religion for the world; for so surely as *Judas* designed the world in becoming religious: so surely did he also sell Religion, and his Master for the same. To answer the question therefore affirmatively, as I perceive you have done, and to accept of as authentick such answer, is both Heathenish, Hypocritical and Devilish, and your reward will be according to your works.† Then they stood stareing one upon another, but had not wherewith to answer *Christian*. *Hopeful* also approved of the soundness of *Christians* answer, so there was a great silence among them. Mr. *By-ends* and his company also staggered, and kept behind, that *Christian* and *Hopeful* might outgo them. Then said *Christian* to his fellow, if these men cannot stand before the sentence of men, what will they do with the sentence of God? & if they are mute when dealt with by vessels of clay, what will they do when they shall be rebuked by the flames of a devouring fire?†

Then *Christian* and *Hopeful* outwent them again, and went till they came at a delicate Plain, called *Ease*, where they went with much content; but that Plain was but *narrow*, so they were quickly got over it. Now at the further side of that Plain, was a little Hill called *Lucre*,† and in that *Hill* a *Silver-Mine*, which some of them that had formerly gone that way, because of the rarity of it, had turned aside to see; but going too near the brink of the pit, the ground being deceitful under

The ease that Pilgrims have is but little in this life.

Lucre *Hill a dangerous Hill.*

them, broke, and they were slain; some also had been maimed there, and could not to their dying day be their own men again.

* Demas *at the Hill* Lucre.

* *He calls to* Christian *and* Hopeful *to come to him.*

Then I saw in my Dream, that a little off the Road, over against the *Silver-Mine*, stood **Demas*,† (*Gentleman*-like) to call to Passengers to come and see: who said to *Christian* and his fellow; *Ho, turn aside hither, and I will shew you a thing.

Chr. *What thing so deserving as to turn us out of the way?*

Dem. Here is a Silver-*Mine*, and some digging in it for Treasure; if you will come, with a little paines you may richly provide for your selves.

Hopeful *tempted to go, but* Christian *holds him back.*

Hopef. Then said Hopeful, *Let us go see*.

Chr. Not I, said *Christian*; I have heard of this place before now, and how many have there been slain; and besides, that Treasure is a snare to those that seek it, for it hindreth them in their Pilgrimage. Then *Christian* called to *Demas*, saying, *Is not the place dangerous? hath it not hindred many in their Pilgrimage?*

Hos. 4. 18.

Dem. Not very dangerous, except to those that are careless: but withal, he *blushed* as he spake.

Chr. Then said *Christian* to *Hopeful*, Let us not stir a step, but still keep on our way.

Hope. *I will warrant you, when* By-ends *comes up, if he hath the same invitation as we, he will turn in thither to see.*

Chr. No doubt thereof, for his principles lead him that way, and a hundred to one but he dies there.

Dem. Then *Demas* called again, saying, But will you not come over and see?

Christian *roundeth up* Demas.

2 Tim. 4. 10.

Chr. Then *Christian* roundly answered, saying, *Demas*, Thou art an Enemy to the right ways of the Lord of this way, and hast been already condemned for thine own turning aside, by one of his Majesties Judges;† and why seekest thou to bring us into the like condemnation? Besides, if we at all turn aside, our Lord the King will certainly hear thereof; and will there put us to shame, where we would stand with boldness before him.

Demas cried again, That he also was one of their fraternity; and that if they would tarry a little, he also himself would walk with them.

Chr. Then said *Christian*, What is thy name? is it not the same by the which I have called thee?

De. Yes, my name is *Demas*, I am the Son of *Abraham*.

Chr. I know you, *Gehazi* was your Great Grandfather, and *Judas* your Father, and you have trod their steps. It is but a devilish prank that thou usest: Thy Father was hanged for a Traitor, and thou deservest no better reward. Assure thy self, that when we come to the King, we will do him word of this thy behaviour. Thus they went their way.

2 Kings 5. 20. Mat. 26. 14, 15. chap. 27. 1, 2, 3, 4, 5, 6.

By this time *By-ends* and his companions was come again within sight, and they at the first beck went over to *Demas*. Now whether they fell into the Pit, by looking over the brink thereof, or whether they went down to dig, or whether they was smothered in the bottom, by the damps that commonly arise, of these things I am not certain: But this I observed, that they never was seen again in the way.

By-ends *goes over to* Demas.

Then Sang Christian,

> By-ends, *and Silver-*Demas, *both agree;*
> *One calls, the other runs, that he may be*
> *A sharer in his Lucre: so these two*
> *Take up in this World, and no further go.*

Now I saw, that just on the other side of this Plain, the Pilgrims came to a place where stood an old *Monument*, hard by the High-way-side, at the sight of which they were both concerned, because of the strangeness of the form therof; for it seemed to them as if it had been a *Woman* transformed into the shape of a Pillar: here therefore they stood looking, and looking upon it, but could not for a time tell what they should make thereof. At last *Hopeful* espied written above upon the head thereof, a Writing in an unusual hand; but he being no Scholar, called to *Christian* (for he was learned) to see if he could pick out the meaning: so he came, and after a little laying of Letters together, he found the same to be this, *Remember Lot's Wife*. So he read it to his fellow; after which, they both concluded, that that was the *Pillar of Salt into which *Lot's Wife* was turned for her looking back with a *covetous heart*, when she was going from *Sodom* for safety. Which sudden and amazing sight, gave them occasion of this discourse.

They see a strange monument.

* Gen. 19. 26.

Chr. Ah my Brother, this is a seasonable sight; it came opportunely to us after the invitation which *Demas* gave us to come over to view the Hill *Lucre*: and had we gone over as he desired us, and as thou wast inclining to do (my Brother) we had, for ought I know, been made our selves a spectacle for those that shall come after to behold.

Hope. I am sorry that I was so foolish, and am made to wonder that I am not now as *Lot's* Wife; for wherein was the difference 'twixt her sin and mine? she only looked back, and I had a desire to go see; let Grace be adored, and let me be ashamed, that ever such a thing should be in mine heart.

Chr. Let us take notice of what we see here, for our help for time to come: *This* woman escaped one Judgment; for she fell not by the destruction of *Sodom*, yet she was destroyed by another; as we see, she is turned into a Pillar of Salt.

Hope. True, and she may be to us both *Caution*, and *Example; Caution* that we should shun her sin, or a sign of what judgment will overtake such as shall not be prevented by this caution: So *Korah, Dathan*, and *Abiram*, with the two hundred and fifty men, that perished in their sin, did also become *a sign, or example to others to beware: but above all, I muse at one thing, to wit, how *Demas* and his fellows can stand so confidently yonder to look for that treasure, which this Woman, but for looking behind her, after (for we read not that she stept one foot out of the way) was turned into a pillar of Salt; specially since the Judgment which overtook her, did make her an example, within sight of where they are: for they cannot chuse but see her, did they but lift up their eyes.

* Numb. 26. 9, 10.

Chr. It is a thing to be wondered at, and it argueth that their heart is grown desperate in the case; and I cannot tell who to compare them to so fitly, as to them that pick Pockets in the presence of the Judge, or that will cut purses under the Gallows. It is said of the men of *Sodom, That they were sinners* exceedingly*, because they were sinners *before the Lord*; that is, in his eye-sight; and notwithstanding the kindnesses that he had shewed them, for the Land of *Sodom*, was now, like the *Garden of *Eden heretofore*. This therefore provoked him the more to jealousie, and made their plague as hot as the fire of the Lord out of Heaven could make it. And it is most rationally

* Gen. 13. 13.

* Vers. 10.

to be concluded, that such, even such as these are, that shall sin in the sight, yea, and that too in despite of such examples that are set continually before them, to caution them to the contrary, must be partakers of severest Judgments.

Hope. Doubtless thou hast said the truth, but what a mercy is it, that neither thou, but especially I, am not made, my self, this example: this ministreth occasion to us to thank God, to fear before him, and always to remember *Lot*'s Wife.

A River.

Psal. 65. 9. Rev. 22. Ezek. 47.

I saw then that they went on their way to a pleasant River, which *David the King* called the *River of God*; but, *John, The River of the water of life*. Now their way lay just upon the bank of the River: here therefore *Christian* and his Companion walked with great delight; they drank also of the water of the River, which was pleasant and enlivening to their weary Spirits: besides, on the banks of this River, on either side, were *green Trees*, that bore all manner of Fruit; and the leaves of the Trees were good for Medicine; with the Fruit of these Trees they were also much delighted; and the leaves they eat to prevent Surfeits, and other Diseases that are incident to those that heat their blood by Travels. On either side of the River was also a Meadow, curiously beautified with Lilies; And it was green all the year long. In this Meadow they lay down and slept, for here they might *lie down safely*. When they awoke, they gathered again of the Fruit of the Trees, and drank again of the Water of the River: and then lay down again to sleep. Thus they did several days and nights. Then they sang,

Trees by the River.

The Fruit and leaves of the trees.

A Meadow in which they lie down to sleep.

Psal. 23. 2. Isa. 14. 30.

Behold ye how these Christal streams do glide
(To comfort Pilgrims) by the High-way side;
The Meadows green, besides their fragrant smell,
Yield dainties for them: And he that can tell
What pleasant Fruit, yea Leaves, these Trees do yield,
Will soon sell all, that he may buy this Field.

So when they were disposed to go on (for they were not, as yet, at their Journeys end) they eat and drank, and departed.

Now I beheld in my Dream, that they had not journied far, but the River and the way, for a time, parted. At which they were not a little sorry, yet they durst not go out of the way.

Numb. 21. 4.

By-Path-Meadow.

One temptation does make way for another.

Strong Christians may lead weak ones out of the way.

Now the way from the River was rough, and their feet tender by reason of their Travels; *So the soul of the Pilgrims was much discouraged, because of the way.* Wherefore still as they went on, they wished for better way. Now a little before them, there was on the left hand of the Road, a *Meadow*, and a Stile to go over into it, and that *Meadow* is called *By-Path-Meadow*. Then said *Christian* to his fellow. If this Meadow lieth along by our way side, lets go over into it. Then he went to the Stile to see, and behold a Path lay along by the way on the other side of the fence. 'Tis according to my wish, said *Christian*, here is the easiest going; come good *Hopeful*, and let us go over.

Hope. *But how if this Path should lead us out of the way?*

Chr. That's not like, said the other; look, doth it not go along by the way side? So *Hopeful*, being perswaded by his fellow, went after him over the Stile. When they were gone over, and were got into the Path, they found it very easie for their feet; and withal, they looking before them, espied a Man walking as they did, (and his name was *Vain-confidence*) so they called after him, and asked him whither that way led? he said, To the Cœlestial Gate. *Look, said *Christian*, did not I tell you so? by this you may see we are right: so they followed, and he went before them. But behold the night came on, and it grew very dark; so that they that were behind, lost the sight of him that went before.

** See what it is too suddenly to fall in with strangers.*

Isa. 9. 16.

A Pit to catch the vain-glorious in.

He therefore that went before (*Vain-confidence* by name) not seeing the way before him, fell into a deep Pit, which was on purpose there made by the Prince of those grounds, to catch *vain-glorious* fools withall; and was dashed in pieces with his fall.

Reasoning between Christian *and* Hopeful.

Now *Christian* and his fellow heard him fall. So they called, to know the matter, but there was none to answer, only they heard a groaning. Then said *Hopeful*, Where are we now? Then was his fellow silent, as mistrusting that he had led him out of the way. And now it began to rain, and thunder, and lighten in a very dreadful manner, and the water rose amain.

Then *Hopeful* groaned in himself, saying, *Oh that I had kept on my way!*

Chr. Who could have thought that this path should have led us out of the way?

Hope. *I was afraid on't at very first, and therefore gave you that gentle caution. I would have spoke plainer, but that you are older then I.*

Chr. Good Brother be not offended, I am sorry I have brought thee out of the way, and that I have put thee into such eminent danger; pray my Brother forgive me, I did not do it of an evil intent.

Christians *repentance for leading of his Brother out of the way.*

Hope. *Be comforted my Brother, for I forgive thee; and believe too, that this shall be for our good.*

Chr. I am glad I have with me a merciful Brother: but we must not stand thus, let's try to go back again.

Hope. *But good Brother let me go before.*

Chr. No, if you please let me go first; that if there be any danger, I may be first therein, because by my means we are both gone out of the way.

Hope. *No, said* Hopeful, *you shall not go first, for your mind being troubled, may lead you out of the way again.* Then for their encouragement, they heard the voice of one, saying, *Let thine Heart be towards the High-way, even the way that thou wentest, turn again.* But by this time the Waters were greatly risen, by reason of which, the way of going back was very dangerous. (Then I thought that it is easier going out of the way when we are in, then going in, when we are out.) Yet they adventured to go back; but it was so dark, and the flood was so high, that in their going back, they had like to have been drowned nine or ten times.

Jer. 31. 21.

They are in danger of drowning as they go back.

Neither could they, with all the skill they had, get again to the Stile that night. Wherefore, at last, lighting under a little shelter, they sat down there till the day brake; but being weary, they fell asleep. Now there was not far from the place where they lay, a *Castle*, called *Doubting-Castle*, the owner whereof was *Giant Despair*,† and it was in his grounds they now were sleeping; wherefore he getting up in the morning early, and walking up and down in his Fields, caught *Christian* and *Hopeful* asleep in his grounds. Then with a *grim* and *surly* voice he bid them awake, and asked them whence they were? and what they did in his grounds? They told him, they were Pilgrims, and that they had lost their way. Then said the *Giant*, You have this night trespassed on me, by trampling in, and

They sleep in the grounds of Giant Despair.

He finds them in his ground, and carries them to Doubting *Castle.*

lying on my grounds, and therefore you must go along with me. So they were forced to go, because he was stronger then they. They also had but little to say, for they knew themselves in a fault. The *Giant* therefore drove them before him, and put them into his Castle, into a very dark Dungeon, nasty and stinking to the spirit of these two men: Here then they lay, from *Wednesday* morning till *Saturday* night, without one bit of bread, or drop of drink, or any light, or any to ask how they did. They were therefore here in evil case, and were far from friends and acquaintance. Now in this place, *Christian* had double sorrow, because 'twas through his unadvised haste that they were brought into this distress.

The Grievousness of their Imprisonment.

Psal. 88. 18.

Now *Giant Despair* had a Wife, and her name was *Diffidence*:† so when he was gone to bed, he told his Wife what he had done, to wit, that he had taken a couple of Prisoners, and cast them into his *Dungeon*, for trespassing on his grounds. Then he asked her also what he had best to do further to them. So she asked him what they were, whence they came, and whither they were bound; and he told her; Then she counselled him, that when he arose in the morning, he should beat them without any mercy: So when he arose, he getteth him a grievous Crab-tree† Cudgel, and goes down into the *Dungeon* to them; and there, first falls to rateing of them as if they were dogs, although they gave him never a word of distaste; then he falls upon them, and beats them fearfully, in such sort, that they were not able to help themselves, or to turn them upon the floor. This done, he withdraws and leaves them, there to condole their misery, and to mourn under their distress: so all that day they spent the time in nothing but sighs and bitter lamentations. The next night she talking with her Husband about them further, and understanding that they were yet alive, did advise him to counsel them, to make away themselves: So when morning was come, he goes to them in a surly manner, as before, and perceiving them to be very sore with the stripes that he had given them the day before; he told them, that since they were never like to come out of that place, their only way would be, forthwith to make *an end of themselves, either with Knife, Halter or Poison: For why, said he, should you chuse life, seeing it is attended with so much bitterness. But

On Thursday *Giant* Despair *beats his Prisoners.*

* *On* Friday *Giant* Despair *counsels them to kill themselves.*

The Pilgrims now, to gratify the Flesh,
Will seek its Ease; but oh how they afresh
Do thereby plunge themselves new Grief into!
Who seeks to please the Flesh, themselves undo.

they desired him to let them go; with that he looked ugly upon them, and rushing to them, had doubtless made an end of them himself, but that he fell into one of his *fits; (for he sometimes in Sun-shine weather fell into fits) and lost (for a time) the use of his hand: wherefore he withdrew, and left them, (as before) to consider what to do. Then did the Prisoners consult between themselves, whether 'twas best to take his counsel or no: and thus they began to discourse.

* *The Giant sometimes has fits.*

* Christian *crushed.*

* Job 7. 15.

Chr. Brother, said *Christian*, *what shall we do? the life that we now live is miserable: for my part, I know not whether is best, to live thus, or to die out of hand. **My soul chuseth strangling rather than life*; and the Grave is more easie for me than this Dungeon: Shall we be ruled by the Giant?

* Hopeful *comforts him.*

Hope. **Indeed our present condition is dreadful, and death would be far more welcome to me than* thus *for ever to abide: but yet let us consider, the Lord of the Country to which we are going, hath said, Thou shalt do no murther,*† *no not to another man's person; much more then are we forbidden to take his counsel to kill our selves. Besides, he that kills another, can but commit murder upon his body; but for one to kill himself, is to kill body and soul at once. And moreover, my Brother, thou talkest of ease in the Grave; but hast thou forgotten the Hell whither, for certain, the murderers go? for no murderer hath eternal life,*† &c. *And, let us consider again, that all the Law is not in the hand of* Giant Despair: *Others, so far as I can understand, have been taken by him, as well as we; and yet have escaped out of his hand: Who knows, but that God that made the world, may cause that* Giant Despair *may die; or that, at some time or other he may forget to lock us in; or, but he may in short time have another of his fits before us, and may lose the use of his limbs; and if ever that should come to pass again, for my part, I am resolved to pluck up the heart of a man, and to try my utmost to get from under his hand. I was a fool that I did not try to do it before, but however, my Brother, let's be patient, and endure a while; the time may come that may give us a happy release: but let us not be our own murderers. With these words,* Hopeful, *at present did moderate the mind of his Brother; so they continued together (in the dark) that day, in their sad and doleful condition.*

Well, towards evening the Giant goes down into the Dungeon again, to see if his Prisoners had taken his counsel; but when he came there, he found them alive, and truly, alive was all: for now, what for want of Bread and Water, and by reason of the Wounds they received when he beat them, they could do little but breath: But, I say, he found them alive; at which he fell into a grievous rage, and told them, that seeing they had disobeyed his counsel, it should be worse with them, than if they had never been born.

At this they trembled greatly, and I think that *Christian* fell into a Swound;† but coming a little to himself again, they renewed their discourse about the *Giants* counsel; and whether yet they had best to take it or no. *Now *Christian* again seemed to be for doing it, but *Hopeful* made his second reply as followeth.

* Christian *still dejected.*

Hope. **My Brother, said he, remembrest thou not how valiant thou hast been heretofore*; Apollyon *could not crush thee, nor could all that thou didst hear, or see, or feel in the Valley of the shadow of Death; what hardship, terror, and amazement hast thou already gone through, and art thou now nothing but fear? Thou seest that I am in the Dungeon with thee, a far weaker man by nature than thou art: Also this Giant has wounded me as well as thee; and hath also cut off the Bread and Water from my mouth; and with thee I mourn without the light: but let's exercise a little more patience. Remember how thou playedst the man† at* Vanity-Fair, *and wast neither afraid of the Chain nor Cage; nor yet of bloody Death: wherefore let us (at least to avoid the shame, that becomes not a Christian to be found in) bear up with patience as well as we can.*

* Hopeful *comforts him again, by calling former things to remembrance.*

Now night being come again, and the *Giant* and his Wife being in bed, she asked him concerning the Prisoners, and if they had taken his counsel: To which he replied, They are sturdy Rogues, they chuse rather to bear all hardship, than to make away themselves. Then said she, Take them into the Castle-yard to morrow, and shew them the *Bones* and *Skulls* of those that thou hast already dispatch'd; and make them believe, e're a week comes to an end, thou also wilt tear them in pieces as thou hast done their fellows before them.

So when the morning was come, the *Giant* goes to them

again, and takes them into the Castle-yard, and shews them, as his Wife had bidden him. *These, said he, were Pilgrims as you are, once, and they trespassed in my grounds, as you have done; and when I thought fit, I tore them in pieces; and so within ten days I will do you. Go get you down to your Den again; and with that he beat them all the way thither: they lay therefore all day on *Saturday* in a lamentable case, as before. Now when night was come, and when Mrs. *Diffidence*, and her Husband, the *Giant*, were got to bed, they began to renew their discourse of their Prisoners: and withal, the old *Giant* wondered, that he could neither by his blows, nor counsel, bring them to an end. And with that his Wife replied, I fear, said she, that they live in hope that some will come to relieve them, or that they have pick-locks about them; by the means of which they hope to escape. And, sayest thou so, my dear, said the *Giant*, I will therefore search them in the morning.

* *On* Saturday *the Giant threatned, that shortly he would pull them in pieces.*

Well, on *Saturday* about midnight they began to *pray*, and continued in Prayer till almost break of day.

Now a little before it was day, good *Christian*, as one half amazed, brake out in this passionate speech, *What a fool, quoth he, am I, thus to lie in a stinking Dungeon, when I may as well walk at liberty?* I have a *Key* in my bosom, called *Promise*,† that will, (I am perswaded) open any Lock in *Doubting-Castle*. Then said *Hopeful*, That's good news; good Brother pluck it out of thy bosom, and try: Then *Christian* pulled it out of his bosom, and began to try at the Dungeon door, whose bolt (as he turned the Key) gave back, and the door flew open with ease, and *Christian* and *Hopeful* both came out. Then he went to the outward door, that leads into the *Castle yard*, and with his Key opened the door also. After he went to the *Iron* Gate, for that must be opened too, but that Lock went *damnable*† hard, yet the Key did open it; then they thrust open the Gate to make their escape with speed; but that Gate, as it opened, made such a creaking, that it waked *Giant Despair*, who hastily rising to pursue his Prisoners, felt his Limbs to fail, for his fits took him again, so that he could by no means go after them. Then they went on, and came to the Kings high way again, and so were safe, because they were out of his Jurisdiction.

A Key in Christians *bosom, called* Promise, *opens any Lock in* Doubting *Castle.*

Now when they were gone over the Stile, they began to contrive with themselves what they should do at that Stile, to prevent those that should come after, from falling into the hands of *Giant Despair*. So they consented to erect there a *Pillar, and to engrave upon the side thereof; *Over this Stile is the way to* Doubting-*Castle, which is kept by* Giant Despair, *who despiseth the King of the Cœlestial Countrey, and seeks to destroy his holy Pilgrims*. Many therefore that followed after, read what was written, and escaped the danger. This done, they sang as follows.

** A Pillar erected by* Christian *and his fellow.*

Out of the way we went, and then we found
What 'twas to tread upon forbidden ground:
And let them that come after have a care,
Lest heedlesness makes them, as we, to fare:
Lest they, for trespassing, his prisoners are,
Whose Castle's Doubting, *and whose name's* Despair.

They went then, till they came to the delectable Mountains, which Mountains belong to the Lord of that Hill of which we have spoken before; so they went up to the Mountains, to behold the Gardens, and Orchards, the Vineyards, and Fountains of water, where also they drank, and washed themselves, and did freely eat of the Vineyards. Now there was on the tops of these Mountains, Shepherds feeding their flocks, and they stood by the high-way side. The Pilgrims therefore went to them, and leaning upon their staves, (as is common with weary Pilgrims, when they stand to talk with any by the way,) they asked, **Whose delectable Mountains are these? and whose be the sheep that feed upon them?*

The delectable mountains.

They are refreshed in the mountains.

** Talk with the Shepherds.*

Shep. These Mountains are *Immanuels Land*,† and they are within sight of his City, and the sheep also are his, and he laid down his life for them.

Joh. 10. 11.

Chr. *Is this the way to the Cœlestial City?*

Shep. You are just in your way.

Chr. *How far is it thither?*

Shep. Too far for any, but those that *shall* get thither indeed.

Chr. *Is the way safe, or dangerous?*

Shep. Safe for those for whom it is to be safe, *but transgressors shall fall therein*.

Hos. 14. 9.

Mountains delectable they now ascend,
Where Shepherds be, which to them do commend
Alluring things, and things that cautious are,
Pilgrims are steddy kept by Faith and Fear.

Chr. *Is there in this place any relief for Pilgrims that are weary and faint in the way?*

Shep. The Lord of these Mountains hath given us a charge, *Not to be forgetful to entertain strangers*: Therefore the good of the place is before you. Heb. 13. 1, 2.

I saw also in my Dream, that when the *Shepherds* perceived that they were way-fairing men, they also put questions to them, (to which they made answer as in other places) as, Whence came you? and, How got you into the way? and, By what means have you so persevered therein? For but few of them that begin to come hither, do shew their face on these Mountains. But when the Shepherds heard their answers, being pleased therewith, they looked very lovingly upon them; and said, **Welcome to the delectable Mountains.*

* *The Shepherds welcome them.*

The Shepherds, I say, whose names were, *Knowledge*, *Experience*, *Watchful*, and *Sincere*, took them by the hand, and had them to their Tents, and made them partake of that which was ready at present. They said moreover, We would that you should stay here a while, to acquaint with us, and yet more to solace your selves with the good of these delectable Mountains. They then told them, That they were content to stay; and so they went to their rest that night, because it was very late.

The names of the Shepherds.

Then I saw in my Dream, that in the morning, the Shepherds called up *Christian* and *Hopeful* to walk with them upon the Mountains: So they went forth with them, and walked a while, having a pleasant prospect on every side. Then said the Shepherds one to another, shall we shew these Pilgrims some *wonders? So when they had concluded to do it, they had them first to the top of an Hill, called *Errour*, which was very steep on the furthest side, and bid them look down to the bottom. So *Christian* and *Hopeful* lookt down, and saw at the bottom several men, dashed all to pieces by a fall that they had from the top. Then said *Christian*, What meaneth this? The Shepherds answered; Have you not heard of them that were made to err, by hearkening to **Hymeneus*, and *Philetus*, as concerning the faith of the Resurrection of the Body? They answered, Yes. Then said the Shepherds, Those that you see lie dashed in pieces at the bottom of this Mountain, *are they*: and they have continued to this day unburied (as you see) for

* *They are sure wonders.*

The Mountain of Errour.

* 2 Tim. 2. 17, 18.

an example to others to take heed how they clamber too high, or how they come too near the brink of this Mountain.

Then I saw that they had them to the top of another Mountain, and the name of that is **Caution*; and bid them look a far off: Which when they did, they perceived, as they thought, several men walking up and down among the Tombs† that were there. And they perceived that the men were blind, because they stumbled sometimes upon the Tombs, and because they could not get out from among them. Then said *Christian*, *What means this?*

* *Mount* Caution.

The Shepherds then answered, Did you not see a little below these Mountains a *Stile* that led into a Meadow on the left hand of this way? They answered, Yes. Then said the Shepherds, From that Stile there goes a path that leads directly to *Doubting-Castle*, which is kept by *Giant Despair*; and these men (pointing to them among the Tombs) came once on Pilgrimage, as you do now, even till they came to that same *Stile*. And because the right way was rough in that place, they chose to go out of it into that Meadow, and there were taken by Giant *Despair*, and cast into *Doubting-Castle*; where, after they had a while been kept in the Dungeon, he at last did put out their eyes, and led them among those Tombs, where he has left them to wander to this very day, that the saying of the wise Man might be fulfilled, *He that wandereth out of the way of understanding, shall remain in the Congregation of the dead*. Then *Christian* and *Hopeful* looked one upon another, with tears gushing out; but yet said nothing to the Shepherds.

Prov. 21. 16.

Then I saw in my Dream, that the Shepherds had them to another place, in a bottom, where was a door in the side of an Hill; and they opened the door, and bid them look in. They looked in therefore, and saw that within it was very dark, and smoaky; they also thought that they heard there a lumbering noise as of fire, and a cry of some tormented, and that they smelt the scent of Brimstone. Then said *Christian*, *what means this?* The Shepherds told them, saying, This is a By-way to Hell, a way that Hypocrites go in at; namely, such as sell their Birthright, with *Esau*: such as sell their Master, with *Judas*: such as blaspheme the Gospel, with *Alexander*; and that lie, and dissemble, with *Ananias* and *Saphira* his wife.†

A by-way to Hell.

Hope. Then said *Hopeful* to the Shepherds, *I perceive that these had on them, even every one, a shew of Pilgrimage as we have now; had they not?*

Shep. Yes, and held it a long time too.

Hope. *How far might they go on Pilgrimage in their day, since they notwithstanding were thus miserably cast away?*

Shep. Some further, and some not so far as these Mountains.

Then said the Pilgrims one to another, *We had need cry to the Strong for strength.*

Shep. Ay, and you will have need to use it when you have it, too.

By this time the Pilgrims had a desire to go forwards, and the Shepherds a desire they should; so they walked together towards the end of the Mountains. Then said the Shepherds one to another, Let us here shew to the Pilgrims the Gates of the Cœlestial City, if they have skill to look through our *Perspective Glass. The Pilgrims then lovingly accepted the motion: So they had them to the top of an high Hill called **Clear*, and gave them their Glass to look. Then they essayed to look, but the remembrance of that last thing that the Shepheards had shewed them, made their hands shake; by means of which impediment they could not look steddily through the Glass; yet they thought they saw something like the Gate, and also some of the Glory of the place. Then they went away and sang.

** The Shepherds Perspective-Glass.*
** The Hill* Clear.
The fruit of slavish fear.

> *Thus by the* Shepherds, *Secrets are reveal'd,*
> *Which from all other men are kept conceal'd:*
> *Come to the* Shepherds *then, if you would see*
> *Things deep, things hid, and that mysterious be.*

When they were about to depart, one of the Shepherds gave them a *note of the way*. Another of them, *bid them *beware of the flatterer*. The third *bid them take heed that they sleep not upon the Inchanted Ground*. And the fourth, *bid them God speed*. So I awoke from my Dream.†

** A two fold Caution.*

And I slept, and Dreamed again, and saw the same two Pilgrims going down the Mountains along the High-way towards the City. Now a little below these Mountains, on the

The Country of Conceit, *out of which came* Ignorance.

left hand, lieth the Countrey of *Conceit*; from which Countrey there comes into the way in which the Pilgrims walked, a little crooked Lane. Here therefore they met with a very brisk Lad, that came out of that Countrey; and his name was *Ignorance*. So *Christian* asked him, *From what parts he came? and whither he was going?*

Christian *and* Ignorance *hath some talk.*

Ign. Sir, I was born in the Countrey that lieth off there, a little on the left hand; and I am going to the Cœlestial City.

Chr. *But how do you think to get in at the Gate, for you may find some difficulty there?*

Ign. As other good People do, said he.

Chr. *But what have you to shew at that Gate, that may cause that the Gate should be opened unto you?*

Ign. I know my Lords will, and I have been a good Liver, I pay every man his own; I Pray, Fast, pay Tithes, and give Alms,† and have left my Countrey, for whither I am going.

Chr. *But thou camest not in at the Wicket-gate, that is, at the head of this way: thou camest in hither through that same crooked Lane, and therefore I fear, however thou mayest think of thy self, when the reckoning day shall come, thou wilt have laid to thy charge, that thou art a Theif and a Robber,† instead of getting admitance into the City.*

He saith to every one, that he is a fool.

Ignor. Gentlemen, ye be utter strangers to me, I know you not, be content to follow the Religion of your Countrey, and I will follow the Religion of mine. I hope all will be well. And as for the Gate that you talk of, all the world knows that that is a great way off of our Countrey. I cannot think that any man in all our parts doth so much as know the way to it; nor need they matter whether they do or no, since we have, as you see, a fine, pleasant, green Lane, that comes down from our Countrey the next way into it.

Pr. 26. 12. Eccl. 10. 3. *How to carry it to a fool.*

When *Christian* saw that the man was wise in his own conceit; he said to *Hopeful*, whisperingly. *There is more hopes of a fool then of him*. And said moreover, *When he that is a fool walketh by the way, his wisdom faileth him, and he saith to every one that he is a fool.* What, shall we talk further with him? or out-go him at present? and so leave him to think of what he hath heard already? and then stop again for him afterwards, and see if by degrees we can do any good of him? Then said *Hopeful*,

Let Ignorance a little while now muse
On what is said, and let him not refuse
Good counsel to imbrace, lest he remain
Still ignorant of what's the chiefest gain.
God saith, Those that no understanding have,
(Although he made them) them he will not save.

Hope. He further added, It is not good, I think to say all to him at once, let us pass him by, if you will, and talk to him anon, *even as he is able to bear it.*†

So they both went on, and *Ignorance* he came after. Now when they had passed him a little way, they entered into a very dark Lane, where they met a man whom seven Devils had bound with seven strong Cords, and were carrying of him back *to the door* that they saw in the side of the Hill. Now good *Christian* began to tremble, and so did *Hopeful* his Companion: Yet as the Devils led away the man, *Christian* looked to see if he knew him, and he thought it might be one *Turn-away* that dwelt in the *Town* of *Apostacy*. But he did not perfectly see his face, for he did hang his head like a Thief that is found: But being gone past, *Hopeful* looked after him, and espied on his back a Paper with this Inscription, *Wanton Professor, and damnable Apostate*. Then said *Christian* to his Fellow, Now I call to remembrance that which was told me of a thing that happened to a good man hereabout. The name of the man was *Little-Faith*, but a good man, and he dwelt in the Town of *Sincere*. The thing was this; at the entering in of this passage there comes down from *Broad-way-gate*, a Lane, called *Deadmans Lane*; so called, because of the Murders that are commonly done there. And this *Little-Faith* going on Pilgrimage, as we do now, chanced to sit down there and slept. Now there happened at that time, to come down that *Lane* from *Broad-way-gate*, three Sturdy Rogues; and their names were *Faint-heart, Mistrust*, and *Guilt*, (three Brothers) and they espying *Little-faith* where he was, came galloping up with speed: Now the good man was just awaked from his sleep, and was getting up to go on his Journey. So they came all up to him, and with threatning Language bid him *stand*. At this *Little faith* look'd as white as a clout,† and had neither power to *fight*, nor

Mat. 12. 45. Prov. 5. 22.

The destruction of one Turn-away.

Christian *telleth his Companion a story of* Little-Faith.

Broad-way-gate. Deadmans Lane.

Little-Faith *robbed by* Faint-heart, Mistrust, *and* Guilt.

flie. Then said *Faint-heart*, Deliver thy Purse; but he making no haste to do it, (for he was loth to lose his Money) *Mistrust* ran up to him, and thrusting his hand into his Pocket, pull'd out thence a bag of Silver. Then he cried out, Thieves,
They got away his Silver, and knockt him down. thieves. With that *Guilt* with a great Club that was in his hand, strook *Little-Faith* on the head, and with that blow fell'd him flat to the ground, where he lay bleeding as one that would bleed to death. All this while the Thieves stood by. But at last, they hearing that some were upon the Road, and fearing lest it should be one *Great-grace* that dwells in the City of *Good-confidence*, they betook themselves to their heels, and left this good man to shift for himself. Now after a while, *Little-faith* came to himself, and getting up, made shift to scrabble on his way. This was the story.

Hope. *But did they take from him all that ever he had?*

Little faith *lost not his best things.* *Chr.* No: the place where his Jewels were, they never ransackt, so those he kept still; but as I was told, the good man was much afflicted for his loss. For the Thieves got most of his spending Money.† That which they got not (as I said) were
1 Pet. 4. 18. Jewels, also he had a little odd Money left, but *scarce* enough to bring him to his Journeys end; nay, (if I was not mis-informed) he was forced to beg as he went, to keep himself alive, (for his
Little-faith *forced to beg to his Journeys end.* Jewels he might not sell.) But beg, and do what he could, *he went* (as we say) *with many a hungry belly* the most part of the rest of the way.

Hope. *But is it not a wonder they got not from him his Certificate, by which he was to receive his admittance at the Cœlestial gate?*

Chr. 'Tis a wonder, but they got not that; though they mist it not through any good cunning of his, for he being dismayed
He kept not his best things by his own cunning. with their coming upon him, had neither power nor skill to hide any thing; so 'twas more by good Providence then by his Indeavour, that they mist of *that good thing*.

2 Tim. 1. 14. Hope. *But it must needs be a comfort to him, that they got not this Jewel from him.*

2 Pet. 1. 19. *Chr.* It might have been great comfort to him, had he used it as he should; but they that told me the story, said, That he made but little use of it all the rest of the way; and that because of the dismay that he had in their taking away his Money: indeed he forgot it a great part of the rest of the Journey; and

besides, when at any time, it came into his mind, and he began to be comforted therewith, then would fresh thoughts of his loss come again upon him, and those thoughts would swallow up all.

Hope. *Alas poor Man! this could not but be a great grief unto him.*

Chr. Grief! Ay, a grief indeed! would it not a been so to any of us, had we been used as he, to be Robbed and wounded too, and that in a strange place, as he was? 'Tis a wonder he did not die with grief, poor heart! I was told, that he scattered almost all the rest of the way with nothing but doleful and bitter complaints. Telling also to all that over-took him, or that he over-took in the way as he went, where he was Robbed, and how; who they were that did it, and what he lost; how he was wounded, and that he hardly escaped with life.

He is pitied by both.

Hope. *But 'tis a wonder that his necessities did not put him upon* selling, or pawning *some of his Jewels, that he might have wherewith to relieve himself in his Journey.*

Chr. Thou talkest like one, upon whose head is the Shell to this very day:† For what should he *pawn* them? or to whom should he sell them? In all that Countrey where he was Robbed his Jewels were not accounted of, nor did he want that relief which could from thence be administred to him; besides, had his Jewels been missing at the Gate of the Cœlestial City, he had (and that he knew well enough) been excluded from an Inheritance there; and that would have been worse to him then the appearance, and villany of ten thousand Thieves.

Christian *snibbeth his fellow for unadvised speaking.*

Hope. *Why art thou so tart my Brother? Esau* sold his Birth-right, *and that for a mess of Pottage; and that Birth-right was his greatest Jewel: and if he, why might not* Little-Faith *do so too?*

Heb. 12. 16.

Chr. Esau did sell his Birth-right indeed, and so do many besides; and by so doing, exclude themselves from the chief blessing, as also that *Caytiff* did. But you must put a difference betwixt *Esau* and *Little-Faith*, and also betwixt their Estates. *Esau*'s Birth-right was Typical,† but *Little-Faith's* Jewels were not so. *Esau*'s belly was his God, but *Little-Faith's* belly was not so. *Esau*'s want lay in his fleshly appetite, *Little-Faith's* did not so. Besides, *Esau* could see no further then to the fulfilling of his lusts; *For I am at the point to dye*, said he, *and*

A discourse about Esau *and* Little-Faith.

Esau *was ruled by his lusts.* Gen. 25. 32.

what good will this Birth-right do me? But *Little-Faith*, though it was his lot to have but a *little faith*, was by his *little faith* kept from such extravagancies; and made to *see* and *prize* his Jewels more, then to sell them, as *Esau* did his Birth-right. You read not any where that *Esau* had *Faith*, no not so much as a *little*: Therefore no marvel, if where the flesh only bears sway (as it will in that man where *no* Faith is to resist) if he sells his *Birth-right*, and his Soul and all, and that to the Devil of Hell; for it is with such, as it is with the Ass, *Who in her occasions cannot be turned away*. When their minds are set upon their Lusts, they will have them what ever they cost. But *Little-faith* was of another temper, his mind was on things Divine; his livelyhood was upon things that were Spiritual, and from above; Therefore to what end should he that is of such a temper sell his Jewels, (had there been any that would have bought them) to fill his mind with empty things? Will a man give a penny to fill his belly with Hay? or can you perswade the *Turtle-dove* to live upon Carrion, like the *Crow*? Though *faithless* ones can for carnal Lusts, pawn, or morgage, or sell what they have, and themselves out right to boot; yet they that have *faith, saving faith*, though but a *little* of it, cannot do so. Here therefore, my Brother, is thy mistake.

Esau *never had Faith.*

Jer. 2. 24.

Little-Faith *could not live upon* Esaus *Pottage.*

A comparison between the Turtle-dove *and the* Crow.

Hope. *I acknowledge it; but yet your severe reflection had almost made me angry.*

Chr. Why, I did but compare thee to some of the Birds that are of the brisker sort, who will run to and fro in untrodden paths with the shell upon their heads: but pass by that, and consider the matter under debate, and all shall be well betwixt thee and me.

Hope. *But* Christian, *These three fellows, I am perswaded in my heart, are but a company of Cowards: would they have run else, think you, as they did, at the noise of one that was coming on the road? Why did not* Little-faith *pluck up a greater heart? He might, methinks, have stood one brush with them, and have yielded when there had been no remedy.*

Hopeful *swaggers.*

Chr. That they are Cowards, many have said, but few have found it so in the time of Trial. As for *a great heart*, *Little-faith* had none; and I perceive by thee, my Brother, hadst thou been the Man concerned, thou art but for a brush, and then to

No great heart for God, where there is but little faith.

yield. And verily, since this is the height of thy Stomach, now they are at a distance from us, should they appear to thee, as they did to him, they might put thee to second thoughts.

We have more courage when out, then when we are in.

But consider again, they are but Journey-men Thieves, they serve under the King of the Bottomless pit; who, if need be, will come in to their aid himself, and his voice is *as the roaring of a Lion*. I my self have been Ingaged as this *Little-faith* was, and I found it a terrible thing. These three Villains set upon me, and I beginning like a *Christian* to resist, they gave but a call and in came their Master: I would, as the saying is, have given my life for a penny; but that, as God would have it, I was cloathed with Armour of proof. Ay, and yet, though I was so harnessed, I found it hard work to quit my self like a man;† no man can tell what in that Combat attends us, but he that hath been in the Battle himself.

1 Pet. 5. 8.

Christian *tells his own experience in this case.*

Hope. *Well, but they ran, you see, when they did but suppose that one* Great-Grace *was in the way.*

Chr. True, they often fled, both they and their Master, when *Great-grace* hath but appeared; and no marvel, for he is *the Kings Champion*: But I tro, you will put some difference between *Little-faith* and the *Kings Champion*; all the Kings Subjects are not his Champions: nor can they, when tried, do such feats of War as he. Is it meet to think that a little child should handle *Goliah* as *David* did?† or that there should be the strength of an *Ox* in a *Wren*? Some are strong, some are weak, some have *great* faith, some have *little*: this man was one of the weak, and therefore he went to the walls.†

The Kings Champion.

Hope. *I would it had been* Great-Grace *for their sakes.*

Chr. If it had been he, he might have had his hands full: For I must tell you, that though *Great-Grace* is excellent good at his Weapons, and has, and can, so long as he keeps them at Swords point, do well enough with them: yet if they get within him, even *Faint-heart, Mistrust*, or the other, it shall go hard but they will throw up his heels.† And when a man is down, you know, what can he do?

Who so looks well upon *Great-graces* face, shall see those Scars and Cuts there that shall easily give demonstration of what I say. Yea once I heard he should say, (and that when he was in the Combat) *We despaired even of life*:† How did these sturdy Rogues and their Fellows make *David* groan, mourn, and roar?† Yea *Heman* and *Hezekiah*† too, though Champions in their day, were forced to bestir them, when by these assaulted; and yet, that notwithstanding, they had their Coats soundly brushed by them. *Peter* upon a time would go try what he could do; but, though some do say of him that he is the Prince of the Apostles, they handled him so, that they made him at last afraid of a sorry Girle.†

Besides, their King is at their Whistle, he is never out of hearing; and if at any time they be put to the worst, he, if possible, comes in to help them: And, of him it is said, *The Sword of him that layeth at him cannot hold: the Spear, the Dart, nor the Habergeon; he esteemeth Iron as Straw, and Brass as rotten Wood. The Arrow cannot make him flie, Sling-stones are turned with him into stubble, Darts are counted as stubble, he laugheth at the shaking of a Spear.* What can a man do in this case? 'Tis true, if a man could at every turn have *Job*s Horse, and had skill and courage to ride him, he might do notable things. *For his neck is clothed with Thunder, he will not be afraid as the Grashoper, the glory of his Nostrils is terrible, he paweth in the Valley, rejoyceth in his strength, and goeth out to meet the armed men. He mocketh at fear, and is not affrighted, neither turneth back from the Sword. The Quiver rattleth against him, the glittering Spear, and the shield. He swalloweth the ground with fierceness and rage, neither believeth he that it is the sound of the Trumpet. He saith among the Trumpets, Ha, ha; and he smelleth the Battel a far off, the thundring of the Captains, and the shoutings.*

Job 41. 26.

Leviathans *sturdiness.*

The excellent mettle that is in Job's *horse.*

Job 39. 19.

But for such footmen as thee and I are, let us never desire to meet with an enemy, nor vaunt as if we could do better, when we hear of others that they have been foiled, nor be tickled at the thoughts of our own manhood, for such commonly come by the worst when tried. Witness *Peter*, of whom I made mention before. He would swagger, Ay he would: He would, as his vain mind prompted him to say, do better, and stand more for his Master, then all men: But who so foiled, and run down with these *Villains* as he?

When therefore we hear that such Robberies are done on the

Kings High-way, two things become us to do: first to go out Harnessed, and to be sure *to take a Shield with us:* For it was for want of that, that he that laid so lustily at *Leviathan*† could not make him yield. For indeed, if that be wanting, he fears us not at all. Therefore he that had skill, hath said, *Above all take the Shield of Faith, wherewith ye shall be able to quench all the fiery darts of the wicked.* Ephes. 6. 16.

'Tis good also that we desire of the King a Convoy, yea that he will go with us himself. This made *David* rejoyce when in the Valley of the shaddows of death; and *Moses* was rather for dying where he stood, then to go one step without his God. O my Brother, if he will but go along with us, what need we be afraid of ten thousands that shall set themselves against us, but without him, *the proud helpers fall under the slain.*

'Tis good to have a Convoy.

Exod. 33. 15. Psal. 3. 5, 6, 7, 8. Psal. 27. 1, 2, 3. Isa. 10. 4.

I for my part have been in the fray before now, and though (through the goodness of him that is best) I am as you see alive: yet I cannot boast of my manhood. Glad shall I be, if I meet with no more such brunts, though I fear we are not got beyond all danger. However, since the Lion and the Bear hath not as yet, devoured me, I hope God will also deliver us from the next uncircumcised *Philistine*.† Then Sang *Christian*.

> *Poor* Little-Faith! *Hast been among the Thieves!*
> *Wast robb'd! Remember this, Who so believes*
> *And gets more faith, shall then a Victor be*
> *Over ten thousand, else scarce over three.*

So they went on, and *Ignorance* followed. They went then till they came at a place where they saw a *way* put it self into their *way*, and seemed withal, to lie as straight as the way which they should go; and here they knew not which of the two to take, for both seemed straight before them, therefore here they stood still to consider. And as they were thinking about the way, behold, a man black of flesh, but covered with a very light Robe,† came to them, and asked them, why they stood there? They answered, They were going to the Cœlestial City, but knew not which of these ways to take. Follow me, said the man, it is thither that I am going. So they followed him in the way that but now came into the road, which by degrees

A way and a way.

Christian *and his fellow deluded.*

They are taken in a Net.

turned, and turned them so from the City that they desired to go to, that in little time their faces were turned away from it; yet they followed him. But by and by, before they were aware, he led them both within the compass of a Net, in which they were both so entangled, that they knew not what to do; and with that, *the white robe fell off the black mans back*: then they saw where they were. Wherefore there they lay crying sometime, for they could not get themselves out.

They bewail. their conditions.

Prov. 29.

Chr. Then said *Christian* to his fellow, Now do I see my self in an errour. Did not the Shepherds bid us beware of the flatterers? As is the saying of the Wise man, so we have found it this day: *A man that flattereth his Neighbour, spreadeth a Net for his feet.*

Psal. 17. 4.

A shining one comes to them with a whip in his hand.

Hope. They also gave us a note of directions about the way, for our more sure finding thereof: but therein we have also forgotten to read, and have not kept our selves from the Paths of the destroyer. Here *David* was wiser then wee; for saith he, *Concerning the works of men, by the word of thy lips, I have kept me from the paths of the destroyer.* Thus they lay bewailing themselves in the Net. At last they espied a shining One coming towards them, with a whip of small cord in his hand. When he was come to the place where they were, he asked them whence they came? and what they did there? They told him, That they were poor Pilgrims, going to *Sion*, but were led out of their way by a black man, cloathed in white; who bid us, said they, follow him; for he was going thither too.

Prov. 29. 5.
Dan. 11. 32.
2 Cor. 11. 13, 14.

They are examined, and convicted of forgetfulness.

Deceivers fine spoken.
Rom. 16. 18.

Then said he with the Whip, it is *Flatterer*, a false Apostle, that hath transformed himself into an Angel of Light. So he rent the Net and let the men out. Then said he to them, Follow me, that I may set you in your way again; so he led them back to the way, which they had left to follow the *Flatterer*. Then he asked them, saying, Where did you lie the last night? They said, with the Shepherds upon the delectable Mountains. He asked them then, If they had not of them Shepherds *a note of direction for the way?* They answered; Yes. But did you, said he, when you was at a stand, pluck out and read your note? They answered, No. He asked them why? They said they forgot. He asked moreover, If the Shepherds did not bid them beware of the *Flatterer*? They answered, Yes: But we did not imagine, said they, that this fine-spoken man had been he.

Then I saw in my Dream, that he commanded them to *lie down*; which when they did, he chastized them sore, to teach them the good way wherein they should walk; and as he chastized them, he said, *As many as I love, I rebuke and chasten; be zealous therefore, and repent*. This done, he bids them go on their way, and take good heed to the other directions of the Shepherds. So they thanked him for all his kindness, and went softly along the right way, Singing.

Deut. 25. 2. 2 Chron. 6. 26, 27. Rev. 3. 19. *They are whipt, and sent on their way.*

Come hither, you that walk along the way;
See how the Pilgrims fare, that go a stray!
They catched are in an intangling Net,
'Cause they good Counsel lightly did forget:
'Tis true, they rescu'd were, but yet you see
They're scourg'd to boot: Let this your caution be.

Now after a while, they perceived afar off, one comeing softly and alone all along the High-way to meet them. Then said *Christian* to his fellow, Yonder is a man with his back toward *Sion*, and he is coming to meet us.

Hope. I see him, let us take heed to our selves now, lest he should prove a *Flatterer* also. So he drew nearer and nearer, and at last came up unto them. His name was *Atheist*, and he asked them whither they were going.

The Atheist *meets them.*

Chr. *We are going to the Mount* Sion.

Then *Atheist* fell into a very great Laughter.

He Laughs at them.

Chr. *What is the meaning of your Laughter?*

Atheist. I laugh to see what ignorant persons you are, to take upon you so tedious a Journey; and yet are like to have nothing but your travel for your paines.

Chr. *Why man? Do you think we shall not be received?*

They reason together.

Atheist. Received! There is no such place as you Dream of, in all this World.

Chr. *But there is in the World to come.*

Atheist. When I was at home in mine own Countrey, I heard as you now affirm, and from that hearing went out to see, and have been seeking this City this twenty years: But find no more of it, then I did the first day I set out.

Jer. 22. 13. Eccl. 10. 15.

Chr. *We have both heard and believe that there is such a place to be found.*

Atheist. Had not I, when at home, believed, I had not come thus far to seek: But finding none, (and yet I should, had there been such a place to be found, for I have gone to seek it further then you) I am going back again, and will seek to refresh my self with the things that I then cast away, for hopes of that, which I now see, is not.

The Atheist *takes up his content in this World.*

Chr. Then said *Christian* to *Hopeful* his Fellow, *Is it true which this man hath said?*

Christian *proveth his Brother.*

Hope. Take heed, he is one of the *Flatterers*; remember what it hath cost us once already for our harkning to such kind of Fellows. What! no Mount *Sion*? Did we not see from the delectable Mountains the Gate of the City? Also, are we not now to walk by Faith? *Let us go on, said *Hopeful*, lest the man with the Whip overtakes us again.

Hopeful's *gracious answer.*

2 Cor. 5. 7.

* *A remembrance of former chastisements is an help against present temptations.*

You should have taught me that Lesson, which I will round you in the ears withal; *Cease, my Son, to hear the Instruction that causeth to err from the words of knowledge.* I say my Brother, ccasc to hear him, and let us believe to the saving of the Soul.

Prov. 19. 27.
Heb. 10. 39.

Chr. *My Brother, I did not put the question to thee, for that I doubted of the Truth of our belief my self: But to prove thee, and to fetch from thee a fruit of the honesty of thy heart. As for this man, I know that he is blinded by the god of this World: Let thee and I go on knowing that we have belief of the Truth, and no lie is of the Truth.*

A fruit of an honest heart.

1 Joh. 2. 21.

Hope. Now do I rejoyce in hope of the glory of God: So they turned away from the man, and he, Laughing at them, went his way.

I saw then in my Dream, that they went till they came into a certain Countrey, whose Air naturally tended to make one drowsie, if he came a stranger into it. And here *Hopeful* began to be very dull and heavy of sleep, wherefore he said unto *Christian*, I do now begin to grow so drowsie, that I can scarcely hold up mine eyes; let us lie down here and take one Nap.

They are come to the inchanted ground.

Hopeful *begins to be drowsie.*

Chr. *By no means*, said the other, *lest sleeping, we never awake more.*

Christian *keeps him awake.*

Hope. Why my Brother? sleep is sweet to the Labouring man; we may be refreshed if we take a Nap.

Chr. *Do you not remember, that one of the Shepherds bid us beware of the Inchanted ground? He meant by that, that we should*

1 Thes. 5. 6.

beware of sleeping; wherefore let us not sleep as do others, but let us watch and be sober.

Hope. I acknowledge my self in a fault, and had I been here alone, I had by sleeping run the danger of death. I see it is true that the wise man saith, *Two are better then one*. Hitherto hath thy Company been my mercy; *and thou shalt have a good reward for thy labour.*†

He is thankful. Eccl. 4. 9.

Chr. *Now then*, said Christian, *to prevent drowsiness in this place, let us fall into good discourse.*

To prevent drowsiness, they fall to good discourse.

Hope. With all my heart, said the other.

Chr. *Where shall we begin?*

Good discourse prevents drowsiness.

Hope. Where God began with us.† But do you begin if you please.

☞ *The Dreamers note.*

When Saints do sleepy grow, let them come hither,
And hear how these two Pilgrims talk together:
Yea, let them learn of them, in any wise
Thus to keep ope their drowsie slumbring eyes.
Saints fellowship, if it be manag'd well,
Keeps them awake, and that in spite of hell.

Chr. Then *Christian* began and said, *I will ask you a question. How *came you to think at first of doing as you do now?*

** They begin at the beginning of their conversion.*

Hope. Do you mean, How came I at first to look after the good of my soul?

Chr. *Yes, that is my meaning.*

Hope. I continued a great while in the delight of those things which were seen, and sold at our *fair*; things which, as I believe now, would have (had I continued in them still) drowned me in perdition and destruction.

Chr. *What things were they?*

Hope. All the Treasures and Riches of the World. *Also I delighted much in Rioting, Revelling, Drinking, Swearing, Lying, Uncleanness, Sabbath-breaking, and what not, that tended to destroy the Soul. But I found at last, by hearing and considering of things that are Divine, which indeed I heard of you, as also of beloved *Faithful*, that was put to death for his Faith and good-living in *Vanity-fair, That the end of these things is death*. And that for these things sake the wrath of God cometh upon the children of disobedience.

* Hopeful's *life before conversion.*

Rom. 6. 21, 22, 23. Ephes. 5. 6.

Chr. *And did you presently fall under the power of this conviction?*

* Hopeful *at first shuts his eyes against the light.*

Hope. No,* I was not willing presently to know the evil of sin, nor the damnation that follows upon the commission of it, but endeavoured, when my mind at first began to be shaken with the word, to shut mine eyes against the light thereof.

Chr. *But what was the cause of your carrying of it thus to the first workings of Gods blessed Spirit upon you?*

* *Reasons of his resisting of light.*

Hope. *The causes were, 1. I was ignorant that this was the work of God upon me. I never thought that by awaknings for sin, God at first begins the conversion of a sinner. 2. Sin was yet very sweet to my flesh, and I was loth to leave it. 3. I could not tell how to part with mine old Companions, their presence and actions were so desirable unto me. 4. The hours in which convictions were upon me, were such troublesome and such heart-affrighting hours that I could not bear, no not so much as the remembrance of them upon my heart.

Chr. *Then as it seems, sometimes you got rid of your trouble.*

Hope. Yes verily, but it would come into my mind again; and then I should be as bad, nay worse then I was before.

Chr. *Why, what was it that brought your sins to mind again?*

Hope. Many things, As,

* *When he had lost his sense of sin, what brought it again.*

1. *If I did but meet a good man in the Streets; or,
2. If I have heard any read in the Bible; or,
3. If mine Head did begin to Ake; or,
4. If I were told that some of my Neighbours were sick; or,
5. If I heard the Bell Toull for some that were dead; or,
6. If I thought of dying my self; or,
7. If I heard that suddain death happened to others.
8. But especially, when I thought of my self, that I must quickly come to Judgement.

Chr. *And could you at any time with ease get off the guilt of sin when by any of these wayes it came upon you?*

Hope. No, not latterly, for then they got faster hold of my Conscience. And then, if I did but think of going back to sin (though my mind was turned against it) it would be double torment to me.

Chr. *And how did you do then?*

Hope. I thought I must endeavour to mend my life, for else thought I, I am sure to be damned.

When he could no longer shake off his guilt by sinful courses, then he endeavours to mend.

Chr. *And did you indeavour to mend?*

Hope. Yes, and fled from, not only my sins, but sinful Company too; and betook me to Religious Duties, as Praying, Reading, weeping for Sin, speaking Truth to my Neighbours, *&c.* These things I did, with many others, too much here to relate.

Chr. *And did you think your self well then?*

Hope. Yes, for a while; but at the last my trouble came tumbling upon me again, and that over the neck of all my Reformations.

Then he thought himself well.

Chr. *How came that about, since you was now Reformed?*

Hope. There were several things brought it upon me, especially such sayings as these; *All our righteousnesses are as filthy rags, By the works of the Law no man shall be justified. When you have done all things, say, We are unprofitable:* with many more the like: From whence I began to reason with my self thus: If *all* my righteousnesses are filthy rags, if by the deeds of the Law, *no* man can be justified; And, if when we have done *all*, we are yet unprofitable: Then 'tis but a folly to think of heaven by the Law. I further thought thus: *If a man runs an 100*l.* into the Shop-keepers debt, and after that shall pay for all that he shall fetch, yet his old debt stands still in the Book uncrossed; for the which the Shop-keeper may sue him, and cast him into Prison till he shall pay the debt.†

Reformation at last could not help, and why. Isa. 64. 6. Gal. 2. 16. Luke 17. 10.

* *His being a debtor by the Law troubled him.*

Chr. *Well, and how did you apply this to your self?*

Hope. Why, I thought thus with my self; I have by my sins run a great way into Gods Book, and that my now reforming will not pay off that score; therefore I should think still under all my present amendments, But how shall I be freed from that damnation that I have brought my self in danger of by my former transgressions?

Chr. *A very good application: but pray go on.*

Hope. Another thing that hath troubled me, even since my late amendments, is, that if I look narrowly into the best of what I do now, I still see sin, new sin, mixing it self with the best of that I do. So that now I am forced to conclude, that

His espying bad things in his best duties, troubled him.

notwithstanding my former fond conceits of my self and duties, I have committed sin enough in one duty to send me to Hell, though my former life had been faultless.

Chr. *And what did you do then?*

This made him break his mind to Faithful, *who told him the way to be saved.*

Hope. Do! I could not tell what to do, till I brake my mind to *Faithful;* for he and I were well acquainted: And he told me, That unless I could obtain the righteousness of a man that never had sinned, neither mine own, nor all the righteousness of the World could save me.

Chr. *And did you think he spake true?*

Hope. Had he told me so when I was pleased and satisfied with mine own amendments, I had called him Fool for his pains: but now, since I see my own infirmity, and the sin that cleaves to my best performance, I have been forced to be of his opinion.

Chr. *But did you think, when at first he suggested it to you, that there was such a man to be found, of whom it might justly be said, That he never committed sin?*

At which he started at present.

Hope. I must confess the words at first sounded strangely, but after a little more talk and company with him, I had full conviction about it.

Chr. *And did you ask him what man this was, and how you must be justified by him?*

Heb. 10. Rom. 4. Col. 1. 1 Pet. 1. * *A more particular discovery of the way to be saved.*

Hope. Yes, and he told me it was the Lord Jesus, that dwelleth on the right hand of the most High: *And thus, said he, you must be justified by him, even by trusting to what he hath done by himself in the days of his flesh, and suffered when he did hang on the Tree. I asked him further, How that mans righteousness could be of that efficacy, to justifie another before God? And he told me, He was the mighty God, and did what he did, and died the death also, not for himself, but for me; to whom his doings, and the worthiness of them should be imputed, if I believed on him.

Chr. *And what did you do then?*

He doubts of acceptation.

Hope. I made my objections against my believing, for that I thought he was not willing to save me.

Chr. *And what said* Faithful *to you then?*

Hope. He bid me go to him and see: Then I said, It was presumption: but he said, No: for I was invited to come. Mat. 11. 28.

*Then he gave me a Book of *Jesus* his inditing, to incourage me the more freely to come: And he said concerning that Book, That every jot and tittle there of stood firmer then Heaven and earth. Then I asked him, What I must do when I came? and he told me, I must intreat upon my knees with all my heart and soul, the Father to reveal him to me. Then I asked him further, How I must make my supplication to him? And he said, Go, and thou shalt find him upon a mercy-seat, where he sits all the year long, to give pardon and forgiveness to them that come. I told him that I knew not what to say when I came: *and he bid me say to this effect, *God be merciful to me a sinner,*† *and make me to know and believe in Jesus Christ; for I see that if his righteousness had not been, or I have not faith in that righteousness, I am utterly cast away: Lord, I have heard that thou art a merciful God, and hast ordained that thy Son Jesus Christ should be the Saviour of the world; and moreover, that thou art willing to bestow him upon such a poor sinner as I am, (and I am a sinner indeed) Lord take therefore this opportunity, and magnifie thy grace in the Salvation of my soul, through thy Son Jesus Christ*. Amen.

** He is better instructed.*

Mat. 24. 35.

Psal. 95. 6. Dan. 6. 10. Jer. 29. 12, 13. Exod. 25. 22. Lev. 16. 9. Numb. 7. 8, 9. Heb. 4. 16.

** He is bid to pray.*

Chr. *And did you do as you were bidden?*

Hope. Yes, over, and over, and over.

Chr. *And did the Father reveal his Son to you?*

Hope. Not at the first, nor second, nor third, nor fourth, nor fifth; no, nor at the sixth time neither.

He prays.

Chr. *What did you do then?*

Hope. What! why I could not tell what to do.

Chr. *Had you not thoughts of leaving off praying?*

Hope. *Yes, an hundred times, twice told.

** He thought to leave off praying.*

Chr. *And what was the reason you did not?*

Hope. *I believed that that was true which had been told me, *to wit*, That without the righteousness of this Christ, all the World could not save me: And therefore thought I with my self, If I leave off, I die; and I can but die at the Throne of Grace. And withall, this came into my mind, *If it tarry, wait for it, because it will surely come, and will not tarry.* So I continued Praying until the Father shewed me his Son.

** He durst not leave off praying, and why.*

Habb. 2. 3.

Chr. *And how was he revealed unto you?*

Hope. I did *not* see him with my bodily eyes, but with the

Ephes. 1. 18, 19. eyes of mine understanding; and thus it was. One day I was very sad, I think sader then at any one time in my life; and this sadness was through a fresh sight of the greatness and vileness of my sins: And as I was then looking for nothing but *Hell*, and the everlasting damnation of my Soul, suddenly, as I thought, I saw the Lord Jesus look down from Heaven upon me,† and saying, *Believe on the Lord Jesus Christ, and thou shalt be saved.*

Christ is revealed to him, and how.

Act. 16. 30, 31.

But I replyed, Lord, I am a great, a very great sinner; and he answered, *My grace is sufficient for thee.*† Then I said But Lord, what is believing? And then I saw from that saying, [*He that cometh to me shall never hunger, and he that believeth on me shall never thirst*] That believing and coming was all one, and that he that came, that is, run out in his heart and affections after Salvation by Christ, he indeed believed in Christ. Then the water stood in mine eyes, and I asked further, But Lord, may such a great sinner as I am, be indeed accepted of thee, and be saved by thee? And I heard him say, *And him that cometh to me, I will in no wise cast out.*† Then I said, But how, Lord, must I consider of thee in my coming to thee, that my Faith may be placed aright upon thee? Then he said, *Christ Jesus came into the World to save sinners. He is the end of the Law for righteousness to every one that believes. He died for our sins, and rose again for our justification: He loved us, and washed us from our sins in his own blood: He is Mediator* between God and us.† *He ever liveth to make intercession for us.* From all which I gathered, that I must look for righteousness in his person, and for satisfaction for my sins by his blood;† that what he did in obedience to his Fathers Law, and in submitting to the penalty thereof, was not for himself, but for him that will accept it for his Salvation, and be thankful. And now was my heart full of joy, mine eyes full of tears, and mine affections running over with love, to the Name, People, and Ways of Jesus Christ.

2 Cor. 12. 9.
John 6. 35.
John 6. 37.
1 Tim. 1. 15.
Rom. 10. 4.
chap. 4.
Heb. 7. 24, 25.

Chr. *This was a Revelation of Christ to your soul indeed: But tell me particularly what effect this had upon your spirit?*

Hope. It made me see that all the World, notwithstanding all the righteousness thereof, is in a state of condemnation. It made me see that God the Father, though he be just, can justly justifie the coming sinner: It made me greatly ashamed of the vileness of my former life, and confounded me with the sence of mine own Ignorance; for there never came thought into mine heart before now, that shewed me so the beauty of Jesus Christ. It made me love a holy life, and long to do something for the Honour and Glory of the Name of the Lord Jesus. Yea I thought, that had I now a thousand gallons of blood in my body, I could spill it all for the sake of the Lord Jesus.†

I then saw in my Dream, that *Hopeful* looked back and saw *Ignorance*, whom they had left behind, coming after. *Look*, said he, to *Christian, how far yonder Youngster loitereth behind.*

Chr. Ay, Ay, I see him; he careth not for our Company.

Hope. *But I tro, it would not have hurt him, had he kept pace with us hitherto.*

Chr. That's true, but I warrant you he thinketh otherwise.

Hope. *That I think he doth, but however let us tarry for him.* So they did. *Young* Ignorance *comes up again.*

Then *Christian* said to him, *Come away man, why do you stay so behind?*

Ign. I take my pleasure in walking alone, even more a great deal then in Company, unless I like it the better. *Their talk.*

Then said *Christian* to *Hopeful*, (but softly) *did I not tell you he cared not for our Company: But however, come up and let us talk away the time in this solitary place.* Then directing his Speech to *Ignorance*, he said, *Come, how do you? how stands it between God and your Soul now?*

Ignor. *I hope well, for I am always full of good motions, that come into my mind to comfort me as I walk. * Ignorance's *hope, and the ground of it.*

Chr. *What good motions? pray tell us.*

Ignor. Why, I think of God and Heaven.

Chr. *So do the Devils, and damned Souls.*

Ignor. But I think of them, and desire them.

Chr. *So do many that are never like to come there:* The Soul of the Sluggard desires and hath nothing.†

Ignor. But I think of them, and leave all for them.

Chr. *That I doubt, for leaving of all, is an hard matter, yea a harder matter then many are aware of. But why, or by what, art thou perswaded that thou hast left all for God and Heaven?*

Ignor. My heart tells me so.

Chr. *The wise man sayes*, He that trusts his own heart is a fool. Prov. 28. 26.

Ignor. That is spoken of an evil heart, but mine is a good one.

Chr. *But how dost thou prove that?*

Ignor. It comforts me in the hopes of Heaven.

Chr. *That may be, through its deceitfulness, for a mans heart may minister comfort to him in the hopes of that thing, for which he yet has no ground to hope.*

Ignor. But my heart and life agree together, and therefore my hope is well grounded.

Chr. *Who told thee that thy heart and life agrees together?*

Ignor. My heart tells me so.

Chr. *Ask my fellow if I be a Thief:*† *Thy heart tells thee so! Except the word of God beareth witness in this matter, other Testimony is of no value.*

Ignor. But is it not a good heart that has good thoughts? And is not that a good life, that is according to Gods Commandments?

Chr. *Yes, that is a good heart that hath good thoughts, and that is a good life that is according to Gods Commandments: But it is one thing indeed to have these, and another thing only to think so.*

Ignor. Pray, what count you good thoughts, and a life according to Gods Commandments?

Chr. *There are good thoughts of divers kinds, some respecting our selves, some God, some Christ, and some other things.*

Ignor. What be good thoughts respecting our selves?

What are good thoughts?

Chr. *Such as agree with the Word of God.*

Ignor. When does our thoughts of our selves, agree with the Word of God?

Chr. *When we pass the same Judgement upon our selves which the Word passes. To explain my self: The Word of God saith of*
Rom. 3. *persons in a natural condition*, There is none Righteous, there is
Gen. 6. 5. none that doth good. *It saith also*, That every imagination of the heart of man is only evil, and that continually. *And again*, The imagination of mans heart is evil from his Youth.† *Now then, when we think thus of our selves, having sense thereof, then are our thoughts good ones, because according to the Word of God.*

Ignor. I will never believe that my heart is thus bad.

Chr. *Therefore thou never hadst one good thought concerning thy self in thy life. But let me go on: As the Word passeth a Judgement upon our HEART, so it passeth a Judgement upon our WAYS; and when our thoughts of our HEARTS and WAYS agree with the Judgement which the Word giveth of both, then are both good, because agreeing thereto.*

Ignor. Make out your meaning.

Chr. *Why, the Word of God saith, That mans ways are crooked ways, not good, but perverse: It saith, They are naturally out of the good way, that they have not known it. Now when a man thus thinketh of his ways, I say when he doth sensibly, and with heart-humiliation thus think, then hath he good thoughts of his own ways, because his thoughts now agree with the judgment of the Word of God.*

Psal. 125. 5. Prov. 2. 15. Rom. 3.

Ignor. What are good thoughts concerning God?

Chr. *Even (as I have said concerning ourselves) when our thoughts of God do agree with what the Word saith of him. And that is, when we think of his Being and Attributes as the Word hath taught: Of which I cannot now discourse at large. But to speak of him with reference to us, Then we have right thoughts of God, when we think that he knows us better then we know our selves, and can see sin in us, when, and where we can see none in our selves; when we think he knows our in-most thoughts, and that our heart, with all its depths is always open unto his eyes: Also when we think that all our Righteousness stinks in his Nostrils, and that therefore he cannot abide to see us stand before him in any confidence, even of all our best performances.*

Ignor. Do you think that I am such a fool, as to think God can see no further then I? or that I would come to God in the best of my performances?

Chr. *Why, how dost thou think in this matter?*

Ignor. Why, to be short, I think I must believe in Christ for Justification.†

Chr. *How! think thou must believe in Christ, when thou seest not thy need of him! Thou neither seest thy original, nor actual infirmities, but hast such an opinion of thy self, and of what thou dost, as plainly renders thee to be one that did never see a necessity of Christs personal righteousness to justifie thee before God: How then dost thou say, I believe in Christ?*

Ignor. I believe well enough for all that.

Chr. *How dost thou believe?*

Ignor. I believe that Christ died for sinners, and that I shall be justified before God from the curse, through his gracious acceptance of my obedience to his Law: Or thus, Christ makes my Duties that are Religious, acceptable to his Father by vertue of his Merits; and so shall I be justified.

Chr. *Let me give an answer to this confession of thy faith.*

The Faith of Ignorance.

1. *Thou believest with a* Fantastical *Faith, for this faith is no where described in the Word.*

2. *Thou believest with a* False *Faith, because it taketh Justification from the personal righteousness of Christ, and applies it to thy own.*

3. *This faith maketh not Christ a Justifier of thy person, but of thy actions; and of thy person for thy actions sake, which is false.*

4. *Therefore this faith is deceitful, even such as will leave thee under wrath, in the day of God Almighty. For true Justifying Faith puts the soul (as sensible of its lost condition by the Law) upon flying for refuge unto Christs righteousness: (which righteousness of* his, *is, not an act of grace, by which he maketh for Justification* thy *obedience accepted with God, but* his *personal obedience to the Law in doing and suffering for us, what that required at our hands.) This righteousness, I say, true faith accepteth, under the skirt*† *of which, the soul being shrouded, and by it presented as spotless before God, it is accepted, and acquit from condemnation.*

Ignor. What! would you have us trust to what Christ in his own person has done without us? This conceit would loosen the reines of our lust, and tollerate us to live as we list: For what matter how we live if we may be Justified by Christs personal righteousness from all, when we believe it?†

Chr. Ignorance *is thy name, and as thy name is, so art thou; even this thy answer demonstrateth what I say.* Ignorant *thou art of what Justifying righteousness is, and, as* Ignorant *how to secure thy Soul through the faith of it from the heavy wrath of God. Yea, thou also art* Ignorant *of the true effects of saving faith in this righteousness of Christ, which is, to bow and win over the heart to God in Christ, to love his Name, his Word, Ways and People, and not as thou* ignorantly *imaginest.*

Hope. Ask him if ever he had Christ revealed to him from Heaven?

Ignor. *What! you are a man for revelations! I believe that what both you, and all the rest of you say about that matter, is but the fruit of distracted braines.*

Ignorance *angles with them.*

Hope. Why man! Christ is so hid in God from the natural apprehensions of all flesh, that he cannot by any man be savingly known, unless God the Father reveals him to them.

Ignor. *That is your faith, but not mine; yet mine I doubt not, is as good as yours: though I have not in my head so many whimzies as you.*

He speaks reproachfully of what he knows not.

Chr. Give me leave to put in a word: You ought not so slightly to speak of this matter: for this I will boldly affirm, (even as my good Companion hath done) that no man can know Jesus Christ but by the Revelation of the Father: yea, and faith too, by which the soul layeth hold upon Christ (if it be right) must be wrought by the exceeding greatness of his mighty power, the working of which faith, I perceive, poor *Ignorance*, thou art ignorant of. Be awakened then, see thine own wretchedness, and flie to the Lord Jesus; and by his righteousness, which is the righteousness of God, (for he himself is God) thou shalt be delivered from condemnation.

Mat. 11. 27. 1 Cor. 12. 3. Eph. 1. 18, 19

Ignor. *You go so fast, I cannot keep pace with you; do you go on before, I must stay a while behind.*

The talk broke up.

Then they said,

> *Well* Ignorance, *wilt thou yet foolish be,*
> *To slight good Counsel, ten times given thee?*
> *And if thou yet refuse it, thou shalt know*
> *Ere long the evil of thy doing so:*
> *Remember man in time, stoop, do not fear,*
> *Good Counsel taken well, saves; therefore hear:*
> *But if thou yet shalt slight it, thou wilt be*
> *The loser* (Ignorance) *I'le warrant thee.*

Then *Christian* addressed thus himself to his fellow.

Chr. Well, come my good *Hopeful*, I perceive that thou and I must walk by our selves again.

So I saw in my Dream, that they went on a pace before, and *Ignorance* he came hobling after. Then said *Christian* to his Companion, *It pities me much for this poor man, it will certainly go ill with him at last.*

Hope. Alas, there are abundance in our Town in his condition; whole Families, yea, whole Streets, (and that of Pilgrims too) and if there be so many in our parts, how many, think you, must there be in the place where he was born?

Chr. *Indeed the Word saith*, He hath blinded their eyes, lest they should see, *&c.*† *But now we are by our selves, what do you think of such men? Have they at no time, think you, convictions of sin, and so consequently fears that their state is dangerous?*

Hope. Nay, do you answer that question your self, for you are the elder man.

Chr. *Then, I say, sometimes (as I think) they may, but they being naturally ignorant, understand not that such convictions tend to their good; and therefore they do desperately seek to stifle them, and presumptuously continue to flatter themselves in the way of their own hearts.*

The good use of fear.

Hope. I do believe as you say, that fear tends much to Mens good, and to make them right, at their beginning to go on Pilgrimage.

Job 28. 28. Psal. 111. 10. Prov. 1. 7. ch. 9. 10.

Chr. *Without all doubt it doth, if it be right: for so says the Word*, The fear of the Lord is the beginning of Wisdom.

Hope. How will you describe right fear?

Right fear.

Chr. *True, or right fear, is discovered by three things.*

1. By its rise. It is caused by saving convictions for sin.

2. It driveth the soul to lay fast hold of Christ for Salvation.

3. It begetteth and continueth in the soul a great reverence of God, his word, and ways, keeping it tender, and making it afraid to turn from them, to the right hand, or to the left, to any thing that may dishonour God, break its peace, grieve the Spirit, or cause the enemy to speak reproachfully.

Hope. Well said, I believe you have said the truth. Are we now almost got past the Inchanted ground?

Chr. *Why, are you weary of this discourse?*

Hope. No verily, but that I would know where we are.

Why ignorant persons stifle convictions.
** 1. In general.*

Chr. *We have not now above two Miles further to go thereon. But let us return to our matter. *Now the Ignorant know not that such convictions that tend to put them in fear, are for their good, and therefore they seek to stifle them.*

Hope. How do they seek to stifle them?

** 2. In particular.*

Chr. *1. They think that those fears are wrought by the

Devil (though indeed they are wrought of God) and thinking so, they resist them, as things that directly tend to their overthrow. 2. They also think that these fears tend to the spoiling of their faith, (when alas for them, poor men that they are! they have none at all) and therefore they harden their hearts against them. 3. They presume they ought not to fear, and therefore, in despite of them, wax presumptuously confident. 4. They see that these fears tend to take away from them their pitiful old self-holiness, and therefore they resist them with all their might.

Hope. I know something of this my self; for before I knew my self it was so with me.

Chr. *Well, we will leave at this time our Neighbour* Ignorance *by himself, and fall upon another profitable question.*

Hope. With all my heart, but you shall still begin.

Talk about one Temporary.

Chr. *Well then, Did you not know about ten years ago, one* Temporary *in your parts, who was a forward man in Religion then?*

Hope. Know him! Yes, he dwelt in *Graceless*, a Town about two miles off of *Honesty*, and he dwelt next door to one *Turn-back*.

Where he dwelt.

Chr. *Right, he dwelt under the same roof with him. Well, that man was much awakened once;* I believe that then he had some sight of his sins, and of the wages that was due thereto.*†

** He was towardly once.*

Hope. I am of your mind, for (my house not being above three miles from him) he would oft times come to me, and that with many tears. Truly I pitied the man, and was not altogether without hope of him; but one may see, it is not every one that cries, *Lord, Lord.*†

Chr. *He told me once, That he was resolved to go on Pilgrimage, as we do now; but all of a sudden he grew acquainted with one* Save-self, *and then he became a stranger to me.*

Hope. Now since we are talking about him, let us a little enquire into the reason of the suddain backsliding of him and such others.

Chr. *It may be very profitable, but do you begin.*

Hope. Well then, there are in my judgement four reasons for it.

Reason, why towardly ones go back.

1. Though the Consciences of such men are awakened, yet their minds are not changed: therefore when the power of

guilt weareth away, that which provoked them to be Religious, ceaseth. Wherefore they naturally turn to their own course again: even as we see the Dog that is sick of what he hath eaten, so long as his sickness prevails, he vomits and casts up all; not that he doth this of a free mind (if we may say a Dog has a mind) but because it troubleth his Stomach; but now when his sickness is over, and so his Stomach eased, his desires being not at all alienate from his vomit, he turns him about,
2 Pet. 2. 22. and licks up all. And so it is true which is written, *The Dog is turned to his own vomit again*. Thus, I say, being hot for Heaven, by virtue only of the sense and fear of the torments of Hell, as their sense of Hell, and the fears of damnation chills and cools, so their desires for Heaven and Salvation cool also. So then it comes to pass, that when their guilt and fear is gone, their desires for Heaven and Happiness die; and they return to their course again.

2ly. Another reason is, They have slavish fears that do overmaster them. I speak now of the fears that they have of men:
Prov. 29. 25. *For the fear of men bringeth a snare.* So then, though they seem to be hot for Heaven, so long as the flames of Hell are about their ears, yet when that terrour is a little over, they betake themselves to second thoughts; namely, that 'tis good to be wise, and not to run (for they know not what) the hazard of loosing all; or at least, of bringing themselves into unavoidable and unnecessary troubles: and so they fall in with the world again.

3ly. The shame that attends Religion, lies also as a block in their way; they are proud and haughty, and Religion in their eye is low and contemptible: Therefore when they have lost their sense of Hell and wrath to come, they return again to their former course.

4ly, Guilt, and to meditate terrour, are grievous to them, they like not to see their misery before they come into it: Though perhaps the sight of it first, if they loved that sight, might make them flie whither the righteous flie and are safe; but because they do, as I hinted before, even shun the thoughts of guilt and terrour, therefore, when once they are rid of their awakenings about the terrors and wrath of God, they harden their hearts gladly, and chuse such ways as will harden them more and more.

Chr. *You are pretty near the business, for the bottom of all is, for want of a change in their mind and will. And therefore they are but like the Fellon that standeth before the Judge: he quakes and trembles, and seems to repent most heartily; but the bottom of all is, the fear of the Halter, not of any detestation of the offence; as is evident, because, let but this man have his liberty, and he will be a Thief, and so a Rogue still; whereas, if his mind was changed, he would be otherwise.*

Hope. Now I have shewed you the reasons of their going back, do you shew me the manner thereof.

Chr. *So I will willingly.*

1. They draw off their thoughts all that they may from the remembrance of God, Death, and Judgement to come. *How the Apostate goes back.*

2. Then they cast off by degrees private Duties, as Closet-Prayer, curbing their lusts, watching, sorrow for Sin, and the like.

3. Then they shun the company of lively and warm Christians.

4. After that, they grow cold to publick Duty, as Hearing, Reading, Godly Conference,† and the like.

5. Then they begin to pick holes, as we say, in the Coats of some of the Godly, and that devilishly that they may have a seeming colour to throw Religion (for the sake of some infirmity they have spied in them) behind their backs.

6. Then they begin to adhere to, and associate themselves with carnal, loose, and wanton men.

7. Then they give way to carnal and wanton discourses in secret; and glad are they if they can see such things in any that are counted honest, that they may the more boldly do it through their example.

8. After this, they begin to play with little sins openly.

9. And then, being hardened, they shew themselves as they are. Thus being lanched again into the gulf of misery, unless a Miracle of Grace prevent it, they everlastingly perish in their own deceivings.†

Now I saw in my Dream, that by this time the Pilgrims were got over the Inchanted Ground, and entering into the Country of *Beulah*,† whose Air was very sweet and pleasant, the way lying directly through it, they solaced themselves there for a Isa. 62. 4. Cant. 2. 10, 11, 12.

season. Yea, here they heard continually the singing of Birds, and saw every day the flowers appear in the earth: and heard the voice of the Turtle in the Land. In this Countrey the Sun shineth night and day; wherefore this was beyond the Valley of the *shadow of death*, and also out of the reach of Giant *Despair*; neither could they from this place so much as see *Doubting-Castle*. Here they were within sight of the City they were going
Angels. to: also here met them some of the Inhabitants thereof. For in this Land the shining Ones commonly walked, because it was upon the Borders of Heaven. In this Land also the contract
Isa. 62. 5. between the Bride and the Bridgroom was renewed: Yea here,
ver. 8. *as the Bridegroom rejoyceth over the Bride, so did their God rejoyce over them*. Here they had no want of Corn and Wine; for in this place they met with abundance of what they had sought for in all their Pilgrimage. Here they heard voices from out of the City, loud voices, saying, *Say ye to the daughter of*
ver. 11. Zion, *Behold thy Salvation cometh, behold his reward is with him*.
ver. 12. Here all the Inhabitants of the Countrey called them, *The holy People, the redeemed of the Lord, Sought out*, &c.

Now as they walked in this Land they had more rejoycing then in parts more remote from the Kingdom, to which they were bound; and drawing near to the City, they had yet a more perfect view thereof.† It was builded of Pearls and Precious Stones, also the Street thereof was paved with Gold, so that by reason of the natural glory of the City, and the reflection of the Sunbeams upon it, *Christian*, with desire fell sick, *Hopeful* also had a fit or two of the same Disease: Wherefore here they lay by it a while, crying out because of their pangs, *If you see my Beloved, tell him that I am sick of love*.†

But being a little strengthned, and better able to bear their sickness, they walked on their way, and came yet nearer and nearer, where were Orchards, Vineyards, and Gardens, and their Gates opened into the Highway. Now as they came up to these places, behold the Gardener stood in the way; to whom
Deut. 23. 24. the Pilgrims said, Whose goodly Vineyards and Gardens are these? He answered, They are the Kings, and are planted here for his own delights, and also for the solace of Pilgrims, So the Gardiner had them into the Vineyards, and bid them refresh themselves with the Dainties; he also shewed them *there* the

Kings Walks and the *Arbors* where he delighted to be: And here they tarried and slept.

Now I beheld in my Dream, that they talked more in their sleep at this time, then ever they did in all their Journey; and being in a muse there-about, the Gardiner said even to me, Wherefore musest thou at the matter? It is the nature of the fruit of the Grapes of these Vineyards to go down so sweetly, as to cause the lips of them that are asleep to speak.

So I saw that when they awoke, they addressed themselves to go up to the City. But, as I said, the reflections of the Sun upon the City, (for the City was pure Gold) was so extreamly glorious, that they could not, as yet, with open face behold it, but through an *Instrument* made for that purpose. So I saw, that as they went on, there met them two men, in Raiment that shone like Gold, also their faces shone as the light.

Rev. 21. 18.

2 Cor. 3. 18.

These men asked the Pilgrims whence they came? and they told them; they also asked them, Where they had lodg'd, what difficulties, and dangers, what comforts and pleasures they had met in the way? and they told them. Then said the men that met them, You have but two difficulties more to meet with, and then you are in the City.

Christian then and his Companion asked the men to go along with them, so they told them they would; but, said they, you must obtain it by your own faith. So I saw in my Dream that they went on together till they came within sight of the Gate.

Death.

Now I further saw, that betwixt them and the Gate was a River, but there was no Bridge to go over; the River was very deep; at the sight therefore of this River, the Pilgrims were much stounded, but the men that went with them, said, You must go through, or you cannot come at the Gate.

Death is not welcome to nature though by it we pass out of this World into glory.

1 Cor. 15. 51, 52.

The Pilgrims then began to enquire if there was no other way to the Gate; to which they answered, Yes; but there hath not any, save two, to wit, *Enoch* and *Elijah*,† been permitted to tread that path, since the foundation of the World, nor shall, until the last Trumpet shall sound. The Pilgrims then, especially *Christian*, began to dispond in his mind, and looked this way and that, but no way could be found by them, by which they might escape the River. Then they asked the men if the Waters were all of a depth. They said no; yet they could not help them in that Case; for said they, *You shall find it deeper or shallower, as you believe in the King of the place.*

Angels help us not comfortably through death.

They then addressed themselves to the Water; and entering, *Christian* began to sink, and crying out to his good friend *Hopeful*; he said, I sink in deep Waters, the Billows go over my head, all his Waves go over me, *Selah*.†

Then said the other, Be of good chear, my Brother, I feel the bottom, and it is good. Then said *Christian*, Ah my friend, the sorrows of death have compassed me about,† I shall not see the Land that flows with Milk and Honey,† And with that, a great darkness and horror fell upon *Christian*,† so that he could not see before him; also here he in great measure lost his senses, so that he could neither remember nor orderly talk of any of those sweet refreshments that he had met with in the way of his Pilgrimage. But all the words that he spake, still tended to discover that he had horror of mind, and hearty fears that he should die in that River, and never obtain entrance in at the Gate: Here also, as they that stood by, perceived, he was much in the troublesome thoughts of the sins that he had committed, both since and before he began to be a Pilgrim. 'Twas also observed, that he was troubled with apparitions of Hobgoblins and Evil Spirits, For ever and anon he would intimate so much by words. *Hopeful* therefore here had much adoe to keep his Brothers head above water, yea sometimes he would be quite gone down, and then ere a while he would rise up again half dead. *Hopeful* also would endeavour to comfort him, saying, Brother, I see the Gate, and men standing by it to receive us. But *Christian* would answer, 'Tis you, 'tis you they wait for, you have been *Hopeful* ever since I knew you: and so have you, said he to *Christian*. Ah Brother, said he, surely if I was right, he would now arise to help me; but for my sins he hath brought me into the snare, and hath left me. Then said *Hopeful*, My Brother, you have quite forgot the Text, where its said of the wicked, *There is no band in their death, but their strength is firm, they are not troubled as other men, neither are they plagued like other men.* These troubles and distresses that you go through in these Waters, are no sign that God hath forsaken

Christians *conflict at the hour of death.*

Psal. 73. 4, 5.

you, but are sent to try you, whether you will call to mind that which heretofore you have received of his goodness, and live upon him in your distresses.

Then I saw in my Dream that *Christian* was as in a muse a while; to whom also *Hopeful* added this word, *Be of good cheer, Jesus Christ maketh thee whole:*† And with that, *Christian* brake out with a loud voice, Oh I see him again! and he tells me, *When thou passest through the waters, I will be with thee, and through the Rivers, they shall not overflow thee*. Then they both took courage, and the enemy was after that as still as a stone, until they were gone over.† *Christian* therefore presently found ground to stand upon; and so it followed that the rest of the River was but shallow. Thus they got over. Now upon the bank of the River, on the other side, they saw the two shining men again, who there waited for them. Wherefore being come up out of the River, they saluted them, saying, *We are ministring Spirits, sent forth to minister for those that shall be Heirs of Salvation.*† Thus they went along towards the Gate, now you must note that the City stood upon a mighty hill, but the Pilgrims went up that hill *with ease*, because they had these two men to lead them up by the Arms; also they had left their *Mortal* Garments behind them in the River: for though they went in with them, they came out without them. They therefore went up here with much agility and speed, though the foundation upon which the City was framed was higher then the Clouds. They therefore went up through the Regions of the Air, sweetly talking as they went, being comforted, because they safely got over the River, and had such glorious Companions to attend them.

Christian *delivered from his fears in death.*

Isa. 43. 2.

The Angels do wait for them so soon as they are passed out of this world.

They have put off mortality.

The talk that they had with the shining Ones, was about the glory of the place, who told them, that the beauty, and glory of it was inexpressible. There, said they, is the Mount *Sion*, the heavenly *Jerusalem*, the inumerable company of Angels, and the Spirits of Just Men made perfect:† You are going now, said they, to the Paradice of God, wherein you shall see the Tree of Life, and eat of the never-fading fruits thereof: And when you come there, you shall have white Robes given you, and your walk and talk shall be every day with the King, even all the days of eternity. There you shall not see again, such things as

Heb. 12. 22, 23, 24.
Rev. 2. 7.
Rev. 3. 4.

Rev. 21. 1.

Now, now look how the holy Pilgrims ride,
Clouds are their Chariots, Angels are their Guide:
Who would not here for him all Hazards run,
That thus provides for his when this World's done!

you saw when you were in the lower Region upon the earth, to wit, sorrow, sickness, affliction, and death, *for the former things are passed away*.† You are going now to *Abraham, to Isaac*, and *Jacob*, and to the Prophets; men that God hath taken away from the evil to come, and that are now resting upon their Beds, each one walking in his rightousness.† The men then asked, What must we do in the holy place? To whom it was answered, You must there receive the comfort of all your toil, and have joy for all your sorrow; you must reap what you have sown, even the fruit of all your Prayers and Tears, and sufferings for the King by the way. In that place you must wear Crowns of Gold, and enjoy the perpetual sight and Visions of the *Holy One, for there you shall see him as he is*. There also you shall serve him continually with praise, with shouting and thanksgiving, whom you desired to serve in the World, though with much difficulty, because of the infirmity of your flesh. There your eyes shall be delighted with seeing, and your ears with hearing, the pleasant voice of the mighty One. There you shall enjoy your friends again, that are got thither before you; and there you shall with joy receive, even every one that follows into the Holy place after you. There also you shall be cloathed with Glory and Majesty, and put into an equipage fit to ride out with the King of Glory. When he shall come with sound of Trumpet in the Clouds, as upon the wings of the Wind, you shall come with him; and when he shall sit upon the Throne of Judgement, you shall sit by him; yea, and when he shall pass Sentence upon all the workers of Iniquity, let them be Angels or Men, you also shall have a voice in that Judgement, because they were his and your Enemies. Also when he shall again return to the City, you shall go too, with sound of Trumpet, and be ever with him.

Isa. 57. 1, 2.
Isa. 65. 14.
Gal. 6. 7.
1 John 3. 2.
1 Thes. 4. 13, 14, 15, 16.
Jude 14.
Da. 7. 9, 10.
1 Cor. 6. 2, 3.

Now while they were thus drawing towards the Gate, behold a company of the Heavenly Host came out to meet them: To whom it was said, by the other two shining Ones, These are the men that have loved our Lord, when they were in the World, and that have left all for his holy Name, and he hath sent us to fetch them, and we have brought them thus far on their desired Journey; that they may go in and look their Redeemer in the face with joy. Then the Heavenly Host gave

Rev. 19. a great shout, saying, *Blessed are they that are called to the Marriage Supper of the Lamb*.

There came out also at this time to meet them, several of the Kings Trumpeters, cloathed in white and shining Rayment, who with melodious noises, and loud, made even the Heavens to eccho with their sound. These Trumpeters saluted *Christian* and his Fellow with ten thousand welcomes from the world: And this they did with shouting, and sound of Trumpet.

This done, they compassed them round on every side; some went before, some behind, and some on the right hand, some on the left (as 'twere to guard them through the upper Regions) continually sounding as they went, with melodious noise, in notes on high; so that the very sight was to them that could behold it, as if Heaven it self was come down to meet them. Thus therefore they walked on together, and as they walked, ever and anon, these Trumpeters, even, with joyful sound, would, by mixing their Musick, with looks and gestures, still signifie to *Christian* and his Brother, how welcome they were into their company, and with what gladness they came to meet them: And now were these two men, as 'twere, in Heaven, before they came at it; being swallowed up with the sight of Angels, and with hearing of their melodious notes. Here also they had the City it self in view, and they thought they heard all the Bells therein to ring, to welcome them thereto: but above all, the warm and joyful thoughts that they had about their own dwelling there, with such company, and that for ever and ever. Oh! by what tongue or pen can their glorious joy be expressed: and thus they came up to the Gate.

Now when they were come up to the Gate, there was written
Rev. 22. 14. over it, in Letters of Gold, *Blessed are they that do his commandments, that they may have right to the Tree of Life; and may enter in through the Gates into the City*.

Then I saw in my Dream, that the shining men bid them call at the Gate, the which when they did, some from above looked over the Gate; to wit, *Enoch, Moses*, and *Elijah, &c.* to whom it was said, These Pilgrims are come from the City of *Destruction*, for the love that they bear to the King of this place: and then the Pilgrims gave in unto them each man his Certificate, which they had received in the beginning; those therefore were

carried into the King, who when he had read them, said, Where are the men? to whom it was answered, They are standing without the Gate. The King then commanded to open the Gate; *That the righteous Nation*, said he, *that keepeth Truth may* Isa. 26. 2.
enter in.

Now I saw in my Dream, that these two men went in at the Gate; and loe, as they entered, they were transfigured, and they had Raiment put on that shone like Gold. There was also that met them with Harps and Crowns, and gave them to them; The Harp to praise withal, and the Crowns in token of honor: Then I heard in my Dream, that all the Bells in the City Rang again for joy; and that it was said unto them, *Enter ye into the joy of your Lord*.† I also heard the men themselves, that they sang with a loud voice, saying, *Blessing, Honour, Glory, and* Rev. 5. 13, 14.
Power, be to him that sitteth upon the Throne, and to the Lamb for ever and ever.

Now just as the Gates were opened to let in the men, I looked in after them; and behold, the City shone like the Sun, the Streets also were paved with Gold, and in them walked many men, with Crowns on their heads, Palms in their hands, and golden Harps† to sing praises withall.

There were also of them that had wings, and they answered one another without intermission, saying, *Holy, Holy, Holy, is the Lord*.† And after that, they shut up the Gates: which when I had seen, I wished my self among them.

Now while I was gazing upon all these things, I turned my head to look back, and saw *Ignorance* come up to the River side: but he soon got over, and that without half that difficulty which the other two men met with. For it happened, that there was then in that place one *Vain-hope* a Ferry-man, that with his Boat helped him over: so he, as the other I saw, did ascend the Hill to come up to the Gate, only he came alone; neither did any man meet him with the least incouragement. When he was come up to the Gate, he looked up to the writing that was above; and then began to knock, supposing that entrance should have been quickly administered to him: But he was asked by the men that lookt over the top of the Gate, Whence came you? and what would you have? He answered, I have eat and drank in the presence of the King, and he has taught in our

Streets.† Then they asked him for his Certificate, that they might go in and shew it to the King. So he fumbled in his bosom for one, and found none. Then said they, Have you none? But the man answered never a word. So they told the King, but he would not come down to see him; but commanded the two shining Ones that conducted *Christian* and *Hopeful* to the City, to go out and take *Ignorance* and bind him hand and foot,† and have him away. Then they took him up, and carried him through the air to the door that I saw in the side of the Hill, and put him in there. Then I saw that there was a way to Hell, even from the Gates of Heaven, as well as from the City of *Destruction*. So I awoke, and behold it was a Dream.

FINIS

THE CONCLUSION

Now Reader, I have told my Dream to thee;
See if thou canst Interpret it to me;
Or to thy self, or Neighbour: but take heed
Of mis-interpreting: for that, instead
Of doing good, will but thy self abuse:
By mis-interpreting evil insues.
Take heed also, that thou be not extream,
In playing with the out-side *of my Dream:*
Nor let my figure, or similitude,
Put thee into a laughter or a feud;
Leave this for Boys *and* Fools; *but as for thee,*
Do thou the substance of my matter see.
Put by the Curtains, look within my Vail;
Turn up my Metaphors and do not fail:
There, if thou seekest them, such things to find,
As will be helpful to an honest mind.
What of my dross *thou findest there, be bold*
To throw away, but yet preserve the Gold.
What if my Gold be wrapped up in Ore?
None throws away the Apple for the Core:
But if thou shalt cast all away as vain,
I know not but 'twill make me Dream again.

THE END

The Pilgrims Progress Pt 2d
Destruction
Sturt sc
Sold by N. Ponder at the Peacock in the Poultry

THE

Pilgrim's Progreſs.

FROM

THIS WORLD

TO

That which is to come

The Second Part.

Delivered under the Similitude of a

DREAM

Wherein is ſet forth

The manner of the ſetting out of *Chri ſtian's* Wife and Children, their Dangerous JOURNEY,

AND

Safe Arrival at the Deſired Country.

By *JOHN BUNYAN.*

I have uſed Similitudes, Hoſ. 12. 10.

LONDON,

Printed for *Nathaniel Ponder* at the *Peacock* in the *Poultry*, near the Church. 1684.

THE AUTHOR'S WAY OF SENDING FORTH HIS SECOND PART OF THE PILGRIM

Go, now my little Book, to every place,
Where my first Pilgrim *has but shewn his Face,*
Call at their door: If any say, who's there?
Then answer thou, Christiana is here.
If they bid thee come in, *then enter thou*
With all thy boys. And then, as thou know'st how,
Tell who they are, also from whence they came,
Perhaps they'l know them, by their looks, or name:
But if they should not, ask them yet again
If formerly they did not Entertain
One Christian *a Pilgrim; If they say*
They did: And was delighted in his way:
Then let them know that those related were
Unto him: Yea, his Wife and Children are.
Tell them that they have left their House and Home,
Are turned Pilgrims, seek a World to come:
That they have *met with hardships in the way,*
That they do *meet with troubles night and Day;*
That they have trod on Serpents, fought with Devils,
Have also overcome a many evils.
Yea tell them also of the rest, who have
Of love to Pilgrimage *been stout and brave*
Defenders of that way, and how they still
Refuse this World, to do their Fathers will.
Go, tell them also of those dainty things,
That Pilgrimage *unto the* Pilgrim *brings,*
Let them acquainted be, too, how they are
Beloved of their King, under his care;
What goodly Mansions *for them he Provides.*

Tho they meet with rough Winds, and swelling Tides,
How brave a calm they will enjoy at last,
Who to their Lord, and by *his ways hold fast.*
Perhaps with heart and hand they will imbrace
Thee, as they did my firstling, and will Grace
Thee, and thy fellows with such chear and fair,
As shew will, they of Pilgrims *lovers are.*

1 *Object*

But how if they will not believe of me
That I am truly thine, 'cause some there be
That Counterfeit the Pilgrim, and his name,†
Seek by disguise to seem the very same.
And by that means have wrought themselves into
The Hands and Houses of I know not who.

Answer

'Tis true, some have of late, to Counterfeit
My *Pilgrim, to their own, my Title set;*
Yea others, half my Name and Title too;
Have stitched to their Book, to make them do;
But yet they by their Features *do declare*
Themselves not mine to be, whose ere they are.
If such thou meetst with, then thine only way
Before them all, is, to say out thy say,
In thine own native Language, which no man
Now useth, nor with ease dissemble can.
If after all, they still of you shall doubt,
Thinking that you like Gipsies *go about,*
In naughty-wise the Countrey to defile,
Or that you seek good People to beguile
With things unwarrantable: Send for me
And I will Testifie, you Pilgrims *be;*
Yea, I will Testifie that only you
My Pilgrims *are; And that alone will do.*

2 *Object*

But yet, perhaps, I may enquire for him,
Of those that wish him Damned life and limb,

What shall I do, when I at such a door,
For *Pilgrims* ask, and they shall rage the more?

Answer

Fright not thy self my Book, for such Bugbears
Are nothing else but ground for groundless fears,
My Pilgrims *Book has travel'd Sea and Land,*†
Yet could I never come to understand,
That it was slighted, or turn'd out of Door
By any Kingdom, were they Rich or Poor.
In France *and* Flanders *where men kill each other*
My Pilgrim *is esteem'd a Friend, a Brother.*
In Holland *too, 'tis said, as I am told,*
My Pilgrim *is with some, worth more than Gold.*
Highlanders, *and* Wild-Irish *can agree,*
My Pilgrim *should familiar with them be.*
'Tis in New-England *under such advance,*
Receives there so much loving Countenance,
As to be Trim'd, new Cloth'd & Deckt with Gems,†
That it might shew its Features, and its Limbs,
Yet more; so comely doth my Pilgrim *walk,*
That of him thousands daily Sing and talk.
If you draw nearer home, it will appear
My Pilgrim *knows no ground of shame, or fear;*
City, and Countrey will him Entertain,
With welcome Pilgrim. *Yea, they can't refrain*
From smiling, if my Pilgrim *be but by,*
Or shews his head in any Company.
Brave Galants do my Pilgrim *hug and love,*
Esteem it much, yea value it above
Things of a greater bulk, yea, with delight,
Say my Larks leg *is beter than a* Kite.†
Young Ladys, and young Gentle-women too,
Do no small kindness to my Pilgrim *shew;*
Their Cabinets, their Bosoms, and their Hearts
My Pilgrim *has, 'cause he to them imparts*
His pretty riddles in such wholsome straines
As yields them profit double to their paines
Of reading. Yea, I think I may be bold

To say some prize him far above their Gold.
The very Children that do walk the street,
If they do but my holy Pilgrim *meet,*
Salute him will, will wish him well and say,
He is the only Stripling *of the Day.*
They that have never seen him, yet admire
What they have heard of him, and much desire
To have his Company, and hear him tell
Those Pilgrim *storyes which he knows so well.*
Yea, some who did not love him at the first,
But cal'd him Fool, *and* Noddy, *say they must*
Now they have seen & heard *him, him commend,*
And to those whom they love, they do him send.
Wherefore my Second Part, *thou needest not be*
Afraid to shew thy Head: None can hurt thee,
That wish but well to him, that went before,
'Cause thou com'st after with a Second store,
Of things as good, as rich, as profitable,
For Young, for Old, for Stag'ring and for stable.

3 *Object*

But some there be that say he laughs too loud;
And some do say his Head is in a Cloud.
Some say, his Words and Storys are so dark,
They know not how, by them, to find his mark.

Answer

One may (I think) say both his laughs & cryes,
May well be guest at by his watry Eyes.
Some things are of that Nature as to make
Ones fancie Checkle while his Heart doth ake,
When Jacob *saw his* Rachel *with the Sheep,*
He did at the same time both kiss and weep.†
Whereas some say a Cloud is in his Head,
That doth but shew how Wisdom's covered
With its own mantles: And to stir the mind
To a search after what it fain would find,
Things that seem to be hid in words obscure,
Do but the Godly mind the more alure;

To study what those Sayings should contain,
That speak to us in such a Cloudy strain.
I also know, a dark Similitude
Will on the Fancie more it self intrude,
And will stick faster in the Heart and Head,
Then things from Similies not borrowed.
Wherefore, my Book, let no discouragement
Hinder thy travels. Behold, thou art sent
To Friends, not foes: to Friends that will give place
To thee, thy Pilgrims, *and thy words imbrace.*
Besides, what my first Pilgrim *left conceal'd,*
Thou my brave Second Pilgrim *hast reveal'd;*
What Christian *left lock't up and went his way,*
Sweet Christiana *opens with her Key.*

4 *Object*

But some love not the method of your first,
Romance they count it, throw't away as dust,
If I should meet with such, what should I say?
Must I slight them as they slight me, or nay?

Answer

My Christiana, *if with such thou meet,*
By all means in all Loving-wise, them greet;
Render them not reviling for revile:†
But if they frown, I prethee on them smile.
Perhaps 'tis Nature, or some ill report
Has made them thus *dispise, or* thus *retort.*
Some love no Cheese, some love no Fish, & some
Love not their Friends, nor their own House or home;
Some start at Pigg, slight Chicken, love not Fowl,
More then they love a Cuckoo or an Owl.
Leave such, my Christiana, *to their choice,*
And seek those, who to find thee will rejoyce;
By no means strive, but in all humble wise,
Present thee to them in thy Pilgrims *guise.*
Go then, my little Book and shew to all
That entertain, and bid thee welcome shall,
What thou shalt keep close, shut up from the rest,

And wish what thou shalt shew them may be blest
To them for good, may make them chuse to be
Pilgrims, better by far, then thee or me.
Go then, I say, tell all men who thou art,
Say, I am Christiana, *and my part*
Is now with my four Sons, to tell you what
It is for men to take a Pilgrims *lot.*
Go also tell them who, *and what they be,*
That now do go on Pilgrimage *with thee;*
Say, here's my neighbour Mercy, *she is one,*
That has long-time with me a Pilgrim *gone:*
Come see her in her Virgin *Face, and learn*
Twixt Idle ones, and Pilgrims *to discern.*
Yea let young Damsels learn of her to prize
The World which is to come, in any wise;
When little Tripping *Maidens follow God,*
And leave old doting Sinners to his Rod;
'Tis like those Days wherein the young ones cri'd
Hosanah to whom old ones did deride.†
Next tell them of old Honest, *who you found*
With his white hairs treading the Pilgrims ground,
Yea, tell them how plain hearted this *man was,*
How after his good Lord he bare his Cross:
Perhaps with some gray Head this may prevail,
With Christ to fall in Love, and Sin bewail.
Tell them also how Master Fearing *went*
On Pilgrimage, and how the time he spent
In Solitariness, with Fears and Cries,
And how at last, he won the Joyful Prize.
He was *a good man, though much down in Spirit,*
He is *a good Man, and doth Life inherit.*†
Tell them of Master Feeblemind *also,*
Who, not before, but still behind would go;
Show them also how he had like been slain,
And how one Great-Heart *did his life regain:*
This man was true of Heart, tho weak in grace,
One might true Godliness read in his Face.
Then tell them of Master Ready-to-halt,
A Man with Crutches, but much without fault:

Tell them how Master Feeblemind, *and he*
Did love, and in Opinions *much agree.*
And let all know, tho weakness was their chance,
Yet sometimes one could Sing, *the other* Dance.
Forget not Master Valiant-for-the-Truth,
That Man of courage, tho a very Youth.
Tell every one his Spirit was so stout,
No Man could ever make him face about,
And how Great-Heart, *& he could not forbear*
But put down Doubting Castle, slay Despair.
Overlook not Master Despondancie.
Nor Much-a-fraid, *his Daughter, tho they ly*
Under such Mantles as may make them look
(With some) as if their God had them forsook.
They softly went, but sure, and at the end,
Found that the Lord of Pilgrims *was their Friend.*
When thou hast told the World of all these things,
Then turn about, my book, and touch these strings,
Which, if but touched will such Musick make,
They'l make a Cripple dance, a Gyant quake.
Those Riddles that lie couch't within thy breast,
Freely propound, expound: and for the rest
Of thy misterious lines, let them remain,
For those whose nimble Fancies shall them gain.
Now may this little Book a blessing be,
To those that love this little Book and me,
And may its buyer have no cause to say,
His Money is but lost or thrown away.
Yea may this Second Pilgrim *yield that Fruit,*
As may with each good Pilgrims *fancie sute,*
And may it perswade some that go astray,
To turn their Foot and Heart to the right way.

Is the Hearty Prayer
of the Author
JOHN BUNYAN

THE PILGRIM'S PROGRESS

IN THE SIMILITUDE OF A

DREAM

THE SECOND PART

COURTEOUS Companions, sometime since, to tell you my Dream that I had of *Christian* the Pilgrim, and of his dangerous Journey toward the Celestial Countrey, was pleasant to me, and profitable to you. I told you then also what I saw concerning his *Wife* and *Children*, and how unwilling they were to go with him on Pilgrimage: Insomuch that he was forced to go on his Progress without them, for he durst not run the danger of that destruction which he feared would come by staying with them, in the City of Destruction: Wherefore, as I then shewed you, he left them and departed.

Now it hath so happened, thorough the Multiplicity of Business, that I have been much hindred, and kept back from my wonted Travels into those Parts whence he went, and so could not till now obtain an opportunity to make further enquiry after whom he left behind, that I might give you an account of them. But having had some concerns that way of late, I went down again thitherward. Now, having taken up my Lodgings in a Wood about a mile off the Place, as I slept I dreamed again.

And as I was in my Dream, behold, an aged Gentleman came by where I lay; and because he was to go some part of the way that I was travelling, me thought I got up and went with him. So as we walked, and as Travellers usually do, it was as if we fell into discourse, and our talk happened to be about *Christian* and his Travels: For thus I began with the Old-man.

Sir, said I, *what Town is that there below, that lieth on the left hand of our way?*

Then said Mr. *Sagasity*, for that was his name, it is the City of *Destruction*, a populous place, but possessed with a very ill conditioned, and idle sort of People.

I thought that was that City, quoth I, *I went once my self through that Town, and therefore know that this report you give of it is true*.

Sag. Too true, I wish I could speak truth in speaking better of them that dwell therein.

Well, Sir, quoth I, *Then I perceive you to be a well meaning man: and so one that takes pleasure to hear and tell of that which is good; pray did you never hear what happened to a man sometime ago in this Town (whose name was* Christian) *that went on Pilgrimage up towards the higher Regions?*

Sag. Hear of him! Aye, and I also heard of the Molestations, Troubles, Wars, Captivities, Cries, Groans, Frights and Fears that he met with, and had in his Journey. Besides, I must tell you, all our Countrey rings of him, there are but few Houses that have heard of him and his doings, but have sought after and got the *Records* of his Pilgrimage; yea, I think I may say, that that his hazzardous Journey has got a many welwishers to his ways: For though when he was here, he was *Fool* in every mans mouth, yet now he is gone, he is highly commended of all. For 'tis said he lives bravely where he is: Yea, many of them that are resolved never to run his hazzards, yet have their mouths water at his gains.

Christians *are well spoken of when gone, tho' called Fools while they are here.*

They may, quoth I, *well think, if they think any thing that is true, that he liveth well where he is, for he now lives at and in the Fountain of Life,*† *and has what he has without Labour and Sorrow, for there is no grief mixed therewith.*

Sag. Talk! The People talk strangely about him. Some say that he *now walks in White*, that he has a Chain of Gold about his Neck, that he has a Crown of Gold,† beset with Pearls upon his Head: Others say, that the shining ones that sometimes shewed themselves to him in his Journey, are become his Companions, and that he is as familiar with them in the place where he is, as here one Neighbour is with another. Besides, 'tis confidently affirmed concerning him, that the King of the place where he is, has bestowed upon him already, a very rich and pleasant Dwelling at Court, and that he every day eateth

Revel. 3. 4. Chap. 6. 11.

Zech. 3. 7.

Luke 14. 15. and drinketh, and walketh, and talketh with him, and receiveth of the smiles and favours of him that is Judge of all there. Moreover, it is expected of some that his Prince, the Lord of that Countrey, will shortly come into *these* parts, and will know

Jude 14, 15. the reason, if they can give any, why his Neighbours set so little by him, and had him so much in derision when they perceived that he would be a Pilgrim. *For they say, that now he is so in the Affections of his Prince, and that his *Soveraign* is so much concerned with the *Indignities* that was cast upon *Christian* when he became a Pilgrim, that he will look upon all as if done

Luke 10. 16. unto himself; and no marvel, for 'twas for the love that he had to his Prince, that he ventured as he did.

* Christians *King will take* Christians *part.*

I dare say, quoth I, *I am glad on't, I am glad for the poor mans*

Revel. 14. 13. *sake, for that now he has rest from his labour, and for that now he*

Psal. 126. 5, 6. *reapeth the benefit of his Tears with Joy; and for that he is got beyond the Gun-shot of his Enemies, and is out of the reach of them that hate him. I also am glad for that a Rumour of these things is noised abroad in this Countrey; Who can tell but that it may work some good effect on some that are left behind? But, pray Sir, while it is fresh in my mind, do you hear any thing of his Wife and Children? poor hearts, I wonder in my mind what they do.*

Sag. Who! *Christiana*, and her Sons! *They are like to do as well as did *Christian* himself, for though they all plaid the Fool at the first, and would by no means be perswaded by either the tears or intreaties of *Christian*, yet second thoughts have wrought wonderfully with them, so they have packt up and are also gone after him.

* *Good tidings of* Christians *Wife and Children.*

Better, and better, quoth I, *But what! Wife and Children and all?*

Sag. 'Tis true, I can give you an account of the matter, for I was upon the spot at the instant, and was throughly acquainted with the whole affair.

Then, said I, *a man it seems may report it for a truth?*

Sag. You need not fear to affirm it, I mean that they are all gon on Pilgrimage, both the good Woman and her four Boys. And being we are, as I perceive, going some considerable way together, I will give you an account of the whole of the matter.

This *Christiana* (for that was her name from the day that she with her Children betook themselves to a *Pilgrims* Life,) after her Husband was gone *over the River*, and she could hear of him no more, her thoughts began to work in her mind; First, for that she had lost her Husband, and for that the loving bond of that Relation was utterly broken betwixt them. For you know, said he to me, nature can do no less but entertain the living with many a heavy Cogitation in the remembrance of the loss of loving Relations. This therefore of her Husband did cost her many a Tear. But this was not all, for *Christiana* did also begin to consider with her self, whether her unbecoming behaviour towards her Husband, was not one cause that she saw him no more, and that in such sort he was taken away from her. And upon this, came into her mind by *swarms*, all her unkind, unnatural, and ungodly Carriages to her dear Friend: Which also clogged her Conscience, and did load her with guilt. She was moreover much broken with recalling to remembrance the restless Groans, brinish Tears and self-bemoanings of her Husband, and how she did harden her heart against all his entreaties, and loving perswasions (of her and her Sons) to go with him, yea, there was not any thing that *Christian* either said to her, or did before her, all the while that his burden did hang on his back, but it returned upon her like a flash of lightning, and rent the Caul of her Heart† in sunder. Specially that bitter out-cry of his, *What shall I do to be saved*,† did ring in her ears most dolefully.

1 Part, pag. 149.

Mark this, you that are Churles to your godly Relations.

1 Part, pag. 10.

Then said she to her Children, Sons, we are all undone. I have sinned away your Father, and he is gone; he would have had us with him; but I would not go my self; I also have hindred you of Life. With that the Boys fell all into Tears, and cryed out to go after their Father. Oh! Said *Christiana*, that it had been but our lot to go with him, then had it fared well with us beyond what 'tis like to do now. For tho' I formerly foolishly imagin'd concerning the Troubles of your Father, that they proceeded of a foolish fancy that he had, or for that he was over run with Melancholy Humours; yet now 'twill not out of my mind, but that they sprang from another cause, to wit, for that the Light of Light was given him, by the help of which, as I perceive, he has escaped the Snares of Death.† Then they all wept again, and cryed out: Oh, Wo, worth the day.†

James 1. 23, 24, 25.

Christiana's *Dream.*

The next night *Christiana* had a Dream, and behold she saw as if a broad Parchment was opened before her, in which were recorded the sum of her ways, and the times, as she thought, look'd *very black upon her*. Then she cryed out aloud in her sleep, Lord have mercy upon me a Sinner, and the little Children heard her.

Luke 18. 13.

After this she thought she saw two very ill favoured ones standing by her Bed-side, and saying, **What shall we do with this Woman? For she cryes out for Mercy waking and sleeping: If she be suffered to go on as she begins, we shall lose her as we have lost her Husband*. Wherefore we must by one way or other, seek to take her off from the thoughts of what shall be hereafter: else all the World cannot help it, but she will become a Pilgrim.

* *Mark this, this is the quintescence of* Hell.

Now she awoke in a great Sweat, also a trembling was upon her, but after a while she fell to sleeping again. *And then she thought she saw *Christian* her Husband in a place of Bliss among many *Immortals*, with an *Harp* in his Hand, standing and playing upon it before one that sate on a Throne with a Rainbow about his Head.† She saw also as if he bowed his Head with his Face to the Pav'd-work that was under the Princes Feet, saying, *I heartily thank my Lord and King for bringing of me into this Place*. Then shouted a Company of them that stood round about, and harped with their Harps: but no man living could tell what they said, but *Christian* and his Companions.

* *Help against Discouragement.*

Revel. 14. 2, 3.

Next Morning when she was up, had prayed to God, and talked with her Children a while, one knocked hard at the door; to whom she spake out saying, *If thou comest in Gods Name, come in*. So he said *Amen*, and opened the Door, and saluted her with *Peace be to this House*.† *The which when he had done, he said, *Christiana*, knowest thou wherefore I am come? Then she blush'd and trembled, also her Heart began to wax warm with desires to know whence he came, and what was his Errand to her. So he said unto her; my name is *Secret*,† I dwell with those that are high. It is talked of where I dwell, as if thou had'st a desire to go thither; also there is a report that thou art aware of the evil thou hast formerly done to thy Husband in hardening of thy Heart against his way, and in keeping of these thy Babes in their Ignorance. *Christiana*, the merciful one has sent me to tell thee that he is a God ready to forgive,

* *Convictions seconded with fresh Tidings of Gods readiness to Pardon.*

and that he taketh delight to multiply pardon to offences. He also would have thee know that he inviteth thee to come into his presence, to his Table, and that he will feed thee with the Fat of his House, and with the Heritage of *Jacob* thy Father.†

There is *Christian* thy Husband, *that was*, with Legions more his Companions, ever beholding that face that doth minister Life to beholders: and they will all be glad when they shall hear the sound of thy feet step over thy Fathers Threshold.

Christiana at this was greatly abashed in her self, and bowing her head to the ground, this *Visitor* proceeded and said, *Christiana*! Here is also a Letter for thee which I have brought from thy Husbands King. So she took it and opened it, but it smelt after the manner of the best Perfume, also it was Written in Letters of Gold. The Contents of the Letter was, *That the King would have her do as did* Christian *her Husband; For that was the way to come to his* City, *and to dwell in his Presence with Joy, forever*. At this the good Woman was quite overcome: So she cried out to her *Visitor, Sir, will you carry me and my children with you, that we also may go and Worship this King?*

Song 1. 3.

Christiana *quite overcome.*

Then said the Visitor, *Christiana! The bitter is before the sweet:* Thou must through Troubles, as did he that went before thee, enter this Celestial City. Wherefore I advise thee, to do as did *Christian* thy Husband: go to the *Wicket Gate* yonder, over the Plain, for that stands in the head of the way up which thou must go, and I wish thee all good speed. Also I advise that thou put this Letter in thy Bosome, that thou read therein to thy self and to thy Children, until you have got it by root-of-Heart.† For it is one of the Songs that thou must Sing while thou art in this House of thy Pilgrimage. Also this thou must deliver in at the *further* Gate.

Further Instruction to Christiana.

Psal. 119. 54.

Now I saw in my Dream that this Old Gentleman, as he told me this Story, did himself seem to be greatly affected therewith. He moreover proceeded and said, So *Christiana* called her Sons together, and began thus to Address her self unto them. *My Sons, I have, as you may perceive, been of late under much exercise in my Soul about the Death of your Father; not for that I doubt at all of his Happiness: For I am satisfied now that he is well. I have also been much affected with the thoughts of mine own State and yours, which I verily

* Christiana *prays well for her Journey.*

believe is by nature miserable: My Carriages also to your Father in his distress, is a great load to my Conscience. For I hardened both mine own heart and yours against him, and refused to go with him on Pilgrimage.

The thoughts of these things would now kill me outright; but that for a Dream which I had last night, and but that for the incouragement that this Stranger has given me this Morning. Come, my Children, let us pack up, and be gon to the Gate that leads to the Celestial Countrey, that we may see your Father, and be with him and his Companions in Peace according to the Laws of that Land.

Then did her Children burst out into Tears for Joy that the Heart of their Mother was so inclined: So their *Visitor* bid them farewel: and they began to prepare to set out for their Journey.

But while they were thus about to be gon, two of the Women that were *Christiana's* Neighbours, came up to her House and knocked at her Dore. To whom she said as before. *If you come in Gods Name, come in.* *At this the Women were stun'd, for this kind of Language they used not to hear, or to perceive to drop from the Lips of *Christiana*. Yet they came in; but behold they found the good Woman a preparing to be gon from her House.

* Christiana's *new language stunds her old Neighbours.*

So they began and said, *Neighbour, pray what is your meaning by this?*

Christiana answered and said to the eldest of them, whose name was Mrs. *Timorous*, I am preparing for a Journey (This *Timorous* was Daughter to him that met *Christian* upon the Hill *Difficulty*; and would a had him gone back for fear of the Lyons.)

1 *Part, pag.* 42.

Timorous *comes to visit* Christiana, *with* Mercie *one of her Neighbours.*

Timorous. For what Journey I pray you?

Chris. *Even to go after my good Husband*, and with that she fell aweeping.

Timo. I hope not so, good Neighbour, pray for your poor Childrens sake, do not so unwomanly cast away your self.

Chris. *Nay, my Children shall go with me; not one of them is willing to stay behind.*

Timo. I wonder in my very Heart, what, or who, has brought you into this mind.

Chris. Oh, Neighbour, knew you but as much as I do, I doubt not but that you would go with me.

Timo. *Prithee what new knowledge hast thou got that so worketh off thy mind from thy Friends, and that tempteth thee to go no body knows where?*

Chris. Then *Christiana* reply'd, I have been sorely afflicted since my Husbands departure from me; but specially since he went *over the River*. But that which troubleth me most, is, my churlish Carriages to him when he was under his distress. Besides, I am *now*, as he was *then*; nothing will serve me but going on Pilgrimage. I was a dreamed† last night, that I saw him. O that my Soul was with him. He dwelleth in the presence of the King of the Country, he sits and eats with him at his Table, he is become a Companion of *Immortals*, and has a House now given him to dwell in, to which, the best Palaces on Earth, if compared, seems to me to be but as a Dunghil. The Prince of the Place has also sent for me, with promise of entertainment if I shall come to him; his messenger was here even now, and has brought me a Letter, which Invites me to come. And with that she pluck'd out her Letter, and read it, and said to them, what now will you say to this?

Death.

2 Cor. 5. 1, 2, 3, 4.

Timo. *Oh the madness that has possessed thee and thy Husband, to run your selves upon such difficulties! You have heard, I am sure, what your Husband did meet with, even in a manner at the first step, that he took on his way, as our Neighbour* Obstinate *yet can testifie; for he went along with him, yea and* Plyable *too, until they, like* wise men, *were afraid to go any further. We also heard over and above, how he met with the Lyons, Apollyon, the Shadow of Death, and many other things: Nor is the danger he met with at* Vanity *fair to be forgotten by thee. For if he, tho' a man, was so hard put to it, what canst thou being but a poor Woman do? Consider also that these four sweet Babes are thy Children, thy Flesh and thy Bones. Wherefore, though thou shouldest be so rash as to cast away thy self, yet for the sake of the Fruit of thy Body, keep thou at home.*

1 *Part, pag.* 16–18.

The reasonings of the flesh.

But *Christiana* said unto her, tempt me not, my Neighbour: I have now a price put into mine hand to get gain, and I should be a Fool of the greatest size, if I should have no heart to strike in with the opportunity. And for that you tell me of all these

** A pertinent reply to fleshly reasonings.*

Troubles that I am like to meet with in the way, *they are so far off from being to me a discouragement, that they shew I am in the right. *The bitter must come before the sweet*, and that also will make the sweet the sweeter. Wherefore, since you came not to my House, *in Gods name*, as I said, I pray you to be gon, and not to disquiet me further.

Mercies *Bowels yearn over* Christiana.

Then *Timorous* all to revil'd her, and said to her Fellow, Come Neighbour *Mercie*, lets leave her in her own hands, since she scorns our Counsel and Company. But *Mercie* was at a stand, and could not so readily comply with her Neighbour: and that for a twofold reason. First, her Bowels yearned† over *Christiana*: so she said with in her self, If my Neighbour will needs be gon, I will go a little way with her, and help her. Secondly, her Bowels yearned over her own Soul, (for what *Christiana* had said, had taken some hold upon her mind.) Wherefore she said within her self again, I will yet have more talk with this *Christiana*, and if I find Truth and Life in what she shall say, my self with my Heart shall also go with her. Wherefore *Mercie* began thus to reply to her Neighbour *Timorous*.

Timorous *forsakes her; but* Mercie *cleaves to her.*

Mercie. Neighbour, *I did indeed come with you, to see* Christiana *this Morning, and since she is, as you see, a taking of her last farewel of her Country, I think to walk this Sun-shine Morning, a little way with her to help her on the way*. But she told her not of her second Reason, but kept that to her self.

Timo. Well, I see you have a mind to go a fooling too; but take heed in time, and be wise: while we are out of danger we are out; but when we are in, we are in. So Mrs. *Timorous* returned to her House, and *Christiana* betook herself to her Journey. But when *Timorous* was got home to her House, she sends for some of her Neighbours, to wit, Mrs. *Bats-eyes*, Mrs. *Inconsiderate*, Mrs. *Light-mind*, and Mrs. *Know-nothing*. So when they were come to her House, she falls to telling of the story of *Christiana*, and of her intended Journey. And thus she began her Tale.

Timorous *acquaints her Friends what the good* Christiana *intends to do.*

Timo. Neighbours, having had little to do this Morning, I went to give *Christiana* a Visit, and when I came at the Door, I knocked, as you know 'tis our Custom: And she answered, *If you come in God's Name, come in*. So in I went, thinking all was well: But when I came in, I found her preparing her self to depart the Town, she and also her Children. So I asked her what was her meaning by that? and she told me in short, That she was now of a mind to go on Pilgrimage, as did her Husband. She told me also of a Dream that she had, and how the King of the Country where her Husband was, had sent her an inviting Letter to come thither.

Then said Mrs. Know-nothing. *And what! do you think she will go?*

Mrs. Know-nothing.

Timo. Aye, go she will, what ever come on't; and methinks I know it by this; for that which was my great Argument to perswade her to stay at home, (to wit, the Troubles she was like to meet with in the way) is one great Argument with her to put her forward on her Journey. For she told me in so many words, *The bitter goes before the sweet*. Yea, and for as much as it so doth, it makes the sweet the sweeter.

Mrs. *Bats-eyes.* Oh this blind and foolish Woman, said she, Will she not take warning by her Husband's Afflictions? For my part, I say if he was here again he would rest him content in a whole Skin, and never run so many hazards for nothing.

Mrs. Bats-eyes.

Mrs. *Inconsiderate* also replied, saying, away with such Fantastical Fools from the Town; a good riddance, for my part I say, of her. Should she stay where she dwels, and retain this her mind, who could live quietly by her? for she will either be dumpish or un-neighbourly, or talk of such matters as no wise body can abide: Wherefore, for my part, I shall never be sorry for her departure; let her go, and let better come in her room: 'twas never a good World since these whimsical Fools dwelt in it.

Mrs. Inconsiderate.

Then Mrs. *Light-mind* added as followeth. Come put this kind of Talk away. I was Yesterday at Madam *Wantons*, where we were as merry as the Maids.† For who do you think should be there, but I, and Mrs. *Love-the-flesh*, and three or four more, with Mr. *Lechery*, Mrs. *Filth*, and some others. So there we had Musick and dancing, and what else was meet to fill up the pleasure. And I dare say my Lady her self is an admirably well-bred Gentlewoman, and Mr. *Lechery* is as pretty a Fellow.

Mrs. Light-mind. *Madam* Wanton, *she that had like to a bin too hard for* Faithful *in time past.*

1 Part, pag. 69.

By this time *Christiana* was got on her way, and *Mercie* went along with her. So as they went, her Children being there also, *Christiana* began to discourse. And, *Mercie*, said *Christiana*, I take this as an unexpected favour, that thou shouldest set foot out of Doors with me to accompany me a little in my way.

Discourse betwixt Mercie *and good* Christiana.

Mercie *inclines to go.*

Mercie. *Then said young* Mercie (*for she was but young*,) *If I thought it would be to purpose to go with you, I would never go near the Town any more.*

Chris. Well *Mercie*, said *Christiana*, cast in thy Lot with me. I well know what will be the end of our Pilgrimage; my Husband is where he would not but be, for all the Gold in the *Spanish* Mines.† Nor shalt thou be rejected, tho thou goest but upon *my Invitation*. The King, who hath sent for me and my Children, is one that delighteth in *Mercie*. Besides, if thou wilt, I will hire thee, and thou shalt go along with me as my servant. Yet we will have all things in common betwixt thee and me, only go along with me.

Christiana *would have her Neighbour with her.*

Mercie *doubts of acceptance.*

Mercie. *But how shall I be ascertained that I also shall be entertained? had I but this hope from one that can tell, I would make no stick at all, but would go, being helped by him that can help, tho' the way was never so tedious.*

Christiana *alures her to the Gate which is Christ, and promiseth there to enquire for her.*

Christiana. Well, loving *Mercie*, I will tell thee what thou shalt do; go with me to the *Wicket Gate*, and there I will further enquire for thee, and if there thou shalt not meet with incouragement, I will be content that thou shalt return to thy place. I also will pay thee for thy Kindness which thou shewest to me and my Children, in thy accompanying of us in our way as thou doest.

Mercie *prays.*

Mercie. *Then will I go thither, and will take what shall follow, and the Lord grant that my Lot may there fall even as the King of Heaven shall have his heart upon me.*

Christiana *glad of* Mercie's *company.*

Christiana then was glad at her heart, not only that she had a Companion, but also for that she had prevailed with this poor Maid to fall in love with her own Salvation. So they went on together, and *Mercie* began to weep. Then said *Christiana*, wherefore weepeth my Sister so?

Mercie *grieves for her carnal Relations.*

Mer. *Alas! said she, who can but lament that shall but rightly consider what a State and Condition my poor Relations are in, that yet remain in our sinful Town: and that which makes my*

Grief the more heavy, is, because they have no Instructor, nor any to tell them what is to come.

Chris. Bowels becometh Pilgrims. And thou dost for thy Friends, as my good *Christian* did for me when he left me; he mourned for that I would not heed nor regard him, but his Lord and ours did gather up his Tears and put them into his Bottle,† and now both I, and thou, and these my sweet Babes, are reaping the Fruit and Benefit of them. I hope, *Mercie*, these Tears of thine will not be lost, for the truth hath said, *That they that sow in Tears shall reap in Joy, in singing. And he that goeth forth and weepeth, bearing precious seed, shall doubtless come again with rejoicing, bringing his Sheaves with him.*

Christian's *Prayers were answered for his Relations after he was dead.*

Psal. 126. 5, 6.

Then said *Mercie*,

> *Let the most blessed be my guide,*
> *If't be his blessed Will,*
> Unto *his Gate*, into *his Fould*,
> Up to *his Holy Hill.*
> *And let him never suffer me*
> *To swarve, or turn aside*
> *From his free grace, and Holy ways,*
> *What ere shall me betide.*
> *And let him gather them of mine,*
> *That I have left behind.*
> *Lord make them pray they may be thine,*
> *With all their heart and mind.*

Now my old Friend proceeded, and said, But when *Christiana* came up to the Slow of *Despond*, she began to be at a stand; for, said she, This is the place in which my dear Husband had like to a been smuthered with Mud. She perceived also, that notwithstanding the Command of the King to make this place for Pilgrims good; yet it was rather worse than formerly. So I asked if that was true? Yes, said the Old Gentleman, too true. For that many there be that pretend to be the Kings Labourers;† and that say they are for mending the Kings High-way, that bring *Dirt* and *Dung* instead of Stones, and so marr, instead of mending. Here *Christiana* therefore, with her Boys, did make a stand: but said *Mercie*, *come let us venture, only let us be wary. Then they looked well to the

1 *Part, pag.* 16–17.

Their own Carnal Conclusions, instead of the word of life.

* Mercie *the boldest at the Slow of* Despond.

Steps, and made a shift to get staggeringly over. Yet *Christiana* had like to a been in, and that not once nor twice. Now they had no sooner got over, but they thought they heard words that said unto them, *Blessed is she that believeth, for there shall be a performance of the things that have been told her from the Lord.*

Luke 1. 45.

Then they went on again; and said *Mercie* to *Christiana*, Had I as good ground to hope for a loving Reception at the *Wicket-Gate*, as you, I think no Slow of *Despond* would discourage me.

Well, said the other, you know *your sore*, and I know *mine*; and, good friend, we shall all have enough evil before we come at our Journeys end.

For can it be imagined, that the people that design to attain such excellent Glories *as we do*, and that are so envied that Happiness *as we are*; but that we shall meet with what Fears and Scares, with what Troubles and Afflictions they can possibly assault us with, that hate us?

Prayer should be made with Consideration, and Fear: As well as in Faith and Hope.

And now Mr. *Sagacity* left me to Dream out my Dream by my self. Wherefore me-thought I saw *Christiana*, and *Mercie* and the *Boys* go all of them up to the Gate. To which when they were come, they betook themselves to a short debate about *how* they must manage their calling at the Gate, and what should be said to him that did open to them. So it was concluded, since *Christiana* was the eldest, that she should knock for entrance, and that she should speak to him that did open, for the rest. So *Christiana* began to knock, and as her poor Husband did, she *knocked* and *knocked* again. But instead of any that answered, they all thought that they heard, as if a Dog† came barking upon them. A Dog, and a great one too, and this made the Women and Children afraid. Nor durst they for a while dare to knock any more, for fear the *Mastiff* should fly upon them. *Now therefore they were greatly tumbled up and down in their minds, and knew not what to do. Knock they durst not, for fear of the Dog: go back they durst not, for fear that the Keeper of that Gate should espy them, as they so went, and should be offended with them. At last they thought of knocking again, and knocked more vehemently then they did at the first. Then said the Keeper of the Gate, who is there? So the *Dog* left off to bark, and he opened unto them.

1 *Part, pag.* 25.

The Dog, the Devil, an Enemy to Prayer.

* Christiana *and her companions perplexed about Prayer.*

Then *Christiana* made low obeysance, and said, Let not our

Lord be offended with his Handmaidens, for that we have knocked at his Princely Gate. Then said the Keeper, Whence come ye, and what is that you would have?

Christiana answered, We are come from whence *Christian* did come, and upon the same *Errand* as he; to wit, to be, if it shall please you, graciously admitted by this Gate, into the way that leads to the Celestial City. And I answer, my Lord, in the next place, that I am *Christiana*, once the Wife of *Christian*, that now is gotten above.

With that the Keeper of the Gate did marvel, saying, *What! is she become now a Pilgrim, that but awhile ago abhorred that Life?* Then she bowed her Head, and said, yes; and so are these my sweet Babes also.

Then he took her by the hand, and led her in, and said also, *Suffer the little Children to come unto me*,† and with that he shut up the Gate. This don, he called to a Trumpeter that was above over the Gate, to entertain *Christiana* with shouting and sound of Trumpet for joy. So he obeyed and sounded, and filled the Air with his melodious Notes.

How Christiana *is entertained at the Gate.* Luke 15. 7.

Now all this while, poor *Mercie* did stand without, trembling and crying for fear that she was rejected. But when *Christiana* had gotten admittance for her self and her Boys: then she began to make Intercession for *Mercy*.

Chris. *And she said, my Lord, I have a Companion of mine that stands yet without, that is come hither upon the same account as my self. *One that is much dejected in her mind, for that she comes, as she thinks, without sending for, whereas I was sent to, by my Husbands King, to come.*

* Christiana's *Prayer for her friend* Mercie.

Now *Mercie* began to be very impatient, for each *minute* was as long to her as an Hour, wherefore she prevented *Christiana* from a fuller interceding for her, by knocking at the Gate her self. And she knocked then so loud, that she made *Christiana* to start. Then said the Keeper of the Gate, Who is there? And said *Christiana*, It is my Friend.

The delays make the hungring Soul the ferventer.

So he opened the Gate, and looked out; *but *Mercie* was fallen down without in a Swoon, for she fainted, and was afraid that no Gate should be opened to her.

* Mercie *faints.*

Then he took her by the hand, and said, *Damsel*, I bid thee arise.

O Sir, said she, I am faint, there is scarce Life left in me. But he answered, That one once said, *When my Soul fainted within me, I remembered the Lord, and my prayer came in unto thee, into thy Holy Temple*. Fear not, but stand upon thy Feet, and tell me wherefore thou art come.

Jonah 2. 7.

Mer. I am come, for *that*, unto which I was never invited, as my Friend *Christiana* was. **Hers* was from the King, and *mine* was but from *her:* Wherefore I fear I presume.

* *The cause of her fainting.*

Did she desire thee to come with her to this Place?

Mer. Yes. And as my Lord sees, I am come. And if there is any Grace and forgiveness of Sins to spare, I beseech that I thy poor Handmaid may be partaker thereof.

Then he took her again by the Hand, and led her gently in, and said: *I pray for all them that believe on me,† by what means soever they come unto me. Then said he to those that stood by: Fetch something, and give it *Mercie* to smell on, thereby to stay her fainting. So they fetcht her a *Bundle* of *Myrrh*,† and a while after she was revived.

* *mark this.*

And now was *Christiana*, and her Boys, and *Mercie*, *received* of the Lord at the head of the way, and spoke kindly unto by him.

Then said they yet further unto him, We are sorry for our Sins, and beg of our Lord his Pardon, and further information what we must do.

I grant Pardon, said he, by word, and deed; by word in the promise of forgiveness: by deed in the way I obtained it. Take the first from my Lips with a kiss, and the other, as it shall be revealed.

Song 1. 2.
John 20. 20.

Now I saw in my Dream that he spake many good words unto them, whereby they were greatly gladed. He also had them up to the top of the Gate and shewed them by what *deed* they were saved, and told them withall that that sight they would have again as they went along in the way, to their comfort.

Christ Crucified seen afar off.

So he left them a while in a Summer-Parler† below, where they entred into talk by themselves. And thus *Christiana* began, **O Lord! How glad am I, that we are got in hither!*

* *Talk between the Christians.*

Mer. *So you well may; but I, of all have cause to leap for joy.*†

Chris. *I thought, one time, as I stood at the Gate (because I had knocked and none did answer) that all our Labour had been lost: Specially when that ugly Curr made such a heavy barking against us.*

Mer. But my worst Fears was after I saw that you was taken into his favour, and that I was left behind: Now thought I, 'tis fulfiled which is Written, *Two Women shall be Grinding together; the one shall be taken, and the other left.* I had much ado to forbear crying out, Undone, undone. Mat. 24. 41.

And afraid I was to knock any more; but when I looked up, to what was Written over the Gate, I took Courage. I also thought that I must either knock again or dye. So I knocked; but I cannot tell how, for my spirit now *struggled* betwixt life and death. *1 Part, pag.* 24–5.

Chris. *Can you not tell how you knocked? I am sure your knocks were so earnest, that the very sound of them made me start. I thought I never heard such knocking in all my Life. I thought you would a come in by violent hand, or a took the Kingdom by storm.* Christiana *thinks her Companion prays better then she.* Mat. 11. 12.

Mer. Alas, to be in my Case, who that so was, could but a done so? You saw that the Door was shut upon me, and that there was a most cruel *Dog* thereabout. Who, I say, that was so faint hearted as I, that would not a knocked with all their might? But pray what said my Lord to my rudeness, was he not angry with me?

Chris. **When he heard your lumbring noise, he gave a wonderful Innocent smile. I believe what you did pleas'd him well enough, for he shewed no sign to the contrary. But I marvel in my heart why he keeps such a Dog; had I known that afore, I fear I should not have had heart enough to a ventured my self in this manner. But now we are in, we are in, and I am glad with all my heart.* * Christ pleased with loud and restless praises.

Mer. I will ask if you please next time he comes down, why he keeps such a filthy Cur in his Yard. I hope he will not take it amiss.

**Ay do, said the Children, and perswade him to hang him, for we are afraid that he will bite us when we go hence.* ** The Children are afraid of the dog.*

So at last he came down to them again, and *Mercie* fell to the Ground on her Face before him and worshipped, and said, Let my Lord accept of the Sacrifice of praise which I now offer unto him, with the calves of my Lips.†

Jer. 12. 1, 2. *So he said to her, peace be to thee, stand up.*

But she continued upon her Face and said, *Righteous art thou O Lord when I plead with thee, yet let me talk with thee of thy Judgments:* *Wherefore dost thou keep so cruel a Dog in thy Yard, at the sight of which, such Women and Children as we, are ready to fly from thy Gate for fear?*

* Mercie *expostulates about the dog.*

He answered, and said: *That Dog* has another *Owner, he also is kept close in an other man's ground; only my Pilgrims hear his barking. He belongs to the Castle which you see there at a distance: but can come up to the Walls of this Place. He has frighted many an honest Pilgrim from worse to better, by the great voice of his roaring. Indeed he that oweth him, doth not keep him of any good will to me or mine; but with intent to keep the Pilgrims from coming to me, and that they may be afraid to knock at this Gate for entrance. Sometimes also he has broken out and has *worried* some that I love; but I take all at present patiently: I also give my Pilgrims timely help, so they are not delivered up to his power to do to them what his Dogish nature would prompt him to. *But what! My purchased one,† I tro, hadst thou known never so much before hand, thou wouldst not a bin afraid of a *Dog*.

* *Devill.*

1 *Part, pag.* 27.

* *A Check to the carnal fear of the Pilgrims.*

The Beggers that go from Door to Door, will, rather then they will lose a supposed Alms, run the hazzard of the bauling, barking, and biting too of a Dog: and shall a Dog, a Dog in an other Mans Yard: a Dog, whose barking I turn to the Profit of Pilgrims, keep any from coming to me? I deliver them from the *Lions*, their Darling from the power of the Dog.†

Mer. Then said *Mercie*, **I confess my Ignorance: I spake what I understood not: I acknowledg that thou doest all things well.*

* Christians *when wise enough acquiesce in the wisdom of their Lord.*

Chris. Then *Christiana* began to talk of their Journey, and to enquire after the way. So he fed them, and washed their feet, and set them in the way of his Steps,† according as he had dealt with her Husband before.

1 *Part, pag.* 28.

So I saw in my Dream, that they walkt on in their way, and had the weather very comfortable to them.

Then *Christiana* began to sing, saying,

Bless't be the Day that I began
A Pilgrim for to be;
And blessed also be that man
That thereto moved me.

'Tis true, 'twas long ere I began
To seek to live for ever:
But now I run fast as I can,
'Tis better late *then* never.† Mat. 20. 6.

Our Tears *to joy, our fears to Faith*
Are turned, as we see:
Thus our beginning, (*as one saith,*)
Shews what our end will be.†

Now there was, on the other side of the Wall that fenced in the way up which *Christiana* and her Companions was to go, a *Garden; and that Garden belonged to him whose was that *Barking Dog*, of whom mention was made before. And some of the Fruit-Trees that grew in that Garden shot their Branches over the Wall, and being mellow, they that found them did gather them up and oft eat of them to their hurt. So *Christiana's* Boys, as Boys are apt to do, being pleas'd with the Trees, and with the Fruit that did hang thereon, did *Plash* them, and began to eat. Their mother did also chide them for so doing; but still the Boys went on.

** The devils garden.*

The Children eat of the Enemies Fruit.

Well, said she, my Sons, you Transgress, for that Fruit is none of ours: but she did not know that they did belong to the Enemy; Ile warrant you if she had, she would a been ready to die for fear. But that passed, and they went on their way. Now by that they were gon about two Bows-shot† from the place that let them into the way: they espyed two very *ill-favoured ones* coming down a pace to meet them. With that *Christiana*, and *Mercie* her Friend, covered themselves with their Vails, and so kept on their Journey: The Children also went on before, so at last they met together. Then they that came down to meet them, came just up to the Women, as if they would imbrace them; but *Christiana* said, Stand back, or go peaceably by as you should. Yet these two, as men that are deaf, regarded not *Christiana's* words; but began to lay hands upon them; at that *Christiana* waxing very wroth, spurned at them with her feet.

Two ill favoured ones.

They assault Christiana.

The pilgrims struggle with them.

Mercie also, as well as she could, did what she could to shift them. *Christiana* again, said to them, Stand back and be gon, for we have no Money to loose being Pilgrims as ye see, and such too as live upon the Charity of our Friends.

Ill-fa. Then said one of the two of the Men, We make no assault upon you for Money; but are come out to tell you, that if you will but grant one small request which we shall ask, we will make Women of you for ever.

Christ. Now *Christiana*, imagining what they should mean, made answer again, *We will neither hear nor regard, nor yield to what you shall ask. We are in haste, cannot stay, our Business is a Business of Life and Death.* So again she and her Companions made a fresh assay to go past them. But they letted them in their way.

Ill-fa. And they said, we intend no hurt to your lives, 'tis an other thing we would have.

Christ. Ay, quoth *Christiana*, you would have us Body and Soul, for I know 'tis for that you are come; but we will die rather upon the spot, then suffer our selves to be brought into such Snares as shall hazzard our well being hereafter. And with that they both *Shrieked* out, and cryed Murder, Murder: and so put themselves under those Laws that are provided for the Protection of Women. But the men still made their approach upon them, with design to prevail against them: They therefore cryed out again.

She cryes out.

Deut. 22. 25, 26, 27.

*Now they being, as I said, not far from the Gate in at which they came, their voice was heard from where they was, thither: Wherefore some of the House came out, and knowing that it was *Christiana*'s Tongue: they made haste to her relief. But by that they was got within sight of them, the Women was in a very great scuffle, the Children also stood crying by. Then did he that came in for their relief, call out to the Ruffins saying, What is that thing that you do? Would you make my Lords People to transgress?† He also attempted to take them; but they did make their escape over the Wall into the Garden of the Man, to whom the great Dog belonged, so the Dog became their Protector. This *Reliever* then came up to the Women, and asked them how they did. So they answered, we thank thy Prince, pretty well, only we

* *'Tis good to cry out when we are assaulted.*

The Reliever *comes.*

The Ill-ones *fly to the devill for releif.*

have been somewhat affrighted; we thank thee also for that thou camest in to our help, for otherwise we had been overcome.

Reliever. So after a few more words, this *Reliever* said as followeth: *I marvelled much when you was entertained at the Gate above, being ye knew that ye were but weak Women, that you petitioned not the Lord there for a Conductor: Then might you have avoided these Troubles, and Dangers: For he would have granted you one.*

The Reliever *talks to the Women.*

Christ. *Alas said *Christiana*, we were so taken with our present blessing, that Dangers to come were forgotten by us; besides, who could have thought that so near the Kings Palace there should have lurked such naughty ones? indeed it had been well for us had we asked our Lord for one; but since our Lord knew 'twould be for our profit, I wonder he sent not one along with us.

** mark this.*

Relie. *It is not always necessary to grant things not asked for, lest by so doing they become of little esteem; but when the want of a thing is felt, it then comes under, in the Eyes of him that feels it, that estimate, that properly is its due, and so consequently will be thereafter used. Had my Lord granted you a Conductor, you would not neither so have bewailed that oversight of yours in not asking for one, as now you have occasion to do. So all things work for good,*† *and tend to make you more wary.*

We lose for want of asking for.

Christ. Shall we go back again to my Lord, and confess our folly and ask one?

Relie. *Your Confession of your folly, I will present him with: To go back again, you need not. For in all places where you shall come, you will find no want at all, for in every of my Lord's Lodgings, which he has prepared for the reception of his Pilgrims, there is sufficient to furnish them against all attempts whatsoever. But, as I said, he will be enquired of by them to do it for them: and 'tis a poor thing that is not worth asking for.* When he had thus said, he went back to his place, and the Pilgrims went on their way.

Ezek. 36. 37.

Mer. Then said *Mercie*, what a sudden blank is here? I made account we had now been past all danger, and that we should never see sorrow more.

The mistake of Mercie.

Christ. Thy *Innocency*, my Sister, said *Christiana* to *Mercie*, may excuse thee much; but as for me, my fault is so much the

Christiana's *Guilt.*

greater, for that I saw this danger before I came out of the Doors, and yet did not provide for it where provision might a been had. I am therefore much to be blamed.

Mer. *Then said* Mercie, *how knew you this before you came from home? pray open to me this Riddle.*

Christ. Why, I will tell you. Before I set Foot out of Doors, one Night, as I lay in my Bed, I had a Dream about this. For methought I saw two men, as like these as ever the World they could look, stand at my *Beds-feet*, plotting how they might prevent my Salvation. I will tell you their very words. They said, ('twas when I was in my Troubles,) *What shall we do with this Woman? for she cries out waking and sleeping for forgiveness. If she be suffered to go on as she begins, we shall lose her as we have lost her Husband.* This you know might a made me take heed, and have provided when Provision might a been had.

Christiana's *Dream repeated.*

Mercie *makes good use of their neglect of duty.*

Mer. Well, said *Mercie, as by this neglect, we have an occasion ministred unto us to behold our own imperfections: So our Lord has taken occasion thereby, to make manifest the Riches of his Grace. For he, as we see, has followed us with un-asked kindness, and has delivered us from their hands that were stronger then we, of his meer good pleasure.*

Thus now when they had talked away a little more time, they drew nigh to an House which stood in the way, which House was built for the relief of Pilgrims as you will find more fully related in the first part of these Records of the *Pilgrims Progress*. So they drew on towards the House (the House of the Interpreter) and when they came to the Door, they heard a great talk in the House; they then gave ear, and heard, as they thought, *Christiana* mentioned by name. For you must know that there went along, even before her, a talk of her and her Childrens going on Pilgrimage. And this thing was the more pleasing to them, because they had heard that she was *Christian*'s Wife; that Woman who was sometime ago so unwilling to hear of going on Pilgrimage. Thus therefore they stood still and heard the good people within commending her, who they little thought stood at the Door. *At last *Christiana* knocked as she had done at the Gate before. Now when she had knocked, there came to the Door a young Damsel and

1 Part, pag. 29.

Talk in the Interpreter's house about Christiana's *going on pilgrimage.*

** She knocks at the Door.*

opened the Door and looked, and behold two Women was there.

The door is opened to them by Innocent.

Damsel. *Then said the Damsel to them, With whom would you speak in this Place?*

Christ. Christiana answered, we understand that this is a priviledged place for those that are become Pilgrims, and we now at this Door are such: Wherefore we pray that we may be partakers of that for which we at this time are come; for the day, as thou seest, is very far spent, and we are loth to night to go any further.

Damsel. Pray what may I call your name, that I may tell it to my Lord within?

Christ. My name is *Christiana*, I was the Wife of that Pilgrim that some years ago did Travel this way, and these be his four Children. This Maiden also is my Companion, and is going on Pilgrimage too.

Innocent. Then ran *Innocent* in (for that was her name) and said to those within, Can you think who is at the Door? There is *Christiana* and her Children, and her Companion, all waiting for entertainment here. *Then they leaped for Joy, and went and told their Master. So he came to the Door, and looking upon her, he said, *Art thou that* Christiana, *whom* Christian, *the Good-man, left behind him, when he betook himself to a Pilgrims Life?*

** Joy in the house of the Interpreter that* Christiana *is turned Pilgrim.*

Christ. I am that Woman that was so hard-hearted as to slight my Husbands Troubles, and that left him to go on in his Journey alone, and these are his four Children; but now I also am come, for I am convinced that no way is right but this.

Inter. *Then is fulfilled that which also is written of the Man that said to his Son, go work to day in my Vineyard, and he said to his Father, I will not; but afterwards repented and went.*

Mat. 21. 29.

Christ. Then said *Christiana*, So be it, *Amen*, God make it a true saying upon me, and grant that I may be found at the last, of him in peace without spot and blameless.†

Inter. *But why standest thou thus at the Door, come in thou Daughter of* Abraham,† *we was talking of thee but now: For tidings have come to us before, how thou art become a Pilgrim. Come Children, come in; come Maiden, come in*; so he had them all into the House.

So when they were within, they were bidden sit down and rest them, the which when they had done, those that attended upon the Pilgrims in the House, came into the Room to see them. And one smiled, and another smiled, and they all smiled for Joy that *Christiana* was become a Pilgrim. They also looked upon the Boys, they stroaked them over the Faces with the Hand, in token of their kind reception of them: they also carried it lovingly to *Mercie*, and bid them all welcome into their Masters House.

Old Saints glad to see the young ones walk in Gods ways.

After a while, because Supper was not ready, *the *Interpreter* took them into his *Significant* Rooms, and shewed them what *Christian*, *Christiana*'s Husband had seen sometime before. Here therefore they saw the *Man* in the *Cage*, the man and his Dream, the man that cut his way thorough his Enemies, and the Picture of the biggest of them all:† together with the rest of those things that were then so profitable to *Christian*.

** The Significant Rooms.*

This done, and after these things had been somewhat digested by *Christiana*, and her Company: the *Interpreter* takes them apart again: and has them first into a Room, *where was a man that could look no way but downwards, with a Muckrake in his hand. There stood also one over his head with a Celestial Crown in his Hand, and proffered to give him that Crown for his Muck-rake; but the man did neither look up, nor regard; but raked to himself the Straws, the small Sticks, and Dust of the Floar.*

The man with the Muck-rake expounded.

Then said *Christiana, I perswade my self that I know somewhat the meaning of this: For this is a Figure of a man of this World: Is it not, good Sir?*

Inter. Thou hast said the right, said he, and his *Muck-rake* doth show his Carnal mind. And whereas thou seest him rather give heed to rake up Straws and Sticks, and the Dust of the Floar, then to what he says that calls to him from above with the Celestial Crown in his Hand; it is to show, That Heaven is but as a Fable to some, and that things here are counted the only things substantial. Now whereas it was also shewed thee, that the man could look no way but downwards: It is to let thee know that earthly things when they are with Power upon Mens minds, quite carry their hearts away from God.

Chris. *Then said* Christiana, *O! deliver me from this Muck-rake.* * Christiana's *prayer against the* Muck-rake.

Inter. That Prayer said the *Interpreter*, has lain by till 'tis almost rusty: *Give me not Riches*, is scarce the Prayer of one of ten thousand. Straws, and Sticks, and Dust, with most, are the great things now looked after. Pro. 30. 8.

With that *Mercie*, and *Christiana* wept, and said, It is alas! too true.

When the *Interpreter* had shewed them this, he has them into the very best Room in the house, (a very brave Room it was) so he bid them look round about, and see if they could find any thing profitable there. Then they looked round and round: For there was nothing there to be seen but a very great *Spider* on the Wall: and that they overlook't.

Mer. *Then said* Mercie, *Sir, I see nothing; but* Christiana *held her peace*.

Inter. But said the *Interpreter*, look again: she therefore lookt again and said, Here is not any thing, but an *ugly Spider*,† who hangs by her Hands upon the Wall. Then said he, Is there but one *Spider* in all this spacious Room? Then the water stood in *Christiana*'s Eyes, for she was a Woman quick of apprehension: and she said, Yes Lord, there is more here then one. Yea, and *Spiders* whose Venom is far more destructive then that which is in her. The *Interpreter* then looked pleasantly upon her, and said, Thou hast said the Truth. This made *Mercie* blush, and the Boys to cover their Faces. For they all began now to understand the Riddle. *Of the Spider.* *Talk about the Spider.*

Then said the *Interpreter* again, *The Spider taketh hold with her hands, as you see, and is in Kings Pallaces*. And wherefore is this recorded; but to show you, that how full of the Venome of Sin soever you be, yet you may by the hand of Faith lay hold of, and dwell in the best Room that belongs to the Kings House above? Pro. 30. 28. *The Interpretation.*

Chris. I thought, said *Christiana*, of something of this; but I could not imagin it all. I thought that we were like *Spiders*, and that we looked like ugly Creatures, in what fine Room soever we were: But that by this *Spider*, this venomous and ill favoured Creature, we were to learn *how to act Faith*, that came not into my mind. And yet she has taken hold with her hands as I see, and dwells in the best Room in the House. God has made nothing in vain.

Then they seemed all to be glad; but the water stood in their Eyes: Yet they looked one upon another, and also bowed before the *Interpreter*.

Of the Hen and Chickens. He had them then into another Room where was a Hen and Chickens, and bid them observe a while. So one of the Chickens went to the Trough to drink, and every time she drank she lift up her head and her eyes towards Heaven. See, said he, what this little Chick doth, and learn of her to acknowledge whence your Mercies come, by receiving them with looking up. Yet again, said he, observe and look: So they gave heed, and perceived that the Hen did walk in a fourfold Method towards her Chickens. 1. She had a *common call*, and that she hath all day long. 2. She had a *special call*, and that she had but sometimes. 3. She had a *brooding note*. And 4. she had an *out-cry*.

Now, said he, compare this *Hen* to your King, and these Chickens to his Obedient ones. For answerable to her, himself has his Methods, which he walketh in towards his People. By his common call, *he gives nothing*, by his special call, he always *has something to give*, he has also a brooding voice, *for them that are under his Wing*. And he has an out-cry, to give *the Alarm when he seeth the Enemy come*. I chose, my Darlings, to lead you into the Room where such things are, because you are Women, and they are easie for you. (Mat. 23. 37.)

Chris. And Sir, said *Christiana*, pray let us see some more: So he had them into the Slaughter-house, where was a *Butcher* a killing of a Sheep: And behold the Sheep was quiet, and took her Death patiently. Then said the *Interpreter*: You must learn of this Sheep, to suffer: And to put up wrongs without murmurings and complaints. Behold how quietly she takes her Death, and without objecting she suffereth her Skin to be pulled over her Ears. Your King doth call you his Sheep. (*Of the Butcher and the Sheep.*)

Of the Garden. After this, he led them into his Garden, where was great variety of Flowers: and he said, do you see all these? So *Christiana* said, yes. Then said he again, Behold the Flowers are divers in *Stature*, in *Quality*, and *Colour*, and *Smell*, and *Virtue*, and some are better then some: Also where the Gardiner has set them, there they stand, and quarrel not one with another.†

Again he had them into his Field, which he had sowed with Wheat and Corn: but when they beheld, the tops of all was cut off, only the Straw remained. He said again, this Ground was Dunged, and Plowed, and Sowed; but what shall we do with the Crop? Then said *Christiana*, burn some and make muck of the rest. Then said the *Interpreter* again, Fruit you see is that thing you look for, and for want of that you condemn it to the Fire, and to be trodden under foot of men: Beware that in this you condemn not your selves.

Of the Field.

Then, as they were coming in from abroad, they espied a little *Robbin* with a great *Spider* in his mouth. So the *Interpreter* said, look here. So they looked, and *Mercie* wondred; but *Christiana* said, what a disparagement is it to such a little pretty Bird as the *Robbin-red-breast* is, he being also a Bird above many, that loveth to maintain a kind of Sociableness with man? I had thought they had lived upon crums of Bread, or upon other such harmless matter. I like him worse then I did.

Of the Robbin *and the* Spider.

The *Interpreter* then replied, This *Robbin* is an Emblem very apt to set forth some Professors† by; for to sight they are as this *Robbin*, pretty of Note, Colour and Carriages, they seem also to have a very great Love for Professors that are sincere; and above all other to desire to sociate with, and to be in their Company, as if they could live upon the good Mans Crums. They pretend also that therefore it is, that they frequent the House of the Godly, and the appointments of the Lord: but when they are by themselves, *as the Robbin*, they can catch and gobble up *Spiders*, they can change their Diet, drink *Iniquity*, and swallow down *Sin* like Water.

So when they were come again into the House, because Supper as yet was not ready, *Christiana* again desired that the *Interpreter* would either *show* or *tell* of some other things that are Profitable.

Pray, and you will get at that which yet lies unrevealed.

Then the *Interpreter* began and said, *The fatter the Sow is, the more she desires the Mire; the fatter the Ox is, the more gamesomly he goes to the Slaughter; and the more healthy the lusty man is, the more prone he is unto Evil.*

There is a desire in Women, to go neat and fine, and it is a comely thing to be adorned with that, that in Gods sight is of great price.†

'Tis easier watching a night or two, then to sit up a whole year together: So 'tis easier for one to begin to profess well, then to hold out as he should to the end.

Every Ship-Master, when in a Storm, will willingly cast that over Board that is of the smallest value in the Vessel; but who will throw the best out first? none but he that feareth not God.

One leak will sink a Ship,† *and one Sin will destroy a Sinner.*

He that forgets his Friend, is ungrateful unto him; but he that forgets his Saviour is unmerciful to himself.

He that lives in Sin, and looks for Happiness hereafter, is like him that soweth Cockle, and thinks to fill his Barn with Wheat, or Barley.†

If a man would live well, let him fetch his last day to him, and make it always his company-Keeper.

Whispering and change of thoughts, proves that Sin is in the World.

If the world which God sets light by, is counted a thing of that worth with men: what is Heaven which God commendeth?

If the Life that is attended with so many troubles, is so loth to be let go by us, What is the Life above?

Every Body will cry up the Goodness of Men; but who is there that is, as he should, affected with the Goodness of God?

We seldom sit down to Meat; but we eat, and leave. So there is in Jesus Christ more Merit and Righteousness then the whole World has need of.

Of the Tree that is rotten at heart.

When the *Interpreter* had done, he takes them out into his Garden again, and had them to a Tree whose *inside* was all rotten,† and gone, and yet it grew and had Leaves. Then said *Mercie*, what means this? This Tree, said he, whose *out-side* is fair, and whose *inside* is rotten; is it to which many may be compared that are in the Garden of God: Who with their mouths speak high in behalf of God, but indeed will do nothing for him: Whose Leaves are fair; but their heart Good for nothing, but to be *Tinder* for the Devils *Tinder-box*.

They are at Supper.

Now Supper was ready, the Table spread, and all things set on the Board; so they sate down and did eat when one had given thanks. And the *Interpreter* did usually entertain those that lodged with him with Musick at Meals, so the Minstrels played. There was also one that did Sing. And a very fine voice he had.

His Song was this.

The Lord is only my support,
And he that doth me feed:
How can I then want any thing
Whereof I stand in need?

When the Song and Musick was ended, the *Interpreter* asked *Christiana, what it was that at first did move her to betake her self to a Pilgrims Life?*

Talk at Supper.

Christiana answered: *First*, the loss of my Husband came into my mind, at which I was heartily grieved: but all that was but natural Affection. Then after that, came the Troubles, and Pilgrimage of my Husband into my mind, and also how like a Churl I had carried it to him as to that. So guilt took hold of my mind, and would have drawn me into the *Pond*; but that opportunely I had a Dream of the well-being of my Husband, and a Letter sent me by the King of that Country where my Husband dwells, to come to him. The Dream and the Letter together so wrought upon my mind, that they forced me to this way.

A Repetition of Christiana's *Experience.*

Inter. *But met you with no opposition afore you set out of Doors?*

Chris. Yes, a Neighbour of mine, one Mrs. *Timerous.* (She was a kin to him that would have perswaded my Husband to go back for fear of the Lions.) She all-to-be-fooled me† for, as she called it, my intended desperate adventure; she also urged what she could, to dishearten me to it, the hardships and Troubles that my Husband met with in the way; but all this I got over pretty well. But a Dream that I had, of two ill-lookt ones, that I thought did Plot how to make me miscarry in my Journey, that hath troubled me much: Yea, it still runs in my mind, and makes me afraid of every one that I meet, lest they should meet me to do me a mischief, and to turn me out of the way. Yea, I may tell my Lord, tho' I would not have every body know it, that between this and the Gate by which we got into the way, we were both so sorely assaulted, that we were made to cry out Murder, and the two that made this assault upon us, were like the two that I saw in my Dream.

Then said the *Interpreter*, Thy beginning is good, thy latter end shall greatly increase.† So he addressed himself to *Mercie*: and said unto her, *And what moved thee to come hither, sweet-heart?*

A question put to Mercie.

Mercie. Then *Mercie* blushed and trembled, and for a while continued silent.

Interpreter. *Then said he, be not afraid, only believe, and speak thy mind.*

Mercys *answer.*

Mer. So she began and said, Truly Sir, my want of Experience, is that that makes me covet to be in silence, and that also that fills me with fears of coming short at last. I cannot tell of Visions, and Dreams as my friend *Christiana* can; nor know I what it is to mourn for my refusing of the Counsel of those that were good Relations.

Interpreter. *What was it then, dear-heart, that hath prevailed with thee to do as thou hast done?*

Mer. Why, when our friend here, was packing up to be gone from our Town, I and another went accidentally to see her. So we knocked at the Door and went in. When we were within, and seeing what she was doing, we asked what was her meaning. She said, she was sent for to go to her Husband, and then she up and told us, how she had seen him in a Dream, dwelling in a curious place among *Immortals* wearing a Crown, playing upon a Harp, eating and drinking at his Princes Table, and singing Praises to him for bringing him thither, *&c.* Now methought, while she was telling these things unto us, my heart burned within me. And I said in my Heart, if this be true, I will leave my Father and my Mother, and the Land of my Nativity, and will, if I may, go along with *Christiana*.

So I asked her further of the truth of these things, and if she would let me go with her: For I saw now that there was no dwelling, but with the danger of ruin, any longer in our Town. But yet I came away with a heavy heart, not for that I was unwilling to come away; but for that so many of my Relations were left behind. And I am come with all the desire of my heart, and will go if I may with *Christiana* unto her Husband and his King.

Inter. Thy setting out is good, for thou hast given credit to the truth, Thou art a *Ruth*, who did for the love that she bore to *Naomi*, and to the Lord her God, leave Father and Mother, and the land of her Nativity to come out, and go with a People that she knew not heretofore. *The Lord recompence thy work, and a full reward be given thee of the Lord God of* Israel, *under whose Wings thou art come to trust.* Ruth 2. 11, 12.

Now Supper was ended, and Preparations was made for Bed, the Women were laid singly alone, and the Boys by themselves. Now when *Mercie* was in Bed, she could not sleep for joy, for that now her doubts of missing at last, were removed further from her than ever they were before. So she lay blessing and Praising God who had had such favour for her. *They address themselves for bed.* Mercy's *good nights rest.*

In the Morning they arose with the *Sun*, and prepared themselves for their departure: But the *Interpreter* would have them tarry a while, for, said he, you must orderly go from hence. Then said he to the Damsel that at first opened unto them, Take them and have them into the Garden, to the *Bath*, and there wash them, and make them clean from the soil which they have gathered by travelling. Then *Innocent* the Damsel took them and had them into the Garden, and brought them to the *Bath*, so she told them that there they must wash and be clean, for so her Master would have the Women to do that called at his House as they were going on *Pilgrimage*. They then went in and washed, yea they and the Boys and all, and they came out of that *Bath* not only sweet, and clean; but also much enlivened and strengthened in their Joynts: So when they came in, they looked fairer a deal, then when they went out to the washing. *The Bath* Sanctification.† *They wash in it.*

When they were returned out of the Garden from the *Bath*, the *Interpreter* took them and looked upon them and said unto them, *fair as the Moon*.† Then he called for the *Seal*† wherewith they used to be *Sealed* that were washed in his *Bath*. So the *Seal* was brought, and he set his Mark upon them, that they might be known in the Places whither they were yet to go: Now the seal was the contents and sum of the Passover which the Children of *Israel* did eat when they came out from the Land of *Egypt*: and the mark was set between their Eyes. This seal greatly added to their Beauty, for it was an Ornament to *They are sealed.* Exo. 13. 8, 9, 10.

their Faces. It also added to their gravity, and made their Countenances more like them of Angels.

Then said the *Interpreter* again to the Damsel that waited upon these Women, Go into the Vestry and fetch out Garments for these People: So she went and fetched out white Rayment, and laid it down before him; so he commanded them to put it on. *It was fine Linnen, white and clean.*† When the Women were thus adorned they seemed to be a Terror one to the other, for that they could not see that glory each one on her self, which they could see in each other. Now therefore they began to esteem each other better then themselves. For, You are fairer then I am, said one, and, You are more comely then I am, said another. The Children also stood amazed to see into what fashion they were brought.

They are clothed.

True humility.

The *Interpreter* then called for a *Man-servant* of his, one *Great-heart*,† and bid him take *Sword*, and *Helmet* and *Shield*, and take these my Daughters, said he, and conduct them to the House called *Beautiful*, at which place they will rest next. So he took his Weapons, and went before them, and the *Interpreter* said, God speed. Those also that belonged to the Family sent them away with many a good wish. So they went on their way, and Sung.

This place has been our second Stage,
Here we have heard and seen
Those good things that from Age to Age,
To others hid have been.
The Dunghil-raker, Spider, Hen,
The Chicken too to me
Hath taught a Lesson, let me then
Conformed to it be.
The Butcher, Garden and the Field,
The Robbin *and his bait,*
Also the Rotten-tree doth yield
Me Argument of weight
To move me for to watch and pray,†
To strive to be sincere,
To take my Cross up day by day,
And serve the Lord with fear.

Now I saw in my Dream that they went on, and *Great-heart* went before them, so they went and came to the place where *Christians* Burthen fell off his Back, and tumbled into a Sepulchre. Here then they made a pause, and here also they blessed God. Now said *Christiana*, it comes to my mind what was said to us at the Gate, to wit, that we should have Pardon, by *Word* and *Deed*; by word, that is, by the promise; by *Deed*, to wit, in the way it was obtained. What the promise is, of that I know something: But what is it to have Pardon by deed, or in the way that it was obtained, Mr. *Great-heart*, I suppose you know; wherefore if you please let us hear you discourse thereof.

1 *Part, pag.* 37.

Great-heart. Pardon by the deed done, is Pardon obtained by some one, for another that hath need thereof: Not by the Person pardoned, but in the way, *saith another*, in which I have obtained it. So then to speak to the question more large, The pardon that you and *Mercie* and these Boys have *attained*, was *obtained* by another, to wit, by him that let you in at the Gate: And he hath obtain'd it in this double way. He has performed Righteousness to cover you, and split blood to wash you in.

A comment upon what was said at the Gate, or a discourse of our being justified by Christ.

Chris. *But if he parts with his Righteousness to us: What will he have for himself?*

Great-heart. He has more Righteousness then you have need of, or then he needeth himself.

Chris. *Pray make that appear*.

Great-heart. With all my heart, but first I must premise that he of whom we are now about to speak, is one that has not his Fellow. He has two Natures in one Person, plain to be *distinguished, impossible* to be *divided.* Unto each of these Natures a Righteousness belongeth, and each Righteousness is essential to that Nature. So that one may as easily cause the Nature to be extinct, as to seperate its Justice or Righteousness from it. Of *these* Righteousnesses therefore, we are not made partakers so, as that they, or any of them, should be put upon us that we might be made just, and live thereby. Besides these there is a Righteousness which this Person has, as these two Natures are joyned in one. And this is not the Righteousness of the *Godhead*, as distinguished from the *Manhood*; nor the Righteousness of the *Manhood*, as distinguished from the *Godhead*; but a Righteousness which standeth in the Union of both Natures:

and may properly be called, the Righteousness that is essential to his being prepared of God to the capacity of the Mediatory Office† which he was to be intrusted with. If he parts with his first Righteousness, he parts with his *Godhead*; if he parts with his second Righteousness, he parts with the purity of his *Manhood*; if he parts with this third, he parts with that perfection that capacitates him to the Office of Mediation. He has therefore another Righteousness which standeth in *performance*, or obedience to a revealed Will: And that is it that he puts upon Sinners, and that by which their Sins are covered. Wherefore he saith, *as by one mans disobedience many were made Sinners: So*
Rom. 5. 19. *by the obedience of one shall many be made Righteous.*

Chris. *But are the other Righteousnesses of no use to us?*

Great-heart. Yes, for though they are essential to his Natures and Office, and so cannot be communicated unto another, yet it is by Virtue of them that the Righteousness that justifies, is for that purpose efficacious. The *Righteousness* of his *God-head* gives *Virtue* to his Obedience; the *Righteousness* of his *Manhood* giveth capability to his obedience to justifie, and the Righteousness that standeth in the Union of these two Natures to his Office, giveth Authority to that Righteousness to do the work for which it is ordained.

So then, here is a Righteousness that Christ, as God, has no need of, for he is God without it: here is a Righteousness that Christ, as Man, has no need of to make him so, for he is perfect Man without it. Again, here is a Righteousness that Christ as God-man has no need of, for he is perfectly so without it. Here then is a Righteousness that Christ, as God, as Man, as God-man has no need of, with Reference to himself, and therefore he can spare it, a justifying Righteousness, that he for himself wanteth not, and therefore he giveth it away. Hence 'tis called
Rom. 5. 17. the *gift of Righteousness.* This Righteousness, since Christ Jesus the Lord, has made himself under the Law, *must* be given away: For the Law doth not only bind him that is under it, *to do justly*; but to use Charity: Wherefore he *must*, he *ought* by the Law, if he hath two Coats, to give one to him that has none.† Now our Lord hath indeed *two Coats*, one for himself, and one to spare: Wherefore he freely bestows one upon those that have none. And thus *Christiana*, and *Mercie*, and the rest of you that

are here, doth your Pardon come by *deed*, or by the work of another man. Your Lord Christ is he that has worked, and given away what he wrought for to the next poor Beggar he meets.

But again, in order to Pardon by *deed*, there must something be paid to God as a price, as well as something prepared to cover us withal. Sin has delivered us up to the just Curse of a Righteous Law: Now from this Curse we must be justified by way of Redemption, a price being paid for the harms we have done, and this is by the Blood of your Lord, who came and stood in your place, and stead, and died your Death for your Transgressions. Thus has he ransomed you from your Transgressions by Blood, and covered your poluted and deformed Souls with Righteousness: For the sake of which, God passeth by you, and will not hurt you, when he comes to Judge the World.

Ro. 4. 24.

Gala. 3. 13.

Chris. *This is brave. Now I see that there was something to be learnt by our being pardoned by* word *and* deed. *Good* Mercie, *let us labour to keep this in mind, and my Children do you remember it also. But, Sir, was not this it that made my good* Christians *Burden fall from off his Shoulder, and that made him give three leaps for Joy?*

Christiana *affected with this way of Redemption.*

Great-heart. *Yes, 'twas the belief of this, that cut those Strings that could not be cut by other means, and 'twas to give him a proof of the Virtue of this, that he was suffered to carry his Burden to the Cross.

** How the Strings that bound Christians burden to him were cut.*

Chris. *I thought so, for tho' my heart was lightful and joyous before, yet it is ten times more lightsome and joyous now. And I am perswaded by what I have felt, tho' I have felt but little as yet, that if the most burdened Man in the World was here, and did see and believe, as I now do, 'twould make his heart the more merry and blithe.*

Great-heart. There is not only comfort, and the ease of a Burden brought to us, by the sight and Consideration of these; but an indeared Affection begot in us by it: For who can, if he doth but once think that Pardon comes, not only by promise, but thus; but be affected with the way and means of his Redemption, and so with the man that hath wrought it for him?

How affection to Christ is begot in the Soul.

1 Part, pag. 37.

Cause of admiration.

Chris. *True, methinks it makes my Heart bleed to think that he should bleed for me. Oh! thou loving one, Oh! thou Blessed one. Thou deservest to have me, thou hast bought me: Thou deservest to have me all, thou hast paid for me ten thousand times more than I am worth. No marvel that this made the Water stand in my Husbands Eyes, and that it made him trudg so nimbly on: I am perswaded he wished me with him; but vile wretch, that I was, I let him come all alone. O* Mercie, *that thy Father and Mother were here, yea, and Mrs.* Timorous *also. Nay I wish now with all my Heart, that here was Madam* Wanton *too. Surely, surely, their Hearts would be affected, nor could the fear of the one, nor the powerful Lusts of the other, prevail with them to go home again, and to refuse to become good Pilgrims.*

To be affected with Christ and with what he has don is a thing special.

Great-heart. You speak now in the warmth of your Affections, will it, think you, be always thus with you? Besides, this is not communicated to every one, nor to every one that did see your Jesus bleed. There was that stood by, and that saw the Blood run from his Heart to the Ground, and yet was so far off this, that instead of lamenting, they laughed at him,† and instead of becoming his Disciples, did harden their Hearts against him. So that all that you have, my Daughters, you have by a peculiar impression made by a Divine contemplating upon what I have spoken to you. Remember that 'twas told you, that the *Hen* by her common call, gives no meat to her *Chickens*. This you have therefore by a special Grace.

Simple *and* Sloth *and* Presumption *hanged, and why.*

Now I saw still in my Dream, that they went on until they were come to the place that *Simple*, and *Sloth* and *Presumption* lay and slept in, when *Christian* went by on Pilgrimage. And behold they were hanged up in Irons a little way off on the other-side.

Mercie. *Then said* Mercie *to him that was their Guide, and Conductor, What are those three men? and for what are they hanged here?*

Great-heart. These three men, were Men of very bad Qualities, they had no mind to be Pilgrims themselves, and whosoever they could they hindred; they were for Sloth and Folly themselves, and whoever they could perswade with, they made so too, and withal taught them to presume that they should do

Behold here how the slothful are a signe
Hung up, cause holy ways they did decline;
See here too how the Child did play the man,
And weak grow strong, when *Great-heart* leads the Van.

well at last. They were asleep when *Christian* went by, and now you go by they are hanged.

Mercie. *But could they perswade any to be of their Opinion?*

Great-heart. Yes, they turned several out of the way. There was *Slow-pace* that they perswaded to do as they. They also prevailed with one *Short-wind*, with one *No-heart*, with one *Linger-after-lust*, and with one *Sleepy-head*, and with a young Woman her name was *Dull*, to turn out of the way and become as they. Besides, they brought up an ill report of your Lord, perswading others that he was a task-Master. They also brought up an evil report of the good Land,† saying, 'twas not half so good as some pretend it was: They also began to villifie his Servants, and to count the very best of them meddlesome, troublesome busie-Bodies: Further, they would call the Bread of God, *Husks*; the *Comforts* of his Children, *Fancies*, the Travel and Labour of Pilgrims, things to no purpose.

Their Crimes.

Who they prevailed upon to turn out of the way.

Chris. *Nay, said* Christiana, *if they were such, they shall never be bewailed by me, they have but what they deserve, and I think it is well that they hang so near the High-way that others may see and take warning. But had it not been well if their Crimes had been ingraven in some Plate of Iron or Brass, and left here, even where they did their Mischiefs, for a caution to other bad Men?*

Great-heart. So it is, as you well may perceive if you will go a little to the Wall.

Mercie. *No no, let them hang and their Names Rot,† and their Crimes live for ever against them; I think it a high favour that they were hanged afore we came hither, who knows else what they might a done to such poor Women as we are?* Then she turned it into a Song, saying,

Now then, you three, hang there and be a Sign
To all that shall against the Truth combine:
And let him that comes after, fear this end,
If unto Pilgrims he is not a Friend.
And thou my Soul of all such men beware,
That unto Holiness Opposers are.

Thus they went on till they came at the foot of the Hill *Difficulty*, where again their good Friend, Mr. *Great-heart*,

1 *Part, pag.* 41.

took an occasion to tell them of what happened there when *Christian* himself went by. So he had them first to the Spring. *Lo*, saith he, *This is the Spring that* Christian *drank of*, before he went up this Hill, and then 'twas clear and good; but now 'tis Dirty with the feet of some that are not desirous that Pilgrims here should quench their Thirst: Thereat *Mercie* said, *And why so ęnvious tro?* But said their Guide, It will do, if taken up, and put into a Vessel that is sweet and good; for then the Dirt will sink to the bottom, and the Water come out by it self more clear. Thus therefore *Christiana* and her Companions were compelled to do. They took it up, and put it into an Earthen-pot and so let it stand till the Dirt was gone to the bottom, and then they drank thereof.

Ezek. 34. 18.

'Tis difficult getting of good Doctrine in erroneous Times.

Next he shewed them the two *by-ways* that were at the foot of the Hill, where *Formality* and *Hypocrisie*, lost themselves. And, said he, these are dangerous Paths: Two were here cast away when *Christian* came by. *And although, as you see, these ways are since stopt up with *Chains*, *Posts* and a *Ditch*: Yet there are that will chuse to adventure here, rather then take the pains to go up this Hill.

** By paths tho barred up will not keep all from going in them.*

1 Part, pag. 41.

Christiana. *The way of Transgressors is hard. 'Tis a wonder that they can get into those ways, without danger of breaking their Necks.*

Pro. 13. 15.

Great-heart. They will venture, yea, if at any time any of the Kings Servants doth happen to see them, and doth call unto them, and tell them that *they* are in the wrong ways, and do bid them beware the danger. Then they will railingly return them answer and say, *As for the Word that thou hast spoken unto us in the name of the King, we will not hearken unto thee; but we will certainly do whatsoever thing goeth out of our own Mouths*, &c. Nay if you look a little farther, you shall see that these ways, are made cautionary enough, not only by these *Posts* and *Ditch* and *Chain*; but also by being hedged up. Yet they will chuse to go there.

Jer. 44. 16, 17.

Christiana. **They are Idle, they love not to take Pains, up-hill-way is unpleasant to them. So it is fulfilled unto them as it is Written, The way of the slothful man is a Hedg of Thorns. Yea, they will rather chuse to walk upon a Snare, then to go up this Hill, and the rest of this way to the City.*

** The reason why some do chuse to go in by-waies.*

Pro. 15. 19.

The Hill puts the Pilgrims to it.

Then they set forward and began to go up the Hill, and up the Hill they went; but before they got to the top, *Christiana* began to *Pant*, and said, I dare say this is a breathing Hill, no marvel if they that love their ease more than their Souls, chuse to themselves a smoother way. Then said *Mercie*, I must sit down, also the least of the Children began to cry. Come, come, said *Great-heart*, sit not down here, for a little above is the Princes *Arbour*. Then took he the little Boy by the Hand, and led him up thereto.

They sit in the Arbour.

1 Part, pag. 42–5.

Mat. 11. 28.

When they were come to the *Arbour* they were very willing to sit down, for they were all in a pelting heat. Then said *Mercie, How sweet is rest to them that Labour!* And how good is the Prince of Pilgrims, to provide such resting places for them! Of *this Arbour* I have heard much; but I never saw it before. But here let us beware of sleeping: For as I have heard, for that it cost poor *Christian* dear.

The little Boys answer to the guide, and also to Mercie.

Then said Mr. *Great-heart* to the little ones, Come my pretty *Boys*, how do you do? what think you now of going on Pilgrimage? Sir, said the least, I was almost beat out of heart; but I thank you for lending me a hand at my need. And I remember now what my Mother has told me, namely, That the way to Heaven is as up a Ladder, and the way to Hell is as down a Hill. But I had rather go up the Ladder to Life, then down the Hill to Death.

Which is hardest up Hill or down Hill?

Then said *Mercie*, But the Proverb is, *To go down the Hill is easie*:† But *James* said (for that was his Name) The day is coming when in my Opinion, *going down Hill will be the hardest of all*. 'Tis a good Boy, said his Master, thou hast given her a right answer. Then *Mercie* smiled, but the little Boy did blush.

They refresh themselves.

Chris. Come, said *Christiana*, will you eat a bit, a little to sweeten your Mouths, while you sit here to rest your Legs? For I have here a piece of Pomgranate which Mr. *Interpreter* put in my Hand, just when I came out of his Doors; he gave me also a piece of an Honey-comb,† and a little Bottle of Spirits.† I thought he gave you something, said *Mercie*, because he called you a to-side. Yes, so he did, said the other, But *Mercie*, It shall still be as I said it should, when at first we came from home: Thou shalt be a sharer in all the good that I have, because thou so willingly didst become my Companion. Then she gave to them, and they did eat, both *Mercie*, and the Boys. And said *Christiana* to Mr. *Great-heart*, Sir will you do as we? But he answered, You are going on Pilgrimage, and presently I shall return; much good may what you have, do to you. At home I eat the same every day. Now when they had eaten and drank, and had chatted a little longer, their guide said to them, The day wears away, if you think good, let us prepare to be going. So they got up to go, and the little Boys went before; but *Christiana* forgat to take her Bottle of Spirits with her, so she sent her little Boy back to fetch it. Then said *Mercie*, I think this is a *losing* Place. Here *Christian* lost his *Role*, and here *Christiana* left her Bottle behind her: Sir, what is the cause of this? so their guide made answer and said, The cause is *sleep*, or *forgetfulness*; some *sleep*, when they should keep *awake*; and some *forget*, when they should *remember*; and this is the very cause, why often at the resting places, some Pilgrims in some things come off losers. Pilgrims should watch and remember what they have already received under their greatest enjoyments: But for want of doing so, oft times their rejoicing ends in Tears, and their Sun-shine in a Cloud: Witness the story of *Christian* at this place.

Christiana *forgets her Bottle of Spirits.*

Mark this.

1 *Part, page* 44.

When they were come to the place where *Mistrust* and *Timorous* met *Christian* to perswade him to go back for fear of the Lions, they perceived as it were a Stage, and before it towards the Road, a broad plate with a Copy of Verses Written thereon, and underneath, the reason of the raising up of that Stage in that place, rendered. The Verses were these.

Let him that sees this Stage take heed,
Unto his Heart and Tongue:
Lest if he do not, here he speed
As some have long agone.

The words underneath the Verses were. *This Stage was built to punish such upon, who through* Timorousness, *or* Mistrust, *shall be afraid to go further on Pilgrimage. Also on this Stage both* Mistrust, *and* Timorous *were burned thorough the Tongue with an hot Iron,*† *for endeavouring to hinder* Christian *in his Journey.*

Then said *Mercie*. This is much like to the saying of the beloved, *What shall be given unto thee? or what shall be done unto* Psal. 120. 3, 4.

thee thou false Tongue? sharp Arrows of the mighty, with Coals of Juniper.

1 Part, pag. 45. So they went on till they came within sight of the Lions. Now Mr. *Great-heart* was a strong man, so he was not afraid of a Lion. But yet when they were come up to the place where the Lions were, the Boys that went before, were now glad to cringe behind, for they were afraid of the Lions, so they stept back and went behind. At this their guide smiled, and said, How now my Boys, do you love to go before when no danger doth approach, and love to come behind so soon as the Lions appear?

An Emblem of those that go on bravely, when there is no danger; but shrink when troubles come.

Of Grim *the* Giant, *and of his backing the Lions.*

Now as they went up, Mr. *Great-heart* drew his Sword with intent to make a way for the Pilgrims in spite of the Lions. Then there appeared one, that it seems, had taken upon him to back the Lions. And he said to the Pilgrims guide, What is the cause of your coming hither? Now the name of that man was *Grim* or *Bloody man*,† because of his slaying of Pilgrims, and he was of the race of the *Gyants*.

Great-heart. Then said the *Pilgrims* guide, these Women and Children, are going on Pilgrimage, and this is the way they must go, and go it they shall in spite of thee and the Lions.

Grim. This is not their way, neither shall they go therein. I am come forth to withstand them, and to that end will back the Lions.

Now to say truth, by reason of the fierceness of the Lions, and of the *Grim*-Carriage of him that did back them, this way had of late lain much un-occupied, and was almost all grown over with Grass.

Christiana. Then said *Christiana*, Tho' the High-ways have been unoccupied heretofore, and tho' the Travellers have been made in time past, to walk thorough by-Paths, it must not be so
Judg. 5. 6, 7. now I am risen, *Now I am Risen a Mother in* Israel.†

Grim. Then he swore *by the Lions*, but it should; and therefore bid them turn aside, for they should not have passage there.

Great-heart. But their guide made first his Approach unto *Grim*, and laid so heavily at him with his Sword, that he forced him to a retreat.

Grim. Then said he (that attempted to back the Lions) will you slay me upon mine own Ground?

Great-heart. 'Tis the Kings High-way that we are in, and in this way it is that thou hast placed thy Lions; but these Women and these Children, tho' weak, shall hold on their way in spite of thy Lions. And with that he gave him again a down-right blow, and brought him upon his Knees. With this blow he also broke his Helmet, and with the next he cut off an Arm. Then did the *Giant Roar* so hideously, that his Voice frighted the Women, and yet they were glad to see him lie sprawling upon the Ground. Now the Lions were chained, and so of themselves could do nothing. Wherefore when old *Grim* that intended to back them was dead, Mr. *Great-heart* said to the Pilgrims, Come now and follow me, and no hurt shall happen to you from the Lions. They therefore went on; but the Women trembled as they passed by them, the Boys also look't as if they would die; but they all got by without further hurt.

A fight betwixt Grim *and* Great-heart.

The Victory.

They pass by the Lyons.

Now then they were within sight of the *Porters* Lodg, and they soon came up unto it; but they made the more haste after this to go thither, because 'tis dangerous travelling there in the Night. So when they were come to the Gate, the guide knocked, and the Porter cried, *who is there*? but as soon as the Guide had said *it is I*, he knew his Voice and came down (For the Guide had oft before that, came thither as a Conductor of Pilgrims). When he was came down, he opened the Gate, and seeing the Guide standing just before it (for he saw not the Women, for they were behind) he said unto him, How now Mr. *Great-heart*, what is your business here so late to Night? I have brought, said he, some Pilgrims hither, where by my Lords Commandment they must Lodg. I had been here some time ago, had I not been opposed by the Giant that did use to back the Lyons. But I after a long and tedious combate with him, have cut him off, and have brought the Pilgrims hither in safety.

They come to the Porters Lodge.

Porter. *Will you not go in, and stay till Morning?*

Great-heart. No, I will return to my Lord to night.

Christiana. Oh Sir, I know not how to be willing you should leave us in our Pilgrimage, you have been so faithful, and so loving to us, you have fought so stoutly for us, you have been so

Great-heart *attempts to go back. The Pilgrims implore his company still.*

hearty in counselling of us, that I shall never forget your favour towards us.

Mercie. Then said *Mercie*, O that we might have thy Company to our Journeys end! How can such poor Women as we, hold out in a way so full of Troubles as this way is, without a Friend, and Defender?

James. Then said *James*, the youngest of the Boys, Pray Sir be perswaded to go with us and help us, because we are so weak, and the way so dangerous as it is.

Help lost for want of asking for.

Great-heart. I am at my Lords Commandment. If he shall allot me to be your Guide quite thorough, I will willingly wait upon you; but here you failed at first; for when he bid me come thus far with you, then you should have begged me of him to have gon quite thorough with you, and he would have granted your request. However, at present I must withdraw, and so good *Christiana, Mercie*, and my brave Children, Adieu.

1 *Part, pag.* 47–8. Christiana *makes her self known to the Porter, he tells it to a damsel.*

Then the Porter, Mr. *Watchfull*, asked *Christiana* of her Country, and of her Kindred, and she said, *I came from the City of* Destruction, *I am a Widdow Woman, and my Husband is dead, his name was* Christian *the Pilgrim*. How, said the Porter, was he your Husband? Yes, said she, and these are his Children: and this, pointing to *Mercie*, is one of my Towns-Women. Then the Porter rang his Bell, as at such times he is wont, and there came to the Door one of the Damsels, whose Name was *Humble-mind*. And to her the Porter said, Go tell it within that *Christiana* the Wife of *Christian* and her Children are come hither on Pilgrimage. She went in therefore and told it. But Oh what a Noise for gladness was there within, when the Damsel did but drop that word out of her Mouth!

Joy at the noise of the Pilgrims coming.

So they came with haste to the Porter, for *Christiana* stood still at the Door; then some of the most grave, said unto her, *Come in* Christiana, *come in thou Wife of that Good Man, come in thou Blessed Woman, come in with all that are with thee*. So she went in, and they followed her that were her Children, and her Companions. Now when they were gone in, they were had into a very large Room, where they were bidden to sit down: So they sat down, and the chief of the House was called to see, and welcome the Guests. Then they came in, and understanding who they were, did Salute each one with a kiss,†

Christians *love is kindled at the sight of one another.*

and said, Welcome ye Vessels of the Grace of God, welcome to us your Friends.

Now because it was somewhat late, and because the Pilgrims were weary with their Journey, and also made faint with the sight of the Fight, and of the terrible Lyons, therefore they desired as soon as might be, to prepare to go to Rest. Nay, said those of the Family, refresh your selves first with a Morsel of Meat. For they had prepared for them a Lamb, with the accustomed Sauce belonging thereto. For the Porter had heard before of their coming, and had told it to them within. So when they had Supped, and ended their Prayer with a Psalm, they desired they might go to rest. But let us, said *Christiana*, if we may be so bold as to chuse, be in that Chamber that was my Husbands, when he was here. So they had them up thither, and they lay all in a Room. When they were at Rest, *Christiana* and *Mercie* entred into discourse about things that were convenient.

Exo. 12. 3, 8. Joh. 1. 29.

1 Part, pag. 53.

Chris. *Little did I think once, that when my Husband went on Pilgrimage I should ever a followed.*

Mercie. And you as little thought of lying in his Bed, and in his Chamber to Rest, as you do now.

Chris. *And much less did I ever think of seeing his Face with Comfort, and of Worshipping the Lord the King with him, and yet now I believe I shall.*

Christs Bosome is for all Pilgrims.

Mercie. Hark, don't you hear a Noise?

Christiana. Yes, 'tis as I believe a Noise of Musick, for Joy *that we are here.*

Musick.

Mer. Wonderful! Musick in the House, Musick in the Heart, and Musick also in Heaven, for joy that we are here.

Thus they talked a while, and then betook themselves to sleep; so in the morning, when they were awake, *Christiana* said to *Mercy*.

Chris. *What was the matter that you did laugh in your sleep to Night? I suppose you was in a Dream?*

Mercy *did laugh in her sleep.*

Mercy. So I was, and a sweet Dream it was; but are you sure I laughed?

Christiana. *Yes, you laughed heartily; But prethee* Mercy *tell me thy Dream?*

Mercy. I was a Dreamed† that I sat all alone in a Solitary

Mercy's *Dream.*

place, and was bemoaning of the hardness of my Heart. Now I had not sat there long, but methought many were gathered about me to see me, and to hear what it was that I said. So they harkened, and I went on bemoaning the hardness of my Heart. At this, some of them laughed at me, some called me Fool, and some began to thrust me about. With that, methought I looked up, and saw one coming with Wings towards me. So he came directly to me, and said *Mercy*, what aileth thee? Now when he had heard me make my complaint; he said, *Peace be to thee:* he also wiped mine Eyes with his Hankerchief, and *clad* me in *Silver* and *Gold*; he put a Chain about my Neck, and Ear-rings in mine Ears, and a beautiful Crown upon my Head. Then he took me by my Hand, and said, *Mercy*, come after me. So he went up, and I followed, till we came at a Golden Gate. Then he knocked, and when they within had opened, the man went in and I followed him up to a Throne, upon which one sat, and he said to me, *welcome Daughter*. The place looked bright, and twinkling like the Stars, or rather like the *Sun*, and I thought that I saw your Husband there, so I awoke from my Dream. But did I laugh?

What her dream was.

Ezek. 16. 8, 9, 10, 11.

Christiana. *Laugh! Ay, and well you might to see your self so well. For you must give me leave to tell you, that I believe it was a good Dream, and that as you have begun to find the first part true, so you shall find the second at last.* God speaks once, yea twice, yet man perceiveth it not. In a Dream, in a Vision of the Night, when deep sleep falleth upon men, in slumbering upon the Bed. *We need not, when a-Bed, lie awake to talk with God; he can visit us while we sleep, and cause us then to hear his Voice. Our Heart oft times wakes when we sleep,*† *and God can speak to that, either by Words, by Proverbs, by Signs, and Similitudes, as well as if one was awake.*

Job 33. 14, 15.

Mercy. Well, I am glad of my Dream, for I hope ere long to see it fulfilled, to the making of me laugh again.

Mercy *glad of her dream.*

Christiana. *I think it is now time to rise, and to know what we must do.*

Mercy. Pray, if they invite us to stay a while, let us willingly accept of the proffer. I am the willinger to stay awhile here, to grow better acquainted with these Maids; methinks *Prudence, Piety* and *Charity*, have very comly and sober Countenances.

Chris. *We shall see what they will do*. So when they were up and ready, they came down. And they asked one another of their rest, and if it was Comfortable, or not?

Mer. *Very good, said* Mercy. *It was one of the best Nights Lodging that ever I had in my Life*.

Then said *Prudence*, and *Piety*, If you will be perswaded to stay here a while, you shall have what the House will afford.

They stay here some time.

Charity. *Ay, and that with a very good will, said* Charity. So they consented, and stayed there about a Month or above: and became very Profitable one to another. And because *Prudence* would see how *Christiana* had brought up her Children, she asked leave of her to Catechise them:† So she gave her free consent. Then she began at the youngest whose Name was *James*.

Prudence *desires to catechise* Christianas *Children.*

Pru. *And she said, Come* James, *canst thou tell who made thee?*

James *Catechised.*

Jam. God the Father, God the Son, and God the Holy-Ghost.

Pru. *Good Boy. And canst thou tell who saves thee?*

Jam. God the Father, God the Son, and God the Holy Ghost.

Pru. *Good Boy still. But how doth God the Father save thee?*

Jam. By his Grace.

Pru. *How doth God the Son save thee?*

Jam. By his Righteousness, Death, and Blood, and Life.

Pru. *And how doth God the Holy Ghost save thee?*

Jam. By his *Illumination*, by his *Renovation*, and by his *Preservation*.

Then said *Prudence* to *Christiana*, You are to be commended for thus bringing up your Children. I suppose I need not ask the rest these Questions, since the youngest of them can answer them so well. I will therefore now apply my self to the Youngest next.

Prudence. Then she said, Come *Joseph*, (for his Name was *Joseph*) will you let me Catechise you?

Joseph *catechised.*

Joseph. With all my Heart.

Pru. *What is Man?*

Joseph. A Reasonable Creature, so made by God, as my Brother said.

Pru. *What is supposed by this Word, saved?*

Joseph. That man by Sin has brought himself into a State of Captivity and Misery.

Pru. *What is supposed by his being saved by the Trinity?*

Joseph. That Sin is so great and mighty a Tyrant, that none can pull us out of its clutches but God, and that God is so good and loving to man, as to pull him indeed out of this Miserable State.

Pru. *What is Gods design in saving of poor Men?*

Joseph. The glorifying of his Name, of his Grace, and Justice, *&c.* And the everlasting Happiness of his Creature.

Pru. *Who are they that must be saved?*

Joseph. Those that accept of his Salvation.

Good Boy *Joseph*, thy Mother has taught thee well, and thou hast harkened to what she has said unto thee.

Then said *Prudence* to *Samuel*, who was the eldest but one.

Samuel *Catechised.*

Prudence. Come *Samuel*, are you willing that I should Catechise you also?

Sam. Yes, forsooth, if you please.

Pru. *What is Heaven?*

Sam. A place, and State most blessed, because God dwelleth there.

Pru. *What is Hell?*

Sam. A Place and State most woful, because it is the dwelling place of Sin, the Devil, and Death.

Prudence. *Why wouldest thou go to Heaven?*

Sam. That I may see God, and serve him without weariness; that I may see Christ, and love him everlastingly; that I may have that fulness of the Holy Spirit in me, that I can by no means here enjoy.

Pru. *A very good Boy also, and one that has learned well.*

Mathew *Catechised.*

Then she addressed her self to the eldest, whose Name was *Mathew*, and she said to him, Come *Mathew*, shall I also Catechise you?

Mat. *With a very good will.*

Pru. *I ask then, if there was ever any thing that had a being, Antecedent to, or before God?*

Mat. No, for God is Eternal, nor is there any thing excepting himself, that had a being until the beginning of the first day. *For in six days the Lord made Heaven and Earth, the Sea and all that in them is.*†

Pru. *What do you think of the Bible?*

Mat. It is the Holy Word of God.

Pru. *Is there nothing Written therein, but what you understand?*

Mat. Yes, a great deal.

Pru. *What do you do when you meet with such places therein, that you do not understand?*

Mat. I think God is wiser then I. I pray also that he will please to let me know all therein that he knows will be for my good.

Pru. *How believe you as touching the Resurrection of the Dead?*

Mat. I believe they shall rise, the same that was buried: The same in *Nature*, tho' not in Corruption. And I believe this upon a double account. First, because God has promised it. Secondly, because he is able to perform it.

Prudences *conclusion upon the Catechising of the Boys.*

Then said *Prudence* to the Boys, You must still harken to your Mother, for she can learn you more. You must also diligently give ear to what good talk you shall hear from others, for for your sakes do they speak good things. Observe also and that with carefulness, what the Heavens and the Earth do teach you; but especially be much in the Meditation of that Book that was the cause of your Fathers becoming a Pilgrim. I for my part, my Children, will teach you what I can while you are here, and shall be glad if you will ask me Questions that tend to Godly edifying.

Mercie *has a sweet heart.*

Now by that these Pilgrims had been at this place a week, *Mercie* had a Visitor that pretended some good Will unto her, and his name was Mr. *Brisk*.† A man of some breeding, and that pretended to Religion; but a man that stuck very close to the World. So he came once or twice, or more to *Mercie*, and offered love unto her. Now *Mercie* was of a fair Countenance, and therefore the more alluring.

Mercies *temper.*

Her mind also was, to be always busying of her self in doing, for when she had nothing to do for her self, she would be making of Hose and Garments for others, and would bestow them upon them that had need. And Mr. *Brisk* not knowing where or how she disposed of what she made, seemed to be greatly taken, for that he found her never Idle. I will warrant her a good Huswife, quoth he to himself.

* *Mercie enquires of the Maids concerning Mr.* Brisk.

**Mercie* then revealed the business to the Maidens that were of the House, and enquired of them concerning him: for they did know him better then she. So they told her that he was a very busie Young-Man, and one that pretended to Religion; but was as they feared, a stranger to the Power of that which was good.

Nay then, said Mercie, *I will look no more on him, for I purpose never to have a clog to my Soul.*

Prudence then replied, That there needed no great matter of discouragement to be given to him, her continuing so as she had began to do for the Poor, would quickly cool his Courage.

Talk betwixt Mercie *and Mr.* Brisk.

So the next time he comes, he finds her at her old work, a making of things for the Poor. Then said he, What always at it? Yes, said she, either for my self, or for others. And what canst thee *earn* a day, quoth he? I do these things, said she,
1 Tim. 6. 17, 18, 19. *That I may be Rich in good Works, laying up in store a good Foundation against the time to come, that I may lay hold on Eternal Life*: Why prethee what dost thou with them? said he; Cloath the naked, said she. With that his Countenance fell.

He forsakes her, and why.

So he forbore to come at her again. And when he was asked the reason why, he said, *That* Mercie *was a pretty lass; but troubled with ill Conditions.*

Mercie *in the practice of* Mercie *rejected; While* Mercie *in the Name of* Mercie, *is liked.*

When he had left her, *Prudence* said, Did I not tell thee that Mr. *Brisk* would soon forsake thee? yea, he will raise up an ill report of thee: For notwithstanding his pretence to Religion, and his seeming love to *Mercie*, yet *Mercie* and he are of tempers so different, that I believe they will never come together.

Mercie. *I might a had Husbands afore now, tho' I spake not of it to any; but they were such as did not like my Conditions, though never did any of them find fault with my Person: So they and I could not agree.*

Prudence. Mercie in our days is little set by, any further then as to its Name: the Practice, which is set forth by thy Conditions, there are but few that can abide.

Mercie. *Well, said* Mercie, *if no body will have me, I will dye a Maid, or my Conditions shall be to me as a Husband. For I cannot change my Nature, and to have one that lies cross to me in this, that I purpose never to admit of, as long as I live. I had a Sister named* Bountiful *that was married to one of these Churles; but he and she could never agree; but because my Sister was resolved to do as she had began, that is, to show Kindness to the Poor, therefore her Husband first cried her down at the Cross,*† *and then turned her out of his Doors.*

Mercie's *resolution.*

How Mercie's *Sister was served by her Husband.*

Pru. And yet he was a Professor, I warrant you?

Mer. *Yes, such a one as he was, and of such as he, the World is now full; but I am for none of them all.*

*Now *Mathew* the eldest Son of *Christiana* fell Sick, and his Sickness was sore upon him, for he was much pained in his Bowels, so that he was with it, at times, pulled as 'twere both ends together. There dwelt also not far from thence, one Mr. *Skill*, an Antient, and well approved Physician. So *Christiana* desired it, and they sent for him, and he came. When he was entred the Room, and had a little observed the Boy, he concluded that he was sick of the Gripes. Then he said to his Mother, *What Diet has* Mathew *of late fed upon*? Diet, said *Christiana*, nothing but that which is wholsome. *The Physician answered, *This Boy has been tampering with something which lies in his Maw undigested, and that will not away without means*. And I tell you he must be purged or else he will dye.

* Mathew *falls sick.*

Gripes of Conscience.

* *The Physicians Judgment.*

Samuel. *Then said *Samuel, Mother, Mother, what was that which my Brother did gather up and eat, so soon as we were come from the Gate, that is at the head of this way? You know that there was an Orchard on the left hand, on the otherside of the Wall, and some of the Trees hung over the Wall, and my Brother did plash and did eat.*

* Samuel *puts his Mother in mind of the fruit his Brother did eat.*

Christiana. True my Child, said *Christiana*, he did take thereof and did eat; naughty Boy as he was, I did chide him, and yet he would eat thereof.

Skill. *I knew he had eaten something that was not wholsome Food. And that Food, to wit, that Fruit is even the most hurtful of all. It is the Fruit of* Belzebubs† *Orchard. I do marvel that none did warn you of it; many have died thereof.*

Christiana. Then *Christiana* began to cry, and she said, O naughty Boy, and O careless Mother, what shall I do for my Son?

Skill. *Come, do not be too much Dejected; the Boy may do well again; but he must purge and Vomit.*

Christiana. Pray Sir try the utmost of your Skill with him whatever it costs.

Heb. 10. 1, 2, 3, 4.

Skill. *Nay, I hope I shall be reasonable*: So he made him a Purge; but it was too weak. 'Twas said, it was made of the Blood of a Goat, the Ashes of an Heifer, and with some of the

** Potion prepared.*

Juice of Hyssop,† *&c.* *When Mr. *Skill* had seen that that Purge was too weak, he made him one to the purpose. 'Twas made

John 6. 54, 55, 56, 57. Mark 9. 49. *The Lattine I borrow.* Heb. 9. 14.

ex Carne & Sanguine Christi.† (You know Physicians give strange Medicines to their Patients) and it was made up into Pills with a Promise or two, and a proportionable quantity of Salt. Now he was to take them three at a time fasting in half a quarter of a Pint of the Tears of Repentance. When this potion

** The boy loth to take the Physick.* Zech. 12. 10.

was prepared, and brought to the Boy; *he was loth to take it, tho' torn with the Gripes, as if he should be pulled in pieces. *Come, come, said the Physician, you must take it.* It goes against my Stomach, said the Boy. *I must have you take it, said his Mother.* I shall Vomit it up again, said the Boy. Pray Sir, said *Christiana* to Mr. *Skill*, how does it taste? It has no ill taste, said the Doctor, and with that she touched one of the pills with

The Mother tasts it, and perswades him.

the tip of her Tongue. Oh *Mathew*, said she, this potion is sweeter then Hony. If thou lovest thy Mother, if thou lovest thy Brothers, if thou lovest *Mercie*, if thou lovest thy Life, take it. So with much ado, after a short Prayer for the blessing of God upon it, he took it; and it wrought kindly with him. It caused him to Purge, it caused him to sleep, and rest quietly, it put him into a fine heat and breathing sweat, and did quite rid him of his Gripes.

A word of God in the hand of his Faith.

So in little time he got up, and walked about with a Staff, and would go from Room to Room, and talk with *Prudence, Piety*, and *Charity* of his Distemper, and how he was healed.

Heb. 13. 11, 12, 13, 14, 15.

So when the Boy was healed, *Christiana* asked Mr. *Skill*, saying, Sir, what will content you for your pains and care to and of my Child? And he said, you must pay the *Master of the Colledge* of Physicians, according to rules made, in that case, and provided.

Chris. *But Sir, said she, what is this Pill good for else?*

Skill. It is an universal Pill, 'tis good against all the Diseases that Pilgrims are incident to, and when it is well prepared it will keep good, *time* out of *mind*.

This Pill an Universal Remedy.

Christiana. Pray Sir, make me up twelve Boxes of them: For if I can get these, I will never take other Physick.

Skill. These *Pills* are good to prevent Diseases, as well as to *cure* when one is Sick. Yea, I dare say it, and stand to it, that if a man will but use this Physick as he should, *it will make him live for ever.*† But, good *Christiana*, thou must give these Pills, *no other way*; *but as I have prescribed: For if you do, they will do no good. So he gave unto *Christiana* Physick for her self, and her Boys, and for *Mercie*: and bid *Mathew* take heed how he eat any more *Green Plums*, and kist them and went his way.

** In a Glass of the Tears of Repentance.*

It was told you before, That *Prudence* bid the Boys, that if at any time they would, they should ask her some Questions, that might be profitable, and she would say something to them.

Mat. Then *Mathew* who had been sick, asked her, *Why for the most part Physick should be bitter to our Palats?*

Of Physick.

Pru. To shew how unwelcome the word of God and the Effects thereof are to a Carnal Heart.

Mathew. *Why does Physick, if it does good, Purge, and cause that we Vomit?*

Of the Effects of Physick.

Prudence. To shew that the Word when it works effectually, cleanseth the Heart and Mind. For look what the one doth to the Body, the other doth to the Soul.

Mathew. *What should we learn by seeing the Flame of our Fire go upwards? and by seeing the Beams, and sweet Influences of the Sun strike downwards?*

Of Fire and of the Sun.

Prudence. By the going up of the Fire, we are taught to ascend to Heaven, by fervent and hot desires. And by the Sun his sending his Heat, Beams, and sweet Influences downwards; we are taught, that the Saviour of the World, tho' high, reaches down with his Grace and Love to us below.

Mathew. *Where have the Clouds their Water?*

Of the Clouds.

Pru. Out of the Sea.

Mathew. *What may we learn from that?*

Pru. That Ministers should fetch their Doctrine from God.

Mat. *Why do they empty themselves upon the Earth?*

Pru. To shew that Ministers should give out what they know of God to the World.

Of the Rainbow.

Mat. *Why is the Rainbow caused by the Sun?*

Prudence. To shew that the Covenant of Gods Grace[†] is confirmed to us in Christ.

Mat. *Why do the Springs come from the Sea to us, thorough the Earth?*

Prudence. To shew that the Grace of God comes to us thorough the Body of Christ.

Of the Springs.

Mat. *Why do some of the Springs rise out of the tops of high Hills?*

Prudence. To shew that the Spirit of Grace shall spring up in *some* that are Great and Mighty, as well as in *many* that are Poor and low.

Of the Candle.

Mat. *Why doth the Fire fasten upon the Candle-wick?*

Pru. To shew that unless Grace doth kindle upon the Heart, there will be no true Light of Life in us.

Mathew. *Why is the Wick and Tallow and all, spent to maintain the light of the Candle?*

Prudence. To shew that Body and Soul and all, should be at the Service of, and spend themselves to maintain in good Condition that Grace of God that is in us.

Of the Pelican.

Mat. *Why doth the Pelican pierce her own Brest with her Bill?*[†]

Pru. To nourish her Young ones with her Blood, and thereby to shew that Christ the blessed, so loveth his Young, his People, as to save them from Death by his Blood.

Of the Cock.

Mat. *What may one learn by hearing the Cock to Crow.*

Prudence. Learn to remember *Peter*'s Sin,[†] and *Peter*'s Repentance. The Cocks crowing, shews also that day is coming on, let then the crowing of the Cock put thee in mind of that last and terrible Day of Judgment.

The weak may sometimes call the strong to Prayers.

Now about this time their month was out, wherefore they signified to those of the House that 'twas convenient for them to up and be going. Then said *Joseph* to his Mother, It is convenient that you forget not to send to the House of Mr. *Interpreter*, to pray him to grant that Mr. *Great-heart* should be sent unto us, that he may be our Conductor the rest of our way. Good *Boy*, said she, I had almost forgot. So she drew up a

Petition, and prayed Mr. *Watchful* the Porter to send it by some fit man to her good Friend Mr. *Interpreter*; who when it was come, and he had seen the contents of the Petitions, said to the Messenger, Go tell them that I will send him.

When the Family where *Christiana* was, saw that they had a purpose to go forward, they called the whole House together to give thanks to their King, for sending of them such profitable Guests as these. Which done, they said to *Christiana*, And shall we not shew thee something, according as our Custom is to do to Pilgrims, on which thou mayest meditate when thou art upon the way? So they took *Christiana*, her Children and *Mercy* into the Closet, and shewed them one of the *Apples* that *Eve* did eat of, and that she also did give to her Husband, and that for the eating of which they both were turned out of Paradice, and asked her what she thought that was? Then *Christiana* said, *'Tis Food, or Poyson*, I know not which; so they opened the matter to her, and she held up her hands and wondered.

They provide to be gone on their way.

Eves *Apple.*

A sight of Sin is amazing. Gen. 3. 6. Ro. 7. 24.

Then they had her to a place, and shewed her *Jacob*'s *Ladder*. Now at that time there were some Angels ascending upon it. So *Christiana* looked and looked, to see the Angels go up, and so did the rest of the Company. Then they were going into another place to shew them something else: But *James* said to his Mother, pray bid them stay here a little longer, for this is a curious sight. So they turned again, and stood feeding their Eyes with this *so pleasant a Prospect*. After this they had them into a place where did hang up a *Golden Anchor*, so they bid *Christiana* take it down; for, said they, you shall have it with you, for 'tis of absolute necessity that you should, that you may lay hold of that within the vail, and stand stedfast, in case you should meet with turbulent weather: So they were glad thereof. Then they took them, and had them to the mount upon which *Abraham* our Father, had offered up *Isaac* his Son, and shewed them the *Altar*, the *Wood*, the *Fire*, and the *Knife*, for they remain to be seen to this very Day. When they had seen it, they held up their hands and blest themselves, and said, Oh! What a man, for love to his Master and for denial to himself, was *Abraham*: After they had shewed them all these things, *Prudence* took them into the Dining-Room, where

Jacob's *Ladder.* Gen. 28. 12.

A sight of Christ is taking.

Golden Anchor.

Joh. 1. 51. Heb. 6. 12, 19.

Gen. 22.

Of Abraham *offering up* Isaac.

Prudences *Virginals.*

stood a pair of Excellent Virginals,† so she played upon them, and turned what she had shewed them into this excellent Song, saying;

> Eve's *Apple we have shewed you,*
> *Of that be you aware:*
> *You have seen* Jacobs *Ladder too,*
> *Upon which Angels are.*
> *An Anchor you received have;*
> *But let not these suffice,*
> *Until with* Abra'm *you have gave,*
> *Your best, a Sacrifice.*

Mr. Great-heart *come again.*

Now about this time one knocked at the Door, So the Porter opened, and behold Mr. *Great-heart* was there; but when he was come in, what Joy was there? For it came now fresh again into their minds, how but a while ago he had slain old *Grim Bloody-man*, the Giant, and had delivered them from the Lions.

He brings a token from his Lord with him.

Then said Mr. *Great-heart* to *Christiana*, and to *Mercie*, My Lord has sent each of you a Bottle of Wine, and also some parched Corn,† together with a couple of Pomgranates. He has also sent the Boys some Figs, and Raisins to refresh you in your way.

Then they addressed themselves to their Journey, and *Prudence*, and *Piety* went along with them. When they came at the Gate, *Christiana* asked the Porter, if any of late went by. He said, No, only one some time since: who also told me that of late there had been a great Robbery committed on the Kings High-way, as you go: But he saith, the Thieves are taken, and will shortly be Tryed for their Lives. Then *Christiana*, and *Mercie*, was afraid; but *Mathew* said, Mother fear nothing, as long as Mr. *Great-heart* is to go with us, and to be our Conductor.

Robbery.

Christiana *takes her leave of the Porter.*

Then said *Christiana* to the Porter, Sir, I am much obliged to you for all the Kindnesses that you have shewed me since I came hither, and also for that you have been so loving and kind to my Children. I know not how to gratifie your Kindness: Wherefore pray as a token of my respects to you, accept of this small mite: So she put a Gold Angel† in his Hand, and he made her a low obeisance, and said, Let thy Garments be always White, and let thy Head want no Ointment. Let *Mercie* live and not die, and let not her Works be few.† And to the Boys he said, Do you fly Youthful lusts,† and follow after Godliness with them that are Grave, and Wise, so shall you put Gladness into your Mothers Heart, and obtain Praise of all that are sober minded. So they thanked the Porter and departed.

The Porters blessing.

Now I saw in my Dream, that they went forward until they were come to the Brow of the Hill, where *Piety* bethinking her self cryed out, *Alas!* I have forgot what I intended to bestow upon *Christiana*, and her Companions. I will go back and fetch it. So she ran, and fetched it. While she was gone, *Christiana* thought she heard in a Grove a little way off, on the Right-hand, a most curious melodious Note, with Words much like these,

Through all my Life thy favour is
So frankly shew'd to me,
That in thy House for evermore
My dwelling place shall be.

And listning still she thought she heard another answer it, saying,

For why, the Lord our God is good,
His Mercy is forever sure:
His truth at all times firmly stood:
And shall from Age to Age endure.†

So *Christiana* asked *Prudence*, what 'twas that made those curious Notes? They are, said she, our Countrey Birds: They sing these Notes but seldom, except it be at the Spring, when the Flowers appear, and the Sun shines warm, and then you may hear them all day long. I often, said she, go out to hear them, we also oft times keep them tame in our House. They are very fine Company for us when we are *Melancholy*, also they make the Woods and Groves, and Solitary places, places desirous to be in.

Song 2. 11, 12.

By this time *Piety* was come again, So she said to *Christiana*, Look here, I have brought thee a *Scheme* of all those things that thou hast seen at our House: Upon which thou

Piety *bestoweth something on them at parting.*

mayest look when thou findest thy self forgetful, and call those things again to remembrance for thy Edification, and comfort.

1 *Part, pag.* 55. Now they began to go down the Hill into the Valley of *Humiliation*. It was a steep Hill, & the way was slippery; but they were very careful, so they got down pretty well. When they were down in the Valley, *Piety* said to *Christiana*, This is the place where *Christian* your Husband met with the foul Fiend *Apollyon*, and where they had that dreadful fight that they had. I know you cannot but have heard thereof. But be of good courage, as long as you have here Mr. *Great-heart* to be your Guide and Conductor, we hope you will fare the better. So when these two had committed the Pilgrims unto the Conduct of their Guide, he went forward, and they went after.

Mr. Great-heart *at the Valley of Humiliation.*

Great-heart. Then said Mr. *Great-heart*, We need not be so afraid of this Valley: For here is nothing to hurt us, unless we procure it to our selves. 'Tis true, *Christian* did here meet with *Apollyon*, with whom he also had a sore Combate; but that *frey*, was the fruit of those slips that he got in his going down the Hill. For they that get *slips there*, must look for *Combats here*. And hence it is that this Valley has got so hard a name. For the common people when they hear that some frightful thing has befallen such an one in such a place, are of an Opinion that that place is haunted with some foul Fiend, or evil Spirit; when alas it is for the fruit of their doing, that such things do befal them there.

1 *Part, pag.* 55.

The reason why Christian *was so beset here.*

This Valley of *Humiliation* is of it self as fruitful a place, as any the Crow flies over; and I am perswaded if we could hit upon it, we might find somewhere here abouts something that might give us an Account why *Christian* was so hardly beset in this place.

A Pillar with an Inscription on it.

Then *James* said to his Mother, Lo, yonder stands a Pillar, and it looks as if something was Written thereon: let us go and see what it is. So they went, and found there Written, *Let* Christian'*s slips before he came hither, and the Battels that he met with in this place, be a warning to those that come after*. Lo, said their Guide, did not I tell you, that there was something here abouts that would give Intimation of the reason why *Christian* was so hard beset in this place? Then turning himself to *Christiana*, he said: No disparagement to *Christian* more than to many others whose Hap and Lot his was. For 'tis easier going *up*, then *down this* Hill; and that can be said but of few Hills in all these parts of the World. But we will leave the good Man, he is at rest, he also had a brave Victory over his Enemy; let him grant that dwelleth above, that we fare no worse when we come to be tryed then he.

But we will come again to this Valley of *Humiliation*. It is the best, and most fruitful piece of Ground in all those parts. It is fat Ground,† and as you see, consisteth much in Meddows: and if a man was to come here in the Summer-time, as we do now, if he knew not any thing before thereof, and if he also delighted himself in the sight of his Eyes, he might see that that would be delightful to him. Behold, how green this Valley is, also how beautified *with Lillies*. I have also known many labouring Men that have got good Estates in this Valley of *Humiliation*. (For God resisteth the Proud; but gives *more, more* Grace to the Humble;) for indeed it is a very fruitful Soil, and doth bring forth by handfuls. Some also have wished that the next way to their Fathers House were here, that they might be troubled no more with either Hills or Mountains to go over; but the way is the way, and there's an end.

This Valley a brave place.

Song 2. 1.
Jam. 4. 6.
1 Pet. 5. 5.

Men thrive in the Valley of Humiliation.

Now as they were going along and talking, they espied a Boy feeding his Fathers Sheep. The Boy was in very mean Cloaths, but of a very fresh and well-favoured Countenance, and as he sate by himself he Sung. Hark, said Mr. *Great-heart*, to what the Shepherds Boy saith. So they hearkned, and he said,

He that is down, needs fear no fall,
He that is low, no Pride:
He that is humble, ever shall
Have God to be his Guide.

Philip. 4. 12, 13.

I am content with what I have,
Little be it, or much:
And, Lord, Contentment still I crave,
Because thou savest such.

Heb. 13. 5.

Fulness to such a burden is
That go on Pilgrimage:
Here little, and hereafter Bliss,
Is best from Age to Age.

Then said their *Guide*, Do you hear him? I will dare to say, that this Boy lives a merrier Life, and wears more of that Herb called *Hearts-ease*† in his Bosom, then he that is clad in Silk and Velvet; but we will proceed in our Discourse.

Christ, when in the Flesh, had his Countrey-House in the Valley of Humiliation.

In this Valley our Lord formerly had his *Countrey-House*, he loved much to be here; He loved also to walk these Medows, for he found the Air was pleasant: Besides here a man shall be free from the Noise, and from the hurryings of this Life; all States are full of Noise and Confusion, only the Valley of *Humiliation* is that empty and Solitary Place. Here a man shall not be so let and hindred in his Contemplation, as in other places he is apt to be. This is a Valley that no body walks in, but those that love a Pilgrims Life. And though *Christian* had the hard hap to meet here with *Apollyon*, and to enter with him a brisk encounter, yet I must tell you, that in former times men have met with Angels here, have found Pearls here, and have in this place found the words of Life.

Hos. 12. 4, 5.

Did I say, our Lord had here in former Days his Countrey-house, and that he loved here to walk? I will add, in this Place, and to the People that live and trace these Grounds, he has left a yearly revenue to be faithfully payed them at certain Seasons, for their maintenance by the way, and for their further incouragement to go on in their Pilgrimage.

Mat. 11. 29.

Samuel. Now as they went on, *Samuel* said to Mr. *Great-heart: Sir, I perceive that in this Valley, my Father and* Apollyon *had their Battel; but whereabout was the Fight, for I perceive this Valley is large?*

Great-heart. Your Father had that Battel with *Apollyon* at a place yonder, before us, in a narrow Passage just beyond *Forgetful-Green*. And indeed that place is the most dangerous place in all these Parts. For if at any time the Pilgrims meet with any brunt, it is when they forget what Favours they have received, and how unworthy they are of them. This was the Place also where others have been hard put to it. But more of the place when we are come to it; for I perswade my self, that to this day there remains either some sign of the Battel, or some Monument to testifie that such a Battle there was fought.

Forgetful-Green.

Humility a sweet Grace.

Mercie. Then said *Mercie*, I think I am as well in this Valley, as I have been any where else in all our Journey: The place methinks suits with my Spirit. I love to be in such places where there is no ratling with Coaches, nor rumbling with Wheels: Methinks here one may without much molestation be thinking what he is, whence he came, what he has done, and to what the King has called him: Here one may think, and break at Heart, and melt in ones Spirit, until ones Eyes become like the *Fish Pools of Heshbon*. They that go rightly thorow this Valley of Baca make it a Well, the Rain that God sends down from Heaven upon them that are here also *filleth the Pools*. This Valley is that from whence also the King will give to his their Vineyards, and they that go through it, shall sing, (as *Christian* did, for all he met with *Apollyon*.)

Song 7. 4.
Psal. 84. 5, 6, 7.
Hos. 2. 15.

Great-heart. 'Tis true, said their Guide, I have gone thorough this Valley many a time, and never was better then when here.

An Experiment of it.

I have also been a Conduct to several Pilgrims, and they have confessed the same; *To this man will I look, saith the King, even to him that is Poor, and of a contrite Spirit, and that trembles at my Word.*†

Now they were come to the place where the afore mentioned Battel was fought. Then said the Guide to *Christiana*, her Children, and *Mercie*: This is the place, on this Ground *Christian* stood, and up there came *Apollyon* against him. And look, did not I tell you, here is some of your Husbands Blood upon these Stones to this day: Behold also how here and there are yet to be seen upon the place, some of the Shivers of *Apollyon*'s Broken *Darts*: See also how they did beat the Ground with their Feet as they fought, to make good their Places against each other, how also with their by-blows they did split the very stones in pieces. Verily *Christian* did here play the Man,† and shewed himself as stout, as could, had he been here, even *Hercules*† himself. When *Apollyon* was beat, he made his retreat to the next Valley, that is called The Valley of the Shadow of Death, unto which we shall come anon.

The place where Christian *and the* Fiend *did fight, some signs of the Battel remains.*

Lo yonder also stands a Monument, on which is Engraven this Battle, and *Christian*'s Victory to his Fame throughout all Ages: So because it stood just on the way-side before them, they stept to it and read the Writing, which word for word was this;

A Monument of the Battel.

Hard by, here was a Battle fought,
Most strange, and yet most true.
Christian *and* Apollyon *sought*
Each other to subdue.

A Monument of Christians *Victory.*

The Man so bravely play'd the Man,
He made the Fiend *to fly:*
Of which a Monument I stand,
The same to testifie.

1 *Part, pag.* 61.

When they had passed by this place, they came upon the Borders of the Shadow of Death, and this Valley was longer then the other, a place also most strangely haunted with evil things, as many are able to testifie: But these Women and Children went the better thorough it, because they had day-light, and because Mr. *Great-heart* was their Conductor.

Groanings heard.

When they were entred upon this Valley, they thought that they heard a groaning as of dead men: a very great groaning. They thought also they did hear Words of Lamentation spoken, as of some in extream Torment. These things made the Boys to quake, the Women also looked pale and wan; but their Guide bid them be of Good Comfort.

The Ground shakes.

So they went on a little further, and they thought that they felt the Ground begin to shake under them, as if some hollow place was there; they heard also a kind of a hissing as of Serpents; but nothing as yet appeared. Then said the Boys, Are we not yet at the end of this doleful place? But the Guide also bid them be of good Courage, and look well to their Feet, lest haply, said he, you be taken in some Snare.

James *sick with fear.*

Now *James* began to be Sick; but I think the cause thereof was Fear, so his Mother gave him some of that Glass of Spirits that she had given her at the *Interpreters* House, and three of the Pills that Mr. *Skill* had prepared, and the Boy began to revive. Thus they went on till they came to about the middle of the Valley, and then *Christiana* said, Methinks I see something yonder upon the Road before us, a thing of a shape such as I have not seen. Then said *Joseph*, Mother, what is it? An ugly thing, Child; an ugly thing, said she. But Mother, what is it like, said he? 'Tis like I cannot tell what, said she. And now it was but a little way off. Then said she, it is nigh.

The Fiend *appears.*

The Pilgrims are afraid.

Well, well, said Mr. *Great-heart*, let them that are most

afraid keep close to me: So the *Fiend* came on, and the Conductor met it; but when it was just come to him, it vanished to all their sights. Then remembered they what had been said sometime agoe. *Resist the Devil, and he will fly from you.*†

Great-heart *incourages them.*

They went therefore on, as being a little refreshed; but they had not gone far, before *Mercie* looking behind her, saw as she thought, something most like a Lion, and it came a great padding pace after; and it had a hollow Voice of Roaring, and at every Roar that it gave, it made all the Valley Eccho, and their Hearts to ake, save the Heart of him that was their Guide. So it came up, and Mr. *Great-heart* went behind, and put the Pilgrims all before him. The Lion also came on apace, and Mr. *Great-heart* addressed himself to give him Battel. But when he saw that it was determined that resistance should be made, he also drew back and came no further.

A Lion.

1 Pet. 5. 8, 9.

Then they went on again, and their Conductor did go before them, till they came at a place where was cast up a pit, the whole breadth of the way, and before they could be prepared to go over that, a great mist and a darkness fell upon them,† so that they could not see: Then said the Pilgrims, Alas! now what shall we do? But their Guide made answer; Fear not, stand still and see what an end will he put to this also; so they stayed there because their Path was marr'd. They then also thought that they did hear more apparently the noise and rushing of the Enemies, the fire also and the smoke of the Pit was much easier to be discerned. Then said *Christiana* to *Mercie*, Now I see what my poor Husband went through. I have heard much of this place, but I never was here afore now; poor man, he went here all alone in the night; he had night almost quite through the way, also these Fiends were busie about him, as if they would have torn him in pieces. Many have spoke of it, but none can tell what the Valley of the Shadow of Death should mean, until they come in it themselves. *The heart knows its own bitterness, and a stranger intermeddleth not with its Joy.*† To be here is a fearful thing.

A pit and darkness.

Christiana *now knows what her Husband felt.*

Greath. This is like doing business in great Waters,† or like going down into the deep; this is like being in the heart of the Sea, and like going down to the Bottoms of the Mountains: Now it seems as if the Earth with its bars were about us for

Great-heart's *Reply.*

ever.† *But let them that walk in darkness and have no light, trust in the name of the Lord, and stay upon their God.*† For my part, as I have told you already, I have gone often through this Valley, and have been much harder put to it than now I am, and yet you see I am alive. I would not boast, for that I am not mine own Saviour. But I trust we shall have a good deliverance. Come let us pray for light to him that can lighten our darkness,† and that can rebuke, not only these, but all the Satans in Hell.

They pray. So they cryed and prayed, and God sent light and deliverance, for there was now no lett in their way, no not there, where but now they were stopt with a pit.

Yet they were not got through the Valley; so they went on still, and behold great stinks and loathsome smells, to the great annoyance of them. Then said *Mercie* to *Christiana*, there is not such pleasant being here as at the *Gate*, or at the Interpreters, or at the House where we lay last.

Mercie *to* Christiana.

One of the Boys Reply. *O but*, said one of the Boys, *it is not so bad to go through here, as it is to* abide *here always, and for ought I know, one reason why we must go this way to the House prepared for us, is, that our home might be made the sweeter to us.*

Well said, *Samuel*, quoth the *Guide*, thou hast now spoke like a man. Why, if ever I get out here again, said the *Boy*, I think I shall prize light and good way better than ever I did in all my life. Then said the *Guide*, we shall be out by and by.

So on they went, and *Joseph* said, *Cannot we see to the end of this Valley as yet?* Then said the *Guide*, Look to your feet, for you shall presently be among the Snares.† So they looked to their feet and went on; but they were troubled much with the Snares. Now when they were come among the Snares, they espyed a Man cast into the Ditch on the left hand, with his flesh all rent and torn. Then said the *Guide*, that is one *Heedless*, that was agoing this way; he has lain there a great while. There was one *Takeheed* with him, when he was taken and slain, but *he* escaped their hands. You cannot imagine how many are killed here about, and yet men are so foolishly venturous, as to set out lightly on Pilgrimage, and to come without a *Guide*. Poor *Christian*, it was a wonder that he here escaped, but he was beloved of his God,† also he had a good heart of his own, or else he could never a-done it. Now they drew towards

Heedless *is slain, and* Takeheed *preserved.*

the end of the way, and just there where *Christian* had seen the Cave when he went by, out thence came forth *Maull* a Gyant.† This *Maull* did use to spoyl young Pilgrims with Sophistry, and he called *Great-heart* by his name, and said unto him, how many times have you been forbidden to do these things? Then said Mr. *Great-heart*, what things? What things, quoth the Gyant, you know what things; but I will put an end to your trade. But pray, said Mr. *Great-heart*, before we fall to it, let us understand wherefore we must fight; (now the Women and Children stood trembling, and knew not what to do); quoth the Gyant, You rob the Countrey, and rob it with the worst of Thefts. These are but Generals, said Mr. *Great-heart*, come to particulars, man.

1 Part, pag. 66.

Maull *a Gyant.*

He quarrels with Great-heart.

Then said the *Gyant*, thou practises the craft of a *Kidnapper*, thou gatherest up Women and Children, and carriest them into a strange Countrey, to the weakning of my Masters Kingdom. But now *Great-heart* replied, I am a Servant of the God of Heaven, my business is to perswade sinners to Repentance, I am commanded to do my endeavour to turn Men, Women and Children, from darkness to light, and from the power of Satan to God,† and if this be indeed the ground of thy quarrel, let us fall to it as soon as thou wilt.

God's Ministers counted as Kidnappers.

Then the *Giant* came up, and Mr. *Great-heart* went to meet him, and as he went, he drew his *Sword*, but the *Giant* had a *Club*: So without more ado they fell to it, and at the first blow the *Giant* stroke Mr. *Great-heart* down upon one of his knees; with that the Women, and Children cried out. So Mr. *Great-heart* recovering himself, laid about him in full lusty manner, and gave the *Giant* a wound in his arm; thus he fought for the space of an hour to that height of heat, that the breath came out of the *Giants* nostrils, as the heat doth out of a boiling Caldron.

The Gyant *and Mr.* Great-heart *must fight.*

Weak folks prayers do sometimes help strong folks cries.

Then they sat down to rest them, but Mr. *Great-heart* betook him to prayer; also the Women and Children did nothing but sigh and cry all the time that the Battle did last.

When they had rested them, and taken breath, they both fell to it again, and Mr. *Great-heart* with a full blow fetch't the *Giant* down to the ground. Nay hold, and let me recover, quoth he. So Mr. *Great-heart* fairly let him get up;† So to it

The Gyant *struck down.*

they went again; and the *Giant* mist but little of all-to-breaking Mr. *Great-heart*'s Scull with his Club.

Mr. *Great-heart* seeing that, runs to him in the full heat of his Spirit, and pierceth him under the fifth rib;† with that the *Giant* began to faint, and could hold up his Club no longer. Then Mr. *Great-heart* seconded his blow, and smit the head of the *Giant* from his shoulders. Then the Women and Children rejoyced, and Mr. *Great-heart* also praised God, for the deliverance he had wrought.

He is slain, and his head disposed of.

When this was done, they amongst them erected a Pillar, and fastned the *Gyant's* head thereon, and wrote underneath in letters that Passengers might read,

He that did wear this head, was one
That Pilgrims did misuse;
He stopt their way, he spared none,
But did them all abuse;
Until that I, Great-heart, *arose,*
The Pilgrims Guide *to be;*
Until that I did him oppose,
That was their Enemy.

Now I saw, that they went to the Ascent that was a little way off cast up to be a Prospect for Pilgrims. (That was the place from whence *Christian* had the first sight of *Faithful* his Brother.) Wherefore here they sat down, and rested, they also here did eat and drink, and make merry; for that they had gotten deliverance from this so dangerous an Enemy. As they sat thus and did eat, *Christiana* asked the *Guide, if he had caught no hurt in the battle.* Then said Mr. *Great-heart, No,* save a little on my flesh; yet that also shall be so far from being to my determent, that it is at present a proof of my love to my Master and you, and shall be a means by Grace to encrease my reward at last.

1 Part, pag. 67.

2 Cor. 4.

Discourse of the fight.

But was you not afraid, good Sir, when you see him come with his Club?

It is my duty, said he, to distrust mine own ability, that I may have reliance on him that is stronger then all. *But what did you think when he fetched you down to the ground at the first blow?*

Why I thought, quoth he, that so my master himself was served, and yet he it was that conquered at the last.

Mat. *here admires* Goodness.

Mat. *When you all have thought what you please, I think God has been wonderful good unto us, both in bringing us out of this Valley, and in delivering us out of the hand of this Enemy; for my part I see no reason why we should distrust our God any more, since he has* now, *and in* such *a place as this, given us such testimony of his love as this.*

Old Honest *asleep under an Oak.*

Then they got up and went forward; now a little before them stood an Oak, and under it when they came to it, they found an old *Pilgrim* fast asleep; they knew that he was a *Pilgrim* by his *Cloths*, and his *Staff*, and his *Girdle*.

So the *Guide* Mr. *Great-heart* awaked him, and the old Gentleman, as he lift up his eyes cried out; What's the matter? who are you? and what is your business here?

Great. Come man be not so hot, here is none but Friends; yet the old man gets up and stands upon his guard, and will know of them what they were. Then said the *Guide*, My name is *Great-heart*, I am the guide of these Pilgrims which are going to the Celestial Countrey.

One Saint sometimes takes another for his Enemy.

Honest. Then said Mr. *Honest*, I cry you mercy;† I feared that you had been of the Company of those that some time ago did rob *Little-faith* of his money; but now I look better about me, I perceive you are honester People.

Talk between Great-heart *and he.*

Greath. *Why what would, or could you adone, to a helped your self, if we indeed had been of that Company?*

Hon. Done! Why I would a fought as long as breath had been in me; and had I so done, I am sure you could never have given me the worst on't, for a *Christian* can never be overcome, unless he shall yield of himself.

Greath. *Well said*, Father Honest, *quoth the Guide, for by this I know that thou art a Cock of the right kind, for thou hast said the Truth.*

Hon. And by this also I know that thou knowest what true Pilgrimage is; for all others do think that we are the soonest overcome of any.

Whence Mr. Honest *came.*

Greath. *Well, now we are so happily met, pray let me crave your Name, and the name of the Place you came from?*

Hon. My Name I cannot, but I came from the Town of

Stupidity; it lieth about four Degrees beyond the City of *Destruction*.

Greath. Oh! *Are you that Country-man then? I deem I have half a guess of you, your Name is old* Honesty, *is it not?* So the old Gentleman blushed, and said, Not Honesty in the *Abstract*, but *Honest* is my Name, and I wish that my *Nature* shall agree to what I am called.

Hon. But Sir, said the old Gentleman, how could you guess that I am such a Man, since I came from such a place?

Stupified ones are worse then those merely Carnal.

Greath. *I had heard of you before, by my Master, for he knows all things that are done on the Earth: But I have often wondered that any should come from your place; for your Town is worse then is the City of* Destruction *it self.*

Hon. Yes, we lie more off from the Sun, and so are more Cold and Sensless; but as a Man in a Mountain of Ice, yet if the Sun of Righteousness will arise† upon him, his frozen Heart shall feel a Thaw; and thus it hath been with me.

Greath. I believe it, Father *Honest*, I believe it, for I know the thing is true.

Then the old Gentleman saluted all the Pilgrims with a holy Kiss of Charity,† and asked them of their Names, and how they had fared since they set out on their Pilgrimage.

Old Honest *and* Christiana *talk.*

Christ. Then said *Christiana*, My name I suppose you have heard of, good *Christian* was my Husband, and these four were his Children. But can you think how the old Gentleman was taken, when she told him who she was! He skip'd, he smiled, and blessed them with a thousand good Wishes, saying,

He also talks with the Boys.

Old Mr. Hon-est's *Blessing on them.*

Mat. 10. 3. Psal. 99. 6. Gen. 39. Acts.

Hon. *I have heard much of your Husband, and of his Travels and Wars which he underwent in his days. Be it spoken to your Comfort, the Name of your Husband rings all over these parts of the World; His Faith, his Courage, his Enduring, and his Sincerity under all, has made his name Famous.* Then he turned him to the Boys, and asked them of their names, which they told him: And then said he unto them, *Mathew*, be thou like *Mathew* the Publican, not in Vice, but Virtue. *Samuel*, said he, be thou like *Samuel* the Prophet, a Man of Faith and Prayer. *Joseph*, said he, be thou like *Joseph* in *Potiphar*'s House, Chast, and one that flies from Temptation. And, *James*, be thou like *James* the *Just*, and like *James* the brother of our Lord.†

Then they told him of *Mercie*, and how she had left her Town and her Kindred to come along with *Christiana*, and with her Sons. At that the old *Honest* man said, *Mercie*, is thy Name? by *Mercie* shalt thou be sustained, and carried thorough all those Difficulties that shall assault thee in thy way; till thou come thither where thou shalt look the Fountain of Mercie in the Face with Comfort. *He blesseth* Mercie.

All this while the Guide Mr. *Great-heart*, was very much pleased, and smiled upon his Companion.

Now as they walked along together, the Guide asked the old Gentleman, *if he did not know one Mr.* Fearing, *that came on Pilgrimage out of his Parts.* *Talk of one Mr.* Fearing.

Hon. Yes, very well, said he; he was a Man that had the Root of the Matter in him,† but he was one of the most troublesome Pilgrims that ever I met with in all my days.

Greath. *I perceive you knew him, for you have given a very right Character of him.*

Hon. Knew him! I was a great Companion of his, I was with him most an end; when he first began to think of what would come upon us hereafter, I was with him.

Greath. *I was his Guide from my Master's House, to the Gates of the Celestial City.*

Hon. Then you knew him to be a troublesom one?

Greath. *I did so, but I could very well bear it: for Men of my Calling are often times intrusted with the Conduct of such as he was.*

Hon. Well then, pray let us hear a little of him, and how he managed himself under your Conduct.

Greath. Why he was always afraid that he should come short of whither he had a desire to go. Every thing frightned him that he heard any body speak of, that had the least appearance of Opposition in it. I heard that he lay roaring at the *Slow of Dispond*, for above a Month together, nor durst he, for all he saw several go over before him, venture, tho they, many of them, offered to lend him their Hand. *He would not go back again neither.* The Celestial City, he said he should die if he came not to it, and yet was dejected at every Difficulty, and stumbled at every Straw that any body cast in his way. Well, after he had layn at the *Slow of Dispond* a great while, as I have told you; one sunshine Morning, I do not know how, he *Mr.* Fearing's *troublesom Pilgrimage.* *His behaviour at the* Slow of Dispond.

ventured, and so got over. But when he was over, he would scarce believe it. He had, I think, a *Slow of Dispond* in his Mind, a *Slow* that he carried every where with him, or else he could never have been as he was. So he came up to the Gate, you know what I mean, that stands at the head of this way, and there also he stood a good while before he would adventure to knock. When the Gate was opened he would give back, and give place to others, and say that he was not worthy. For, for all he gat before some to the Gate, yet many of them went in before him. There the poor man would stand shaking and shrinking; I dare say it would have pitied ones Heart to have seen him: *Nor would he go back again*. At last he took the Hammer that hanged on the Gate in his hand, and gave a small Rapp or two; then one opened to him, but he shrunk back as before. He that opened, stept out after him, and said, Thou trembling one, what wantest thou? with that he fell to the Ground. He that spoke to him wondered to see him so faint. So he said to him, Peace be to thee; up, for I have set open the Door to thee; come in, for thou art blest. With that he gat up, and went in trembling, and when he was in, he was ashamed to show his Face. Well, after he had been entertained there a while, as you know how the manner is, he was bid go on his way, and also told the way he should take. So he came till he came to our House, but as he behaved himself at the Gate, so he did at my master the *Interpreters* Door. He lay thereabout in the Cold a good while, before he would adventure to call; *Yet he would not go back*. And the Nights were long and cold then. Nay he had a Note of *Necessity* in his Bosom to my Master, to receive him, and grant him the Comfort of his House, and also to allow him a stout and valiant Conduct, because he was himself so *Chickin-hearted* a Man; and yet for all that he was afraid to call at the Door. So he lay up and down there abouts, till, poor man, he was almost starved; yea so great was his Dejection, that tho he saw several others for knocking got in, yet he was afraid to venture. At last, I think I looked out of the Window, and perceiving a man to be up and down about the Door, I went out to him, and asked what he was; but poor man, the water stood in his Eyes. So I perceived what he wanted. I went therefore in, and told it in the House, and we

His behavior at the Gate.

His behavior at the Interpreters Door.

shewed the thing to our Lord; So he sent me out again, to entreat him to come in, but I dare say I had hard work to do it. At last he came in, and I will say that for my Lord, he carried it wonderful lovingly to him. There were but a few good bits at the Table, but some of it was laid upon his Trencher. Then he presented the *Note*, and my Lord looked thereon and said, His desire should be granted. So when he had bin there a good while, he seemed to get some Heart, and to be a little more Comfortable. For my Master, you must know, is one of very tender Bowels, especially to them that are afraid, wherefore he carried it so towards him, as might tend most to his Incouragement. Well, when he had had a sight of the things of the place, and was ready to take his Journey to go to the City, my Lord, as he did to *Christian* before, gave him a Bottle of Spirits, and some comfortable things to eat. Thus we set forward, and I went before him; but the man was but of few Words, only he would sigh aloud.

How he was entertained there.

He is a little encouraged at the Interpreters house.

When we were come to where the three Fellows were hanged, he said, that he doubted that that would be his end also. Only he seemed glad when he saw the Cross and the Sepulcher. There I confess he desired to stay a little, to look; and he seemed for a while after to be a little *Cheary*. When we came at the Hill *Difficulty*, he made no stick at that, nor did he much fear the Lyons. For you must know that his Trouble *was not about such things as those*, his Fear was about his Acceptance at last.

He was greatly afraid when he saw the Gibbit, Cheary when he saw the Cross.

I got him in at the House *Beautiful*, I think before he was willing; also when he was in, I brought him acquainted with the Damsels that were of the Place, but he was ashamed to make himself much for Company, he desired much to be alone, yet he always loved good talk, and often would get behind the *Screen* to hear it; he also loved much to see *antient* things, and to be *pondering* them in his Mind. He told me afterwards, that he loved to be in those two Houses from which he came last, to wit, at the Gate, and that of the *Interpreters*, but that he durst not be so bold to ask.

Dumpish at the house Beautiful.

When we went also from the House *Beautiful*, down the Hill, into the Valley of *Humiliation*, he went down as well as ever I saw man in my Life, for he cared not how mean he was,

He went down into, and was very Pleasant in the Valley of Humiliation.

so he might be happy at last. Yea, I think there was a kind of a Sympathy betwixt that Valley and him. For I never saw him better in all his Pilgrimage, then when he was in that Valley.

Lam. 3. 27, 28, 29.

Here he would lie down, embrace the Ground, and kiss the very Flowers that grew in this Valley. He would now be up every Morning by break of Day, tracing, and walking to and fro in this Valley.

Much perplexed in the Valley of the Shadow of Death.

But when he was come to the entrance of the Valley of the Shadow of Death, I thought I should have lost my Man; not for that he had any Inclination to go back, that he alwayes abhorred, but he was ready to dy for Fear. O, the *Hobgoblins* will have me, the *Hobgoblins* will have me, cried he; and I could not beat him out on't. He made such a noyse, and such an outcry here, that, had they but heard him, 'twas enough to encourage them to come and fall upon us.

But this I took very great notice of, that this Valley was as quiet while he went thorow it, as ever I knew it before or since. I suppose, those Enemies here, had now a special Check from our Lord, and a Command not to meddle until Mr. *Fearing* was pass'd over it.

His behaviour at Vanity-Fair.

It would be too tedious to tell you of all; we will therefore only mention a Passage or two more. When he was come at *Vanity Fair*, I thought he would have fought with all the men in the Fair; I feared there we should both have been knock'd o'th Head, so hot was he against their Fooleries; upon the inchanted Ground, he also was very wakeful. But when he was come at the *River* where was no Bridge, there again he was in a heavy Case; now, now he said he should be drowned for ever, and so never see that Face with Comfort, that he had come so many miles to behold.

His Boldness at last.

And here also I took notice of what was very remarkable, the Water of that River was lower at this time, than ever I saw it in all my Life; so he went over at last, not much above wet-shod. When he was going up to the Gate, Mr. *Great-heart* began to take his Leave of him,† and to wish him a good Reception above; So he said, *I shall, I shall.* Then parted we asunder, and I saw him no more.

Honest. *Then it seems he was well at last.*

Greath. Yes, yes, I never had doubt about him, he was a man of a choice Spirit, only he was always kept very low, and that made his Life so burthensom to himself, and so troublesom to others. He was above many, tender of Sin; he was so afraid of doing Injuries to others, that he often would deny himself of that which was lawful, because he would not offend.

Psal. 88.

Rom. 14. 21. 1 Cor. 8. 13.

Hon. *But what should be the reason that such a good Man should be all his days so much in the dark?*

Greath. There are two sorts of Reasons for it; one is, The wise God will have it so. Some must *Pipe*, and some must *Weep*: Now Mr. *Fearing* was one that play'd upon *this Base*. He and his fellows sound the *Sackbut*, whose Notes are more doleful than the Notes of other Musick are. Tho indeed some say, the Base is the ground of Musick. And for my part, I care not at all for that Profession that begins not in heaviness of Mind. The first string that the Musitian usually touches, *is the Base*, when he intends to put all in tune; God also plays upon this string first, when he sets the Soul in tune for himself. Only here was the imperfection of Mr. *Fearing*, he could play upon no other Musick but this, till towards his latter end.

Reason why good men are so in the dark.

Mat. 11. 16, 17, 18

I make bold to talk thus Metaphorically, for the ripening of the Wits of young Readers, and because in the Book of the Revelations, the Saved are compared to a company of Musicians that play upon their *Trumpets* and Harps, and sing their Songs before the Throne.

Revel. 8. 2. *Chap.* 14. 2, 3.

Hon. *He was a very zealous man, as one may see by what Relation you have given of him. Difficulties, Lyons, or Vanity-Fair, he feared not at all: 'Twas only Sin, Death and Hell, that was to him a Terror*; because he had some Doubts about his Interest in that Celestial Country.

Greath. You say right. *Those* were the things that were his Troublers, and they, as you have well observed, arose from the weakness of his Mind there about, not from weakness of Spirit as to the practical part of a Pilgrims Life. I dare believe, that as the Proverb is, he could have bit a Firebrand,† had it stood in his way: But the things with which he was oppressed, no man ever yet could shake off with ease.

A Close about him.

Christiana. *Then said* Christiana, *This Relation of Mr.* Fearing *has done me good. I thought no body had been like me, but I see*

Christiana's *Sentence.*

there was some Semblance 'twixt this good man and I, only we differed in two things. His Troubles were so great they brake out, but mine I kept within. His also lay so hard upon him, they made him that he could not knock at the Houses provided for Entertainment; but my Trouble was always such, as made me knock the lowder.

Mercie*'s Sentence.*

Mer. If I might also speak my Heart, I must say that something of him has also dwelt in me. For I have ever been more afraid of the Lake† and the loss of a place in *Paradice*, then I have been of the loss of other things. Oh, thought I, may I have the Happiness to have a Habitation *there*, 'tis enough, though I part with all the World to win it.

Mathew*'s Sentence.*

Mat. *Then said* Mathew, *Fear was one thing that made me think that I was far from having that within me that accompanies Salvation, but if it was so with such a good man as he, why may it not also go well with me?*

James*'s Sentence.*

Jam. No fears, no Grace, said *James*. Though there is not always Grace where there is the fear of Hell; yet to be sure there is no Grace where there is no fear of God.

Greath. *Well said*, James, *thou hast hit the Mark, for the fear of God is the beginning of Wisdom;*† *and to be sure they that want the* beginning, *have neither* middle *nor* end. *But we will here conclude our Discourse of Mr.* Fearing, *after we have sent after him this Farewel.*

Their Farewell about him.

Well, Master Fearing, *thou didst fear*
Thy God, and wast afraid
Of doing any thing, while here,
That would have thee betray'd.
And didst thou fear the Lake and Pit?
Would others did so too;
For, as for them that want thy Wit,
They do themselves undo.

Of Mr. Self-will

Now I saw, that they still went on in their Talk. For after Mr. *Great-heart* had made an end with Mr. *Fearing*, Mr. *Honest* began to tell them of another, but his Name was Mr. *Selfwil*. He pretended himself to be a *Pilgrim*, said Mr. *Honest*; But I perswade my self, he never came in at the Gate that stands at the head of the way.

Greath. *Had you ever any talk with him about it?*

Hon. Yes, more then once or twice; but he would always be like himself, *self-willed*. He neither cared for man, nor Argument, nor yet Example; what his Mind prompted him to, that he would do, and nothing else could he be got to.

Old Honest *had talked with him.*

Greath. *Pray what Principles did he hold, for I suppose you can tell?*

Hon. He held that a man might follow the Vices as well as the Virtues of the Pilgrims, and that if he did both, he should be certainly saved.

Self-will's *Opinions.*

Greath. How! *If he had said, 'tis possible for the best to be guilty of the Vices, as well as to partake of the Virtues of Pilgrims, he could not much a been blamed: For indeed we are exempted from no Vice absolutely, but on condition that we Watch and Strive. But this I perceive is not the thing: But if I understand you right, your meaning is, that he was of that Opinion, that it was allowable so to be.*

Hon. Ai, ai, so I mean, and so he believed and practised.

Greath. *But what Ground had he for his so saying?*

Hon. Why, he said he had the Scripture for his Warrant.

Greath. *Prethee, Mr.* Honest, *present us with a few particulars.*

Hon. So I will. He said, to have to do with other mens Wives, had been practised by *David*, Gods Beloved, and therefore he could do it. He said, to have more Women then one, was a thing that *Solomon* practised, and therefore he could do it. He said, that *Sarah* and the godly Midwives of *Egypt* lyed, and so did saved *Rahab*, and therefore he could do it. He said, that the Disciples went at the bidding of their Master, and took away the Owners *Ass*, and therefore he could do so too. He said, that *Jacob* got the Inheritance of his Father in a way of Guile and Dissimulation, and therefore he could do so too.†

Greath. *High base! indeed, and you are sure he was of this Opinion?*

Hon. I have heard him plead for it, bring Scripture for it, bring Argument for it, *&c.*

Greath. *An Opinion that is not fit to be, with any Allowance, in the World.*

Hon. You must understand me rightly: He did not say that

any man might do this; but that those that had the Virtues of those that did such things, might also do the same.

Greath. *But what more false then such a Conclusion? For this is as much as to say, that because good men heretofore have sinned of Infirmity, therefore, he had allowance to do it of a presumptuous Mind. Or if because a Child, by the blast of the Wind, or for that it stumbled at a stone, fell down and so defiled it self in Myre, therefore he might wilfully ly down and wallow like a Bore therein. Who could a thought that any one could so far a bin blinded by the power of Lust? But what is written must be true: They stumble at*
1 Pet. 2. 8. *the Word, being disobedient, whereunto also they were appointed.*

His supposing that such may have the godly Mans Virtues, who addict themselves to their Vices, is also a Delusion as strong as the other. 'Tis just as if the Dog *should say, I have, or may have the* Qualities *of the* Child, *because I lick up its stinking Excrements.*
Hos. 4. 8. *To eat up the Sin of Gods People, is no sign of one that is possessed with their Virtues. Nor can I believe that one that is of this Opinion, can at present have Faith or Love in him. But I know you have made strong Objections against him, prethee what can he say for himself?*

Hon. Why, he says, To do this by way of Opinion, seems abundance more honest, then to do it, and yet hold contrary to it in Opinion.

Greath. *A very wicked Answer, for tho to let loose the Bridle to Lusts, while our Opinion are against such things, is bad; yet to sin, and plead a Toleration so to do, is worse; the one stumbles Beholders accidentally, the other pleads them into the Snare.*

Hon. There are many of this mans mind, that have not this mans mouth, and *that* makes going on Pilgrimage of so little esteem as it is.

Greath. *You have said the Truth, and it is to be lamented. But he that feareth the King of Paradice, shall come out of them all.*

Christiana. There are strange Opinions in the World. I know one that said 'twas time enough to repent when they came to die.

Greath. *Such are not over wise. That man would a bin loath, might he have had a week to run twenty mile in for his Life, to have deferred that Journey to the last hour of that Week.*

Hon. You say right, and yet the generality of them that

count themselves Pilgrims, do indeed do thus. I am, as you see, an old Man, and have bin a Traveller in this Rode many a day; and I have taken notice of many things.

I have seen some that have set out as if they would drive all the World afore them, who yet have in few days, dyed as they in the Wilderness, and so never gat sight of the promised Land.†

I have seen some that have promised nothing at first setting out to be Pilgrims, and that one would a thought could not have lived a day, that have yet proved very good Pilgrims.

I have seen some that have run hastily forward, that again have after a little time, run just as fast back again.

I have seen some who have spoke very well of a Pilgrims Life at first, that after a while, have spoken as much against it.

I have heard some, when they first set out for Paradice, say positively, there is such a place, who when they have been almost there, have come back again, and said there is none.

I have heard some vaunt what they would do in case they should be opposed, that have even at a false Alarm fled Faith, the Pilgrims way, and all.

Now as they were thus in their way, there came one runing to meet them, and said, Gentlemen, and you of the weaker sort, if you love Life, shift for your selves, for the Robbers are before you.

Fresh News of trouble. 1 *Part, pag.* 121–2.

Greath. Then said Mr. *Great-heart*, They be the three that set upon *Littlefaith* heretofore. Well, said he, we are ready for them; so they went on their way. Now they looked at every Turning when they should a met with the Villains. But whether they heard of Mr. *Great-heart*, or whether they had some other Game, they came not up to the Pilgrims.

Greatheart*'s Resolution.*

Chris. Christiana then wished for an Inn for her self and her Children, because they were weary. Then said Mr. *Honest*, there is one a little before us, where a very honourable Disciple, one *Gaius*† dwells. So they all concluded to turn in thither; and the rather, because the old Gentleman gave him so good a Report. So when they came to the Door, they went in, not knocking for folks use not to knock at the Door of an Inn. Then they called for the Master of the House, and he came to them. *So they asked if they might lie there that Night?*

Christiana *wisheth for an Inn.* Rom. 16. 23. Gaius.

They enter into his House.

Gaius *Entertains them, and how.*

Gaius. Yes Gentlemen, if you be true Men, for my House is for none but Pilgrims. Then was *Christiana*, *Mercie*, and the *Boys*, the more glad, for that the Inn-keeper was a lover of Pilgrims. So they called for Rooms; and he shewed them one for *Christiana*, and her Children, and *Mercy*, and another for Mr. *Great-heart* and the old Gentleman.

Greath. *Then said Mr.* Great-heart, *good* Gaius, *what hast thou for Supper? for these Pilgrims have come far to day, and are weary.*

Gaius. It is late, said *Gaius*; so we cannot conveniently go out to seek Food; but such as we have you shall be welcome to, if that will content.

Greath. *We will be content with what thou hast in the House, for as much as I have proved thee; thou art never destitute of that which is convenient.*

Gaius *his Cook.*

Then he went down, and spake to the Cook, whose Name was *Taste-that-which-is-good*, to get ready Supper for so many Pilgrims. This done, he comes up again, saying, come my good Friends, you are welcome to me, and I am glad that I have an House to entertain you; and while Supper is making ready, if you please, let us entertain one another with some good Discourse. So they all said, content.

Talk between Gaius *and his Guests.*

Gaius. *Then said* Gaius, *Whose Wife is this aged Matron? and whose Daughter is this young Damsel?*

Greath. The Woman is the Wife of one *Christian*, a Pilgrim of former times, and these are his four Children. The Maid is one of her Acquaintance; one that she hath perswaded to come with her on Pilgrimage. The Boys take all after their Father, and covet to tread in his Steps. Yea, if they do but see any place where the old Pilgrim hath lain, or any print of his Foot, it ministreth Joy to their Hearts, and they covet to lie, or tread in the same.

Mark this.

Act. 11. 26.

Of Christian*'s Ancestors.*

Gaius. Then said *Gaius*, is this *Christian*'s Wife, and are these *Christian*'s Children? I knew your Husband's Father, yea, also, his Fathers Father. Many have been good of this stock, their Ancestors dwelt first at *Antioch*.† *Christian*'s Progenitors (I suppose you have heard your Husband talk of them) were very worthy men. They have above any that I know, shewed themselves men of great Virtue and Courage, for the Lord of the

Pilgrims, his ways, and them that loved him. I have heard of many of your Husbands Relations that have stood all Tryals for the sake of the Truth. *Stephen* that was one of the first of the Family from whence your Husband sprang, was knocked o'th' Head with Stones. *James*, an other of this Generation, was slain with the edge of the Sword. To say nothing of *Paul* and *Peter*,† men antiently of the Family from whence your Husband came. There was *Ignatius*, who was cast to the Lyons, *Romanus*, whose Flesh was cut by pieces from his Bones; and *Policarp*, that played the man in the Fire. There was he that was hanged up in a Basket in the Sun, for the Wasps to eat; and he who they put into a Sack and cast him into the Sea, to be drowned.† 'Twould be impossible, utterly to count up all of that Family that have suffered Injuries and Death, for the love of a Pilgrims Life. Nor can I, but be glad, to see that thy Husband has left behind him four such Boys as these. I hope they will bear up their Fathers Name, and tread in their Fathers Steps, and come to their Fathers End.

Acts 7. 59, 60.
Cha. 12. 2.

Greath. *Indeed Sir, they are likely Lads, they seem to chuse heartily their Fathers Ways.*

Gaius. That is it that I said, wherefore *Christians* Family is like still to spread abroad upon the face of the Ground, and yet to be numerous upon the Face of the Earth. Wherefore let *Christiana* look out some Damsels for her Sons, to whom they may be Betroathed, *&c.* that the Name of their Father, and the House of his Progenitors may never be forgotten in the World.

Advice to Christiana *about her Boys.*

Hon. *'Tis pity this Family should fall and be extinct.*

Gaius. Fall it cannot, but be diminished it may; but let *Christiana* take my Advice, and that's the way to uphold it.

And *Christiana*, said *This* Inn-keeper, I am glad to see thee and thy Friend *Mercie* together here, a lovely Couple. And may I advise, take *Mercie* into a nearer Relation to thee. If she will, let her be given to *Mathew* thy eldest Son. 'Tis the way to preserve you a posterity in the Earth.† So this match was concluded, and in process of time they were married. But more of that hereafter.

Mercie *and* Matthew *Marry.*

Gaius also proceeded, and said, I will now speak on the behalf of Women, to take away their Reproach. For as Death and the Curse came into the World by a Woman, so also did

Gen. 3. Gal. 4. Life and Health; *God sent forth his Son, made of a Woman.* Yea, to shew how much those that came after did abhor the Act of their Mother, this Sex, in the old Testament, coveted Children, if happily this or that Woman might be the Mother of the Saviour of the World. I will say again, that when the Saviour was come, Women rejoyced in him, before either Man or Angel. I read not that ever any man did give unto Christ so much as one *Groat*, but the Women followed him, and ministered to him of their Substance. 'Twas a Woman that washed his Feet with Tears, and a Woman that anointed his Body to the Burial. They were Women that wept when he was going to the Cross; And Women that followed him from the Cross, and that sat by his Sepulcher when he was buried. They were Women that was first with him at his Resurrection *morn*, and Women that brought Tidings first to his Disciples that he was risen from the Dead. Women therefore are highly favoured, and shew by these things that they are sharers with us in the Grace of Life.

Why Women of old so much desired Children.

Luke 2.

Chap. 8. 2, 3. chap. 7. 37, 50. Joh. 11. 2. chap. 12. 3. Luke 23. 27. Matt. 27. 55, 56, 61. Luke 24. 22, 23.

Supper ready.

Now the Cook sent up to signifie that Supper was almost ready, and sent one to lay the Cloath, the Trenshers, and to set the Salt and Bread in order.

Then said *Mathew*, *The sight of this Cloath, and of this Forerunner of the Supper, begetteth in me a greater Appetite to my Food then I had before.*

What to be gathered from laying of the Board with the Cloath and Trenshers.

Gaius. So let all ministring Doctrines *to* thee in this Life, beget *in* thee a greater desire to sit at the Supper of the great King in his Kingdom; for all Preaching, Books, and Ordinances here, are but as the laying of the Trenshers, and as setting of Salt upon the Board, when compared with the Feast that our Lord will make for us when we come to his House.

Levit. 7. 32, 33, 34. *Chap.* 10. 14, 15. Psal. 25. 1. Heb. 13. 15.

So Supper came up, and first a *Heave-shoulder*, and a *Wave-breast*† was set on the Table before them, to shew that they must begin their *Meal* with Prayer and Praise to God. The *Heave-shoulder David* lifted his Heart up to God with, and with the *Wave-breast, where his heart lay*, with that he used to lean upon his Harp when he played. These two Dishes were very fresh and good, and they all eat heartily-well thereof.

Deut. 32. 14. Judg. 9. 13.

The next they brought up, was a Bottle of Wine, red as Blood. So *Gaius* said to them, Drink freely, this is the Juice of the true

Vine, that makes glad the Heart of God and Man.† So they drank and were merry. Joh. 15. 1.

The next was a Dish of Milk well crumbed. But *Gaius* said, *Let the Boys have that, that they may grow thereby*. 1 Pet. 2. 1, 2.

Then they brought up in course a Dish of *Butter* and *Hony*. Then said *Gaius*, Eat freely of *this*, for this is good to chear up, and strengthen your Judgments and Understandings: This was our Lords Dish when he was a Child; *Butter and Hony shall he eat, that he may know to refuse the Evil, and choose the Good*. *A Dish of Milk. Of Honey and Butter.* Isa. 7. 15.

Then they brought them up a Dish of Apples, and they were very good tasted Fruit. Then said *Mathew*, May we eat Apples, since they were such, by, and with which the Serpent beguiled our first Mother? *A Dish of Apples.*

Then said *Gaius*,

> *Apples were they* with *which we were beguil'd,*
> *Yet* Sin, *not Apples hath our Souls defil'd.*
> *Apples forbid, if eat, corrupts the Blood:*
> *To eat such, when commanded, does us good.*
> *Drink of his Flagons then, thou, Church, his Dove,*
> *And eat* his *Apples, who art sick of Love*.†

Then said *Mathew, I made the Scruple, because I a while since was sick with eating of Fruit.*

Gaius. Forbidden Fruit will make you sick, but not what our Lord has tolerated.

While they were thus talking, they were presented with an other Dish; and 'twas a dish of *Nuts*. Then said some at the Table, *Nuts* spoyl tender Teeth; especially the Teeth of Children. Which when *Gaius* heard, he said, Song 6. 11. *A dish of* Nuts.

> *Hard* Texts *are* Nuts (*I will not call them* Cheaters,)
> *Whose* Shells *do keep their* Kirnels *from the* Eaters.
> *Ope then the Shells, and you shall have the Meat,*
> *They here are brought, for you to crack and eat.*

Then were they very Merry, and sate at the Table a long time, talking of many things. Then said the old Gentleman, My good Landlord, while we are cracking your *Nuts*, if you please, do you open this Riddle,

A Riddle put forth by old Honest.

A man there was, tho some did count him mad,
The more he cast away, the more he had.

Then they all gave good heed, wondring what good *Gaius* would say, so he sat still a while, and then thus replyed:

Gaius *opens it.*

He that bestows his Goods upon the Poor,
Shall have as much again, and ten times more.

Joseph *wonders.*

Then said *Joseph*, I dare say Sir, I did not think you could a found it out.

Oh! said *Gaius*, I have bin trained up in this way a great while: Nothing teaches like Experience; I have learned of my Lord to be kind, & have found by experience that I have gained thereby: *There is that scattereth, yet increaseth, and there is that withholdeth more then is meet, but it tendeth to Poverty. There is that maketh himself Rich, yet hath nothing; there is that maketh himself poor, yet hath great Riches.*

Prov. 11. 24. *Chap.* 13. 7.

Then *Samuel* whispered to *Christiana* his Mother, and said, Mother, this is a very good mans House, let us stay here a good while, and let my Brother *Matthew* be married here to *Mercy*, before we go any further.

The which *Gaius* the Host overhearing, said, *With a very good Will my Child.*

Mathew *and* Mercie *are Married.*

So they stayed there more then a Month, and *Mercie* was given to *Mathew* to Wife.

While they stayed here, *Mercy* as her Custom was, would be making Coats and Garments to give to the Poor, by which she brought up a very good Report upon the Pilgrims.

The boys go to Bed, the rest sit up.

But to return again to our Story. After Supper, the *Lads* desired a Bed, for that they were weary with Travelling. Then *Gaius* called to shew them their Chamber, but said *Mercy*, I will have them to Bed. So she had them to Bed, and they slept well, but the rest sat up all Night. For *Gaius* and they were such sutable Company, that they could not tell how to part. Then after much talk of their Lord, themselves, and their Journey, Old Mr. *Honest*, he that put forth the Riddle to *Gaius*, began to *nod*. Then said *Great-heart*, What Sir, you begin to be drouzy, come rub up, now here's a *Riddle* for you. Then said Mr. *Honest*, let's hear it.

Old Honest *Nods.*

Then said Mr. *Great-heart*,

He that will kill, must first be overcome:
Who live abroad would, first must die at home.

A Riddle.

Huh, said Mr. *Honest*, it is a hard one, hard to expound, and harder to practise. But come Landlord, said he, I will, if you please, leave my part to you, do you expound it, and I will hear what you say.

No, said *Gaius*, 'twas put to you, and 'tis expected that you should answer it.

Then said the old Gentleman,

He first by Grace must conquer'd be,
That Sin would mortifie.
And who, that lives, would convince me,
Unto himself must die.

The Riddle opened.

It is right, said *Gaius*; good Doctrine, and Experience teaches this. For first, until Grace displays it self, and overcomes the Soul with its Glory, it is altogether without Heart to oppose Sin. Besides, if Sin is Satan's Cords, by which the Soul lies bound, how should it make Resistance, before it is loosed from that Infirmity?

Secondly, Nor will any that knows either Reason or Grace, believe that such a man can be a living Monument of Grace, that is a Slave to his own Corruptions.

And now it comes in my mind, I will tell you a Story, worth the hearing. There were two Men that went on Pilgrimage, the one began when he was young, the other when he was old. The young man had strong Corruptions to grapple with, the old mans were decayed with the decays of Nature. The young man trod his steps as even as did the old one, and was every way as light as he; who now, or which of them had their Graces shining clearest, since both seemed to be alike?

A Question worth the minding.

Honest. *The young mans doubtless. For that which heads it against the greatest Opposition, gives best demonstration that it is strongest. Specially when it also holdeth pace with that that meets not with half so much: as to be sure old Age does not.*

A Comparison.

Besides, I have observed that old men have blessed themselves with this mistake; Namely, taking the decays of Nature for a gracious Conquest over Corruptions, and so have been apt to beguile themselves. Indeed old men that are gracious,

A Mistake.

are best able to give Advice to them that are young, because they have seen most of the emptiness of things. But yet, for an old and a young to set out both together, the young one has the advantage of the fairest discovery of a work of Grace within him, tho the old mans Corruptions are naturally the weakest.

Thus they sat talking till break of Day. Now when the Family was up, *Christiana* bid her Son *James* that he should read a Chapter; so he read the 53 of *Isaiah*. When he had done, Mr. *Honest* asked why it was said, *That the Savior is said to come out of a dry ground, and also that he had no Form nor Comliness in him?*

Another Question.

Greath. Then said Mr. *Great-heart*, To the first I answer, Because, the Church of the Jews, of which Christ came, had then lost almost all the Sap and Spirit of Religion. To the Second I say, The Words are spoken in the Person of the Unbelievers, who because they want *that* Eye that can see into our Princes Heart, therefore they judg of him by the meanness of his Outside.

Just like those that know not that precious Stones are covered over with a homely *Crust*; who when they have found one, because they know not what they have found, cast it again away as men do a common Stone.

Well, said *Gaius*, Now you are here, and since, as I know, Mr. *Great-heart* is good at his Weapons, if you please, after we have refreshed our selves, we will walk into the Fields, to see if we can do any good. About a mile from hence, there is one *Slaygood*, a *Gyant*, that doth much annoy the Kings High-way in these parts. And I know whereabout his Haunt is, he is Master of a number of Thieves; 'twould be well if we could clear these Parts of him.

Gyant Slaygood *assaulted and slain.*

So they consented and went, Mr. *Great-heart* with his *Sword, Helmet* and *Shield*, and the rest with Spears and Staves.

When they came to the place where he was, they found him with one *Feeble-mind* in his Hands, whom his Servants had brought unto him, having taken him in the Way; now the Gyant was rifling of him, with a purpose after that to pick his Bones. For he was of the nature of *Flesh-eaters*.

He is found with one Feeble-mind *in his hands.*

Well, so soon as he saw Mr. *Great-heart*, and his Friends, at the mouth of his Cave with their Weapons, he demanded what they wanted?

Greath. We want thee; for we are come to revenge the Quarrel of the many that thou hast slain of the Pilgrims, when thou hast dragged them out of the Kings High-way; wherefore come out of thy Cave. So he armed himself and came out, and to a Battle they went, and fought for above an Hour, and then stood still to take Wind.

Slaygood. *Then said the Gyant, Why are you here on my Ground?*

Greath. To revenge the Blood of Pilgrims, as I also told thee before; so they went to it again, and the Gyant made Mr. *Great-heart* give back, but he came up again, and in the greatness of his Mind, he let fly with such stoutness at the Gyants Head and Sides, that he made him let his Weapon fall out of his Hand. So he smote him, and slew him, and cut off his Head, and brought it away to the *Inn*. He also took *Feeble-mind* the Pilgrim, and brought him with him to his Lodgings. When they were come home, they shewed his Head to the Family, and then set it up as they had done others before, for a Terror to those that should attempt to do as he, hereafter.

One Feeble-mind *rescued from the Gyant.*

Then they asked Mr. *Feeble-mind* how he fell into his hands?

Feeblem. Then said the poor man, I am a sickly man, as you see, and because *Death* did usually once a day *knock at my Door*, I thought I should never be well at home. So I betook my self to a Pilgrims life; and have travelled hither from the Town of *Uncertain*, where I and my Father were born. I am a man of no strength at all, of Body, nor yet of Mind, but would, if I could, tho I can but *craul*, spend my Life in the Pilgrims way. When I came at the Gate that is at the head of the Way, the Lord of that place did entertain me freely. Neither objected he against my weakly Looks, nor against my *feeble Mind*; but gave me such things that were necessary for my Journey, and bid me hope to the end.† When I came to the House of the *Interpreter*, I received much Kindness there, and because the Hill *Difficulty* was judged too hard for me, I was carried up that by one of his Servants. Indeed I have found much Relief from Pilgrims, tho none was willing to go so softly as I am forced to do. Yet still as they came on, they bid me be of good Chear, and said that it

How Feeble-mind *came to be a Pilgrim.*

1 Thess. 5. 14. was the will of their Lord, that Comfort should be given to the *feeble minded*, and so went on their *own* pace. When I was come up to *Assault-Lane*, then this *Gyant* met with me, and bid me prepare for an *Incounter*; but alas, feeble one that I was, I had more need of a *Cordial*. So he came up and took me, I conceited he should not kill me; also when he had got me into his Den, since I went not with him *willingly*, I believed I should come out alive again. For I have heard, that not any Pilgrim that is taken Captive by violent Hands, if he keeps Heart-whole towards his Master, is by the Laws of Providence to die by the Hand of the Enemy. *Robbed*, I looked to be, and Robbed to be sure I am; but I am as you see escaped with Life, for the which I thank my King as Author, and you as the Means. Other Brunts I also look for, but this I have resolved on, to wit, to *run* when I can, to *go* when I cannot *run*, and to *creep* when I cannot *go*. As to the main, I thank him that loves me, I am fixed; my way is before me, my Mind is beyond the *River* that has no Bridg, tho I am as you see, but of a *feeble Mind*.

Mark this.

Mark this.

Hon. *Then said old Mr.* Honest, *Have not you some time ago, been acquainted with one Mr.* Fearing, *a* Pilgrim?

Mr. Fearing *Mr.* Feeble-mind's *Uncle.*

Feeble. Acquainted with him? Yes. He came from the Town of *Stupidity*, which lieth *four Degrees* to the Northward of the City of *Destruction*, and as many off, of where I was born; Yet we were well acquainted, for indeed he was mine Uncle, my Fathers Brother; he and I have been much of a Temper, he was a little shorter then I, but yet we were much of a Complexion.

Feeble-mind *has some of Mr.* Fearing's *Features.*

Hon. *I perceive you knew him, and I am apt to believe also that you were related one to another; for you have his whitely Look, a Cast like his with your Eye, and your Speech is much alike.*

Feebl. Most have said so, that have known us both, and besides, what I have read in him, I have for the most part found in my self.

Gaius *Comforts him.*

Gaius. *Come Sir, said good* Gaius, *be of good Chear, you are welcome to me, and to my House; and what thou hast a mind to, call for freely; and what thou would'st have my Servants do for thee, they will do it with a ready Mind.*

Feebl. Then said Mr. *Feeble-mind*, This is unexpected Favour, and as the Sun shining out of a very dark Cloud. Did Gyant *Slay-good* intend me this Favour when he stop'd me, and resolved to let me go no further? Did he intend that after he had rifled my Pockets, I should go to *Gaius mine Host?* Yet so it is.

Notice to be taken of Providence.

Now, just as Mr. *Feeble-mind*, and *Gaius* was thus in talk; there comes one running, and called at the Door, and told, That about a Mile and an half off, there was one Mr. *Not-right* a Pilgrim, struck dead upon the place where he was, with a *Thunder-bolt*.

Tidings how one Not-right *was slain with a Thunderbolt, and Mr.* Feeble-mind's *Comment upon it.*

Feebl. Alas! said Mr. *Feeble-mind*, is he slain? he overtook me some days before I came so far as hither, and would be my Company-keeper. He also was with me when *Slay-good* the Gyant took me, but he was nimble of his Heels, and escaped. But it seems, he escaped to die, and I was took to live.

> *What, one would think, doth seek to slay* outright,
> *Ofttimes, delivers from the saddest* Plight.
> *That very* Providence, *whose Face is* Death,
> *Doth ofttimes, to the lowly,* Life bequeath.
> *I taken was, he did escape and flee,*
> *Hands Crost, gives Death to him, and Life to me.*

Now about this time *Mathew* and *Mercie* was Married; also *Gaius* gave his Daughter *Phebe* to *James*, *Mathew's* Brother, to Wife; after which time, they yet stayed above ten days at *Gaius*'s House, spending their time, and the Seasons, like as Pilgrims use to do.

When they were to depart, *Gaius* made them a Feast, and they did eat and drink, and were merry. Now the Hour was come that they must be gon, wherefore Mr. *Great-heart* called for a Reckoning. But *Gaius* told him, that at his House, it was not the Custom for *Pilgrims* to pay for their Entertainment. He boarded them by the year, but looked for his pay from the good *Samaritan*, who had promised him at his return, whatsoever Charge he was at with them, faithfully to repay him. Then said Mr. *Great-heart* to him,

The Pilgrims prepare to go forward.

Luke 10. 33, 34, 35.

How they greet one another at parting.

Greath. *Beloved, thou dost faithfully, whatsoever thou dost, to the Brethren and to Strangers, which have born Witness of thy*

3 John 6.

Charity before the Church. Whom if thou (yet) bring forward on their Journey after a Godly sort, thou shalt do well.

Then *Gaius* took his leave of them all, and of his Children, Gaius *his last kindness to* Feeble-mind. and particularly of Mr. *Feeble-mind*. He also gave him something to drink by the way.

Now Mr. *Feeble-mind*, when they were going out of the Door, made as if he intended to linger. The which, when Mr. *Great-heart* espied, he said, come Mr. *Feeble-mind*, pray do you go along with us, I will be your *Conductor*, and you shall fare as the rest.

Feeble-mind *for going behind.* Feebl. *Alas, I want a sutable Companion, you are all lusty and strong, but I, as you see, am weak; I chuse therefore rather to come behind, lest, by reason of my many Infirmities, I should be both a Burthen to my self, and to you. I am, as I said, a man of a weak and feeble Mind, and shall be offended and made weak at that which others can bear. I shall like no Laughing, I shall like no* *His Excuse for it.* *gay Attire, I shall like no unprofitable Questions. Nay, I am so weak a Man, as to be offended with that which others have a liberty to do. I do not yet know all the Truth; I am a very ignorant* Christian-man; *sometimes if I hear some rejoyce in the Lord, it troubles me because I cannot do so too. It is with me, as it is with a weak Man among the strong, or as with a sick Man among the* Job 12. 5. *healthy, or as a Lamp despised. (He that is ready to slip with his Feet, is as a Lamp despised, in the Thought of him that is at ease.)* So that I know not what to do.

Great-heart's *Commission.* 1 Thess. 5. 14. *Greath.* But Brother, said Mr. *Great-heart*. I have it in Commission, to comfort the *feeble minded*, and to support the weak. You must needs go along with us; we will wait for you, Rom. 14. 1 Cor. 8. Chap. 9. 22. *A Christian Spirit.* we will lend you our help, we will deny our selves of some things, both *Opinionative* and *Practical*, for your sake; we will not enter into doubtful Disputations before you, we will be made all things to you, rather then you shall be left behind.

Now, all this while they were at *Gaius*'s Door; and behold as they were thus in the heat of their Discourse, Mr. *Ready-to-Psa. 38. 17. *Promises.* hault*† came by, with his *Crutches* in his hand, and he also was going on Pilgrimage.

Feeble-mind *glad to see* Ready-to-hault *come by.* Feebl. *Then said Mr.* Feeble-mind *to him, Man! how camest thou hither? I was but just now complaining that I had not a sutable Companion, but thou art according to my Wish. Wel-*

come, welcome, good Mr. Ready-to-hault, *I hope thee and I may be some help.*

Ready-to. I shall be glad of thy Company, said the other; and good Mr. *Feeble-mind*, rather then we will part, since we are thus happily met, I will lend thee one of my Crutches.

Feebl. *Nay, said he, tho I thank thee for thy good Will, I am not inclined to hault before I am Lame. How be it, I think when occasion is, it may help me against a Dog.*

Ready-to. If either my *self*, or my *Crutches*, can do thee a pleasure, we are both at thy Command, good Mr. *Feeble-mind.*

Thus therefore they went on, Mr. *Great-heart* and Mr. *Honest* went before, *Christiana* and her Children went next, and Mr. *Feeble-mind* and Mr. *Ready-to-hault* came behind with his Crutches. Then said Mr. *Honest*,

Hon. *Pray Sir, now we are upon the Road, tell us some profitable things of some that have gon on Pilgrimage before us.* *New Talk.*

Greath. With a good Will. I suppose you have heard how *Christian* of old, did meet with *Apollyon* in the Valley of *Humiliation*, and also what hard work he had to go thorow the Valley of the Shadow of Death. Also I think you cannot but have heard how *Faithful* was put to it with *Madam Wanton*, with *Adam* the first, with one *Discontent*, and *Shame*; four as deceitful Villains, as a man can meet with upon the Road. *1 Part* from *pag.* 69, to *pag.* 73.

Hon. *Yes, I have heard of all this; but indeed, good* Faithful *was hardest put to it with* Shame, *he was an unwearied one.*

Greath. Ai, for as the Pilgrim well said, He of all men had the wrong Name.

Hon. *But pray Sir, where was it that* Christian *and* Faithful *met* Talkative? *that same was also a notable one.*

Greath. He was a confident Fool, yet many follow his wayes.

Hon. *He had like to a beguiled* Faithful?

Greath. Ai, But *Christian* put him into a way quickly to find him out. Thus they went on till they came at the place where *Evangelist* met with *Christian* and *Faithful*, and prophecyed to them of what should befall them at Vanity-Fair. *1 Part, pag.* 74, *pag.* 83, *pag.* 85.

Greath. Then said their Guide, Hereabouts did *Christian* and *Faithful* meet with *Evangelist*, who Prophesied to them of what Troubles they should meet with at *Vanity-Fair.*

Hon. *Say you so! I dare say it was a hard Chapter that then he did read unto them.*

1 *Part, pag.* 92 &c. *Greath.* 'Twas so, but he gave them Incouragement withall. But what do we talk of them, they were a couple of Lyonlike Men; they had set their Faces like Flint.† Don't you remember how undaunted they were when they stood before the Judg?

Hon. *Well* Faithful, *bravely suffered!*

Greath. So he did, and as brave things came on't: For *Hopeful* and some others, as the Story relates it, were Converted by his Death.

Hon. *Well, but pray go on; for you are well acquainted with things.*

1 *Part, pag.* 97. *Greath.* Above all that *Christian* met with after he had passed throw *Vanity-Fair*, one *By-ends* was the arch one.

Hon. *By-ends; what was he?*

Greath. A very arch Fellow, a downright Hypocrite; one that would be Religious, which way ever the World went, but so cunning, that he would be sure neither to lose, nor suffer for it.

He had his *Mode* of Religion for every fresh occasion, and his Wife was as good at it as he. He would turn and change from Opinion to Opinion; yea, and plead for so doing too. But so far as I could learn, he came to an ill End with his *By-ends*, nor did I ever hear that any of his Children were ever of any Esteem with any that truly feared God.

They are come within sight of Vanity. Psa. 12. 2. Now by this time, they were come within sight of the Town of *Vanity*, where Vanity Fair is kept. So when they saw that they were so near the Town, they consulted with one another how they should pass thorow the Town, and some said one thing, and some another. At last Mr. *Greatheart* said, I have, as you may understand, often been a *Conductor* of Pilgrims thorow *this* Town; Now I am acquainted with one Mr. *Mnason*,† a *Cyprusian* by Nation, an old Disciple, at whose House we may Lodg. If you think good, said he, we will turn in there.

They enter into one Mr. Mnasons *to Lodg.*

Content, said old *Honest*; Content, said *Christiana*; Content, said Mr. *Feeble-mind*; and so they said all. Now you must think it was *Even-tide*, by that they got to the outside of the Town, but Mr. *Great-heart* knew the way to the Old man's House. So thither they came; and he called at the Door, and the old Man within knew his Tongue so soon as ever he heard it; so he opened, and they all came in. Then said *Mnason* their Host, How far have ye come to day? So they said, From the House of *Gaius* our Friend. I promise you, said he, you have gone a good stitch, you may well be a-weary; sit down. So they sat down.

Greath. *Then said their Guide, Come what Chear Sirs, I dare say you are welcome to my Friend.*

Mna. I also, said Mr. *Mnason*, do bid you Welcome; and whatever you want, do but say, and we will do what we can to get it for you.

They are glad of entertainment.

Hon. *Our great Want, a while since, was Harbor, and good Company, and now I hope we have both.*

Mna. For Harbour, you see what it is, but for good Company, that will appear in the Tryal.

Greath. *Well, said Mr.* Great-heart, *will you have the Pilgrims up into their Lodging?*

Mna. I will, said Mr. *Mnason*. So he had them to their respective Places; and also shewed them a very fair Dining-Room, where they might be and sup together, until time was come to go to Rest.

Now when they were set in their places, and were a little cheary after their Journey, Mr. *Honest* asked his Landlord if there were any store of good People in the Town?

Mna. We have a few, for indeed they are but a few, when compared with them on the other side.

Hon. *But how shall we do to see some of them? for the sight of good men to them that are going on Pilgrimage, is like to the appearing of the Moon and the Stars to them that are sailing upon the Seas.*

They desire to see some of the good People in the Town.

Mna. Then Mr. *Mnason* stamped with his Foot, and his Daughter *Grace* came up; so he said unto her, *Grace*, go you, tell my Friends, Mr. *Contrite*, Mr. *Holy-man*, Mr. *Love-saint*, Mr. *Dare-not-ly*, and Mr. *Penitent*; that I have a Friend or two at my House, that have a mind this Evening to see them.

Some sent for.

So *Grace* went to call them, and they came, and after Salutation made, they sat down together at the Table.

Then said Mr. *Mnason* their Landlord, My Neighbours, I

have, as you see, a company of *Strangers* come to my House, they are *Pilgrims*: They come from afar, and are going to Mount *Sion*. But who, quoth he, do you think this is? pointing with his Finger to *Christiana*. It is *Christiana*, the Wife of *Christian*, that famous Pilgrim, who with *Faithful* his brother were so shamefully handled in our Town. At that they stood amazed, saying, We little thought to see *Christiana*, when *Grace* came to call us, wherefore this is a very comfortable Surprize. Then they asked her of her welfare, and if these young men were her Husbands Sons. And when she had told them they were; they said, The King whom you love, and serve, make you as your Father, and bring you where he is in Peace.

Some Talk betwixt Mr. Honest *and* Contrite.

Hon. Then Mr. *Honest (when they were all sat down) asked Mr.* Contrite *and the rest, in what posture their Town was at present*?

** The Fruit of Watchfulness.*

Cont. You may be sure we are full of Hurry, in Fair time. *'Tis hard keeping our Hearts and Spirits in any good Order, when we are in a cumbred condition. He that lives in such a place as this is, and that has to do with such as we have, has need of an Item to caution him to take heed, every moment of the Day.

Hon. *But how are your Neighbors for quietness?*

Persecution not so hot at Vanity Fair as formerly.

Cont. They are much more moderate now then formerly. You know how *Christian* and *Faithful* were used at our Town; but of late, I say, they have been far more moderate. I think the Blood of *Faithful* lieth with load upon them till now; for since they burned him, they have been ashamed to burn any more: In *those* days we were afraid to walk the Streets, but *now* we can shew our Heads. *Then* the Name of a Professor was odious, *now*, specially in some parts of our Town (for you know our Town is large) Religion is counted Honourable.

Then said Mr. Contrite *to them, Pray how faireth it with you in your Pilgrimage, how stands the Country affected towards you?*

Hon. It happens to us, as it happeneth to Way-fairing men; sometimes our way is clean, sometimes foul; sometimes up-hill, sometimes down-hill; We are seldom at a Certainty. The Wind is not alwayes on our Backs, nor is every one a Friend that we meet with in the Way. We have met with some notable

Rubs already; and what are yet behind we know not, but for the most part we find it true, that has been talked of of old, *A good Man must suffer Trouble*.†

Contrit. *You talk of Rubs, what Rubs have you met withal?*

Hon. Nay, ask Mr. *Great-heart* our Guide, for he can give the best Account of that.

Greath. We have been beset three or four times already: First *Christiana* and her Children were beset with two Ruffians, that they feared would a took away their Lives; We was beset with Gyant *Bloody-man*, Gyant *Maul*, and Gyant *Slay-good*. Indeed we did rather beset the last, then were beset of him: And thus it was. After we had been some time at the House of *Gaius, mine Host, and of the whole Church*,† we were minded upon a time to take our Weapons with us, and go see if we could light upon any of those that were Enemies to Pilgrims; (for we heard that there was a notable one thereabouts.) Now *Gaius* knew his *Haunt* better than I, because he dwelt thereabout, so we looked and looked, till at last we discerned the mouth of his Cave; then we were glad and pluck'd up our Spirits. So we approached up to his *Den*, and lo when we came there, he had dragged by meer force into his Net, this *poor man*, Mr. *Feeble-mind*, and was about to bring him to his End. But when he saw us, supposing as we thought, he had had an other Prey, he left the poor man in his Hole, and came out. So we fell to it full sore, and he lustily laid about him; but in conclusion, he was brought down to the Ground, and his Head cut off, and set up by the Way side for a Terror to such as should after practise such Ungodliness. That I tell you the Truth, here is the man himself to affirm it, who was as a Lamb taken out of the Mouth of the Lyon.

Feebl. *Then said Mr.* Feeble-mind, *I found this true to my Cost, and Comfort; to my Cost, when he threatned to pick my Bones every moment; and to my Comfort, when I saw Mr.* Great-heart *and his Friends with their Weapons approach so near for my* Deliverance.

Mr. Holy-man's *Speech.*

Holym. Then said Mr. *Holy-man*, There are two things that they have need to be possessed with that go on Pilgrimage, *Courage* and an *unspotted Life*. If they have not *Courage*, they can never hold on their way; and if their Lives be *loose*, they will make the very Name of a *Pilgrim* stink.

Mr. Love-saint's *Speech.*

Loves. Then said Mr. *Love-saint*; I hope this Caution is not needful amongst you. But truly there are many that go upon the Road, that rather declare themselves Strangers to Pilgrimage, then Strangers and Pilgrims in the Earth.†

Mr. Dare-not-ly *his Speech.*

Darenot. *Then said Mr.* Dare-not-ly, *'Tis true; they neither have the Pilgrims* Weed, *nor the Pilgrims Courage; they go not uprightly, but all* awrie *with their Feet, one Shoo goes* inward, *an other* outward, *and their Hosen out behind*; there a *Rag*, and there a *Rent*, to the Disparagement of their Lord.

Mr. Penitent *his Speech.*

Penit. These things, said Mr. *Penitent*, they ought to be troubled for, nor are the Pilgrims like to have that Grace put upon them and their pilgrims Progress, as they desire, until the way is cleared of such Spots and Blemishes.

Thus they sat talking and spending the time, until Supper was set upon the Table. Unto which they went and refreshed their weary Bodys, so they went to Rest. Now they stayed in this Fair a great while, at the House of this Mr. *Mnason*, who in process of time gave his Daughter *Grace* unto *Samuel, Christiana*'s Son, to Wife, and his Daughter *Martha* to *Joseph*.

The time, as I said, that they lay here, was long (for it was not now as in former times.) Wherefore the *Pilgrims* grew acquainted with many of the good people of the Town, and did them what Service they could. *Mercie*, as she was wont, laboured much for the Poor, wherefore their Bellys and Backs blessed her, and she was there an Ornament to her Profession. And to say the truth, for *Grace, Phebe*, and *Martha*, they were all of a very good Nature, and did much good in their place. They were also all of them very Fruitful, so that *Christian's* Name, as was said before, was like to live in the World.

A Monster.

While they lay here, there came a *Monster* out of the Woods,† and slew many of the People of the Town. It would also carry away their Children, and teach them to suck its Whelps. Now no man in the Town durst so much as Face this *Monster*; but all Men fled when they heard of the noise of his coming.

Rev. 17. 3. *His Shape.* His Nature.

The *Monster* was like unto no one Beast upon the Earth. Its Body was like a Dragon, and it had seven Heads and ten Horns, *It made great havock of Children, and yet it was governed by a Woman*. This *Monster* propounded Conditions to men; and such men as loved their Lives more then their Souls, accepted of those Conditions. So they came under.

Now this Mr. *Great-heart*, together with these that came to visit the Pilgrims at Mr. *Mnason*'s House, entred into a Covenant to go and ingage this Beast, if perhaps they might deliver the People of this Town, from the Paws and Mouths of this so devouring a Serpent.

Then did Mr. *Great-heart*, Mr. *Contrite*, Mr. *Holy-man*, Mr. *Dare-not-ly*, and *Mr. Penitent*, with their Weapons go forth to meet him. Now the *Monster* at first was very Rampant, and looked upon these Enemies with great Disdain, but they so belabored him, being sturdy men at Arms, that they made him make a Retreat: so they came home to Mr. *Mnasons* House again. *How he is ingaged.*

The *Monster*, you must know, had his certain Seasons to come out in, and to make his Attempts upon the Children of the People of the Town, also these Seasons did these valiant Worthies watch him in, and did still continually assault him, in so much, that in process of time, he became not only wounded, but lame; also he has not made that havock of the Towns mens Children, as formerly he has done. And it is verily believed by some, that this Beast will die of his Wounds.

This therefore made Mr. *Great-heart* and his Fellows, of great Fame in this Town, so that many of the People that wanted their tast of things, yet had a Reverend Esteem and Respect for them. Upon this account therefore it was that these Pilgrims got not much hurt here. True, there were some of the baser sort that could see no more then a *Mole*, nor understand more then a Beast, these had no reverence for these men, nor took they notice of their Valour or Adventures.

Well, the time drew on that the Pilgrims must go on their way, wherefore they prepared for their Journey. They sent for their Friends, they conferred with them, they had some time set apart therein to commit each other to the Protection of their Prince. There was again, that brought them of such things as they had, that was fit for the weak, and the strong, for the Women, and the men; and so *laded* them with such things as was necessary. Act. 28. 10.

Then they set forwards on their way, and their Friends accompanying them so far as was convenient; they again committed each other to the Protection of their King, and parted.

They therefore that were of the Pilgrims Company went on, and Mr. *Great-heart* went before them; now the Women and Children being weakly, they were forced to go as they could bear, by this means Mr. *Ready-to-hault* and Mr. *Feeble-mind* had more to sympathize with their Condition.

When they were gone from the Towns-men, and when their Friends had bid them farewel, they quickly came to the place where *Faithful* was put to Death: There therefore they made a stand, and thanked him that had enabled him to bear his Cross so well, and the rather, because they now found that they had a benefit by such a manly Suffering as his was.

They went on therefore after this, a good way further, talking of *Christian* and *Faithful*, and how *Hopeful* joyned himself to *Christian* after that *Faithful* was dead.

1 Part, pag. 103. Now they were come up with the *Hill Lucre*, where the *Silver-mine* was, which took *Demas* off from his Pilgrimage, and into which, as some think, *By-ends* fell and perished; wherefore they considered that. But when they were come to the old Monument that stood over against the *Hill Lucre*, to wit, to the Pillar of Salt that stood also within view of *Sodom*, and its stinking Lake; they marvelled, as did *Christian* before, that men of that Knowledge and ripeness of Wit as they was, should be so blinded as to turn aside here. Only they considered again, that Nature is not affected with the Harms that others have met with, specially if that thing upon which they look, has an attracting Virtue upon the foolish Eye.

1 Part, pag. 107. I saw now that they went on till they came at the River that was on this side of the Delectable Mountains. To the River where the fine Trees grow on both sides, and whose Leaves, if taken inwardly, are good against Surfits; where the Medows are green all the year long, and where they might lie down safely. [Psal. 23.]

By this River side in the Medow, there were Cotes and Folds for Sheep, an House built for the *nourishing* and bringing up of those Lambs, the Babes of those Women that go on Pilgrimage. Also there was here one that was intrusted with them, who [Heb. 5. 2.]

could have compassion, and that could gather these Lambs with his Arm, and carry them in his Bosom, and that could gently lead those that were with young. Now to the Care of *this Man, Christiana* admonished her four Daughters to commit their little ones; that by these Waters they might be housed, harbored, suckered and nourished, and that none of them might *be lacking in time to come*. This man, if any of them go astray, or be lost, he will bring them again, he will also bind up that which was broken, and will strengthen them that are sick. Here they will never want Meat, and Drink and Cloathing, here they will be kept from Thieves and Robbers, for this man will dye before one of those committed to his Trust, shall be lost. Besides, here they shall be sure to have good *Nurture* and Admonition, and shall be taught to walk in right Paths, and that you know is a Favour of no small account. Also here, as you see, are delicate *Waters*, pleasant *Medows*, dainty *Flowers*, variety of *Trees*, and such as bear *wholsom Fruit*. Fruit, not like that that *Matthew* eat of, that fell over the Wall out of *Belzebubs* Garden, but Fruit that procureth Health where there is none, and that continueth and increaseth it where it is.

Isa. 40. 11.

Jer. 23. 4.

Ezek. 34. 11, 12, 13, 14, 15, 16.

John 10. 16.

So they were content to commit their little Ones to him; and that which was also an Incouragement to them so to do, was, for that all this was to be at the Charge of the King, and so was an Hospital to young Children, and *Orphans*.

Now they went on: And when they were come to *By-path* Medow, to the Stile over which *Christian* went with his Fellow *Hopeful*, when they were taken by *Gyant-Dispair*, and put into *Doubting*-Castle, they sat down and consulted what was best to be done, to wit, now they were so strong, and had got such a man as Mr. *Great-heart* for their Conductor; whether they had not best to make an Attempt upon the Gyant, demolish his Castle, and if there were any Pilgrims in it, to set them at liberty before they went any further. So one said one thing, and an other said the contrary. One questioned if it was lawful to go upon *unconsecrated* Ground, an other said they might, provided their end was good; but Mr. *Great-heart* said, Though that Assertion offered last, cannot be universally true, yet I have a Comandment to resist Sin, to overcome Evil, to fight the good Fight of Faith.† And I pray, with whom should

They being come to By-path *Stile, have a mind to have a pluck with* Gyant Dispair.

1 *Part, pag.* 108, 109.

I fight this good Fight, if not with *Gyant-dispair*? I will therefore attempt the taking away of his Life, and the demolishing of *Doubting* Castle. Then said he, who will go with me? Then said old *Honest*, I will, And so will we too, said *Christian*'s four Sons, *Mathew, Samuel, James* and *Joseph*, for they were young men and strong.

1 John 2. 13, 14.

So they left the Women in the Road, and with them Mr. *Feeble-mind*, and Mr. *Ready-to-halt*, with his Crutches, to be their *Guard*, until they came back, for in that place tho *Gyant-Dispair* dwelt so near, they keeping in the Road, *A little Child might lead them.*

Isa. 11. 6.

So Mr. *Great-heart*, old *Honest*, and the four young men, went to go up to *Doubting* Castle, to look for *Gyant-Dispair*. When they came at the Castle Gate, they knocked for Entrance with an unusual Noyse. At that the old Gyant comes to the Gate, and *Diffidence* his Wife follows. Then said he, Who, and what is he, that is so hardy, as after this manner to molest the *Gyant-Dispair*? Mr. *Great-heart* replyed, It is I, *Great-heart*, one of the King of the Celestial Countries Conductors of Pilgrims to their Place. And I demand of thee that thou open thy Gates for my Entrance, prepare thy self also to Fight, for I am come to take away thy Head, and to demolish *Doubting* Castle.

Despair *has overcome Angels.*

Now *Gyant-Dispair*, because he was a *Gyant*, thought no man could overcome him, and again, thought he, since heretofore I have made a Conquest of Angels, shall *Great-heart* make me afraid? So he harnessed himself and went out. He had a Cap of Steel upon his Head, a Brestplate of Fire girded to him, and he came out in Iron Shoos, with a great Club in his Hand. Then these six men made up to him, and beset him behind and before; also when *Diffidence*, the *Gyantess*, came up to help him, old Mr. *Honest* cut her down at one Blow. Then they fought for their Lives, and *Gyant-Dispair* was brought down to the Ground, *but was very loth to die*. He strugled hard, and had, as they say, as many Lives as a Cat,† but *Great-heart* was his death, for he left him not till he had severed his head from his shoulders.

Despair *is loth to die.*

Doubting-Castle *demolished.*

Then they fell to demolishing *Doubting* Castle, and that you know might with ease be done, since *Gyant-Dispair* was dead. They were seven Days in destroying of that; and in it of

Tho doubting Castle be demolished
And the Gyant dispair hath lost his head
Sin can rebuild the Castle, make't remaine,
And make despair the Gyant live againe.

Pilgrims, they found one Mr. *Dispondencie*, almost starved to Death, and one *Much-afraid* his Daughter; these two they saved alive. But it would a made you a wondered to have seen the dead Bodies that lay here and there in the Castle Yard, and how full of dead mens Bones the Dungeon was.

When Mr. *Great-heart* and his Companions had performed this Exploit, they took Mr. *Despondencie*, and his Daughter *Much-afraid*, into their Protection, for they were honest People, tho they were Prisoners in *Doubting* Castle, to that Tyrant *Gyant-Dispair*. They therefore I say, took with them the Head of the *Gyant* (for his Body they had buried under a heap of Stones) and down to the Road and to their Companions they came, and shewed them what they had done. Now when *Feeble-mind*, and *Ready-to-hault* saw that it was the Head of *Gyant-Dispair* indeed, they were very jocond and merry. Now *Christiana*, if need was, could play upon the *Vial*, and her Daughter *Mercie* upon the *Lute*: So, since they were so merry disposed, she plaid them a Lesson, and *Ready-to-halt* would Dance. So he took *Dispondencie*'s Daughter, named *Much-afraid*, by the Hand, and to dancing they went in the Road. True, he could not Dance without one Crutch in his Hand, but I promise you, he footed it well; also the Girl was to be commended, for she answered the Musick handsomely.

They have Musick and dancing for joy.

As for Mr. *Despondencie*, the Musick was not much to him, he was for feeding rather then dancing, for that he was almost starved. So *Christiana* gave him some of her bottle of Spirits for present Relief, and then prepared him something to eat; and in little time the old Gentleman came to himself, and began to be finely revived.

Now I saw in my Dream, when all these things were finished, Mr. *Great-heart* took the Head of *Gyant-Dispair*, and set it upon a Pole by the Highway side, right over against the Piller that *Christian* erected for a *Caution* to Pilgrims that came after, to take heed of entering into his Grounds.

Then he writ under it upon a *Marble* stone, these Verses following.

A Monument of Deliverance.

This is the Head *of* him, *whose* Name *only,*
In former times, did Pilgrims *terrify.*

His Castle'*s down, and* Diffidence *his Wife,*
Brave Master Great-heart *has bereft of Life.*
Dispondencie, *his Daughter* Much-afraid,
Great-heart, *for them, also the Man has plaid.*†
Who hereof doubts, if he'l but cast his Eye.
Up hither, may his Scruples satisfy,
This Head, also when doubting Cripples dance,
Doth shew from Fears they have Deliverance.

When these men had thus bravely shewed themselves against *Doubting-Castle*, and had slain *Gyant-Dispair*, they went forward, and went on till they came to the *Delectable* Mountains, where *Christian* and *Hopeful* refreshed themselves with the Varieties of the Place. They also acquainted themselves with the Shepherds there, who welcomed them as they had done *Christian* before, unto the Delectable Mountains.

Now the Shepherds seeing so great a train follow Mr. *Great-heart* (for with him they were well acquainted;) they said unto him, Good Sir, you have got a goodly Company here; pray where did you find all these?

Then Mr. *Great-heart* replyed,

The Guides Speech to the Shepherds.

First here's Christiana *and her train,*
Her Sons, and her Sons Wives, who like the Wain
Keep by the Pole, and do by Compass stere,
From Sin to Grace, else they had not been here.
Next here's old Honest *come on Pilgrimage,*
Ready-to-halt *too, who I dare ingage,*
True hearted is, and so is Feeble-mind,
Who willing was, not to be left behind.
Dispondencie, *good-man, is coming after,*
And so also is Much-afraid, *his Daughter.*
May we have Entertainment here, or must
We further go? let's know whereon to trust.

Their Entertainment. Matt. 25. 40.

Then said the Shepherds; This is a comfortable Company, you are welcome to us, for we have for the *Feeble*, as for the *Strong*; our Prince has an Eye to what is done to the least of these. Therefore Infirmity must not be a block to our Entertainment. So they had them to the Palace Door, and then said unto them, Come in Mr. *Feeble-mind*, come in Mr. *Ready-to-*

halt, come in Mr. *Dispondencie*, and Mrs. *Much-afraid* his Daughter. *These* Mr. *Great-heart*, said the Shepherds to the Guide, we call in by Name, for that they are most subject to draw back; but as for you, and the rest that are *strong*, we leave you to your wonted Liberty. Then said Mr. *Great-heart*, This day I see that Grace doth shine in your Faces, and that you are my Lords Shepherds indeed; for that you have not *pushed* these Diseased neither with Side nor Shoulder, but have rather strewed their way into the Palace with Flowers, as you should.

A Description of false Shepherds. Ezek. 34. 21.

So the Feeble and Weak went in, and Mr. *Great-heart*, and the rest did follow. When they were also set down, the Shepherds said to those of the weakest sort, What is it that you would have? For said they, all things must be managed here, to the supporting of the weak, as well as to the warning of the Unruly.

So they made them a Feast of things easy of Digestion, and that were pleasant to the Palate, and nourishing; the which when they had received, they went to their rest, each one respectively unto his proper place. When Morning was come, because the Mountains were high, and the day clear; and because it was the Custom of the Shepherds to shew to the Pilgrims, before their Departure, some Rarities; therefore after they were ready, and had refreshed themselves, the Shepherds took them out into the Fields, and shewed them first, what they had shewed to *Christian* before.

Mount-Marvel.

Then they had them to some new places. The first was to *Mount-Marvel*, where they looked, and behold a man at a Distance, *that tumbled the Hills about with Words.*† Then they asked the Shepherds what that should mean? So they told him, that that man was the Son of one *Great-grace*, of whom you read in the first part of the Records of the *Pilgrims Progress*. And he is set there to teach Pilgrims how to believe down, or to tumble out of their ways, what Difficulties they shall meet with, by faith. Then said Mr. *Great-heart*, I know him, he is a man above many.

1 Part, pag. 125. Mar. 11. 23, 24.

Mount-Innocent.

Then they had them to another place, called *Mount-Innocent*. And there they saw a man cloathed all in White; and two men, *Prejudice*, and *Ill-will*, continually casting Dirt upon him. Now behold the Dirt, whatsoever they cast at him, would in little time fall off again, and his Garment would look as clear as if no Dirt had been cast thereat.

Then said the Pilgrims what means this? The Shepherds answered, This man is named *Godly-man*, and this Garment is to shew the Innocency of his Life. Now those that throw Dirt at him, are such as hate his *Well-doing*, but as you see the Dirt will not stick upon his Clothes, so it shall be with him that liveth truly Innocently in the World. Whoever they be that would make such men dirty, they labor all in vain; for God, by that a little time is spent, will cause that their *Innocence* shall break forth as the Light, and their Righteousness as the Noon day.

Then they took them, and had them to *Mount-Charity*, where they shewed them a man that had a bundle of Cloth lying before him, out of which he cut Coats and Garments, for the Poor that stood about him; yet his Bundle or Role of Cloth was never the less.

Mount-Charity.

Then said they, what should this be? This is, said the Shepherds, to shew you, That he that has a Heart to give of his Labor to the Poor, shall never want where-withal. He that watereth shall be watered himself. And the Cake that the Widdow gave to the Prophet, did not cause that she had ever the less in her Barrel.†

They had them also to a place where they saw one *Fool*, and one *Want-wit*, washing of an *Ethiopian* with intention to make him white,† but the more they washed him, the blacker he was. They then asked the Shepherds what that should mean. So they told them, saying, Thus shall it be with the vile Person; all means used to get such an one a good Name, shall in Conclusion tend but to make him more abominable. Thus it was with the *Pharises*, and so shall it be with all Hypocrites.

The Work of one Fool, *and one* Want-witt.

Then said *Mercie* the Wife of *Mathew* to *Christiana* her Mother, Mother, I would, if it might be, see the Hole in the Hill; or that, commonly called, the *By-way* to Hell. So her Mother brake her mind to the Shepherds. Then they went to the Door; it was in the side of an Hill, and they opened it, and bid *Mercie* harken awhile. So she harkened, and heard one saying, *Cursed be my Father for holding of my Feet back from the way of Peace and Life*; and another said, *O that I had been*

1 Part, pag. 118.
Mercie *has a mind to see the hole in the Hill.*

torn in pieces before I had, to save my life, lost my Soul; and another said, *If I were to live again, how would I deny my self rather then come to this place*. Then there was as if the very Earth had groaned, and quaked under the Feet of this young Woman for fear; so she looked white, and came trembling away, saying, Blessed be he and she that is delivered from this Place.

Now when the Shepherds had shewed them all these things, then they had them back to the Palace, and entertained them with what the House would afford; But *Mercie* being a young, and breeding Woman, Longed for something which she saw there, but was ashamed to ask. Her Mother-in-law then asked her what she ailed, for she looked as one not well. Then said *Mercy, There is a Looking-glass hangs up in the Dining-room*, off of which I cannot take my mind; if therefore I have it not, I think I shall Miscarry. Then said her Mother, I will mention thy Wants to the Shepherds, and they will not deny it thee. But she said, I am ashamed that these men should know that I longed. Nay my Daughter, said she, it is no Shame, but a Virtue, to long for such a thing as that; so *Mercie* said, Then Mother, if you please, ask the Shepherds if they are willing to sell it.

Mercie *longeth, and for what.*

Now the Glass was one of a thousand. It would present a man, one way, with his own Feature exactly, and turn it but an other way, and it would shew one the very Face and Similitude of the Prince of Pilgrims himself. Yea I have talked with them that can tell, and they have said, that they have seen the very Crown of Thorns upon his Head, by looking in that Glass, they have therein also seen the holes in his Hands, in his Feet, and his Side. Yea such an excellency is there in that Glass, that it will shew him to one where they have a mind to see him; whether living or dead, whether in Earth or Heaven, whether in a State of Humiliation, or in his Exaltation, whether coming to Suffer, or coming to Reign.

It was the Word of God.

Jam. 1. 23.

1 Cor. 13. 12.

2 Cor. 3. 18.

Christiana therefore went to the Shepherds apart. (Now the Names of the Shepherds are *Knowledge, Experience, Watchful,* and *Sincere*), and said unto them, There is one of my Daughters a breeding Woman, that, I think doth long for some thing that she hath seen in this House, and she thinks she shall miscarry if she should by you be denyed.

1 *Part, pag.* 117.

Experience. Call her, call her, She shall assuredly have what we can help her to. So they called her, and said to her, *Mercie*, what is that thing thou wouldest have? Then she blushed and said, The great Glass that hangs up in the Dining-room: So *Sincere* ran and fetched it, and with a joyful Consent it was given her. Then she bowed her Head, and gave Thanks, and said, By this I know that I have obtained Favour in your Eyes.

She doth not lose her Longing.

They also gave to the other young Women such things as they desired, and to their Husbands great Commendations, for that they joyned with Mr. *Great-heart* to the slaying of *Gyant-Dispair*, and the demolishing of *Doubting-Castle*.

About *Christiana*'s Neck, the Shepherds put a Bracelet, and so they did about the Necks of her four Daughters, also they put Ear-rings in their Ears, and Jewels on their Fore-heads.†

How the Shepherds adorn the Pilgrims.

When they were minded to go hence, they let them go in Peace, but gave not to them those certain Cautions which before was given to *Christian* and his Companion. The Reason was, for that these had *Great-heart* to be their Guide, who was one that was well acquainted with things, and so could give them their Cautions more seasonably, to wit, even then when the Danger was nigh the approaching.

1 Part, pag. 119.

What Cautions *Christian* and his Companions had received of the Shepherds, they had also lost, by that the time was come that they had need to put them in practice. Wherefore here was the Advantage that this Company had over the other.

1 Part, pag. 128.

From hence they went on Singing, and they said,

Behold, how fitly *are the Stages set!*
For their Relief, that Pilgrims are become;
And how they us *receive without* one *let,*
That make the other *Life our* Mark *and Home.*
What Novelties *they have, to us they give,*
That we, tho *Pilgrims, joyful Lives may live.*
They do upon us too such things bestow,
That shew we Pilgrims are, where ere we go.

When they were gone from the Shepherds, they quickly came to the Place where *Christian* met with one *Turn-a-way*, that dwelt in the Town of *Apostacy*. Wherefore of him Mr. *Great-heart* their Guide did now put them in mind; saying,

1 *Part, pag.* 121. This is the place where *Christian* met with one *Turn-a-way*, who carried with him the Character of his Rebellion at his Back. And this I have to say concerning this man, He would harken to no Counsel, but once a falling, perswasion could not stop him. When he came to the place where the Cross and the Sepulcher was, he did meet with one that did bid him *look there*, but he gnashed with his Teeth, and stamped, and said, he was resolved to go back to his own Town. Before he came to the Gate, he met with *Evangelist*, who offered to lay Hands on him, to turn him into the way again. But this *Turn-a-way resisted him*, and having done much *despite* unto him, he got away over the Wall, and so escaped his Hand.

How one Turn-a-way *managed his Apostacy.*

Heb. 10. 26, 27, 28, 29.

Then they went on, and just at the place where *Little-faith* formerly was Robbed, there stood a man with his Sword drawn, and his Face all bloody. Then said Mr. *Great-heart*, What art thou? The man made Answer, saying, I am one whose Name is *Valiant-for-Truth*, I am a Pilgrim, and am going to the Celestial City. Now as I was in my way, there was three men did beset me, and propounded unto me these three things. 1. Whether I would become one of them? Or go back from whence I came? Or die upon the Place? To the first I answered, I had been a true Man a long Season, and therefore, it could not be expected that I now should cast in my Lot with Thieves. Then they demanded what I would say to the Second. So I told them that the Place from whence I came, had I not found Incommodity there, I had not forsaken it at all, but finding it altogether unsutable to me, and very unprofitable for me, I forsook it for this Way. Then they asked me what I said to the third. And I told them, my Life cost more dear far, then that I should lightly give it away. Besides, you have nothing to do thus to put things to my Choice; wherefore at your Peril be it, if you meddle. Then these three, to wit, *Wild-head, Inconsiderate*, and *Pragmatick*, drew upon me, and I also drew upon them.

One Valiant-for-truth *beset with Thieves.*

Prov. 1. 10, 11, 12, 13, 14.

So we fell to it, one against three, for the space of above three Hours. They have left upon me, as you see, some of the Marks of their Valour, and have also carried away with them some of mine. They are but just now gone. I suppose they might, as the saying is, hear your Horse dash, and so they betook them to flight.

How he behaved himself, and put them to flight.

Greath. *But here was great Odds, three against one.*

Valiant. 'Tis true, but *little* and *more*, are nothing to him that has the Truth on his side. *Though an Host should encamp against me, said one, My Heart shall not fear. Tho War should rise against me, in this will I be Confident*, etc. Besides, said he, I have read in some Records, that one man has fought an Army; and how many did *Sampson* slay with the Jaw Bone of an Ass?†

Psal. 27. 3.

Great-heart *wonders at his Valour.*

Greath. *Then said the Guide, Why did you not cry out, that some might a came in for your Succour?*

Valiant. So I did, to my King, who I knew could hear, and afford invisible Help, and that was sufficient for me.

Greath. *Then said* Great-heart *to Mr.* Valiant-for-Truth, *Thou hast worthily behaved thy self; Let me see thy Sword; so he shewed it him.*

Has a mind to see his Sword, and spends his Judgment on it.

When he had taken it in his Hand, and looked thereon a while, he said, Ha! *It is a right* Jerusalem *Blade.*

Isa. 2. 3.

Valiant. It is so. Let a man have one of *these Blades*, with a Hand to wield it, and skill to use it, and he may venture upon an Angel with it. He need not fear its holding, if he can but tell how to lay on. Its Edges will never blunt. It will cut *Flesh*, and *Bones*, and *Soul*, and *Spirit*, and all.

Ephes. 6. 12, 13, 14, 15, 16, 17.

Heb. 4. 12.

Greath. *But you fought a great while, I wonder you was not weary?*

Valiant. I fought till my Sword did cleave to my Hand, and when they were joyned together, as if a Sword grew out of my Arm, and when the Blood run thorow my Fingers, then I fought with most Courage.

2 Sam. 23. 10.

The Word. The Faith. Blood.

Greath. *Thou hast done well, thou hast resisted unto Blood, striving against Sin.*† *Thou shalt abide by us, come in, and go out with us; for we are thy Companions.*

Then they took him and washed his Wounds, and gave him of what they had, to refresh him, and so they went on together. Now as they went on, because Mr. *Great-heart* was delighted in him (for he loved one greatly that he found to be a man of his Hands†) and because there was with his Company, them that was feeble and weak, therefore he questioned with him about many things; as first, *What Country-man he was?*

What Countrey man Mr. Valiant *was.*

Valiant. I am of *Dark-land*, for there I was born, and there my Father and Mother are still.

Greath. *Dark-land*, said the Guide, *Doth not that ly upon the same Coast with the City of* Destruction?

How Mr. Valiant *came to go on Pilgrimage.*

Valiant. Yes it doth. Now that which caused me to come on Pilgrimage, was this: We had one Mr. *Tell-true* came into our parts, and he told it about, what *Christian* had done, that went from the City of *Destruction*. Namely, how he had forsaken his *Wife* and *Children*, and had betaken himself to a *Pilgrims* Life. It was also confidently reported how he had killed a *Serpent*† that did come out to resist him in his Journey, and how he got thorow to whither he intended. It was also told what Welcome he had at all his Lords Lodgings; specially when he came to the Gates of the Celestial City. For there, said the man, He was received with sound of Trumpet, by a company of shining ones. He told it also, how all the Bells in the City did ring for Joy at his Reception, and what Golden Garments he was cloathed with; with many other things that now I shall forbear to relate. In a word, that man so told the Story of *Christian* and his Travels, that my Heart fell into a burning hast to be gone after him, nor could Father or Mother stay me, so I got from them, and am come thus far on my Way.

Greath. *You came in at the Gate, did you not?*

He begins right.

Valiant. Yes, yes. For the same man also told us, that all would be nothing if we did not begin to enter this way at the Gate.

Christian's *Name famous.*

Greath. *Look you, said the Guide to* Christiana, *The Pilgrimage of your Husband, and what he has gotten thereby, is spread abroad far and near.*

Valiant. Why, is this *Christian*'s Wife?

Greath. *Yes, that it is, and these are also her four Sons.*

Valiant. What! and going on Pilgrimage too?

Greath. *Yes verily, they are following after.*

He is much rejoyced to see Christian's *Wife.*

Valiant. It glads me at the Heart! Good man! How Joyful will he be, when he shall see them that would not go with him, yet to enter after him, in at the Gates into the City!

Greath. *Without doubt it will be a Comfort to him; for next to the Joy of seeing himself there, it will be a Joy to meet there his Wife and his Children.*

Valiant. But now you are upon that, pray let me see your Opinion about it. Some make a question whether we shall know one another when we are there.

Whether we shall know one another when we come to Heaven.

Greath. *Do they think they shall know themselves then? Or that they shall rejoyce to see themselves in that Bliss? and if they think they shall know and do these; Why not know others, and rejoyce in their Welfare also?*

Again, Since Relations are our second self, tho that State will be dissolved there, yet why may it not be rationally concluded that we shall be more glad to see them there, then to see they are wanting?

Valiant. Well, I perceive whereabouts you are as to this. Have you any more things to ask me about my beginning to come on Pilgrimage?

Greath. *Yes, Was your Father and Mother willing that you should become a Pilgrim?*

Valiant. Oh, no. They used all means imaginable to perswade me to stay at Home.

Greath. *Why, what could they say against it?*

Valiant. They said it was an idle Life, and if I my self were not inclined to Sloath and Laziness, I would never countenance a Pilgrim's Condition.

The great Stumbling-Blocks that by his Friends were laid in his way.

Greath. *And what did they say else?*

Valiant. Why, They told me that it was a dangerous Way, yea the most dangerous Way in the World, said they, is that which the Pilgrims go.

Greath. *Did they shew wherein this Way is so dangerous?*

Valiant. Yes. And that in many Particulars.

Greath. *Name some of them.*

Valiant. They told me of the Slow of *Dispond*, where *Christian* was well nigh Smuthered. They told me that there were Archers standing ready in *Belzebub-Castle*, to shoot them that should knock at the *Wicket* Gate for Entrance. They told me also of the Wood, and dark Mountains, of the Hill *Difficulty*, of the Lyons, and also of the three Gyants, *Bloodyman, Maul*, and *Slay-good*. They said moreover, That there was a foul *Fiend* haunted the Valley of *Humiliation*, and that *Christian* was, by him, almost bereft of Life. Besides, said they, You must go over the *Valley of the Shadow of Death*, where the *Hobgoblins* are, where the Light is Darkness, where the Way is full of Snares,

The first Stumbling-Block.

Pits, Traps and Ginns. They told me also of *Gyant Dispair*, of *Doubting Castle*, and of the *Ruins* that the Pilgrims met with there. Further, They said, I must go over the enchanted Ground, which was dangerous. And that after all this I should find a River, over which I should find no Bridg, and that that River did lie betwixt me and the Celestial Countrey.

Greath. *And was this all?*

The Second. *Valiant*. No, They also told me that this way was full of *Deceivers*, and of Persons that laid await there, to turn good men out of the Path.

Greath. *But how did they make that out?*

The Third. *Valiant*. They told me that Mr. *Worldly-wise-man* did there lie in wait to deceive. They also said that there was *Formality* and *Hypocrisie* continually on the Road. They said also that *By-ends, Talkative*, or *Demas*, would go near to gather me up; that the Flatterer would catch me in his Net, or that with greenheaded *Ignorance* I would presume to go on to the Gate, from whence he always was sent back to the Hole that was in the side of the Hill, and made to go the By-way to Hell.

Greath. *I promise you, this was enough to discourage. But did they make an end here?*

The Fourth. *Valiant*. No, stay. They told me also of many that had tryed that way of old, and that had gone a great way therein, to see if they could find something of the Glory there, that so many had so much talked of from time to time; and how they came back again, and be-fooled themselves for setting a Foot out of Doors in that Path, to the Satisfaction of all the Country. And they named several that did so, as *Obstinate*, and *Plyable, Mistrust*, and *Timerous, Turn-a-way*, and old *Atheist*, with several more; who, they said, had, some of them, gone far to see if they could find, but not one of them found so much Advantage by going, as amounted *to the weight of a Fether*.

Greath. *Said they any thing more to discourage you?*

The Fifth. *Valiant*. Yes, They told me of one Mr. *Fearing*, who was a Pilgrim, and how *he* found this way so Solitary, that he never had comfortable Hour therein, also that Mr. *Dispondency* had like to been starved therein; Yea, and also, which I had almost forgot, that *Christian* himself, about whom there has been such a Noise, after all his Ventures for a Celestial Crown, was certainly drowned in the black River, and never went foot further, however it was smuthered up.

Greath. *And did none of these things discourage you?*

Valiant. No. They seemed but as so many Nothings to me.

Greath. *How came that about?*

Valiant. Why, I still believed what Mr. *Tell-True* had said, and that carried me beyond them all.

How he got over these Stumbling-Blocks.

Greath. *Then this was your Victory, even your Faith?*

Valiant. It was so, I believed and therefore came out, got into the Way, fought all that set themselves against me, and by believing am come to this Place.

Who would true Valour see
Let him come hither;
One here will Constant be,
Come Wind, come Weather.
There's no Discouragement,
Shall make him once Relent,
His first avow'd Intent,
To be a Pilgrim.
Who so beset him round,
With dismal Storys,
Do but themselves Confound;
His Strength the more is.
No Lyon *can him fright,*
He'l with a Gyant *Fight,*
But he will have a right,
To be a Pilgrim.
Hobgoblin, *nor foul* Fiend,
Can daunt *his Spirit:*
He knows, he at the end,
Shall Life Inherit.
Then Fancies fly away,
He'l fear not what men say,
He'l labour Night and Day,
To be a Pilgrim.

By this time they were got to the *enchanted Ground*, where the Air naturally tended to make one *Drowzy*. And that place was all grown over with Bryers and Thorns; excepting *here* and

1 Part, pag. 130.

there, where was an *inchanted Arbor*, upon which, if a Man sits, or in which if a man sleeps, 'tis a question, say some, whether ever they shall rise or wake again in this World. Over this Forrest therefore they went, both one with an other, and Mr. *Great-heart* went before, for that he was the Guide, and Mr. *Valiant-for-truth*, he came behind, being there a Guard, for fear lest paradventure some *Fiend*, or *Dragon*, or *Gyant*, or *Thief*, should fall upon their Rere, and so do Mischief. They went on here each man with his Sword drawn in his Hand; for they knew it was a dangerous place. Also they cheared up one another as well as they could. *Feeble-mind*, Mr. *Great-heart* commanded should come up after him, and Mr. *Dispondency* was under the Eye of Mr. *Valiant*.

Now they had not gone far, but a great Mist and a darkness fell upon them all; so that they could scarce, for a great while, see the one the other. Wherefore they were forced for some time, to feel for one another, by Words; for they walked not by Sight.†

But any one must think, that here was but sorry going for the best of them all, but how much worse for the Women and Children, who both of *Feet* and *Heart* were but tender. Yet so it was, that, thorow the incouraging Words of he that led in the Front, and of him that brought them up behind, they made a pretty good shift to wagg along.

The Way also was here very wearysom, thorow Dirt and Slabbiness. Nor was there on *all* this Ground, so much as one *Inn*, or *Victualling-House*, therein to refresh the feebler sort. Here therefore was *grunting*, and *puffing*, and *sighing*: While one tumbleth over a Bush, another sticks fast in the Dirt, and the Children, some of them, lost their Shoos in the Mire. While one crys out, I am down, and another, Ho, Where are you? and a third, The Bushes have got such fast hold on me, I think I cannot get away from them.

An Arbor *on the Inchanting Ground.*

Then they came at an *Arbor*, warm, and promising much Refreshing to the Pilgrims; for it was finely wrought above-head, beautified with *Greens*, furnished with *Benches*, and *Settles*. It also had in it a soft Couch whereon the weary might lean. This, you must think, all things considered, was tempting; for the Pilgrims already began to be foyled with the badness of the way; but there was not one of them that made so much as a motion to stop there. Yea, for ought I could perceive, they continually gave so good heed to the Advice of their Guide, and he did so faithfully tell them of *Dangers*, and of the *Nature* of Dangers when they were at them, that usually when they were nearest to them, they did most pluck up their Spirits, and hearten one another to deny the Flesh. This *Arbor* was called *The sloathfuls Friend*, on purpose to allure, if it might be, some of the Pilgrims there, to take up their Rest when weary.

The Name of the Arbor.

I saw then in my Dream, that they went on in this their *solitary* Ground, till they came to a place at which a man is apt to lose his Way. *Now*, tho when it was light, their Guide could well enough tell how to miss those ways that led wrong, yet in the dark he was put to a stand: But he had in his Pocket a Map of all ways leading to, or from the Celestial City; wherefore he strook a Light (for he never goes also without his Tinder-box) and takes a view of his Book or Map; which bids him be careful in that place to turn to the right-hand-way. And had he not here been careful to look in his Map, they had all, in probability, been smuthered in the Mud, for just a little before them, and that at the end of the cleanest Way too, was a Pit, none knows how deep, full of nothing but Mud; there made on purpose to destroy the Pilgrims in.

The way difficult to find.

The Guide has a Map of all ways leading to or from the City.

Then thought I with my self, who, that goeth on Pilgrimage, but would have one of these Maps about him, that he may look when he is at a *stand*, which is the way he must take?

God's Book.

They went on then in this *inchanted* Ground, till they came to where was an other *Arbor*, and it was built by the High-way-side. And in that *Arbor* there lay two men whose Names were *Heedless* and *Too-bold*. These two went thus far on Pilgrimage, but here being wearied with their Journey, they sat down to rest themselves, and so fell fast asleep. When the Pilgrims saw them, they stood still and shook their Heads; for they knew that the Sleepers were in a pitiful Case. Then they consulted what to do; whether to go on and leave them in their Sleep, or to step to them and try to awake them. So they concluded to go to them and wake them; that is, if they could; but with this Caution, namely, to take heed that themselves did not sit down, nor imbrace the offered Benefit of that *Arbor*.

An Arbor and two asleep therein.

The Pilgrims try to wake them.

So they went in and spake to the men, and called each by his Name, (for the Guide, it seems, did know them) but there was no Voice nor Answer. Then the Guide did shake them, and do what he could to disturb them. Then said one of them, *I will pay you when I take my Mony*; At which the Guide shook his Head. *I will fight so long as I can hold my Sword in my Hand*, said the other. At that, one of the Children laughed.

Their Endeavour is fruitless.

Then said *Christiana*, What is the meaning of this? The Guide said, *They talk in their Sleep*. If you strike them, beat them, or whatever else you do to them, they will answer you after this fashion; or as one of them said in old time, when the Waves of the Sea did beat upon him, and he slept as one upon the Mast of a Ship, *When I awake I will seek it again*. You know when men talk in their Sleeps, they say any thing; but their Words are not governed, either by Faith or Reason. There is an *Incoherencie* in their Words *now*, as there was before betwixt their going on Pilgrimage, and sitting down here. This then is the Mischief on't, when *heedless* ones go on Pilgrimage, 'tis twenty to one, but they are served thus. For this *inchanted* Ground is one of the last Refuges that the Enemy to Pilgrims has; wherefore it is as you see, placed almost at the end of the Way, and so it standeth against us with the more advantage. For when, thinks the Enemy, will these Fools be so desirous to sit down, as when they are weary; and when so like to be weary, as when almost at their Journys end? Therefore it is, I say, that the *inchanted* Ground is placed so nigh to the Land *Beulah*, and so neer the end of their Race. Wherefore let Pilgrims look to themselves, lest it happen to them as it has done to these, that, as you see, are fallen asleep, and none can wake them.

Prov. 23. 34, 35.

The light of the Word. 2 Pet. 1. 19.

Then the Pilgrims desired with trembling to go forward, only they prayed their Guide to strike a Light, that they might go the rest of their way by the help of the light of a Lanthorn. So he strook a light, and they went by the help of that thorow the rest of this way, tho the Darkness was very great.

The Children cry for weariness.

But the Children began to be sorely weary, and they cryed out unto him that loveth Pilgrims, to make their way more Comfortable. So by that they had gone a little further, a Wind arose that drove away the Fog, so the Air became more clear.

Yet they were not off (by much) of the *inchanted* Ground;

only now they could see one an other better, and the way wherein they should walk.

Now when they were almost at the end of this Ground, they perceived that a little before them, was a *solemn* Noise, as of one that was much concerned. So they went on and looked before them, and behold, they saw, as they thought, *a Man upon his Knees*, with Hands and Eyes lift up, and speaking, as they thought, earnestly to one that was above. They drew nigh, but could not tell what he said; so they went softly till he had done. When he had done, he got up and began to run towards the Celestial City. Then Mr. *Great-heart* called after him, saying, So-ho, Friend, let us have your Company, if you go, as I suppose you do, to the Celestial City. So the man stoped, and they came up to him. But as soon as Mr. *Honest* saw him, he said, I know this man. Then said Mr. *Valiant-for-truth*, Prethee who is it? 'Tis one, said he, that comes from whereabouts I dwelt, his Name is *Stand-fast*, he is certainly a right good Pilgrim.

Standfast *upon his Knees in the Inchanted Ground.*

The Story of Standfast.

So they came up one to another, and presently *Stand-fast* said to old *Honest*, Ho, Father *Honest*, are you there? Ai, said he, that I am, as sure as you are there. Right glad am I, said Mr. *Stand-fast*, that I have found you on this Road. And as glad am I, said the other, that I espied you upon your Knees. Then Mr. *Stand-fast* blushed, and said, But why, did you see me? Yes, that I did, quoth the other, and with my Heart was glad at the Sight. Why, what did you think, said *Stand-fast*? Think, said old *Honest*, what should I think? I thought we had an honest Man upon the Road, and therefore should have his Company by and by. *If you thought not amiss, how happy am I! But if I be not as I should, I alone must bear it.* That is true, said the other; but your fear doth further confirm me that things are right betwixt the Prince of Pilgrims and your Soul. For he saith, *Blessed is the Man that feareth always*.†

Talk betwixt him and Mr. Honest.

Valiant. Well, But Brother, I pray thee tell us what was it that was the cause of thy being upon thy Knees, even now? Was it for that some special Mercy laid Obligations upon thee, or how?

They found him at Prayer.

Stand. Why we are as you see, upon the *inchanted Ground*,

What it was that fetched him upon his Knees.

and as I was coming along, I was musing with my self of what a dangerous Road, the Road in this place was, and how many that had come even thus far on Pilgrimage, had here been stopt, and been destroyed. I thought also of the manner of the Death with which this place destroyeth Men. Those that die here, die of no violent Distemper; the Death which such die, is not grievous to them. For he that goeth away in a *Sleep*, begins that Journey with Desire and Pleasure. Yea, such acquiesce in the Will of that Disease.

Hon. *Then Mr.* Honest *Interrupting of him said, Did you see the two Men asleep in the Arbor?*

Prov. 10. 7.

Stand. Ai, ai, I saw *Heedless*, and *Too-bold* there; and for ought I know, there they will ly till they Rot. But let me go on in my Tale: As I was thus Musing, as I said, there was one in very pleasant Attire, *but old*, that presented her self unto me, and offered me three things, to wit, her *Body*, her *Purse*, and her *Bed*. Now the Truth is, I was both a weary, and sleepy, I am also as poor as a *Howlet*, and that, perhaps, the *Witch* knew. Well, I repulsed her once and twice, but she put by my Repulses, and smiled. Then I began to be angry, but she mattered that nothing at all. Then she made Offers again, and said, If I would be ruled by her, she would make me great and happy. For, said she, I am the Mistriss of the World, and men are made happy by me. Then I asked her Name, and she told me it was *Madam Bubble*. This set me further from her; but she still followed me with Inticements. Then I betook me, as you see, to my Knees, and with Hands lift up, and crys, I pray'd to him that had said, he would help. So just as you came up, the Gentlewoman went her way. Then I continued to give thanks for this my great Deliverance; for I verily believe she intended no good, but rather sought to make stop of me in my Journey.

Madam Buble, *or this vain World.*

Hon. *Without doubt her Designs were bad. But stay, now you talk of her, methinks I either have seen her, or have read some story of her.*

Standf. Perhaps you have done both.

Hon. *Madam Buble! Is she not a tall comely Dame, something of a Swarthy Complexion?*

Standf. Right, you hit it, she is just such an one.

Hon. *Doth she not speak very smoothly, and give you a Smile at the end of a Sentence?*

Standf. You fall right upon it again, for these are her very Actions.

Hon. *Doth she not wear a great Purse by her Side, and is not her Hand often in it fingering her Mony, as if that was her Hearts delight?*

Standf. 'Tis just so. Had she stood by all this while, you could not more amply set her forth before me, nor have better described her Features.

Hon. Then he that drew her Picture was a good *Limner*, and he that wrote of her, said true.

Greath. This Woman is a *Witch*, and it is by Virtue of her *Sorceries* that this Ground is *enchanted*; whoever doth lay their Head down in *her Lap*, had as good lay it down upon that Block over which the Ax doth hang; and whoever lay their Eyes upon her Beauty, are counted the Enemies of God. This is she that maintaineth in their Splendor, all those that are the Enemies of Pilgrims. Yea, This is she that has bought off many a man from a Pilgrims Life. She is a great *Gossiper*, she is always, both she and her Daughters, at one Pilgrim's Heels or other, now Commending, and then preferring the excellencies of this Life. She is a bold and impudent Slut; She will talk with any Man. She always laugheth Poor Pilgrims to scorn, but highly commends the Rich. If there be one cunning to get Mony in a Place, she will speak well of him, from House to House. She loveth Banqueting, and Feasting, mainly well; she is always at one full Table or another. She has given it out in some places, that she is a Goddess, and therefore some do Worship her. She has her times and open places of Feasting, and she will say and avow it, that none can shew a Food comparable to hers. She promiseth to dwell with Childrens Children, if they will but love and make much of her. She will cast out of her Purse, Gold like Dust, in some places, and to some Persons. She loves to be sought after, spoken well of, and to ly in the Bosoms of Men. She is never weary of commending of her Commodities, and she loves them most that think best of her. She will promise to some Crowns, and Kingdoms, if they will but take her Advice, yet

The World.

Jam. 4. 4.

1 John 2. 15.

many has she brought to the Halter, and ten thousand times more to Hell.

Standf. *O! Said* Stand-fast, *What a Mercy is it that I did resist her; for whither might she a drawn me?*

Greath. Whither! Nay, none but God knows whither. But in general to be sure, she would a drawn thee *into many foolish and*
1 Tim. 6. 9. *hurtful Lusts, which drown men in Destruction and Perdition.*

'Twas she that set *Absalom* against his Father, and *Jeroboam* against his Master. 'Twas she that perswaded *Judas* to sell his Lord, and that prevailed with *Demas* to forsake the godly Pilgrims Life;† none can tell of the Mischief that she doth. She makes Variance betwixt Rulers and Subjects, betwixt Parents and Children, 'twixt Neighbor and Neighbor, 'twixt a Man and his Wife, 'twixt a Man and himself, 'twixt the Flesh and the Heart.

Wherefore good Master *Stand-fast*, be as your Name is, and when you have done all, *stand.*†

At this Discourse there was among the Pilgrims a mixture of Joy and Trembling, but at length *they brake* out and Sang:

What Danger is the Pilgrim in,
How many are his Foes,
How many ways there are to Sin,
No living Mortal knows.
Some of the Ditch, shy are, yet can
Lie tumbling in the Myre:
Some tho they shun the Frying-pan,
Do leap into the Fire.

1 *Part, pag.* 145–6. After this I beheld, until they were come into the Land of *Beulah*, where the Sun shineth Night and Day. Here, because they was weary, they betook themselves a while to Rest. And because this Country was common for Pilgrims, and because the Orchards and Vineyards that were here, belonged to the King of the Celestial Country; therefore they were licensed to make bold with any of his things.

But a little while soon refreshed them here, for the Bells did so ring, and the Trumpets continually sound so Melodiously, that they could not sleep, and yet they received as much refreshing, as if they had slept their Sleep never so soundly.

Here also all the noise of them that walked the Streets, was, *More Pilgrims are come to Town*. And an other would answer, saying, And so many went over the Water, and were let in at the Golden Gates to Day. They would cry again, There is now a Legion of Shining ones, just come to Town; by which we know that there are more Pilgrims upon the Road, for here they come to wait for them and to comfort them after all their Sorrow. Then the Pilgrims got up and walked to and fro: But how were their Ears now filled with heavenly Noises, and their Eyes delighted with Celestial Visions! In this Land, they *heard* nothing, *saw* nothing, *felt* nothing, *smelt* nothing, *tasted* nothing, that was offensive to their Stomach or Mind; only when they tasted of the Water of the River, over which they were to go, they thought that tasted a little Bitterish to the Palate, but it proved sweeter when 'twas down.

Death bitter to the Flesh, but sweet to the Soul.

In this place there was a Record kept of the Names of them that had been Pilgrims of old, and a History of all the famous Acts that they had done. It was here also much discoursed how the *River* to some had had its *flowings*, and what *ebbings* it has had while others have gone over. It has been in a manner *dry* for some, while it has overflowed its Banks for others.

Death has its Ebbings and Flowings like the Tide.

In this place, the Children of the Town would go into the Kings Gardens and gather Nose-gaies for the Pilgrims, and bring them to them with much affection. Here also grew *Camphire*, with *Spicknard*, and *Saffron*, *Calamus*, and *Cinamon*, with all its Trees of *Frankincense*, *Myrrhe*, and *Aloes*, with all *chief* Spices.† With these the Pilgrims Chambers were perfumed, while they stayed here; and with these were their Bodys anointed to prepare them to go over the *River* when the time appointed was come.

Now, while they lay here, and waited for the good Hour; there was a Noyse in the Town, that there was a *Post* come from the Celestial City, with Matter of great Importance, to one *Christiana*, the Wife of *Christian* the Pilgrim. So Enquiry was made for her, and the House was found out where she was, so the Post presented her with a Letter; the Contents whereof was, *Hail, Good Woman, I bring thee Tidings that the Master calleth for thee, and expecteth that thou*

A Messenger of Death sent to Christiana.

His Message.

shouldest stand in his Presence, in Cloaths of Immortality, within this ten Days.

How welcome is Death to them that have nothing to do but to dy.

When he had read this Letter to her, he gave her therewith a *sure* Token that he was a true Messenger, and was come to bid her make hast to be gone. The Token was, *An Arrow with a Point sharpened with Love, let easily into her Heart, which by degrees wrought so effectually with her, that at the time appointed she must be gone.*

Her Speech to her Guide.

When *Christiana* saw that her time was come, and that she was the first of this Company that was to go over: She called for Mr. *Great-heart* her Guide, and told him how Matters were. So he told her he was heartily glad of the News, and could a been glad had the Post came for him. Then she bid that he should give Advice, how all things should be prepared for her Journey.

So he told her, saying, Thus and thus it must be, and we that Survive will accompany you to the Riverside.

To her Children.

Then she called for her Children, and gave them *her Blessing*; and told them that she yet read with Comfort the Mark that was set in their Foreheads, and was glad to see them with her there, and that they had kept their Garments so white. Lastly, She bequeathed to the Poor that little she had, and commanded her Sons and her Daughters to be ready against the Messenger should come for them.

To Mr. Valiant.

When she had spoken these Words to her Guide and to her Children, she called for Mr. *Valiant-for-truth*, and said unto him, Sir, You have in all places shewed your self true-hearted, be Faithful unto Death, and my King will give you a Crown of Life. I would also intreat you to have an Eye to my Children, and if at any time you see them faint, speak comfortably to them. For my Daughters, my Sons Wives, they have been Faithful, and a fulfilling of the Promise upon them, will be their end. But she gave Mr. *Stand-fast* a Ring.

To Mr. Stand-fast.

To old Honest.

Then she called for old Mr. *Honest*, and said of him, Behold an Israelite indeed, in whom is no Guile.† Then said *he*, I wish you a fair Day when you set out for Mount *Sion*, and shall be glad to see that you go over the River dry-shod. But she answered, Come *Wet*, come *Dry*, I long to be gone; for however the Weather is in my Journey, I shall have time enough when I come there to sit down and rest me, and dry me.

Then came in that good Man Mr. *Ready-to-halt* to see her. So she said to him, Thy Travel hither has been with Dificulty, but that will make thy Rest the sweeter. But watch, and be ready, for at an Hour when you think not, the Messenger may come.†

To Mr. Ready-to-halt.

After him, came in Mr. *Dispondencie*, and his Daughter *Much-a-fraid*. To whom she said, You ought with Thankfulness for ever, to remember your Deliverance from the Hands of Gyant *Dispair*, and out of *Doubting-Castle*. The effect of that Mercy is, that you are brought with Safety hither. Be ye watchful, and cast away Fear; be sober, and hope to the End.†

To Dispondencie, *and his Daughter.*

Then she said to Mr. *Feeble-Mind*, Thou was delivered from the Mouth of Gyant *Slay-good*, that thou mightest live in the Light of the Living for ever,† and see thy King with Comfort. Only I advise thee to repent thee of thy aptness to fear and doubt of his Goodness before he sends for thee, lest thou shouldest when he comes, be forced to stand before him for that Fault with Blushing.

To Feeble-mind.

Now the Day drew on that *Christiana* must be gone. So the Road was full of People to see her take her Journey. But behold all the Banks beyond the River were full of Horses and Chariots, which were come down from above to accompany her to the City-Gate. So she came forth and entered the *River* with a *Beck'n* of Fare well, to those that followed her to the River side. The last word she was heard to say here was, *I come Lord, to be with thee and bless thee.*

Her last Day, and manner of Departure.

So her Children and Friends returned to their Place, for that those that waited for *Christiana*, had carried her out of their Sight. So she went, and called, and entered in at the Gate with all the Ceremonies of Joy that her Husband *Christian* had done before her.

At her Departure her Children wept, but Mr. *Great-heart*, and Mr. *Valiant*, played upon the well tuned Cymbal and Harp for Joy. So all departed to their respective Places.

In process of time there came a *Post* to the Town again, and his Business was with Mr. *Ready-to-halt*. So he enquired him out, and said to him, I am come to thee in the Name of him whom thou hast Loved and Followed, tho upon *Crutches*. And

Ready-to-halt *Summoned.*

my Message is to tell thee, that he expects thee at his Table to Sup with him in his Kingdom the next Day after *Easter*. Wherefore prepare thy self for this Journey.

Eccles. 12. 6. Then he also gave him a Token that he was a true Messenger, saying, *I have broken thy golden Bowl*, and loosed *thy silver Cord*.

After this Mr. *Ready-to-halt* called for his Fellow Pilgrims, and told them, saying, I am sent for, and God shall surely visit you also. So he desired Mr. *Valiant* to make his *Will*. And because he had nothing to bequeath to them that should Survive him, but his *Crutches*, and his good *Wishes*, therefore thus he said: *These Crutches, I bequeath to my Son that shall tread in my Steps with an hundred warm Wishes that he may prove better then I have done.* *Promises.* *His Will.*

Then he thanked Mr. *Great-heart*, for his Conduct, and Kindness, and so addressed himself to his Journey. When he came at the brink of the River, he said, Now I shall have no more need of these *Crutches*, since yonder are Chariots and Horses for me to ride on. The last Words he was heard to say, was, *Welcome Life*.† So he went his Way. *His last words.*

Feeble-mind *Summoned.* After this, Mr. *Feeble-mind* had Tidings brought him, that the Post sounded his Horn at his Chamber Door. Then he came in and told him, saying, I am come to tell thee that the Master has need of thee, and that in very little time thou must behold his Face in Brightness. And take this as a Token of the Truth of my Message. *Those that look out at the Windows shall be darkned.* Eccles. 12. 3.

Then Mr. *Feeble-mind* called for his Friends, and told them what Errand had been brought unto him, and what Token he had received of the truth of the Message. Then he said, Since I have nothing to bequeath to any, to what purpose should I make a Will? As for my *feeble Mind*, that I will leave behind me, for that I shall have no need of that in the place whither I go; nor is it worth bestowing upon the poorest Pilgrim: Wherefore when I am gon, I desire, that you Mr. *Valiant*, would bury it in a Dunghil. This done, and the Day being come, in which he was to depart; he entered the *River* as the rest. His last Words were, *Hold out Faith and Patience*. So he went over to the other Side. *He makes no Will.* *His last words.*

When Days, had many of them passed away: Mr. *Dispondencie* was sent for. For a *Post* was come, and brought this Message to him; *Trembling Man, These are to summon thee to be ready with thy King, by the next Lords Day, to shout for Joy for thy Deliverance from all thy Doubtings.*

Mr. Dispondencie's *Summons.*

And said the Messenger, That my Message is true, take this for a Proof. So he gave him *The Grashopper to be a Burthen unto him.* Now Mr. *Dispondencie*'s Daughter, whose Name was *Much-a-fraid*, said, when she heard what was done, that she would go with her Father. Then Mr. *Dispondencie* said to his Friends; My self and my Daughter, you know what we have been, and how troublesomly we have behaved our selves in every Company. My Will and my Daughters is, that our *Disponds*, and slavish Fears, be by no man ever received, from the day of our Departure, for ever; For I know that after my Death they will offer themselves to others. For, to be plain with you, they are *Ghosts*, the which we entertained when we first began to be Pilgrims, and could never shake them off after. And they will walk about and seek Entertainment of the Pilgrims, but for our Sakes, shut ye the Doors upon them.

Eccl. 12. 5.

His Daughter goes too.

His Will.

When the time was come for them to depart, they went to the Brink of the *River*. The last Words of Mr. *Dispondencie*, were, *Farewel Night, welcome Day*. His Daughter went thorow the River singing, but none could understand what she said.

His last words.

Then it came to pass, a while after, that there was a *Post* in the Town that enquired for Mr. *Honest*. So he came to the House where he was, and delivered to his Hand these Lines: *Thou art Commanded to be ready against this Day seven Night, to present thy self before thy Lord, at his Fathers House*. And for a Token that my Message is true, *All thy Daughters of Musick shall be brought low*. Then Mr. *Honest* called for his Friends, and said unto them, I Die, but shall make no Will. As for my Honesty, it shall go with me; let him that comes after be told of this. When the Day that he was to be gone, was come, he addressed himself to go over the *River*. Now the *River* at that time overflowed the Banks in some places. But Mr. *Honest* in his Life time had spoken to one *Good-conscience* to meet him

Mr. Honest *Summoned.*

Eccl. 12. 4.

He makes no Will.

Good-conscience *helps* Mr. Honest *over the River.*

there, the which he also did, and lent him his Hand, and so helped him over. The last Words of Mr. *Honest* were, *Grace Reigns*. So he left the World.

Mr. Valiant *Summoned.*

After this it was noised abroad that Mr. *Valiant-for-truth* was taken with a Summons, by the same *Post* as the other; and had this for a Token that the Summons was true, *That his*

Eccl. 12. 6.

Pitcher was broken at the Fountain. When he understood it, he called for his Friends, and told them of it. Then said he, I am going to my Fathers, and tho with great Difficulty I am got hither, yet now I do not repent me of all the Trouble I have

His Will.

been at to arrive where I am. *My Sword*, I give to him that shall succeed me in my Pilgrimage, and my *Courage* and *Skill*, to him that can get it. My *Marks* and *Scarrs* I carry with me, to be a witness for me, that I have fought his Battels, who now will be my Rewarder. When the Day that he must go hence, was come, many accompanied him to the River side, into which, as he went, he said, *Death, where is thy Sting?* And as he

His last words.

went down deeper, he said, *Grave where is thy Victory?*† So he passed over, and the Trumpets sounded for him on the other side.

Mr. Stand-fast *is summoned.*

Then there came forth a Summons for Mr. *Stand-fast*, (This Mr. *Stand-fast*, was he that the rest of the Pilgrims found upon his Knees in the *inchanted* Ground.) For the *Post* brought it him open in his Hands. The Contents whereof were, *That he must prepare for a change of Life, for his Master was not willing that he should be so far from him any longer*. At this Mr. *Stand-fast* was put into a Muse; Nay, said the Messenger, you need not doubt of the truth of my Message; for here is a Token of

Eccl. 12. 6.

the Truth thereof, *Thy Wheel is broken at the Cistern*. Then

He calls for Mr. Great-Heart. *His Speech to him.*

he called to him Mr. *Great-heart*, who was their Guide, and said unto him, Sir, Altho it was not my hap to be much in your good Company in the Days of my Pilgrimage, yet since the time I knew you, you have been profitable to me. When I came from home, I left behind me a Wife, and five small Children. Let me entreat you, at your Return (for I know that you will go, and return to your Masters House, in Hopes that you may yet be a Conductor to more of the Holy Pilgrims,) that you send to my Family, and let them be acquainted with all that hath, and shall happen unto me. Tell them moreover, of my happy Arrival to this Place, and of the present late blessed Condition that I am in. Tell them also of *Christian*, and of *Christiana* his Wife, and how *She* and her Children came after her Husband. Tell them also of what a happy End she made, and whither she is gone. I have little or nothing to send to my Family, except it be Prayers, and Tears for them; of which it will suffice, if thou acquaint them, if paradventure they may prevail. When Mr. *Stand-fast* had thus set things in order, and the time being come for him to hast him away; he also went down to the River. Now there was a great Calm at that time in the River, wherefore Mr. *Stand-fast*, when he was about half way in, he stood a while and talked to his Companions that had waited upon him thither. And he said,

His Errand to his Family.

This River has been a Terror to many, yea the thoughts of it also have often frighted me. But now methinks I stand easie, my Foot is fixed upon that, upon which the Feet of the Priests that bare the Ark of the Covenant stood while *Israel* went over this *Jordan*. The Waters indeed are to the Palate bitter, and to the Stomack cold; yet the thoughts of what I am going to, and of the Conduct that waits for me on the other side, doth lie as a glowing Coal at my Heart.

His last words

Jos. 3. 17.

I see my self now at the *end* of my Journey, my *toilsom* Days are ended. I am going now to see *that* Head that was Crowned with Thorns, and *that* Face that was spit upon,† for me.

I have formerly lived by Hear-say, and Faith, but now I go where I shall live by sight, and shall be with him, in whose Company I delight my self.

I have loved to hear my Lord spoken of, and wherever I have seen the print of his Shooe in the Earth, there I have coveted to set my Foot too.

His Name has been to me as a *Civit-Box*, yea sweeter then all Perfumes. His Voice to me has been most sweet, and his Countenance, I have more desired then they that have most desired the Light of the Sun. His Word I did use to gather for my Food, and for Antidotes against my Faintings. He has held me, and I have kept me from mine Iniquities:† Yea, my Steps hath he strengthened in his Way.

Now while he was thus in Discourse his Countenance changed, his *strong men* bowed under him,† and after he had said, *Take me, for I come unto thee*, he ceased to be seen of them.

But glorious it was, to see how the open Region was filled with Horses and Chariots, with Trumpeters and Pipers, with Singers, and Players on stringed Instruments, to welcome the Pilgrims as they went up and followed one another in at the beautiful Gate of the City.

As for *Christian*'s Children, the four Boys that *Christiana* brought with her, with their Wives and Children, I did not stay where I was, till they were gone over. Also since I came away, I heard one say, that they were yet alive, and so would be for the Increase of the Church in that Place where they were for a time.

Shall it be my Lot to go that way again, I may give those that desire it, an Account of what I here am silent about; mean time I bid my Reader *Adieu*.

FINIS

EXPLANATORY NOTES

Abbreviations

Brown	John Brown, *John Bunyan (1628–88): His Life, Times and Work*, rev. Frank Mott Harrison (1928)
Foxe	John Foxe, *Acts and Monuments of Matters most Special and Memorable, Happening in the Church, with an Universall Historie of the Same*, 3 vols. (1632 edn.)
GA	John Bunyan, *Grace Abounding with Other Spiritual Autobiographies*, ed. John Stachniewski with Anita Pacheco (Oxford World's Classics, 1998)
HW	John Bunyan *The Holy War*, ed. Roger Sharrock and James F. Forrest, Oxford English Texts (Oxford, 1980)
Misc. Works	*The Miscellaneous Works of John Bunyan*, gen. ed. Roger Sharrock, 13 vols. (Oxford, 1976–94)
Mr. B	John Bunyan, *The Life and Death of Mr. Badman*, ed. James F. Forrest and Roger Sharrock, Oxford English Texts (Oxford, 1988)
OET	*The Pilgrim's Progress*, ed. James Blanton Wharey, rev. Roger Sharrock, Oxford English Texts, 2nd edn. (Oxford, 1960)
PP	*The Pilgrim's Progress* (page references to the present edition)

Quotations from the Bible are from the Authorized Version, first published in 1611. This was Bunyan's main text, though he occasionally quotes from, or remembers the phrasing of, the Geneva Bible, first published in 1560.

THE FIRST PART

3 *writing of the Way | And Race of Saints*: the work referred to here is almost certainly Bunyan's *The Heavenly Footman: or, A Description of the Man that gets to Heaven* (posthumously published in 1698), a sermon-treatise developing Paul's metaphor of the Christian life as a race to obtain salvation: 'so run, that ye may obtain' (1 Cor. 9: 24).

Still as I pull'd, it came: the way a spinner would pull flax or wool from the distaff with her finger and thumb, twisting it to make the thread.

5 *Lime-twigs, light and bell*: lime-twigs were twigs smeared with bird-lime (a very sticky substance) for catching birds. In his *Sports and Pastimes of the People of England* (1801 edn., p. 31), Joseph Strutt quotes from an early seventeenth-century description of a method of catching birds like woodcocks and partridges on very dark nights, which involved carrying a bright light and ringing a bell to startle them. 'What with the bell, and what with the light, the birds will be so amazed, that when you come near them, they will turn up their white bellies: your companions shall then lay their nets quietly upon them, and take them.'

5 *Pearl may in a Toads-head dwell*: it was popularly believed that the toad had a precious stone in its head. See *As You Like It*, II. i. 12–14.

Types, Shadows: in interpretation of the Bible, persons, events, and things in the Old Testament were often regarded as 'types' or 'shadows' of persons, events, and things in the Christian dispensation, the latter being referred to as 'antitypes', or fulfilments of the types (see Introduction, p. xxv). In *GA*, Bunyan explains how he came to read the Bible typologically. So, for example, he learned to interpret the 'clean' and 'unclean' beasts in the Old Testament as 'types of men; the clean types of them that were the People of God; but the unclean types of such as were the children of the wicked One' (*GA*, 22). Faithful offers a similar interpretation of the Mosaic text (see above, p. 98). Examples of typological interpretation of Scripture may be found in nearly everything Bunyan wrote. See *Misc. Works*, vii, pp. xv–xliii; viii, pp. xliii–l; xii, pp. xxxviii–xlii.

6 *pins and loops . . . blood of Lambs*: Bunyan here gives a list of references from the Old Testament which may be interpreted typologically. The 'pins and loops' refer to details of the furnishings of the tabernacle (Exod. 26: 4–5, 27: 19). According to Henry Ainsworth, in his *Annotations upon the Five Books of Moses* (London, 1639), the pins (or stakes) signify 'the stability of the Church, and the ministry of God's Word fastening the same', while the 'loops' (used to fasten curtains together) teach us how 'by faith and love in Christ, the Saints are fastened'. The animals, birds, and herbs mentioned by Bunyan were used in the Passover feast, and were regarded as 'types' of Christ's sacrifice on the cross. For calves, see Lev. 16: 3, 14, 15 (and also Heb. 9: 12, 19); for sheep, Lev. 1: 10, 22: 19; for heifers, Deut. 21: 3–9; for rams, Exod. 29: 15–32, Lev. 5: 15–16; for birds, Lev. 14: 4–7; for herbs and blood of lambs, Exod. 12: 3–8.

of our souls bereave: i.e. 'from our souls take (or snatch) away'.

holy Writ . . . (Dark Figures, Allegories): earlier Puritan authors of allegorical works had often defended their method of writing by citing biblical precedent. See, for example, Richard Bernard's postscript to his immensely popular allegory *The Isle of Man: or, The Legall Proceedings in Man-shire against Sinne* (1627; 7th edn. 1630): '*Nathan* did teach *David* by an allegorie . . . *Ezekiel* taught the Jews so too, and . . . our Saviour spake many parables to his hearers.'

Silver Shrines: a reference to the silver shrines made to the goddess Diana at Ephesus, Acts 19: 24.

7 *Sound words . . . refuse*: see 1 Tim. 4: 6–7, 'thou shalt be a good minister of Jesus Christ, nourished up in the words of faith and of good doctrine . . . But refuse profane and old wives' fables.'

Dialogue-wise: many Puritan writers in the seventeenth century wrote works in dialogue form. For example, in Arthur Dent's *The Plaine Mans Path-way to Heaven* (1601, and numerous subsequent editions), four characters, Theologus (a divine), Philagathus (an honest man), Asunetus (an ignorant man), and Antilegon (a caviller), discuss religious matters. This was one of two books Bunyan's first wife brought him as part of her dowry (*GA*, 9).

taught us first to Plow: see Isa. 28: 24–6, 'Doth the ploughman plow all day to sow? . . . his God doth instruct him to discretion, and doth teach him also.' Also, 1 Cor. 9: 10, 'For our sakes, no doubt, this is written: that he that ploweth should plow in hope.'

8 *the everlasting Prize*: see 1 Cor. 9: 24, 'Know ye not that they which run in a race run all, but one receiveth the prize? So run that ye may obtain'; and Phil. 3: 14, 'I press toward the mark for the prize of the high calling of God in Christ Jesus.'

stick like Burs: a proverbial expression.

picking meat: trifles, dainty portions of food.

10 (marg.) *The Gaol*: this marginal note identifying the 'Denn' as a prison first appeared in the third edition (1679). Bunyan probably wrote most of the first part of *PP* towards the end of his twelve-year term as a prisoner in Bedford county gaol, 1660–72 (see OET, pp. xxi–xxxv). The dungeon in Doubting Castle is also referred to as a 'Den'; see above, p. 114.

Raggs . . . burden: the imagery of rags, to represent worthless claims to righteousness, and a great burden, as representing human sinfulness, is borrowed from some of the biblical texts cited by Bunyan in the margin. See Isa. 64: 6, 'we are all as an unclean thing, and all our righteousnesses are as filthy rags', and Psalm 38: 4, 'mine iniquities are gone over mine head: as an heavy burden they are too heavy for me.'

what shall I do?: see Acts 2: 37, 'Men and brethren, what shall we do?' and Acts 16: 30, 'Sirs, what must I do to be saved?'

11 *Evangelist*: he represents a minister of the gospel, as does Great-heart in Part Two. In these representations of the ideal Christian minister, Bunyan is no doubt recalling the spiritual guidance he himself received from the first pastor of the Bedford Independent congregation, John Gifford, 'whose doctrine, by God's grace, was much for my stability' (see *GA*, 24, 34).

Tophet: the name means 'place of burning' (see Isa. 30: 33), and is often used symbolically for Hell. See *Paradise Lost*, I. 404.

Wicket-gate: a 'wicket' is a small, narrow gate or door. As Evangelist later explains to Christian (p. 23), the Wicket Gate here is the 'strait gate' of Matt. 7: 13–14 and Luke 13: 24—'Enter ye in at the strait gate . . . which leadeth unto life'—and entry thus represents the beginning of the process of conversion for Christian. Early in his own conversion experience, Bunyan had a vision in which he had to pass with great difficulty through a 'narrow gap, like a little door-way' in a wall (*GA*, 18–19). He published a sermon entitled *The Strait Gate, or, Great Difficulty of Going to Heaven* (1676), based on Luke 13: 24; *Misc. Works*, v. 69–130.

13 *City of Destruction*: Bunyan borrows the name from Isa. 19: 18, where reference is made to a city called 'the city of destruction'.

Christian: this name is given to him only after the process of conversion has begun; his previous name was Graceless (see p. 47).

14 *wiser* . . . *reason*: see Prov. 26: 16, 'The sluggard is wiser in his own conceit than seven men that can render a reason.'

16 *Dispond*: the temptation to despair was a recognized stage in the process of conversion, as Help explains (p. 17). Much of Bunyan's account of his own conversion is taken up with his anguished struggles against despair of his salvation, and he often speaks of 'sinking', and of finding himself 'as on a miry bog, that shook if I did but stir' (see especially *GA*, 24–33, 38–66).

(marg.) *The Promises*: these are texts from the Bible giving assurance of salvation by faith. Bunyan frequently refers to such texts as 'promises' (see e.g. *GA*, 70–1).

17 *this sixteen hundred years*: i.e. since the gospel began to be proclaimed at the time of Christ.

18 *Mr. Worldly-Wiseman*: as Evangelist explains to Christian on p. 24, Mr Worldly-Wiseman represents reliance on moral behaviour, or 'good works' according to the Old Testament law, rather than true saving grace. His lofty tone and confident manner contrast tellingly with Christian's agonized uncertainty. In his portrait of Worldly-Wiseman, Bunyan may have had in mind some of the views of Edward Fowler, rector of Northill in Bedfordshire. In a book entitled *The Design of Christianity* (1671), Fowler described the 'Precepts of the Gospel' as being to 'perform good Actions . . . after a right manner, with right ends', following the pattern of 'our Saviour's most Excellent Life'. Bunyan strongly attacked these views in *A Defence of the Doctrine of Justification, by Faith* (1672), describing Fowler's idea of natural human righteousness as 'Diametrically opposite to the simplicity of the Gospel of Christ'. For more details, see OET, 314–15; *Misc. Works*, iv, pp. xx–xxv, 1–130.

19 *Wearisomness* . . . *death*: this list of the troubles the pilgrims will have to endure draws upon the apostle Paul's account in 2 Cor. 11: 23–7 of the afflictions he suffered: 'in labours more abundant, in stripes above measure, in prisons more frequent, in deaths oft . . . in perils of waters, in perils of robbers . . . in weariness and painfulness, in watchings often, in hunger and thirst, in fastings often, in cold and nakedness.'

20 *yonder high hill*: the hill is Mount Sinai, where Moses received the Ten Commandments (Exod. 19: 20–5, 20: 1–21). It represents the moral law that condemns all mortals because it cannot be fulfilled. This is why it so terrifies Christian and makes his burden heavier.

lest the Hill should fall on his head: in *GA* Bunyan describes his own fear during his unregenerate days that the church tower at Elstow might fall on him (*GA*, 13).

23 *foot from the way of peace*: see Luke 1: 79, 'to guide our feet into the way of peace'.

the administration of Death: see 2 Cor. 3: 7–9, where 'the ministration of Death', that is, the Mosaic law, is contrasted with 'the ministration of righteousness', the new covenant of grace.

25 *Good-will*: as the one who opens the gate to Christian, Good-will stands for divine grace, Christ's mercy by which sinners are saved.

Mount Zion: Zion (or Sion) is frequently used in the Bible to refer to the city of Jerusalem, and its people, the Israelites (the sons or daughters of Zion). Figuratively, it represents the celestial city, or the kingdom of Heaven, as in Heb. 12: 22: 'ye are come unto mount Sion, and unto the city of the living God, the heavenly Jerusalem.' See note to p. 149.

27 *Belzebub*: more usually known as Beelzebub, the Old Testament god identified in the New Testament as 'the prince of the devils', that is, Satan (Matt. 12: 24, Mark 3: 22, Luke 11: 15).

open Door . . . shut it: see Rev. 3: 8, 'I have set before thee an open door, and no man can shut it.'

28 *Patriarchs*: the Old Testament leaders of Israel: Abraham, Isaac, Jacob, and his twelve sons. See Acts 7: 8.

29 *house of the Interpreter*: during his own conversion Bunyan received instruction from John Gifford, pastor of the Bedford nonconformist congregation: '*Mr. Gifford* . . . took occasion to talke with me . . . he invited me to his house, where I should hear him confer with others about the dealings of God with the Soul: from all which I . . . began to see something of the vanity and inward wretchedness of my wicked heart' (*GA*, 24).

that which will be profitable to thee: the Interpreter instructs Christian by means of a series of emblems, pictures, or tableaux representing some spiritual truth. Books of emblems, made up of allegorical pictures interpreted in accompanying verses, were very popular in the seventeenth century, and it is likely that Bunyan was remembering images from these (for details, see OET, 316–17). Bunyan himself later produced an emblem book, *A Book for Boys and Girls*, first published in 1688. (See *Misc. Works*, vi. 183–269.)

Law of Truth . . . upon its lips: see Mal. 2: 6, 'The law of truth was in his mouth, and iniquity was not found in his lips.'

33 (marg.) *The valiant man*: he is a precursor of Great-heart and Valiant-for-Truth in Part Two, and wears 'the whole armour of God' described in Eph. 6: 11–17: 'take the helmet of salvation, and the sword of the Spirit, which is the word of God.'

the Three: presumably Enoch, Moses, and Elijah, who greet the pilgrims on their arrival at the Celestial City (see p. 152).

34 *Professor*: the word 'professor' was a Puritan term for one who made an open declaration of religious belief, but it was often used negatively, to

imply mere outward profession as opposed to the true practice of religion. Bunyan was particularly hostile to 'formal' professors, those who 'confess Christ with their mouthes, and profess that they know God, but deny him in their works' (*Misc. Works*, i. 91). One of his sermon-treatises, published in 1673, was entitled *The Barren Fig-Tree: or, The Doom and Downfal of the Fruitless Professor* (*Misc. Works*, v. 1–64).

34 *a Man of Despair . . . I cannot*: in this powerful portrayal of the misery of the man in the iron cage, Bunyan is influenced by his reading of *A Relation of the Fearful Estate of Francis Spira, in the Year 1548* (1649, and many editions thereafter). Spira was an Italian Protestant who had renounced his faith and returned to Catholicism, and had later died in despair. In *GA* Bunyan describes the effect on him of reading about Spira: 'every Sentence in that book, every groan of that man . . . his tears, his prayers, his gnashing of teeth, his wringing of hands . . . was as Knives and Daggers in my Soul' (*GA*, 45). Elsewhere Bunyan describes the effect of committing the unpardonable 'Sin against the Holy Ghost' as being 'in the Iron cage, out of which there is neither deliverance nor redemption' (*Misc. Works*, ix. 303). The words of the Man of Despair here—'I cannot get out; O now I cannot'—echo Spira's lamentation at his inability to repent: '*I cannot do it: O now I cannot do it*', quoted by Bunyan in *The Barren Fig-Tree* (1673). See *Misc. Works*, v. 58.

watch, and be sober: see 1 Thess. 5: 6, 'let us not sleep, as do others; but let us watch and be sober'.

35 *I Dreamed . . . Agony*: in *GA* Bunyan describes his own 'fearful dreams': 'I have in my bed been greatly afflicted, while asleep, with the apprehensions of Devils, and wicked spirits, who still, as I then thought, laboured to draw me away with them' (*GA*, 7).

36 *The Comforter*: Christ promised his disciples that when he was gone they would have the Holy Spirit as a 'comforter'; see John 14: 16, 26; 15: 26; 16: 7.

37 *shining ones*: i.e. angels.

a Roll with a Seal upon it: this represents salvation, as is explained on p. 45: 'this Roll was the assurance of his life, and acceptance at the desired Haven'. In *GA* Bunyan speaks of receiving 'an evidence for Heaven, with many Golden Seals thereon' (*GA*, 37). At the end of *PP*, Christian and Hopeful each hand in their 'Certificate' (or roll) to gain admission to the Celestial City, but Ignorance has no certificate to show and is refused entry (pp. 152–4).

39 *Every Fatt must stand upon his own bottom*: a proverbial expression (sometimes as 'every tub'), meaning 'everyone must look after himself'.

Formalist: in *The Strait Gate* (1676), Bunyan describes a 'formalist' as 'a man that hath *lost all* but the *shell* of religion' (*Misc. Works*, v. 125).

42 *wide field . . . dark Mountains*: see Jer. 13: 16, 'before your feet stumble

upon the dark mountains'. A 'field' here refers to a stretch of open land, as opposed to woodland.

a couple of Lions: the lions represent the civil and ecclesiastical persecution of Dissenters which began in 1660 after the restoration of Charles II to the throne. See Introduction, p. xvii. In his preface to *GA*, Bunyan refers to his own imprisonment as being '*between the Teeth of the Lions in the Wilderness*' (*GA*, 3).

44 *Israel . . . Red-Sea*: as a punishment for their 'murmuring', the Children of Israel were ordered by God to return to 'the wilderness, by the way of the Red Sea' (Num. 14: 25; Deut. 1: 40).

45 *doleful Creatures*: see Isa. 13: 21, 'their houses shall be full of doleful creatures'.

Palace . . . Beautiful: the 'Palace' represents the separatist congregation, and Christian's stay there represents the fellowship and mutual support of believers.

47 *Japhet . . . Shem*: the text cited by Bunyan, Gen. 9: 27, reads, 'God shall enlarge Japheth, and he shall dwell in the tents of Shem.' The meaning seems to be that Japheth gets the great favour of being brought into the family of Shem.

51 *Holy, Holy, Holy*: see Isa. 6: 2–3, where six seraphim stand before the throne of God, 'and one cried unto another, and said, Holy, holy, holy, is the Lord of hosts: the whole earth is full of his glory'.

Wife and four small Children: Bunyan had four children by his first wife who died in 1658. In *GA* he describes his distress at being parted from them when he chose to go to prison rather than give up preaching (*GA*, 89–90).

52 *precise*: scrupulous, particularly in matters of religion. Puritans were often referred to as 'precisians'.

fat things . . . refined: see Isa. 25: 6, 'in this mountain shall the Lord of hosts make unto all people a feast of fat things, a feast of wines on the lees, of fat things full of marrow, of wine on the lees well refined'.

stript himself of his glory . . . for the Poor: an allusion to 2 Cor. 8: 9, 'ye know the grace of our Lord Jesus Christ, that, though he was rich, yet for your sakes he became poor, that ye through his poverty might be rich'. (See also Phil. 2: 7.)

53 *Ancient of Days*: this was the name given to God in Dan. 7: 9, 'I beheld till the thrones were cast down, and the Ancient of days did sit, whose garment was white as snow'.

54 *Sword . . . Shooes*: these go to make up the 'whole armour of God', as described by Paul in Eph. 6: 13–18.

Moses Rod . . . Man of Sin: see, in turn, Exod. 4: 2–5, 17; Judg. 4: 21, 7: 16–24, 3: 31, 15: 14–17; 1 Sam. 17: 38–51; 2 Thess. 2: 3–8.

54 *Immanuels Land*: the name Immanuel, or Emmanuel (from the Hebrew meaning 'God [is] with us'), is found in the Old Testament in Isa. 7: 14: 'Behold, a virgin shall conceive, and bear a son, and shall call his name Immanuel.' In Matt. 1: 20–3, this is taken as prophesying the birth of Christ. It is perhaps significant that Emmanuel was a favourite name for Christ among the millenarian group known as Fifth Monarchists, and was the name used for Christ in *HW*.

55 *Bread . . . Wine . . . Raisins*: Bunyan is remembering the food brought by Ziba in 2 Sam. 16: 1, 'two hundred loaves of bread, and an hundred bunches of raisins . . . and a bottle of wine'.

Apollyon: in Rev. 9: 11 there is a description of 'the angel of the bottomless pit, whose name in the Hebrew tongue is Abaddon but in the Greek tongue hath his name Apollyon'. The Greek word means 'the destroyer'. As well as symbolizing the power of the devil, Apollyon also represents the oppressive power of the state. In *An Exposition on the Ten First Chapters of Genesis* (1692), Bunyan refers to 'King *Apollion*' as one of the 'brood of Cain' who persecute the faithful (*Misc. Works*, xii. 179). In *HW*, 'Lord Apollyon' is one of the captains in the army of Diabolus (pp. 12, 174–5, 187, 226, 228).

57 *scales . . . Lion*: in his description of Apollyon Bunyan puts together details from the description of Leviathan in Job 41 ('his scales are his pride . . . out of his nostrils goeth smoke . . . his breath kindleth coals, and a flame goeth out of his mouth') and the beast of Rev. 13: 2 ('the beast which I saw was like unto a leopard, and his feet were as the feet of a bear, and his mouth as the mouth of a lion'). The fight between Christian and Apollyon draws upon descriptions of combats between knights and dragons or giants in popular romances such as Richard Johnson's *Seven Champions of Christendom* (1597). See OET, 322–3 for details. Although later strongly disapproving of them (see *Mr. B*, 40 and *HW*, 31), Bunyan would have read chapbook versions of these romances in his youth. In *A Few Sighs from Hell* (1658), he refers to '*George* on horseback' and '*Bevis* of *Southampton*' (*Misc. Works*, i. 333).

changed a bad for a worse: the more usual form of this proverb is 'to go from bad to worse'. Bunyan may have been remembering the similar proverb, 'to change the bad for the better'.

58 *desirous of vain-glory*: see Gal. 5: 26, 'Let us not be desirous of vain glory.'

59 *the Kings High-way, the way of Holiness*: see Isa. 35: 8, 'And an highway shall be there . . . and it shall be called The way of holiness.' (See also Num. 20: 17.)

61 *Michael*: the Archangel Michael is mentioned in Dan. 10: 13, 21 and 12: 1, as helper of the people of Israel, but the reference here is more likely to the account in Rev. 12: 7 of the war in Heaven, when 'Michael and his angels fought against the dragon'.

Tree of Life: one of the two trees planted by God in the Garden of Eden;

see Gen. 2: 9, 'the tree of life also in the midst of the garden, and the tree of knowledge of good and evil'. Just as Christian is healed by leaves from this tree, so too St George was healed by leaves from a miraculous tree in the *Seven Champions of Christendom* (see OET, 322). In Spenser's *The Faerie Queene*, I. xi. 46–50, the Red Cross Knight is healed by balm from the Tree of Life.

62 *Satyrs*: Bunyan is probably thinking of biblical, not classical satyrs. See Isa. 13: 21 and 34: 14 for descriptions of the desert, where 'satyrs shall dance' and 'the satyr shall cry to his fellows'.

blind have led the blind: see Matt. 15: 14, 'Let them alone: they be blind leaders of the blind' (and also Luke 6: 39). The 'Ditch' represents doctrinal error (the spiritually unenlightened lead the blind into it).

63 *King David once did fall*: the reference here is to David's sin in committing adultery with Bathsheba; see 2 Sam. 11, 12. The 'Quagg' thus represents moral failing.

I will walk in the strength of the Lord God: see Psalm 71: 16, 'I will go in the strength of the Lord God.'

65 *suggested many grievous blasphemies to him*: in *GA* Bunyan describes how he was 'distressed with blasphemies': 'whole flouds of Blasphemies, both against God, Christ, and the Scriptures, was poured upon my spirit, to my great confusion and astonishment' (*GA*, 29, 31).

I will fear none ill: in the Authorized Version of the Bible, this verse from Psalm 23 is rendered as 'I will fear no evil'. Bunyan is evidently remembering here the words of the metrical version by Thomas Sternhold and John Hopkins: 'Yet though I walk in vail of death | Yet will I fear none ill.' First published in 1549, *The Whole Book of Psalms: Collected into English Meeter* was one of the most popular and frequently reprinted books of the seventeenth century.

66 *till more of you be burned*: Giant Pope is referring to the burning of hundreds of Protestants during the reign of the Roman Catholic Queen Mary (1553–8). The heroic suffering of the martyrs was commemorated in the third volume of John Foxe's *Acts and Monuments*, better known as the 'Book of Martyrs' (first published in Latin in 1559, and in English in 1563). An edition of *Acts and Monuments* published in 1632 was the only book, apart from the Bible, that Bunyan had with him in prison (Brown, pp. 153–4). He refers frequently to Foxe in his writings. See *GA*, 77; *Misc. Works*, iii. 134, 154, 306 n., 308 n.; v. 167, 193 n.; vii. 159–63; viii. 383–4; x. 22, 55, 64, 245 n.; xiii. 497.

67 *Avenger of Blood*: see Deut. 19: 6, 'lest the avenger of the blood pursue the slayer' (and also Josh. 20: 5, 9).

last was first: see Matt. 19: 30, 'many that are first shall be last, and the last shall be first'.

69 *it may be writ for a wonder*: it would be surprising.

69 *Adam the first*: in Rom. 5: 12–14 and 1 Cor. 15: 21–2, Paul presents the first (or old) Adam as representing sin and corruption which can only be redeemed by the sacrifice of Christ, the second (or new) Adam.

70 *Put off . . . deeds*: see Col. 3: 9, 'Lie not one to another, seeing that ye have put off the old man with his deeds.'

the Man: i.e. Moses, here representing the moral law as tabulated in the Ten Commandments, and under which all men, without the intervention of Christ, would be condemned.

71 *made a hand of*: made an end of, destroyed. The phrase occurs elsewhere in Bunyan. See *HW*, 250; *Misc. Works*, xiii. 434.

72 *haughty spirit before a fall*: see Prov. 16: 18, 'Pride goeth before destruction, and an haughty spirit before a fall.'

want of understanding in all natural Science: a topical remark, since the Royal Society had received its charter in 1662.

73 *Fools for the Kingdom of Heaven, are wisest*: see 1 Cor. 3: 18–19, 'If any man among you seemeth to be wise in this world, let him become a fool, that he may be wise.'

74 *valiant for the Truth upon the Earth*: see Jer. 9: 3, 'but they are not valiant for the truth upon the earth; for they proceed from evil to evil, and they know not me, saith the Lord'.

cried to God . . . troubles: see Psalm 34: 6, 'This poor man cried, and the Lord heard him, and saved him out of all his troubles.'

76 *of Grace, not of works*: Talkative is referring to Eph. 2: 8–9, 'For by grace are ye saved, through faith . . . not of works, lest any man should boast.'

77 *A Saint abroad, and a Devil at home*: a proverbial saying, sometimes as 'an angel abroad'.

79 *the true Gospel sense of those Texts*: Faithful has interpreted the Old Testament texts 'typologically', revealing their application to the experiences of believers. See note on p. 5 above, and Introduction, p. xxv.

80 *You lie at the catch*: you are watching for an opportunity to catch me out.

When Christ said . . . Blessed are ye if ye do them: see John 13: 17, 'If ye know these things, happy are ye if ye do them.'

81 *sight and sense*: i.e. knowledge, consciousness. The phrase was a favourite one of Bunyan's (see *Misc. Works*, viii. 204, xii. 367; *Mr. B*, 149).

82 *For, not he that . . . the Lord commendeth*: 2 Cor. 10: 18.

83 *From such withdraw thy self*: see 1 Tim. 6: 5, 'Perverse disputings of men of corrupt minds, and destitute of the truth, supposing that gain is godliness: from such withdraw thyself.'

I have dealt plainly . . . perisheth: see Ezek. 3: 18–21, where the prophet is told that if he neglects to warn the wicked man, 'his blood will I require at thine hand'.

peace be to your helpers: see 1 Chron. 12: 18, 'peace, peace be unto thee, and peace be to thine helpers'.

84 *you have not resisted . . . on your side*: this passage is an amalgam of phrases taken from a number of biblical texts. See Heb. 12: 4, 'Ye have not yet resisted unto blood, striving against sin'; Heb. 11: 1, 'faith is the substance of things hoped for, the evidence of things not seen'; Jer. 17: 9, 'The heart is deceitful above all things, and desperately wicked'; Isa. 50: 7, 'the Lord God will help me . . . therefore have I set my face like a flint'; Matt. 28: 18, 'Jesus came and spake unto them, saying, All power is given unto me in heaven and in earth.'

85 *many tribulations . . . abide in you*: see Acts 14: 22, 'we must through much tribulation enter into the kingdom of God'; Acts 20: 23, 'the Holy Ghost witnesseth in every city, saying that bonds and afflictions abide me'.

seal the testimony . . . Crown of life: see Rev. 6: 9, 'I saw . . . the souls of them that were slain for the word of God, and for the testimony which they held'; Rev. 2: 10, 'be thou faithful unto death, and I will give thee a crown of life'.

Vanity-Fair: a fair was held every year in Bunyan's native Elstow, and he may have visited the famous Bartholomew Fair held at Smithfield in London, but in his account of Vanity Fair he is almost certainly drawing upon his knowledge of the fair held every September at Stourbridge near Cambridge. The greatest of English fairs, it was organized on a vast scale, with booths or tents arranged in rows resembling streets. All kinds of goods were on sale, by traders from countries in Europe as well as England and Scotland, and actors, jugglers, puppet-shows, and such like provided entertainment. The fair had its own court, where offenders would be brought before local magistrates for summary trial. See Brown, 254–5.

All that cometh is vanity: Eccles. 11: 8.

Almost five thousand years agone, there were Pilgrims: Bunyan's source here is Heb. 11, where an account is given of the first 'strangers and pilgrims on the earth' from Abel onwards through the patriarchs. The Geneva Bible included a chronology of the world from Adam to the year 1560, which made a total of 5,534 years.

Legion: in Mark 5: 9 and Luke 9: 30 an account is given of a man who dwelt among tombs, possessed by unclean spirits named Legion.

86 *the Ware of Rome*: i.e. Roman Catholicism.

87 *Language of Canaan . . . Barbarians*: the phrase 'language of Canaan' is found in Isa. 19: 18, and the reference to 'barbarians' is taken from 1 Cor. 14: 11, 'if I know not the meaning of the voice, I shall be to him that speaketh a barbarian, and he that speaketh shall be a barbarian unto me'. Puritans were often mocked for their habits of speech and dress. For example, Ben Jonson's comedy *Bartholomew Fair* (1614), which was frequently r[illegible]ed after the Restoration, included a famous caricature of a Jacob[illegible]n, Zeal-of-the-Land Busy.

88 *not rendering . . . blessing*: see 1 Pet. 3: 9, 'not rendering evil for evil, or railing for railing: but contrariwise blessing'.

90 *their Tryal . . . Their Indictment*: some of the procedures and formulae here follow those of an English criminal trial of the seventeenth century, though in having Faithful put to death Bunyan is also drawing upon the accounts of trials and martyrdoms in Foxe. When he himself appeared before the magistrates at the quarter-sessions in Bedford in 1661, the 'bill of indictment' against him charged: 'That John Bunyan of the town of Bedford, labourer . . . hath . . . devilishly and perniciously abstained from coming to church to hear divine service, and is a common upholder of several unlawful meetings and conventicles, to the great disturbance and distraction of the good subjects of this kingdom, contrary to the laws of our sovereign lord the king, &c' (*GA*, 105–6). The portrait of Lord Hategood may recall the behaviour of Sir John Kelyng, chairman of the bench, who was noted for his severity and for his bullying manner. For an example of the way nonconformists could be treated in court, see the account of Richard Baxter's trial before the infamous Lord Chief Justice Jeffreys in 1685 (*The Autobiography of Richard Baxter*, ed. N. H. Keeble (London, 1974), 257–66).

their Prince: i.e. the Devil, 'the prince of this world'; see John 12: 31, 14: 30, 16: 11.

him that is higher then the highest: see Eccles. 5: 8, 'If thou seest the oppression of the poor, and violent perverting of judgment and justice in a province, marvel not at the matter: for he that is higher than the highest regardeth; and there be higher than they.'

91 *Pickthank*: one who 'picks a thank', i.e. flatters, or curries favour. See Shakespeare, *1 Henry IV*, III. ii. 25.

a very pestilent fellow: see Acts 24: 5, 'We have found this man [Paul] a pestilent fellow, and a mover of sedition among all the Jews.'

92 *Thou Runagate, Heretick, and Traitor*: Bunyan may be remembering here the account in Foxe of the trial of George Wishart, who was repeatedly described by his prosecutor as a 'heretike, runnagate, traitor and theefe' (Foxe, ii. 617–20).

95 *they Scourged him . . . at the Stake*: in having Faithful tortured in this way, Bunyan would have had in mind some of the gruesome woodcuts in Foxe. In the first volume of the *Acts and Monuments*, between pages 44 and 45, there is a large fold-out woodcut illustration entitled 'Persecutions of the Primitive Church under the Heathen Tyrants of Rome', which depicts martyrs suffering all the tortures inflicted on Faithful, and others such as having their eyes bored out, and being boiled and roasted alive. In volume iii of Foxe there are many illustrations of Marian martyrs being tortured and burned at the stake.

a Chariot and a couple of Horses: in 2 Kings 2: 11, a 'chariot of fire, and horses of fire' descend and take Elijah up to heaven.

97 *By-ends*: a 'by-end' is a secondary consideration. In the figure of By-ends Bunyan may be satirizing former Puritan clergymen who set aside their principles and conformed to the re-established Church of England in 1662 in order to escape being ejected and losing their livelihoods.

a Water-man, looking one way, and Rowing another: a proverbial expression.

98 *if the Sun shines*: the phrase 'where the sun shines there resort' was proverbial.

99 *Mr. Save-all*: i.e. a miserly person who saves all his money. Bunyan may also intend this character to represent the belief that Christ died for all, not only the elect.

Mr. Gripe-man: a 'gripe' was a covetous person, especially a usurer.

righteous over-much: see Eccles. 7: 16, 'Be not righteous over much.'

100 *hazzarding all for God*: cf. Acts 15: 26, 'Men that have hazarded their lives for the name of our Lord Jesus Christ.'

wise as Serpents: in Matt 10: 16 Christ tells his disciples, 'Behold, I send you forth as sheep in the midst of wolves; be ye therefore wise as serpents, and harmless as doves.'

make hay when the Sun shines: proverbial.

God sends . . . sometimes Sunshine: see Matt. 5: 45, '[God] maketh his sun to rise on the evil and on the good, and sendeth rain on the just and the unjust.'

Job saies . . . lay up gold as dust: see Job 22: 23–4, where Eliphaz (not Job) says, 'If thou return to the Almighty . . . then shalt thou lay up gold as dust.'

101 *making no question for conscience sake*: see 1 Cor. 10: 25, 27, 'whatsoever is set before you, eat, asking no question for conscience sake'.

102 *unlawful to follow Christ for loaves . . . Joh. 6*: see John 6: 26, where, after the feeding of the five thousand, Christ rebukes those who sought him 'not because ye saw the miracles, but because ye did eat of the loaves and were filled'.

make . . . religion a stalking horse: a proverbial expression. It appears elsewhere in Bunyan's writings; see *Misc. Works*, v. 91; *Mr. B*, 68.

103 *Judas the Devil . . . Son of perdition*: Judas, described as 'a devil' in John 6: 70, betrayed Christ for thirty pieces of silver. See Matt. 26: 14–16; John 17: 12.

your reward . . . your works: see Matt. 16: 27, 'the Son of man shall come in the glory of his Father with his angels; and then he shall reward every man according to his works'.

flames of a devouring fire: the phrase is taken from Isa. 29: 6, 30: 30.

Lucre: Bunyan may be alluding here to Samuel's sons, who 'turned aside after lucre' (1 Sam. 8: 3), but he must also have had in mind the denunciations of 'filthy lucre' in the New Testament (1 Tim. 3: 3, 8; Tit. 1: 7, 11; 1 Pet. 5: 2).

104 *Demas*: Paul writes in 2 Tim. 4: 10 that 'Demas hath forsaken me, having loved this present World'.

one of his Majesties Judges: as the marginal reference indicates, this is the apostle Paul.

109 *Doubting-Castle . . . Giant Despair*: the temptation to doubt his own salvation was something with which Bunyan himself had to struggle for a long time. In *GA* he describes a period of two years during which he believed that he had committed the unpardonable sin (*GA*, 40–66). Giant Despair resembles the giants of folk-tale and popular romance (see OET, 331), but he also acts very much like an English landowner dealing with trespassers.

110 *Diffidence*: not 'reticence' as now, but want of faith or confidence, mistrust, distrust, doubt.

Crab-tree: the common apple-tree, which was particularly crooked and knotty.

112 *Thou shalt do no murther*: Jesus repeats this commandment in Matt. 19: 18.

no murderer hath eternal life: see 1 John 3: 15, 'ye know that no murderer hath eternal life abiding in him'.

113 *they trembled greatly, and . . . Christian fell into a Swound*: in the depths of his own despair, Bunyan was 'struck into a very great trembling . . . I felt also such a clogging and heat at my stomach by reason of this my terrour, that I was . . . as if my breast-bone would have split in sunder' (*GA*, 46).

playedst the man: Bunyan is no doubt recalling from Foxe's *Acts and Monuments* the famous words of Bishop Latimer to Bishop Ridley as they were being burned at the stake in Oxford in 1555. 'Be of good comfort M[aster] Ridley, and play the man, we shall this day light such a Candle by Gods grace in England, as I trust shall never be put out' (iii. 503).

114 *Key . . . called Promise*: Bunyan's allegorical point is that the pilgrims had no need to despair because biblical verses (keys) assure them of their salvation. The account of their escape is reminiscent of Peter's miraculous escape from prison, when his chains fell off and the outer gate 'opened . . . of his own accord' (Acts 12: 6–10). In *GA* Bunyan speaks of the Scriptures as being 'the Keys of the Kingdom of Heaven' (*GA*, 69), borrowing the phrase from Matt. 16: 19.

damnable: i.e. damnably, used as a strong intensive. Cf. *The Winter's Tale*, III. ii. 185. As is suggested in OET, 332, Bunyan may be indulging in some 'grim theological punning'. In many nineteenth-century editions of *PP*, the word was omitted or changed to phrases such as 'desperately hard'.

115 *Immanuels Land*: see note to p. 54 above.

118 *men walking . . . among the Tombs*: the allusion is to the story in Mark 5: 2–6 of the 'man with an unclean spirit, who had his dwelling among the tombs . . . And always, night and day, he was in the mountains, and in the tombs, crying, and cutting himself with stones.' In his time of greatest despair, Bunyan compared himself to this man (*GA*, 53).

Esau . . . and Saphira his wife: see, in turn, Gen. 25: 29–34 (Esau); Matt. 26: 14–16, 21–5, 47–50 (Judas); 2 Tim. 4: 14–15 (Alexander); Acts 5: 1–10 (Ananias and Sapphira).

119 *So I awoke from my Dream*: this curious interruption has been explained as referring to Bunyan's release from his first period of imprisonment in 1672 (see OET, pp. xxxi, 333).

120 *I pray . . . and give Alms*: these words of Ignorance's echo those of the Pharisee who prayed in the temple, 'I fast twice in the week, I give tithes of all that I possess', Luke 18: 12.

a Theif and a Robber: see John 10: 1, 'He that entereth not by the door into the sheepfold, but climbeth up some other way, the same is a thief and a robber.'

121 *even as he is able to bear it*: see 1 Cor. 3: 2, 'I have fed you with milk, and not with meat: for hitherto you were not able to bear it.'

as white as a clout: a proverbial expression, more usually in the form 'as pale as a clout'. (A clout was a sheet.) See *Romeo and Juliet*, II. iii. 188.

122 *his Jewels . . . his spending Money*: as is clear from Christian's later explanation, the 'jewels' represent Little-faith's saving faith. Although he may doubt it, his salvation is in fact secure.

123 *one, upon whose head is the Shell to this very day*: alluding to the proverbial lapwing (or plover) chick that 'runs away with the shell on its head'. See *Hamlet*, v. ii. 139.

Esau's Birth-right was Typical: Esau's 'birthright' as the first-born son meant that he should have been particularly consecrated and given unto God (Exod. 22: 29), but instead he sold his birthright to his brother Jacob (Gen. 25: 29–34). In *GA*, Bunyan gives an account of the terrifying effect on him of the verses in Heb. 12: 16–17 describing Esau's fate: 'For ye know how that afterward, when he would have inherited the blessing, he was rejected: for he found no place of repentance, though he sought it carefully with tears.' He later came to understand the 'New Testament stile and sence' of the passage: 'so far as I could conceive, this was the mind of God, That the *Birth-right* signified *Regeneration*, and the *Blessing* the *Eternal Inheritance*' (*GA*, 65).

125 *quit my self like a man*: see 1 Cor. 16: 13, 'stand fast in the faith, quit you like men, be strong'.

handle Goliah as David did: for the story of how David slew the giant Goliath with a sling stone, see 1 Sam. 17: 4–51.

one of the weak, and therefore he went to the walls: the saying 'the weakest go to the wall' was proverbial. (In medieval churches, which did not have pews, benches were set along the walls for the aged and infirm.)

125 *throw up his heels*: a wrestling term. See *As You Like It*, III. ii. 193.

126 *We despaired even of life*: see 2 Cor. 1: 8, 'we were pressed out of measure, above strength, insomuch that we despaired even of life'.

made David groan, mourn, and roar: many references could be cited here, but see Psalm 38, where David speaks of 'groaning' (v. 9) and 'mourning' (v. 6) because of his sins, and says, 'I have roared by reason of the disquietness of my heart' (v. 8).

Heman and Hezekiah: Psalm 88, a cry to God for help in trouble, was traditionally ascribed to Heman, grandson of Samuel. The story of King Hezekiah and his struggle with the Assyrians is recounted in 2 Kings 18–19.

Peter . . . sorry Girle: having declared that he would stand by Christ, Peter, when questioned by a young woman, denied knowing him. See Matt. 26: 33–5, 69–75; Mark 14: 29–31, 66–72; Luke 22: 31–4, 55–62.

127 *Leviathan*: see Job 41 for a description of the great leviathan, or sea animal, often taken to represent the Devil (see Isa. 27: 1).

uncircumcised Philistine: see 1 Sam. 17: 26, 36, where David describes Goliath as an 'uncircumcised Philistine'.

man black of flesh . . . light Robe: this figure of a black man dressed in a white robe seems to represent false ministers, who would mislead and entangle believers. As the shining one with the whip points out (p. 128), the source of the image is 2 Cor. 11: 13–14: 'such are false apostles, deceitful workers, transforming themselves into the apostles of Christ. And no marvel; for Satan himself is transformed into an angel of light.' (For details of various other interpretations, see OET, 335.)

131 *Two are better . . . for thy labour*: see Eccles. 4: 9–10, 'Two are better than one; because they have a good reward for their labour. For if they fall, the one will lift up his fellow.'

Where God began with us: i.e the subject of their conversation is to be their conversion experiences. Members of Dissenting congregations such as the one in Bedford were required to give an oral account of their conversions, and these were often published as spiritual autobiographies. Hopeful's account here follows the pattern of Bunyan's own experiences as recorded in *GA*.

133 *the Shop-keeper may . . . cast him into Prison till he shall pay the debt*: ever since the Middle Ages, creditors in England had had the right to have debtors put in prison and kept there until they paid their debts. The system was not abolished until the nineteenth century.

135 *God be merciful to me a sinner*: this was the cry of the publican in Christ's parable of the Pharisee and the publican, Luke 18: 13.

136 *I saw the Lord Jesus look down from Heaven upon me*: in *GA* Bunyan

describes how on one occasion he 'looked up to Heaven, and was as if I had with the eyes of my understanding, seen the Lord Jesus looking down upon me, as being very hotly displeased with me' (*GA*, 10).

My grace is sufficient for thee: this text was important to Bunyan during his own struggles with religious despair: 'one day as I was in a Meeting of God's people, full of sadness and terrour . . . these words did with great power suddainly break in upon me, *My grace is sufficient for thee, my grace is sufficient for thee, my grace is sufficient for thee*; three times together; and O methought that every word was a mighty word unto me' (*GA*, 59).

him that cometh to me, I will in no wise cast out: Bunyan himself had derived great comfort from this text, even though 'Satan would greatly labour to pull this promise from me, telling of me, that Christ did not mean me' (*GA*, 61).

He died for our sins . . . between God and us: see Rom. 4: 25, 'Who was delivered for our offences, and was raised again for our justification'; Rev. 1: 5, 'Unto him that loved us, and washed us from our sins in his own blood'; 1 Tim. 2: 5, 'there is . . . one mediator between God and men, the man Christ Jesus'.

satisfaction for my sins by his blood: the doctrine of 'satisfaction', i.e. the atonement made by Christ for the sins of the world by his death on the cross, was a key element in Bunyan's theology, according to which the justice of God had to be fully 'satisfied'.

137 *Yea I thought . . . for the sake of the Lord Jesus*: the words here are very close to Bunyan's own in *GA*: 'then I thought, had I had a thousand gallons of blood within my veins, I could freely have spilt it all at the command and feet of this my Lord and Saviour' (*GA*, 55).

The Soul of the Sluggard . . . hath nothing: quotation from Prov. 13: 4.

138 *Ask my fellow if I be a Thief*: a proverbial saying, sometimes as 'ask my companion'.

The imagination of mans heart is evil from his Youth: Gen. 8: 21.

139 *Justification*: in Protestant theology, to be 'justified' was to be completely acquitted of sin before God and pronounced just. Justification freed the sinner from the guilt of sin, the condemnation of God's law, and the threat of eternal punishment. This justification was accomplished by the 'imputation' of Christ's righteousness to the sinner and earned by faith alone. See Introduction, p. xxvii.

140 *under the skirt*: there may be an allusion here to Ruth 3: 9, where Boaz spreads the 'skirt' of his garment over Ruth as a sign that he has 'redeemed' her (see also Ruth 4: 1–13).

What! . . . believe it: Ignorance here accuses Christian of antinomianism, or the belief that Christians are by grace set free from the obligation to obey the moral law. These beliefs were put into practice by groups such as the Ranters in the seventeenth century. In *GA* Bunyan describes meeting a Ranter, who 'gave himself up to all manner of filthiness, especially

Uncleanness . . . when I laboured to rebuke his wickedness, he would laugh' (*GA*, 16).

142 *He hath blinded their eyes, lest they should see*: see John 12: 40, 'He hath blinded their eyes, and hardened their heart; that they should not see with their eyes, nor understand with their heart, and be converted.'

143 *sins, and of the wages that was due thereto*: see Rom. 6: 23, 'For the wages of sin is death.'

not every one that cries, Lord, Lord: see Matt. 7: 21, 'Not every one that saith unto me, Lord, Lord, shall enter into the kingdom of heaven.'

145 *Hearing, Reading, Godly Conference*: i.e. hearing sermons, reading the Bible, discussing religious matters with other believers.

perish in their own deceivings: see 2 Pet. 2: 13, where the ungodly are described as 'sporting themselves with their own deceivings'.

the Country of Beulah: see Isa. 62: 4, 'thou shalt be called Hephzibah [meaning "for the Lord delighteth in thee"], and thy land Beulah [meaning "married"]'.

146 *the City . . . view thereof*: this view of the Celestial City draws upon the elaborate descripton of the New Jerusalem in Rev. 21: 10–27, where the walls were 'garnished with all manner of precious stones' and the 'twelve gates were twelve pearls . . . and the street of the city was pure gold'. Bunyan had earlier written a lengthy millenarian treatise on the New Jerusalem, *The Holy City* (1665). See *Misc. Works*, iii. 69–196.

If you see . . . sick of love: see S. of S. 5: 8, 'I charge you, O daughters of Jerusalem, if ye find my beloved, that ye tell him, that I am sick of love.'

147 *Enoch and Elijah*: neither Enoch nor Elijah experienced death. Enoch was 'translated that he should not see death' while Elijah 'went up by a whirlwind into heaven' (Gen. 5: 24; Heb. 11: 5; 2 Kings 2: 11).

148 *I sink in deep waters . . . Selah*: Bunyan is combining phrases from Psalm 42: 7, 'all thy waves and billows are gone over me', Psalm 69: 2, 'I am come into deep waters, where the floods overflow me', and Psalm 88: 7, 'thou hast afflicted me with all thy waves. Selah'.

the sorrows of death have compassed me about: see Psalm 18: 4–5, 'The sorrows of death compassed me . . . the sorrows of hell compassed me about.'

the Land that flows with Milk and Honey: Canaan, the promised land to which the Israelites journeyed from Egypt through the wilderness, was often described as 'a land flowing with milk and honey' (Exod. 3: 8, 17, 13: 5, 33: 1–3). It came to be used symbolically for Heaven, the land to which saints journey through the wilderness of this world (Heb. 11: 16), as at the end of Bunyan's preface to *GA*, 'My dear Children, The Milk and Honey is beyond this Wilderness' (*GA*, 5).

a great darkness and horror fell upon Christian: an allusion to Gen. 15: 12, 'a deep sleep fell upon Abram; and lo, an horror of great darkness fell upon him'.

149 *Jesus Christ maketh thee whole*: these are the words of Peter to Aeneas, Acts 9: 34.

the enemy . . . gone over: see Exod. 15: 16, 'Fear and dread shall fall upon [the Canaanites]; by the greatness of thine arm they shall be as still as a stone; till thy people pass over.'

ministring Spirits . . . Heirs of Salvation: see Heb. 1: 14, 'Are they not all ministering spirits, sent forth to minister for them who shall be heirs of salvation?'

Mount Sion . . . made perfect: see Heb. 12: 22–4, 'But ye are come unto Mount Sion, and unto the city of the living God, the heavenly Jerusalem, and to an innumerable company of angels, to the general assembly and church of the firstborn, which are written in heaven, and to God the Judge of all, and to the spirits of just men made perfect.' These verses were particularly important in Bunyan's own assurance of salvation. In *GA* he describes how, one night, they 'came bolting in upon me' to his great joy: 'These words also have oft since this time been great refreshment to my Spirit' (*GA*, 74–5).

151 *sorrow, sickness . . . passed away*: see Rev. 21: 4, 'And God shall wipe away all tears from their eyes; and there shall be no more death, neither sorrow, nor crying, neither shall there be any more pain: for the former things are passed away.'

resting upon their Beds . . . rightousness: see Isa. 57: 2, 'they shall rest in their beds, each one walking in his uprightness'.

153 *Enter ye into the joy of your Lord*: these are the words of the lord of the servants to the good and faithful servants in the parable of the talents, Matt. 25: 21, 23.

Crowns . . . Palms . . . Harps: the 'four and twenty elders' who sit around the throne in Rev. 4: 4 and 5: 8 are described as wearing 'crowns of gold' and as having 'every one of them harps'. In Rev. 7: 9 there is a description of a 'great multitude, which . . . stood before the throne . . . clothed with white robes, and palms in their hands'.

them that had wings . . . is the Lord: see Rev. 4: 8, 'the four beasts had each of them six wings about him . . . and they rest not day and night, saying Holy, holy, holy, Lord God Almighty'.

154 *I have eat . . . in our Streets*: see Luke 13: 25–7, 'Then shall ye begin to say, We have eaten and drunk in thy presence, and thou has taught in our streets. But he shall say . . . I know you not.'

bind him hand and foot: see Matt. 22: 13, 'Bind him hand and foot, and take him away, and cast him into outer darkness.'

THE SECOND PART

160 *Counterfeit the Pilgrim, and his name*: Bunyan is referring here to Thomas Sherman, a General Baptist preacher who published *The Second Part of*

The Pilgrim's Progress in 1682. There were many subsequent imitations and adaptations, a testimony to the amazing popularity of Bunyan's work. (For details, see OET, 339.) In 1688, Bunyan's publisher, Nathaniel Ponder, complained about pirates who 'put the two first letters of [Bunyan's] name ... to their rhimes and ridiculous books, suggesting to the world as if they were his' (Brown, 435).

161 *My Pilgrims Book has travel'd Sea and Land*: the first American edition of *The Pilgrim's Progress* was published in Boston in 1681. There were translations into Dutch in 1682 and French in 1685.

Trim'd ... Gems: i.e. handsomely bound.

my Larks leg is beter than a Kite: a proverbial saying, usually in the form 'A leg of a lark is better than the body of a kite.'

162 *Jacob ... weep*: see Gen. 29: 9–11, 'Rachel came with her father's sheep ... and Jacob kissed Rachel, and lifted up his voice, and wept.'

163 *Render them not reviling for revile*: see 1 Pet. 2: 23, 'Who, when he was reviled, reviled not again.'

164 *young ones cri'd Hosanah ... did deride*: see Matt. 21: 15, 'when the chief priests and scribes saw ... the children crying in the temple, and saying, Hosanna to the Son of David; they were sore displeased'.

Life inherit: see Matt. 19: 29, 'shall inherit everlasting life'.

167 *Fountain of Life*: see Psalm 36: 9, 'For with thee is the fountain of life.'

Chain of Gold ... Crown of Gold: see Gen. 41: 42, where Pharaoh 'put a gold chain about [Joseph's] neck'; Psalm 21: 3, 'thou settest a crown of pure gold on his head'.

169 *rent the Caul of her Heart*: see Hos. 13: 8, 'I ... will rend the caul of their heart.' (A caul is any membrane enclosing organs of the body, in particular the heart, and the foetus before birth.)

What shall I do to be saved: see note to p. 10 above.

Snares of Death: see 2 Sam. 22: 6, 'The sorrows of hell compassed me about; the snares of death prevented me' (also in Psalm 8: 5).

Wo, worth the day: Ezek. 30: 2, 'Son of man, prophesy and say, Thus saith the Lord God; Howl ye, Woe worth the day!'

170 *on a Throne with a Rainbow about his Head*: see Rev. 4: 2–3, 'one sat on the throne ... and there was a rainbow round about the throne'.

Peace be to this House: Luke 10: 5, 'into whatsoever house ye enter, first say, Peace be to this house'.

Secret: in naming this character 'Secret', Bunyan may be alluding to Paul's description of the gospel as 'the mystery, which was kept secret since the world began, But now is made manifest' (Rom. 16: 25–6).

171 *feed thee ... thy Father*: see Isa. 58: 14, 'I will ... feed them with the heritage of Jacob thy father.'

by root-of-Heart: the phrase brings together 'by rote' and 'by heart', but it is not a coinage of Bunyan's; there are earlier examples.

173 *I was a dreamed*: i.e. I dreamt. The idiom was a common one. See Henry Fielding, *Pasquin* (1736, iv. i), 'I was a-dreamed I overheard a ghost.'

174 *her Bowels yearned*: the word 'bowels' (which then meant simply the internal organs of the body, and not just the intestines) is often used figuratively in the Authorized Version of the Bible to represent the seat of compassion or kindness. See, for example, 1 Kings 3: 26, 'For her bowels yearned upon her son.'

175 *as merry as the Maids*: a proverbial expression.

176 *all the Gold in the Spanish Mines*: i.e. gold mines in South America.

177 *Tears and put them into his Bottle*: see Psalm 56: 8, 'O God . . . put thou my tears into thy bottle.'

pretend to be the Kings Labourers: i.e. pretend to be ministers of the gospel.

178 *a Dog*: see Psalm 22: 20, 'Deliver . . . my darling from the power of the dog.' On p. 182 it is explained that Satan is the owner of the dog.

179 *Suffer the little Children to come unto me*: these are Christ's words, addressed to the disciples when they rebuked people bringing children to be touched by him. See Mark 10: 14; Luke 18: 16.

180 *I pray for all them that believe on me*: see John 17: 20, '[I pray] for them also which shall believe on me.'

Bundle of Myrrh: See S. of S. 1: 13, 'A bundle of myrrh is my wellbeloved unto me.'

Summer-Parler: an apartment for use in summer.

leap for joy: see Luke 6: 23, 'Rejoice in that day, and leap for joy.'

181 *Let my Lord . . . calves of my Lips*: see Heb. 13: 15, 'let us offer the sacrifice of praise to God'; Hos. 14: 2, 'so will we render the calves [i.e. sacrificial offerings] of our lips'.

182 *purchased one*: see Acts 20: 28, 'the church of God, which he hath purchased with his own blood'.

Darling from the power of the Dog: see note to p. 178 above.

set them in the way of his Steps: see Psalm 85: 13, 'Righteousness . . . shall set us in the way of his steps.'

183 *better late then never*: a proverbial expression.

our beginning . . . end will be: see Job 8: 7, 'Though thy beginning was small, yet thy latter end should greatly increase.'

two Bows-shot: i.e. twice the length an arrow can be shot from a bow.

184 *make my Lords People to transgress*: see 1 Sam. 2: 24, 'ye make the Lord's people to transgress'.

185 *all things work for good*: see Rom. 8: 28, 'all things work together for good to them that love God'.

187 *found . . . blameless*: see 2 Pet. 3: 14, 'be diligent, that ye may be found of him in peace, without spot, and blameless'.

187 *Daughter of Abraham*: Abraham, the father of the Children of Israel (see Gen. 17), is referred to as a 'type' of Christ, the father of the faithful, in Gal. 3: 6–9: 'Even as Abraham believed God . . . they which are of faith [i.e. believers in Christ], the same are the children of Abraham.'

188 *the Picture of the biggest of them all*: i.e. the picture of the 'very grave Person', Evangelist (p. 29), the first of the emblems shown to Christian in Part One.

189 *an ugly Spider*: in his emblem book, *A Book for Boys and Girls* (1686), Bunyan included a lengthy poem entitled 'The Sinner and the Spider', making the same point as here about sinners being saved despite the enormity and ugliness of their sin. See *Misc. Works*, vi. 214–21.

191 *his Garden . . . one with another*: Bunyan frequently used the metaphor of the church as a garden. See, for example, *Christian Behaviour* (1663), '*When Christians stand every* one *in their places . . . they are like the flowers in the Garden*, that stand *and grow where the Gardner hath* planted them' (*Misc. Works*, iii. 10; see also v. 20. xi. 67; xii. 122; xiii. 45).

Professors: see note to p. 34 above.

192 *a desire in Women . . . of great price*: see 1 Pet. 3: 1–4, where wives are warned against outward adornment, and advised to let their adornment be 'a meek and quiet spirit, which is in the sight of God of great price'.

One leak will sink a Ship: a proverbial expression, usually in the form 'a small leak . . .'.

soweth Cockle . . . Barley: cockle is a weed that grows in cornfields, especially among wheat. The phrase 'sowed cockle reaped no corn' was proverbial (see *Love's Labour's Lost*, IV. iii. 357). Bunyan may also be remembering Job 31: 40, 'Let thistles grow instead of wheat, and cockle instead of barley.'

a Tree . . . all rotten: Bunyan had earlier elaborated on this image in a treatise on the theme of the hypocritical professor, *The Barren Fig-Tree* (1673). See *Misc. Works*, v. 1–64.

193 *all-to-be-fooled me*: called me a complete fool.

194 *Thy beginning . . . greatly increase*: see note to p. 183 above.

195 (marg.) *The Bath Sanctification*: the theological concept of sanctification, the process by which the believer is made holy by the divine grace of the Holy Spirit, is here represented by a cleansing bath. The bath may also represent adult baptism by immersion, but it is important to note that Bunyan differed from many of his Baptist co-religionists in not insisting on baptism by water as a prerequisite for church membership, and indeed entered into controversy with some of them on this point. See *Differences in Judgment about Water-Baptism no Bar to Communion* (1673), *Misc. Works*, iv. 189–264.

fair as the Moon: see S. of S. 6: 10, 'Who is she that looketh forth as the morning, fair as the moon.'

the Seal: in Eph. 1: 13, the redeemed are said to be 'sealed with that holy Spirit of promise, which is the earnest of our inheritance until the redemption of the purchased possession'. As Bunyan notes below, the Old Testament feast of the Passover, a 'type' of the Christian redemption, was to be for the Israelites 'a memorial between thine eyes . . . for with a strong hand hath the Lord brought thee out of Egypt' (Exod. 13: 9).

196 *fine Linnen, white and clean*: see Rev. 19: 8, 'she should be arrayed in fine linen, clean and white: for the fine linen is the righteousness of saints'.

Great-heart: like Evangelist in Part One, Great-heart represents a minister of the gospel, wearing 'the whole armour of God': the 'shield of faith . . . the helmet of salvation, and the sword of the spirit' (Eph. 6: 13–17).

watch and pray: this was Christ's repeated injunction to his disciples in the Garden of Gethsemane. See Matt. 26: 41; Mark 13: 33, 14: 38.

198 *the Mediatory Office*: see 1 Tim. 2: 5, 'there is . . . one mediator between God and men, the man Christ Jesus'.

two Coats . . . none: see Luke 3: 11, 'He that hath two coats, let him impart to him that hath none.'

200 *they laughed at him*: accounts of Christ's crucifixion in the Gospels describe how he was mocked and reviled by onlookers.

202 *evil report of the good Land*: an allusion to the 'evil report' of the land of Canaan brought back by the two spies sent out by Moses. See Num. 13: 32, 14: 36–7.

their Names Rot: see Prov. 10: 7, 'the name of the wicked shall rot'.

204 *To go down the Hill is easie*: a proverbial saying, more often in the form 'it is easy to bowl down the hill'.

a piece of an Honey-comb: when Christ appeared to his disciples after the Resurrection, they gave him 'a piece of a broiled fish, and of an honeycomb' (Luke 24: 42).

Bottle of Spirits: Bunyan may intend an allusion to 1 Cor. 12: 13, 'For by one Spirit are we all baptized into one body . . . and have been all made to drink into one Spirit.'

205 *burned thorough the Tongue with an hot Iron*: mutilation was a common punishment in the seventeenth century. In a famous case in 1656, a Quaker leader, James Nayler, was convicted of blasphemy for riding into Bristol on a mule in a manner recalling Christ's entry into Jerusalem. He had his tongue bored, and was flogged, made to stand in the pillory, had the letter B branded on his forehead, and was imprisoned.

206 *Grim or Bloody man*: Grim may be taken to represent the state authorities behind the 'lions' of persecution (see above, note to p. 42). That the lions are fiercer than in Part One may be a reference to the intensified persecution of Dissenters during the early 1680s, following the 'Exclusion Crisis', when an attempt to exclude the Catholic James, Duke of

York, from succeeding to the throne was defeated. In *The Holy War*, the army that attacks Mansoul includes 'Bloodmen' (*HW*, 227–35).

206 *Now I am Risen a Mother in Israel*: Christiana is quoting the words of Deborah, the ruler of Israel who, with Barak, won a great victory over the Canaanites. See Judg. 5: 7.

208 *Salute . . . with a kiss*: see Rom. 16: 16, 'Salute one another with an holy kiss.'

209 *I was a Dreamed*: see note to p. 173 above.

210 *Heart . . . wakes when we sleep*: see S. of S. 5: 2, 'I sleep, but my heart waketh.'

211 *to Catechise them*: a catechism as a preparation for confirmation was included in the Prayer Book, and many other catechisms were published in the seventeenth century. The catechizing of children was regarded as an important duty in Puritan households. Bunyan himself published a catechism, *Instruction for the Ignorant* (1675). See *Misc. Works*, viii. 1–44.

213 *For in six days . . . them is*: Exod. 20: 11.

Mr. Brisk: the word 'brisk' at this time carried strongly pejorative overtones, suggesting rakish behaviour, as in Etheredge's *The Man of Mode*: 'He has been, as the sparkish word is, Brisk upon the Ladies already' (OET, 345). There is a Lord Brisk among the Diabolonians in *HW* (p. 202).

215 *cried her down at the Cross*: this refers to the practice in the seventeenth century by which a man could take his wife to the local market cross (sometimes leading her by a symbolic halter) and sell her to the highest bidder. Although wholly illegal, it was widely sanctioned by folk-custom as a legitimate form of divorce, which was otherwise unavailable to any but the very wealthy.

Belzebubs: see note to p. 27 above.

216 *Blood of a Goat . . . Juice of Hyssop*: see Heb. 9, where Old Testament sacrifices are interpreted as 'types' of the sacrificial blood of Christ which alone can 'purge' sin. 'If the blood of bulls and of goats, and the ashes of an heifer . . . sanctifieth to the purifying of the flesh: how much more shall the blood of Christ . . . purge your conscience from dead works to serve the living God', Heb. 9: 13–14.

ex Carne & Sanguine Christi: 'from the flesh and blood of Christ'.

217 *it will make him live for ever*: see John 6: 51, 'if any man eat of this bread, he shall live for ever'.

218 *the Rainbow . . . the Covenant of Gods Grace*: after the Flood, God set a rainbow in the cloud as 'a token of a covenant between me and the earth', Gen. 9: 13.

the Pelican . . . with her Bill: according to popular belief, pelicans fed their young with their blood (a fallacy arising from the fact that the parent bird takes food from the large bag under its bill and gives it to the young), and hence in Christian art the pelican was often an emblem of Christ.

Peter's Sin: Peter denied being a disciple of Christ's. See Matt. 26: 69–75; Mark 14: 66–72; Luke 22: 55–62; John 18: 25–7.

220 *Virginals*: the virginal (or, more usually, pair or set of virginals) was an early form of the harpsichord. It was a very popular instrument in the sixteenth and seventeenth centuries.

parched Corn: see 1 Sam. 17: 17, 'Take now . . . this parched corn.'

a Gold Angel: a gold coin, worth from 6*s*. 8*d*. to 10*s*., so named because of its device, the Archangel Michael slaying the dragon.

221 *Let thy Garments . . . few*: see Eccles. 9: 8, 'Let thy garments be always white; and let thy head lack no ointment'; Deut. 33: 6, 'Let Reuben live, and not die; and let not his men be few.'

fly Youthful lusts: see 2 Tim. 2: 22, 'Flee also youthful lusts.'

Through all my Life . . . to Age endure: the two stanzas here are from Psalms 23: 6 and 100: 5, in the metrical version of Sternhold and Hopkins (see note to p. 65 above).

223 *fat Ground*: see 1 Chron. 4: 40, 'they found fat pasture and good'.

224 *Hearts-ease*: the common name of the wild pansy, *Viola tricolor*.

225 *To this man . . . Word*: Isa. 66: 2.

play the Man: see note to p. 113 above.

Hercules: the Roman version of Heracles, the most famous of legendary Greek heroes. His many exploits included the twelve 'labours'.

227 *Resist the Devil . . . you*: Jas. 4: 7.

a great mist . . . upon them: see Acts 13: 11, 'immediately there fell on him a mist and a darkness'.

The heart knows . . . Joy: Prov. 14: 10.

doing business in great Waters: see Psalm 107: 23, 'they that go down to the sea in ships, that do business in great waters'.

228 *the Bottoms . . . for ever*: see Jonah 2: 6, 'I went down to the bottoms of the mountains; the earth with her bars was about me for ever.'

them that walk in darkness . . . God: see Isa. 50: 10, 'who is among you that . . . walketh in darkness, and hath no light? Let him trust in the name of the Lord, and stay upon his God.'

lighten our darkness: see 2 Sam. 22: 29, 'the Lord will lighten my darkness'.

Look to your feet . . . Snares: see Psalm 73: 2, 'my feet had almost gone; my steps had well nigh slipped', and Psalm 141: 9, 'keep me from the snares which they have laid for me'.

beloved of his God: see Neh. 13: 26, 'Solomon . . . was beloved of his God.'

229 *Maull a Gyant*: it has been suggested that this giant represents the power of the Roman Catholic Church. The charge of sophistry was certainly one often levelled at Jesuits, but there is little else to suggest that Bunyan had such a specific reference in mind. It seems just as likely that Maul (a maul being a heavy hammer) represents a more general enemy of Pilgrims. In *Good News for the Vilest of Men* (1688), the temptation to doubt one's salvation is described as Satan's '*Maul*, his *Club*, his Master-piece' (*Misc. Works*, xi. 76).

to turn . . . to God: see Acts 26: 18, 'to turn them from darkness to light, and from the power of Satan unto God'.

fairly let him get up: this may be another echo of popular romance. In *Guy of Warwick*, Guy chivalrously allows the giant Colebrand to refresh himself with water during their combat (OET, 348).

230 *under the fifth rib*: Abner slew Asahel by smiting him 'under the fifth rib' and was himself killed by a blow in the same place. See 2 Sam. 2: 23, 3: 27.

231 *I cry you mercy*: I beg your pardon.

232 *the Sun of Righteousness will arise*: see Mal. 4: 2, 'unto you that fear my name shall the sun of righteousness arise with healing in his wings'.

holy Kiss of Charity: see 1 Pet. 5: 14, 'Greet ye one another with a kiss of charity', and Rom. 16: 16, 'Salute one another with an holy kiss.'

James the Just . . . brother of our Lord: these are usually taken to be the same person. (A separate James, the elder brother of St John, was put to death by Herod in AD 44 (Acts 12: 2).) The James referred to as the brother of Christ in Matt. 13: 55 and Mark 6: 3 was converted at the Resurrection and became a leader of the Christian church at Jerusalem. He was known as 'the Just', and was stoned to death in AD 62. Bunyan would have read an account of his character and martyrdom in Foxe, i. 43–4.

233 *the Root of the Matter in him*: Bunyan borrows this phrase from Job 19: 28, 'Why persecute we him, seeing the root of the matter is found in me?'

236 *Mr. Great-Heart began to take his Leave of him*: Bunyan seems to forget that Great-heart is the narrator here.

237 *as the Proverb is, he could have bit a Firebrand*: this striking expression is not listed in any of the standard dictionaries of proverbs.

238 *the Lake*: the 'lake of fire' into which all are cast whose names are not written in the book of life. See Rev. 20: 10–15; 21: 8.

fear of God . . . Wisdom: Psalm 111: 10; Prov. 9: 10.

239 *He said . . . could do so too*: for the biblical precedents cited by Self-will, see 2 Sam. 11 (David); 1 Kings 11: 1–3 (Solomon); Gen. 12: 11–20 (Sarah); Exod. 1: 16–17 (the midwives); Joshua 2: 1–6 (Rahab); Matt. 21: 1–7 (the disciples); Gen. 25: 28–34, 27: 1–36 (Jacob).

241 *dyed as they in the Wilderness . . . promised Land*: some of the Children of

Israel were left in the wilderness and never entered into Canaan. See Num. 14: 11–35; Heb. 3: 7–19.

241 *Gaius*: Paul's host, described as 'the well-beloved' in Rom. 16: 23, and praised for his charity in 3 John 1–6.

242 *their Ancestors dwelt first at Antioch*: the followers of Christ were first called Christians at Antioch in Syria (Acts 11: 26).

243 *Paul and Peter*: Paul was said to have been beheaded at Rome during the reign of Nero in about AD 65. At about the same time, and also at Rome, Peter was, according to tradition, crucified upside down. Bunyan would have read accounts of their deaths in Foxe (i. 45–6).

Ignatius . . . drowned: Bunyan's knowledge of the sufferings of the early Christian martyrs came from reading Foxe's *Acts and Monuments*. In *Come, and Welcome, to Jesus Christ* (1678) he describes the heroic fortitude of Ignatius, Romanus, and other martyrs, citing Foxe as his source (*Misc. Works*, viii. 383–4). Ignatius (*c.*35–*c.*107), bishop of Antioch, was taken to Rome where, in Foxe's words, he was 'thrown to the beasts' (i. 52). Romanus, a deacon at Caesarea in Palestine, was martyred at Antioch in *c.*304. Foxe describes how he was first whipped, then lanced with knives 'until the bones appeared white', then had his teeth knocked out and his beard plucked from the flesh on his face, then was scourged 'in so much as the bare bones appeared', then had his tongue pulled out, before finally being strangled (i. 116–17). Polycarp (*c.*69–*c.*155), bishop of Smyrna, was burned to death at Smyrna. 'When they would have nailed him to the stake with iron hoopes, he said, let me alone as I am, for he that hath given me strength to suffer and abide the fire, shall also give power, that without this your provision of nailes, I shall abide, and not stir in the middest of this fire' (i. 56). Marcus, bishop of Arethusa, was put to death during the reign of the Emperor Julian the Apostate (332–63). After various tortures had been inflicted on him he was put into a basket, 'and being annointed with hony and broth, they hung him abroade in the heat of the sunne as meate for wasps and flies to feede upon' (i. 128).

a posterity in the Earth: see Gen. 45: 7, 'God sent me before you to preserve you a posterity in the earth.'

244 *a Heave-shoulder, and a Wave-breast*: a 'heave shoulder' was so named because the shoulder of the animal was 'heaved' or elevated in sacrifice. Similarly, a 'wave breast' was 'waved' by the priest when being presented in sacrifice.

245 *that makes glad the Heart of God and Man*: see Psalm 104: 15, 'wine that maketh glad the heart of man'.

Drink of his Flagons . . . sick of Love: See S. of S. 2: 5, 'Stay me with flagons, comfort me with apples: for I am sick of love.'

249 *hope to the end*: see 1 Pet. 1: 13, 'be sober, and hope to the end'.

252 *Mr. Ready-to-hault*: as the marginal reference indicates, Bunyan took the

name from Psalm 38: 17, 'For I am ready to halt, and my sorrow is continually before me.'

254 *set their Faces like Flint*: see note to p. 84 above.

Mnason: see Acts 21: 16, where Paul was taken to the house of 'one Mnason of Cyprus, an old disciple, with whom we should lodge'.

257 *A good Man must suffer Trouble*: perhaps alluding to Job 5: 7, 'man is born unto trouble, as the sparks fly upward'.

Gaius, mine Host, and of the whole Church: Rom. 16: 23.

258 *Strangers and Pilgrims in the Earth*: see Heb. 11: 13–16, where the Old Testament patriarchs are described as 'strangers and pilgrims on the earth', who 'desire a better country, that is, an heavenly'.

a Monster out of the Woods: Bunyan's account of this monster draws upon the description in Rev. 17 of a 'scarlet coloured beast . . . having seven heads and ten horns'. A woman sits on the beast, 'and upon her forehead was a name written, MYSTERY, BABYLON THE GREAT, THE MOTHER OF HARLOTS AND ABOMINATIONS OF THE EARTH. And I saw the woman drunken with the blood of the saints, and with the blood of the martyrs of Jesus.' This woman was believed by Protestants to represent Antichrist, the Church of Rome. In a posthumously published treatise, *Of Antichrist, and his Ruine* (1692), Bunyan gave an extended account of the rise and (shortly expected) fall of Antichrist. See *Misc. Works*, xiii. 421–504.

261 *fight the good Fight of Faith*: 1 Tim. 6: 12.

262 *as many Lives as a Cat*: cats are proverbially said to have nine lives.

265 *the Man has plaid*: see note to p. 113 above.

266 *tumbled the Hills about with Words*: this is Bunyan's rendering of Christ's words in Mark 11: 23, 'whosoever shall say unto this mountain, Be thou removed, and be thou cast into the sea; and shall not doubt in his heart, but shall believe that those things which he saith shall come to pass; he shall have whatsoever he saith'.

267 *Cake . . . Barrel*: see 1 Kings 17: 8–16, where the poor widow gives Elijah a cake, and in return is promised that her 'barrel of meal shall not waste'.

washing of an Ethopian . . . white: the phrase 'to wash an Ethiop (or blackamoor) white' was proverbial.

269 *a Bracelet . . . Fore-heads*: Bunyan is remembering Ezek. 16: 11–12, 'I put bracelets upon thy hands . . . and I put a jewel upon thy forehead, and earrings in thine ears.'

271 *Sampson . . . Ass*: see Judg. 15: 15, 'And he [Samson] found a new jawbone of an ass, and put forth his hand, and took it, and slew a thousand men therewith.'

resisted . . . Sin: see Heb. 12: 4, 'Ye have not yet resisted unto blood, striving against sin.'

a man of his Hands: a proverbial expression, more usually in the form 'a tall man . . .'.

272 *killed a Serpent*: this would seem to refer to Apollyon, though in fact he was not killed by Christian.

276 *they walked not by Sight*: see 2 Cor. 5: 7, 'For we walk by faith, not by sight.'

279 *Blessed is the Man that feareth always*: see Prov. 28: 14, 'Happy is the man that feareth alway.' Bunyan is quoting from, or remembering, the Geneva Bible version, which reads 'Blessed is the man . . .'.

282 *set Absalom . . . Pilgrims Life*: for accounts of the four biblical characters mentioned here, see 2 Sam. 15 (Absalom); 1 Kings 12: 25–33 and 2 Chron. 13: 1–20 (Jeroboam); Matt. 26: 14–16 (Judas); 2 Tim. 4: 10 (Demas).

when you have done all, stand: see Eph. 6: 13, 'and having done all, to stand'.

283 *Camphire . . . chief Spices*: see S. of S. 4: 13–14, 'Thy plants are an orchard of pomegranates, with pleasant fruits; camphire, with spikenard, spikenard and saffron; calamus and cinnamon, with all trees of frankincense; myrrh and aloes, with all the chief spices.'

284 *Behold an Israelite . . . no Guile*: these words are spoken of Nathanael by Jesus. See John 1: 47.

285 *watch . . . may come*: see Matt. 24: 42–4, 'Watch therefore . . . be ye also ready; for in such an hour as ye think not the Son of man cometh.'

be sober, and hope to the End: 1 Pet. 1: 13.

live in the Light of the Living for ever: see Psalm 56: 13, 'thou has delivered my soul from death; wilt not thou deliver my feet from falling, that I may walk before God in the light of the living?'

286 *Welcome Life*: in a woodcut illustration of the martyrdom of Laurence Sanders in Foxe, Sanders's last words are given as 'Welcome Life'. Like Ready-to-halt, Sanders had 'seemed so fearfull and feeble spirited that he shewed himselfe in appearance, like either to fall quite from God and his word . . . or at least to betake him to his heeles, and to flye the land' (ii. 140).

288 *Death . . . where is thy Victory?*: 1 Cor. 15: 55.

289 *Head . . . spit upon*: see Matt. 27: 27–8, 'And when they had platted a crown of thorns, they put it upon his head . . . And they spit upon him.' See also Mark 15: 17–19.

I have kept me from mine Iniquities: see 2 Sam. 22: 24, 'I . . . have kept myself from mine iniquity.'

his strong men bowed under him: Bunyan is adapting a phrase from Eccles. 12: 3, 'In the day when the keepers of the house shall tremble, and the strong men shall bow themselves . . .'.

GLOSSARY

[colloq.] = colloquialism; [dial.] = dialectal usage; [obs.] = obsolete form; [var.] = variant form; a page reference indicates that a specific usage is glossed.

a [colloq.] have (e.g. p. 28)
accoutred equipped
addressed prepared (p. 147)
affront attack, assault (p. 61)
ai [var.] aye
amain with full force, vehemently
amuse puzzle (p. 87)
angerly [var.] angrily
apes fools (p. 86)
arch (i) notable, chief; (ii) clever, cunning (p. 254)
a toside [var.] atoneside, on one side

back support, encourage (p. 206)
beck'n gesture, wave
bedabled spattered
bedlams madmen
befooled themselves called themselves fools
bemired soiled, smeared with mud
beshrow [var.] beshrew, curse, blame
betterment difference for the better
bin [dial.] been
blank disappointment, nonplus (p. 185)
boot, to into the bargain, besides
bore [var.] boar
born [var.] borne (e.g. p. 94)
bottom valley floor, stretch of low-lying land (p. 39)
bowels (i) the seat of tender feeling (p. 174); (ii) pity, sympathy, compassion (p. 177)
brast [dial.] burst
brave (i) fashionable, dashing (p. 72); (ii) worthy, noble (p. 161)
bravadoes boastings, defiant assertions
breathing exhausting (p. 204)
breeding pregnant (p. 268)
brest [var.] breast
brisk cheerful, sprightly, lively (p. 120)
broken distressed by remorse (p. 169)
brought him caused him to be (p. 235)
bruit [var.] brute
brunts violent blows
but except (p. 3)
butt [var.] abut, join
by-blows blows which miss their mark
by that by the time that

carriages conduct, behaviour
caytiff [var.] caitiff, wretch
cheapen bargain for
checkle [dial.] chuckle
churl boorish, insensitive person
civit-box [var.] civet box, box of perfume
clap, at a in one go, at once (p. 100)
clogged burdened (p. 169)
colour pretext, excuse (p. 145)
commixes mingles, mixes up
compassed surrounded, encircled
complement compliment, or ceremonial bow
conceited supposed, imagined (p. 250)
concluded determined upon (p. 90)
conditions habits, personal qualities (p. 214)
condole lament
conje bow (French, *congée*)
contrive excogitate, think out (p. 115)
convenient suitable, appropriate (p. 36)

conversation dealings with others, behaviour (p. 52)
courage ardour (p. 214)
cousenage [var.] cozenage, deception, cheating
covet desire eagerly
coxcombs fools
crumbed covered with crumbs
cut steal by cutting a purse from a belt (p. 106)

damp stifle (p. 51)
dash splash through puddles (p. 270)
delicate pleasant, delightful (p. 103)
discretion discernment, good judgement
disserting [var.] deserting
distemper disorder, derangement
do deliver (p. 105)
dumpish sad, dejected
dumps perplexity, bewilderment (p. 28)

engins (i) contrivances (p. 5); (ii) implements (p. 54)
equipage state (or possibly carriage) (p. 151)
experiment proof, example (p. 225)
experimental founded on personal experience, experiential

fact misdemeanour (p. 44)
fall fade away, decline to extinction (p. 243)
fancies delusions (p. 202)
fantastical imaginary, illusory
fat (i) rich, appetizing, nourishing (p. 52); (ii) fertile (p. 223)
fatt tub
figures (i) prefiguring types (p. 6); (ii) emblems, symbols (p. 31)
firy [obs.] fiery
followed prosecuted, went on with (p. 59)
fondness foolishness (p. 72)
forrest wilderness, waste land (p. 276)
foyled discomfited, worn out
frey [var.] fray (i.e. assault, attack)
friend relation, kinsman (pp. 10, 169)

gat [var.] got
gins traps, snares
Gospel-day day of the Christian dispensation
gratifie reward, recompense (p. 220)
greenheaded inexperienced, foolish
groat a small coin, worth four pence; groats were not issued after 1662
guest [var.] guessed (p. 162)

handmaiden servant
hands, man of his courageous and dexterous swordsman
hap luck, fortune
hast [var.] haste (p. 10)
have take, put (p. 246)
hazarding running the risk of incurring (p. 23)
heady passionate, violent
heart-whole whole-heartedly, sincerely
hectoring swaggering, domineering
hosen [dial.] hose, stockings
howlet [dial.] owlet
humane human
humours disposition, moods

ill-favoured ugly
imploy employment, occupation
increase prosper (p. 194)
item admonition, reminder (p. 256)

journey-men hirelings (p. 125)
jumps completely agrees (p. 99)

kind, in his naturally, in his way (p. 77)

lanched [obs.] launched
lavished spent recklessly
learn teach (p. 213)
leered walked stealthily with averted look
lesson musical piece, recital (p. 264)

let hinder (pp. 88, 184)
limner portrait painter
loose [var.] lose
lumbring rumbling
lusty lively (p. 86)

mainly [dial.] mighty (p. 281)
mantles cloaks
marr'd impaired (p. 227)
mattered was concerned about, paid heed to
merchandizers merchants, stall-keepers
mistrusting being afraid, suspecting (p. 108)
most an end [dial.] almost all the time
mystery, in a mystically, symbolically (p. 24)

naughty wicked
naughty-wise wickedly, viciously
next nearest (p. 223)
noddy simpleton
noised rumoured
none-age [var.] nonage (i.e. before coming of age)
notion opinions, theoretical beliefs (p. 82)

ordinances religious observances, particularly the sacraments (p. 40)
outlandish-men strange-looking foreigners
over-run overtake
oweth [dial.] owneth (p. 182)

pair set (p. 220)
passengers passers-by, travellers (p. 230)
pelting sweating, excessively hot
perspective glass spy-glass, telescope
pitied grieved, moved to pity (p. 234)
plaid [var.] played
plash bend or break down
plat [dial.] place, patch of ground
plow [var.] plough
pluck bout (p. 261)
post courier, messenger (p. 283)
pretty (i) fine (p. 76); (ii) clever, ingenious (p. 161)
price sum of money
proof tried and tested strength (p. 55)
prove test the genuineness of (p. 13)
purpose, to thoroughly (p. 17)

quagg [var.] quag, quagmire

rack drive before the wind (p. 35)
rateing chiding angrily, reproving vehemently
refined clarified (p. 52)
renovation spiritual renewal and purification (p. 211)
ridged [var.] rigid, dogmatically strict (p. 99)
role [var.] roll (p. 205)
round whisper (p. 130)
roundeth up rebukes (p. 104)
roundly bluntly, sharply, severely
rub up revive
rude superficial, unskilled (p. 6)
ruffins [var.] ruffians
runagate renegàde, villain

sackbut bass trumpet
scheme conspectus, summary (p. 221)
scrub [colloq.] shabby wretch (p. 95)
sentence pithy saying, maxim (p. 237)
settle wooden bench with arms and back (p. 44)
sight awareness, consciousness (p. 81)
slabbiness muddiness
slow [var.] slough (p. 16)
sneaking skulking, cringing (p. 17)
snibbeth [dial.] rebukes, reproves
sober temperate
spends utters (p. 271)
stage scaffold (p. 205)
stitch, a good [dial.] a considerable distance to walk
straight [var.] strait, dilemma (p. 4)
strodled [dial.] straddled
stroke [var.] struck (p. 229)

strook [var.] struck
stumble form an obstacle to belief for (p. 83)
stounded [dial.] bewildered, at a loss (p. 147)
stun'd [var. dial.] stounded, astonished, stupefied (p. 172)
sutable [var.] suitable
sute [var.] suit
swet [var.] sweat
swound [dial.] swoon

then [var.] than (e.g. p. 25)
thorow [var.] through
through [var.] thorough (p. 76)
thorough all the way, to the end (p. 208)
tinder-box box containing inflammable material and steel and flint with which to strike a spark
tollerate allow, permit (p. 140)
toull [var.] toll
tracing ranging over, making his way about (p. 236)
travailer [var.] traveller (e.g. p. 8)
travel [var.] travail, labour (p. 30)
trenshers [var.] trenchers, platters
tro [var.] trow, believe
Turk barbarian, savage (p. 77)
twice told counted twice

unwarrantable not genuine, fraudulent (p. 160)

venturous daring, bold
vestry a room where clothes are kept (p. 196)
vial [obs.] viol (p. 264)

wagg [colloq.] stagger
wain [var.] wane (p. 83)
Wain Great Bear constellation (p. 265)
walk behave, conduct herself (p. 190)
way-fairing [var.] wayfaring
weed clothing, attire (p. 258)
wet-shod [dial.] what would wet the feet
wotted knew

INDEX

The Oxford World's Classics Website

www.worldsclassics.co.uk

- Browse the full range of Oxford World's Classics online
- Sign up for our monthly e-alert to receive information on new titles
- Read extracts from the Introductions
- Listen to our editors and translators talk about the world's greatest literature with our Oxford World's Classics audio guides
- Join the conversation, follow us on Twitter at OWC_Oxford
- Teachers and lecturers can order inspection copies quickly and simply via our website

www.worldsclassics.co.uk

MORE ABOUT **OXFORD WORLD'S CLASSICS**

American Literature

British and Irish Literature

Children's Literature

Classics and Ancient Literature

Colonial Literature

Eastern Literature

European Literature

Gothic Literature

History

Medieval Literature

Oxford English Drama

Poetry

Philosophy

Politics

Religion

The Oxford Shakespeare

A complete list of Oxford World's Classics, including Authors in Context, Oxford English Drama, and the Oxford Shakespeare, is available in the UK from the Marketing Services Department, Oxford University Press, Great Clarendon Street, Oxford OX2 6DP, or visit the website at www.oup.com/uk/worldsclassics.

In the USA, visit www.oup.com/us/owc for a complete title list.

Oxford World's Classics are available from all good bookshops. In case of difficulty, customers in the UK should contact Oxford University Press Bookshop, 116 High Street, Oxford OX1 4BR.

A SELECTION OF **OXFORD WORLD'S CLASSICS**

	The Anglo-Saxon World
	Beowulf
	Lancelot of the Lake
	The Paston Letters
	Sir Gawain and the Green Knight
	Tales of the Elders of Ireland
	York Mystery Plays
GEOFFREY CHAUCER	**The Canterbury Tales** **Troilus and Criseyde**
HENRY OF HUNTINGDON	**The History of the English People 1000–1154**
JOCELIN OF BRAKELOND	**Chronicle of the Abbey of Bury St Edmunds**
GUILLAUME DE LORRIS and JEAN DE MEUN	**The Romance of the Rose**
WILLIAM LANGLAND	**Piers Plowman**
SIR THOMAS MALORY	**Le Morte Darthur**

A SELECTION OF **OXFORD WORLD'S CLASSICS**

	Bhagavad Gita
	The Bible Authorized King James Version *With Apocrypha*
	Dhammapada
	Dharmasūtras
	The Koran
	The Pañcatantra
	The Sauptikaparvan (from the Mahabharata)
	The Tale of Sinuhe and Other Ancient Egyptian Poems
	Upaniṣads
ANSELM OF CANTERBURY	**The Major Works**
THOMAS AQUINAS	**Selected Philosophical Writings**
AUGUSTINE	**The Confessions** **On Christian Teaching**
BEDE	**The Ecclesiastical History**
HEMACANDRA	**The Lives of the Jain Elders**
KĀLIDĀSA	**The Recognition of Śakuntalā**
MANJHAN	**Madhumalati**
ŚĀNTIDEVA	**The Bodhicaryāvatāra**

A SELECTION OF **OXFORD WORLD'S CLASSICS**

	Classical Literary Criticism
	The First Philosophers: The Presocratics and the Sophists
	Greek Lyric Poetry
	Myths from Mesopotamia
APOLLODORUS	**The Library of Greek Mythology**
APOLLONIUS OF RHODES	**Jason and the Golden Fleece**
APULEIUS	**The Golden Ass**
ARISTOPHANES	**Birds and Other Plays**
ARISTOTLE	**The Nicomachean Ethics** **Physics** **Politics**
BOETHIUS	**The Consolation of Philosophy**
CAESAR	**The Civil War** **The Gallic War**
CATULLUS	**The Poems of Catullus**
CICERO	**Defence Speeches** **The Nature of the Gods** **On Obligations** **The Republic and The Laws**
EURIPIDES	**Bacchae and Other Plays** **Medea and Other Plays** **Orestes and Other Plays** **The Trojan Women and Other Plays**
GALEN	**Selected Works**
HERODOTUS	**The Histories**
HOMER	**The Iliad** **The Odyssey**

A SELECTION OF **OXFORD WORLD'S CLASSICS**

HORACE	The Complete Odes and Epodes
JUVENAL	The Satires
LIVY	The Dawn of the Roman Empire The Rise of Rome
MARCUS AURELIUS	The Meditations
OVID	The Love Poems Metamorphoses Sorrows of an Exile
PETRONIUS	The Satyricon
PLATO	Defence of Socrates, Euthyphro, and Crito Gorgias Phaedo Republic Symposium
PLAUTUS	Four Comedies
PLUTARCH	Greek Lives Roman Lives Selected Essays and Dialogues
PROPERTIUS	The Poems
SOPHOCLES	Antigone, Oedipus the King, and Electra
STATIUS	Thebaid
SUETONIUS	Lives of the Ceasars
TACITUS	Agricola and Germany The Histories
VIRGIL	The Aeneid The Eclogues and Georgics

A SELECTION OF **OXFORD WORLD'S CLASSICS**

	An Anthology of Elizabethan Prose Fiction
	An Anthology of Seventeenth-Century Fiction
	Early Modern Women's Writing
	Three Early Modern Utopias (Utopia; New Atlantis; The Isle of Pines)
FRANCIS BACON	**Essays**
APHRA BEHN	**Oroonoko and Other Writings** **The Rover and Other Plays**
JOHN BUNYAN	**Grace Abounding** **The Pilgrim's Progress**
JOHN DONNE	**The Major Works** **Selected Poetry**
BEN JONSON	**The Alchemist and Other Plays** **The Devil is an Ass and Other Plays** **Five Plays**
JOHN MILTON	**Selected Poetry**
SIR PHILIP SIDNEY	**The Old Arcadia**
IZAAK WALTON	**The Compleat Angler**

A SELECTION OF **OXFORD WORLD'S CLASSICS**

	Women's Writing 1778–1838
WILLIAM BECKFORD	**Vathek**
JAMES BOSWELL	**Life of Johnson**
FRANCES BURNEY	**Camilla** **Cecilia** **Evelina** **The Wanderer**
LORD CHESTERFIELD	**Lord Chesterfield's Letters**
JOHN CLELAND	**Memoirs of a Woman of Pleasure**
DANIEL DEFOE	**A Journal of the Plague Year** **Moll Flanders** **Robinson Crusoe** **Roxana**
HENRY FIELDING	**Joseph Andrews and Shamela** **A Journey from This World to the Next and The Journal of a Voyage to Lisbon** **Tom Jones**
WILLIAM GODWIN	**Caleb Williams**
OLIVER GOLDSMITH	**The Vicar of Wakefield**
MARY HAYS	**Memoirs of Emma Courtney**
ELIZABETH HAYWOOD	**The History of Miss Betsy Thoughtless**
ELIZABETH INCHBALD	**A Simple Story**
SAMUEL JOHNSON	**The History of Rasselas** **The Major Works**
CHARLOTTE LENNOX	**The Female Quixote**
MATTHEW LEWIS	**Journal of a West India Proprietor** **The Monk**
HENRY MACKENZIE	**The Man of Feeling**
ALEXANDER POPE	**Selected Poetry**

A SELECTION OF **OXFORD WORLD'S CLASSICS**

ANN RADCLIFFE	**The Italian** **The Mysteries of Udolpho** **The Romance of the Forest** **A Sicilian Romance**
SAMUEL RICHARDSON	**Pamela**
FRANCES SHERIDAN	**Memoirs of Miss Sidney Bidulph**
RICHARD BRINSLEY SHERIDAN	**The School for Scandal and Other Plays**
TOBIAS SMOLLETT	**The Adventures of Roderick Random** **The Expedition of Humphry Clinker** **Travels through France and Italy**
LAURENCE STERNE	**The Life and Opinions of Tristram Shandy, Gentleman** **A Sentimental Journey**
JONATIIAN SWIFT	**Gulliver's Travels** **A Tale of a Tub and Other Works**
HORACE WALPOLE	**The Castle of Otranto**
MARY WOLLSTONECRAFT	**Mary and The Wrongs of Woman** **A Vindication of the Rights of Woman**